Huntsman

HOUSE OF MISFITS

CAMBRIA HEBERT

Once upon a Time...

A boy is sired with poison in his veins. He
cannot outrun the venom in his blood, so he
escapes from those who put it there. Secreting
away his darkest tendencies, he grows to
become a friend, brother, bartender
Huntsman.
A man who becomes exactly what he ran from,
a villain of his own making.
A villain who falls in love with the one woman
he is told to steer clear of.
Enchanted by a girl with hair as brilliant as the
sun and innocence as potent as his corruption.
A girl locked away in a tower and told she will
never walk again.
This boy doesn't want to be the villain in her
story. For once, he desires to be a hero.
Regrettably, his past creeps in like thick,
winding fog, reaching wickedly for the one he
loves the most. A hero is no match for the
rotten tree from which he fell.
Once a huntsman, always a huntsman.
Poisoning guaranteed.

Note to the Reader:

Just a brief note to let you fabulous readers know that I recommend reading *Ivory White* (House of Misfits #1) before *Huntsman*. No, you don't have to, but it will help you understand the dynamics between Earth and his family (especially Neo) much better.
You do not have to read *Prince* (House of Misfits #2) for this book, but Earth, as well as all the other misfits, are in it! Thank you so much for reading my work. I appreciate you.

Huntsman

HOUSE OF MISFITS

CAMBRIA HEBERT

A beauty locked away in a tower lit up her own darkness
while a villain clutching a bloodstained blade embraced
his.

Against all odds, they fell in love.

Prologue

VILLAIN

SOMEWHERE IN ASIA...

"The past is calling."

The unmistakable light of amusement in my assistant's eyes faded and snuffed out completely when I lifted my eyes, shifting deeper into the high-backed wingchair behind my desk.

"Excuse me?"

Clearing his throat, gaze lowered to the expensive handwoven rug stretching nearly wall to wall over the glossy and meticulously laid dark wood floors, he spoke loud enough to project his next sentence to me even though his chin remained downcast.

"You have a call. From America."

Interest piqued with suspicion, I replied, "We haven't dealt with anyone that far west in a long time."

He made a sound of agreement.

"If you know that, then why would you put the call through?"

His tremble was visible, as was the way his Adam's apple bobbed when he swallowed. "I didn't at first."

"I shouldn't have to ask for an explanation."

Dark eyes snapped up. He knew I was losing

patience. Clenching his hands in front of him, he nearly tripped over his words, making haste. "It's been the same call for a few weeks now. I keep hanging up, but she keeps calling back."

She?

"I was curious how she could even get this number, let alone be persistent enough to call every single day."

"Americans think the world revolves around them."

"She says she knows someone, someone you've been trying to find."

I tilted my head. "Who?"

"She refused to tell me, insisting she would only speak to you."

"Get out."

The second I spoke, he jolted and spun, the black jacket momentarily puffing out around his slim hips. He scurried like a rat in search of food, making my upper lip curl.

As if he felt the snarl, his hip caught the edge of a decorative table on his way past. The crystal vase atop it fell over with a sharp snap. The rush of water splashed over the edge, carrying with it a long-stemmed black rose. The water and the once pristine flower plopped onto the floor.

With a low gasp and a sheer look of horror, the man dropped to his knees, which only amplified the mess.

"I a-a-apologize," he stammered, trying to scoop up the water with his hands.

My five-inch heels were soundless as I walked over the carpet, my presence only realized when the pointed toes stepped up to the edge of the mess he was trying to clean.

All attempts to fix what he'd done ceased, and the shoulders beneath his suit jacket slumped. The way his head hung on his neck was pathetic, as though he'd already accepted his fate.

Simpering. Spineless. Good help was hard to find these days.

The only surefire way to get the kind I need is to create it. And sometimes, not even that is foolproof.

That thought made the anger burning inside me hotter.

"Chul," I beckoned without even lifting my voice.

The white-paneled door opened immediately, a large man filling its frame. With a single, stoic glance, he took in the employee on the floor and the mess surrounding him.

"I don't want to see him again."

His nod was curt, and when his hand cupped under the arm of the now-former employee, the acceptance of his fate crumpled and he started to whimper, dragging it out into a God-awful wail.

"P-pleeease," he keened. "I'll do anything."

Chul kept going, the man's feet dragging over the floor as he went.

"You."

Chul stopped, and the sniveling man looked up, hope blossoming over his red face.

"That joke wasn't funny," I informed him.

Hope shriveled, and realization dawned once more. "I'm sorry! Give me another chance!" he wailed as Chul hauled him away, shutting the door quietly behind him and cutting off his pathetic and useless pleas.

Silence descended once more, and I bent to pick up the rose. A thorn pricked deep into my flesh, stinging me with pain and drawing forth a swell of blood.

I stared down at the wounded finger and the sharp thorn, which was now smeared with red. Chuckling, I carefully placed the onyx-topped stem on the table and sucked my finger between my painted lips.

Metallic, sharp, and slightly pungent, my own blood burst over my tongue. Remembering the call, I went back to my desk to lift the gleaming black phone and press a button.

"Yes?" My voice was cool.

"I know where he is." I did not recognize her voice. But her tone? That was something else entirely.

Distinguished. Powerful. Petty.

And most importantly… filled with revenge.

"Who?" I faked disinterest.

"The man you've spent the last ten years searching for."

The hand not holding the phone curled around the edge of my desk, squeezing until every small joint in every finger ached and burned. The back of my neck tingled, making my eyes narrow into slits.

It couldn't be.

"Who is this?" I demanded, power radiating from my core.

"Mirror, mirror on the wall," the woman murmured, "who's the most powerful of them all?"

Was she challenging me?

"Listen to me." I began, thinking this woman had no idea who she was playing with.

"New York City. The Grimms. I don't know what you call him, but here, he goes by Earth."

I jolted upright, my already perfect posture going so rigid it was painful. I opened my lips to demand more, but the buzzing of the line against my ear cut me off.

She'd hung up.

Replacing the receiver, I stood at the side of my wooden desk, staring blindly at the deep-gray walls covered in ornate wainscoting. I also didn't see the authentic Leonardo Da Vinci painting that hung between the moldings, the candle sconces, or the tall, leafy green tree that was potted in the corner.

All the high-priced elegance of this office faded away until there was nothing in front of me but an empty street cloaked by the obscurity of night and brought alive only by thick silver-gray fog that drifted above the pavement, concealing where the ground ended and the air began.

The sound of a gunshot boomed through the memory, ripping it away and knocking me back onto my butt. One high heel flipped off, landing on its side nearby, while the other dangled half on, half off my foot as I sprawled on the floor, hand clutching my chest.

Pain so vivid and real tore through me. I began tearing at the white silk jacket, ripping its oversized fit away from my body to find a blooming patch of red.

"I've been shot!" I wailed.

Across the room, the door shuddered open. Behind me, the paneled black bookshelves slid soundlessly in, and a man rushed out.

Surrounded at once, chaos thundered throughout the room as my men filled the space. The one who'd come from the bookcase dropped to his knees beside me.

"I've been shot!" I yelled. "Don't just stand there! Find the gunman!"

The men all shuffled uncomfortably, and the one at my side grabbed my hands to hold them. "There was no gunshot. The estate is secure."

Ripping my hands free, I moved to show him the blood.

There was none.

A broken cry ripped from my throat.

"Out!" the man at my side roared. "Do a perimeter search!"

"What happened?" he demanded when everyone was gone.

No blood. No pain. No dark street. Just me on the floor in my office.

Just me being weak.

Shoving his hands off, I stood. Without the five-inch heels, my height was insignificant, something I hated. Knowing this, he did not stand. Instead, he placed my shoes in front of me, offering one wide shoulder to use as I slid them on.

Only then did he stand, his height still more than mine but a much more tolerable difference.

"What happened?" he repeated.

The past called. My former assistant had no idea how right that statement was.

Except it wasn't because it was still yesterday in America, but it was because that brief unknown caller had managed to shove me ten years into the past without even giving her name.

But she had given *a* name.

Could it really be?

My eyes lifted. "Call Daeshim. I want him here now."

One

*E*ARTH

T*HE* *FAINT* *RINGING* *OF* *A* *PHONE* *TUCKED* *AWAY* *IN* *MY* office stilled my movements and tilted my head.

It was the third time I'd heard that thing ringing today. Even though I'd retired from the business of killing, I still kept the phone.

I still heard it ringing from time to time.

And sometimes, I still had the urge to answer.

The muffled chimes silenced, and I grunted, going back to pushing the broom over the bar floor. It wasn't even that late in the day. "Someone must really want someone dead," I muttered as I finished sweeping up the discarded peanut shells from the night before.

From his bed against the wall, Snort lifted his head, the tags on his collar jangling with the movement.

"What are you looking at?" I asked.

Living up to his name, he gave a loud snort and then rolled onto his side.

I didn't ever advertise my career as an assassin. Doing so would make me shitty at what I did. In fact, just getting my phone number took a lot of work, especially because I changed it often.

Finished with the cleanup, I went to the back to grab

a few cases of beer to stock behind the bar for when we opened later tonight.

The Rotten Apple didn't open until late afternoon and closed when the last person left. Or when I was fed up with them all and kicked them out.

The sound of clinking bottles was interrupted by more ringing. Stiffening inside the cooler, I drew up, equal parts in awe and annoyed at this asshole's persistence.

But then I realized the ringing was much louder than before, and it wasn't the phone hidden away in my office but my actual cell phone lying on the bar. I sneered at the irritating thing but still leaned over to see who it was.

It could be Fletcher. He might need something. And before you go joining in with the rest of my family saying I had a soft spot for my baby brother, you're wrong. I just worried about him is all.

It wasn't Fletch, but I did a double take when I saw who it was.

Neo.

My eyes widened in shock. I mean, sure, he was family, but the rift between us meant barely ever seeing that name flash on my screen.

"What's wrong?" I spat into the line the second I accepted the call. Even if I was concerned, I wouldn't show it.

The brief pause on the other side was filled with a lot of background noise that did not sound like the city I was familiar with.

"Why would something be wrong?" Neo retorted.

"Because you're calling."

"I need a favor."

I barked a laugh, the sound harsh. I didn't have to say

told you so for him to know that was exactly what I was thinking. Once upon a time we were so close words weren't always needed.

"Never mind," Neo muttered, and I could practically see him pulling the phone away from his ear.

"Neo! Think about Virginia." Ivory's voice echoed through the line.

My brows drew together, my fingers tightening on the phone. "Virginia?" I asked. "Is something wrong with your sister?"

The sound of some kind of announcement echoed loudly in the background. *Where is he?*

"Neo," I demanded.

His voice came back on the line, loud and clear. "I went to California with Ivory for a business thing. We were supposed to be back by now."

All of the background noise suddenly made sense. He was at an airport.

"Where are you?"

"Texas. There's some freak storm, and all the flights have been grounded. We'd hoped to be on a plane by now, but it's not looking good. We might not get out of here until tomorrow."

"What's that have to do with Virginia?" I asked.

"She has an appointment later this afternoon with a specialist. We can't really cancel because these appointments are set up months in advance."

"Okay," I said, not really understanding his point.

"I want you to take her in my place."

Jolting upright, I pulled the phone away from my ear to stare at it. "What?" My voice was incredulous. "I thought you forbade me to go near her."

"I did. But I'm not as pissed at you as before. And…"

"And what?" I pressed when he faltered.

"I know you won't let anyone mess with her."

I felt my upper lip curl. "I guess it's convenient to have someone like me around sometimes."

Ivory gasped. "That's not true!"

Did she have her ear pressed to the phone? Ever since I'd heard the name *Ivory White,* my life began to unravel. She was nosy, bossy, and impossible to kill. And now? She was family.

Her voice was muffled like she'd pulled back to scold Neo. "Tell him that's not true!"

She was also far more forgiving than my brother.

Neo grunted. "After the meeting with the doctor, she's seeing a new physical therapist. You gotta watch them. Some of them get handsy."

My back teeth snapped together. I couldn't even muster up surprise because I knew damn well that there were more people in the world who took advantage of others than not. But the idea of anyone doing that to Virginia made fire singe my belly.

"I know we aren't back to where we used to be... *yet.* But this is my sister, and I can't be there. I know you will protect her."

I was silent for a few beats, digesting everything he said and trying to settle all the emotion churning inside me. Truth was the rift between Neo and me bothered me. I didn't like it. I also didn't like that I didn't like it.

This was a chance to make it up to him. An opportunity to gain back some of the trust I'd broken.

"Where and what time?"

Neo's exhale sounded like wind blowing straight through the phone. "I'll text you the address. You'll need to pick her up soon. It takes a little longer when traveling with—"

I grunted, cutting him off. "I get it."

"I'm not sure you do." The words were spoken softly, almost as if they weren't meant for my ears. The underlying pain in them was audible, but I didn't feel bad for Neo.

Still, I heard myself saying, "Don't worry about her. I'll make sure she's okay."

"Thanks."

I pulled the phone away from my ear, but hearing him call my name brought it back up. "What?"

"I didn't call you because it was convenient. If anything, calling someone else would have been a hell of a lot easier."

My eyes focused on the large sign hanging behind the bar. *Poisoning Guaranteed.* "Then why didn't you?"

"Because I trust you with her safety. Don't make me regret it."

The call disconnected, and I held the phone up until it vibrated in my hand, signaling the text he'd promised to send. Noting the time and location of the appointment, I glanced at the clock and went to change.

I'd been waiting a long time to rebuild my relationship with my brother, and finally, *finally*, he was giving me a chance.

Two

THE FAMILIAR SCENT OF NAIL POLISH WAFTED UP AS I stroked the short, paint-covered brush over my toenail. A sunny shade of yellow was left in its wake as I went back again with another long stroke to add even more of the shiny color.

As I leaned over in concentration, my long hair slipped over my shoulder, pooling in my lap. I pushed the brush back into the small square bottle, carefully swiping it before bending back to my toes.

Just as I placed the brush on my nail, my foot slipped off the side of the bed where I'd propped it and fell like dead weight toward the floor.

I giggled, bending again at the waist to stare at my foot, which was adorned with a long stripe of yellow polish all the way up my toe.

"Maybe I'll start a new trend," I mused, glancing over to the small lit-up glass cage where Zilla lived.

Hearing my voice, the leopard gecko turned her head to glance in my direction.

"What do you think, Zilla? Perhaps I should just add some brown dots and then we can match!"

She stared another moment longer, then went into the little tent at the side of her cage.

"I'll take that as a yes," I called after her.

Setting aside the polish, I lifted my fallen leg, propping it up on the side of my bed once more. The quilt I used was colorful and patterned, so if I accidentally got a little polish on it now and then, no one would even notice.

Giving my legs a tap, I made sure they were steady and went back to finishing my task. Soon, all ten toenails were glossy yellow and radiating warmth just like the sun. I imagined how it would feel to wiggle them under the summer rays outside and maybe even how it would feel to burrow them into heated sand on the beach.

My cell phone lit up, a photo of my brother filling the screen. I sighed even as I reached for it. So overprotective. He was going to be here soon, but he was calling too!

"I didn't forget about the appointment," I said ruefully instead of just saying hello.

"I'm glad, but... I didn't make it back in time," Neo replied, also forgoing a standard greeting.

I gasped lightly, pushing at my hair. "What? Is everything okay?"

"Everything's fine." He assured me. "The flights all got canceled in Texas because of weather."

"Oh," I said, listening to all the sounds in the background and wondering what it would be like to wander around a busy airport. "Well, that's okay. I can handle this one on my own."

"No."

I pursed my lips. "No?"

"I called my bro—" A bunch of static interrupted his voice, cackling through the line.

"Neo?"

"... V. The signal is b...d."

He tried to say something else, but all I heard was more static and his frustration.

"Listen!" I said loud into the line. Talking louder wasn't going to make a difference, but my voice rose just the same. "Don't worry about me. I'll handle myself and tell you all about it later. Be safe, okay, and give my love to Ivory!"

"Vir—" *Garble, garble, garble.* "I cal—" The call dropped.

Pulling the cell away from my ear, I stared at the screen as it went black. I debated calling him back, but there really was no point. Tossing the phone into my lap, I couldn't help but feel a little tingle of excitement as I realized I would be doing something independently today.

Quickly adjusting my legs so they were resting back on the footrests on my wheelchair, I rolled across the room to Zilla's cage. The special lamp that kept her warm glowed down, and inside the glass enclosure looked like a small tropical paradise.

"Zill!" I exclaimed, tapping lightly on the glass. The small spotted gecko poked her head out of the tent, nose first. "Can you believe it? I get to be on my own today!"

She moved forward, coming right up to the glass where I was. Smiling, I reached into her warm climate and stroked her on the top of her head. "Maybe I'll even make a stop to get you some tasty crickets."

Her tail swished a little at that, signaling she was as excited as me.

This was the first time ever I was going to go out to an appointment or do anything alone. Neo was probably beside himself with the knowledge, but secretly, I was thrilled. No overprotective big brother watching every move I made. No one telling me to be careful or ask me if I was okay every second.

Just me out there in the city, taking care of myself. *The way it was supposed to be.*

Zilla went back into her tent, and I wheeled over to the brightly painted dresser near my bed. Reaching into the drawer, I pulled out a long cotton maxi dress and a small white T-shirt.

Even though I was in my room with the door closed, I felt awkward just stripping off my nightgown in the middle of the room. Anyone could walk in at any moment. It was just how it was when you lived in a care facility.

As much as I loved the staff here—and as much of me as they'd admittedly seen of me before—I still wanted to retain some sense of privacy. Taking my clothes, I wheeled into the wide bathroom, pushing the door closed behind me.

There was a floor-to-ceiling mirror propped along one wall. Neo brought it in especially for me so I could check my outfits without any trouble. And yes, he bolted it to the wall because he was terrified it would fall over on me.

I tried to tell him I wasn't a toddler and I wasn't going to be climbing on it, but he insisted.

Stripping off my nightgown and draping it over the back of my wheelchair, I tugged on the short-sleeved baby T-shirt and then the green maxi dress that had thin spaghetti straps and was patterned with white daisies with yellow centers.

Maxi dresses were my favorite thing to wear. Not only were they so soft and comfy, but they were very convenient. It was a lot easier to tug that down and under my bum and legs than trying to maneuver myself into jeans.

Once I had the dress worked down below my hips, I worked to adjust it until it fell over my legs.

Sometimes I missed the feel of the cotton swishing against my ankles.

Using the mirror, I checked to make sure that the dress definitely was on properly, pulled under my butt, and covering everything it should. It was super embarrassing when one side got caught and showed things I didn't mean to show.

Satisfied, I opened the bathroom door and then made my way back into my small room, smiling at the huge mural of a tower in a field of flowers that covered the largest wall. My laptop was open on my bed, a movie I'd seen a hundred times playing on the screen.

Reaching for a white plastic basket and my brush, I got started on my hair.

Did I mention I had like *a lot* of hair? When Neo lifted me, it hung well past my butt. It was the color of wheat, a golden hue but not nearly as bright as the sun. It was thick and soft and prone to tangles.

I loved it, though. The long blond locks represented a part of me that could grow and change. A part of me that held even just a little of the sun I often missed so much, a part that could become a field of flowers or filled with waves like the ocean. Brushing through the lengthy strands was a calming ritual, and I also found it to be the most soothing memory when I needed it most.

Despite the copious amounts of hair, I was very skilled with my fingers and brush. In no time, I had it brushed out and parted down the center, my nimble fingers French braiding it into two very long pigtails.

Once they were done, I loosened the braids a bit and

set about pinning small flower clips along the plaits. When I was done, my pale-gold hair was transformed into a field of purple and white daisies.

A swift knock on the door was followed by it pushing in swiftly (See what I mean? No privacy!), and my favorite nurse, Emogen, peeked her head in.

"You decent?" Most of the space her head occupied was taken up by the wild black coils of hair, perfect springy spirals that seemed to burst off her head to create this explosive beauty to surround an equally stunning face. Her skin was polished ebony, smooth and clear, and her vivid dark eyes never missed a thing.

"Funny you should ask that *after* you come in." I teased.

White but not perfectly straight teeth flashed when her full lips pulled into a smile. "I ain't asking for me, girl."

Eyes widening, I realized that she was still just peeking inside, having made no move to fling it open wide. "Who's out there?" I asked.

"Your brother."

My nose wrinkled. "My brother? But Neo is in Tex—"

"I'm not her brother," an extremely disgruntled voice grumped from out in the hall.

Even though it had been quite a while since I'd heard that particular voice, I recognized it instantly. "Earth!" I exclaimed.

A loud thud vibrated the wood when he slapped his hand on the other side of the door and pushed. The old hinges creaked as it swung in, revealing Emogen standing there in a pair of lavender scrubs with a glowering Asian man behind her.

"I thought y'all were family," Emogen retorted, swinging around to look at him.

But he was looking at me, coal-black eyes sweeping from head to toe almost as if he were checking to see if I'd changed at all since I'd seen him last.

He was still the same. Intense. *So* intense. With the kind of piercing stare that paralyzed your lungs but made you forget to panic because suddenly breathing wasn't all that necessary. His hair seemed maybe a bit longer, the inky strands looking like he'd run his hands through them more than once.

High cheekbones. Short dark eyelashes. Wide lips and strong dark eyebrows. He was dressed all in black, exactly the same as he always was. There was a rip in the right knee of his jeans. His black boots probably added two inches to his height, and the only way I knew where his black T-shirt ended and black leather jacket began was because of the slight sheen to the leather.

"She's not my ₁sister," Earth said again, stepping around Emogen to move farther into the room. "Hey, V," he said, eyes finally leaving me to gaze around the space.

Remembering to breathe, I sucked in some air, fingers finding the end of my braid curled in my lap to fidget with the elastic at the base. "Earth, what are you doing here?"

He swung back, glancing down to where I sat. I was used to being on a lower level, so why did the way he towered over me make me feel shy?

"You didn't know I was coming?"

"Should I?"

"Neo didn't call you?"

"Well, yeah, he called, but I couldn't understand anything he said before the call dropped."

Jamming his hands into the pockets of his jeans, Earth sighed. "He asked me to take you to your appointment today."

My shoulders jerked, the words flinging me back. "He what?"

Earth scowled.

"But why would he do that?" I continued. "I'm perfectly capable of getting myself there and back with no problem."

I glanced at Emogen so she could back me up. She laughed.

"Why is that so funny?" I demanded, punctuating my irritation by tightly crossing my arms over my chest.

"Because this is Neo we're talking about. In the entire time I've been your nurse, that boy has not once ever let you go anywhere alone."

I groaned. "But I thought—"

"I gave him my word," Earth interrupted, voice flat. "I realize being stuck with me is probably not what you want, but… I gave him my word. I can't go back on it."

Pursing my lips, I studied him for long moments. He thought that I wouldn't want to be around him. *Why?* Obviously, I knew he and Neo had a big falling-out, but no one would tell me why. Not even Ivory. She never listened to Neo, but this time, even her lips remained quiet.

If no one else would tell me, maybe Earth would.

Shrugging, I said, "Okay. You can come."

Surprise flashed in his eyes before it disappeared.

Looking at Emogen, I asked, "Could you call a taxi for us? We'll need it since my brother isn't here to drive."

"No." Earth stopped Emogen before she could even agree.

"No?" Her wild curls bounced.

"I brought my car. I'll drive."

I gaped. "You have a car?"

The surprise on my face seemed to amuse him

because those wide lips curled up into a satisfied smile. "Sure do. There's lots of things you don't know about me."

Exhilaration bloomed in my chest as my hands curled over the sides of my wheelchair. I wondered what else I might learn today about my brother who wasn't my brother and who also stopped coming to visit due to a mysterious feud with my actual brother.

As I leaned forward, a mischievous smile played on my lips. "Can we leave now?"

Three

WHY ISN'T SHE ACTING SCARED?

Why is she acting excited?

Why—

"Is that your car?" she exclaimed. Her wheelchair halted in the middle of the sidewalk as she gaped at the vintage black Dodge Charger at the curb.

If most people—okay, literally *any* people—were to exclaim at my car like that, I'd be tempted to leave tread marks on their forehead as I sped off on the way to not giving a flying fuck.

But Virginia wasn't any people. She was Neo's little sister. So I bit back the biting reply to scratch behind my ear. "Well, I know it's not exactly the cushy SUV Neo probably uses—"

"It's way better!" Her arms flung up over her head in excitement. As they dropped, she rotated at the waist to find me with sparkling chestnut eyes. "Can I drive?"

It took me a heartbeat to digest the fact she liked the car and then another to realize she just asked to drive. *Cheeky.*

"Nobody drives my car but me." I scowled.

Her lashes batted. "But I'm a really good driver."

A con artist. Just like her brother.

"Don't listen to her. She just ran over old Mr. Donaldson's foot last week. The man acted like he was dying for days," Emogen cracked from near the entrance to the Tower.

"Such a drama queen," Virginia muttered. "He was wearing shoes."

My lips curled inward so the scowl I favored so much couldn't morph into a smile.

"Besides. It's this clunky thing's fault." V patted the side of her wheelchair. "It's clearly not as superb as this." Her hands spread wide as if introducing the car.

"You wouldn't be able to reach the pedals," I told her on my way past to open up the passenger door.

A sound of horror filled the air. "How dare you discriminate against me because I'm short!"

I couldn't help it. I smiled. Good thing I was facing inside the car when it happened. Wiping it off my face, I spun back, boots stomping over the uneven pavement as I closed the distance between us.

I didn't like the way she craned her neck to stare up at me, and before I'd realized it, I'd dropped into a crouch in front of her chair, bringing us to eye level.

A little fissure of surprise flickered in her expression, but it was gone before I could really grasp hold.

Leaning in, I whispered, "I hate to be the bearer of bad news, but… your legs don't work."

A delicate, small-fingered hand with yellow-painted nails flew up to cover her mouth. The shock pouring from her eyes made me frown. Had I gone too far?

A prickle of unfamiliar conscience stung the back of my neck, and my tongue started to move in apology before my lips even parted. "V—"

A little giggle bubbled out around the hand pressed against her lips.

My stare whipped up. Her eyes were glimmering, not with upset… but with humor.

More giggles burst out, and her narrow shoulders shook with it. A summer breeze blew down the street, tugging at a long strand of hair that had come loose from the braids she always wore. It wiggled around behind her like it, too, was laughing.

Her hand dropped, revealing a warm smile. "I missed you."

Pause.

Those words were like a magic wand, the kind so powerful that, with just one flourish, it could put everything to sleep around you. Suddenly, the obnoxious city quieted. The scent of garbage always lingering in the streets disappeared. My fingers curled into my palms, tightening my hands into fists.

"I miss all of you. It gets boring here."

A loud horn broke through the quiet. The wind picked up, smacking me in the face with the foul odor of trash. Just like that, the world started up again, leaving me with nail prints in my palms and a bitter taste on my tongue.

"We should go. We're going to be late," I said, straightening from the crouch.

Her face lifted, following my movements, and then her eyes strayed to the open door of the car. "Emogen?" she called out, turning toward the nurse still watching us from the entrance. "I might need help."

Before the nurse was even two steps forward, I reached down to lift her easily out of the wheelchair.

She gasped at the same time her arms looped around my neck. "What are you doing?"

"Why are you so light?" I demanded.

Her eyes snapped up at my aggressive tone. "What?"

"Don't you eat? You're practically weightless!"

Emogen was halfway between the Tower and where we stood, frozen in place, staring.

My eyes narrowed. "Don't you people feed her?"

Emogen's eyes flashed, and her hands planted firmly on her hips.

"Don't be ridiculous! Of course I eat. And the staff here at the Tower are wonderful!"

A sound of disbelief rumbled deep in my chest.

Pat. Pat.

I glanced down to where her palm tapped lightly against my chest. My eyebrow lifted.

"Be nice," she scolded softly.

"I got it from here," I told Emogen. "Maybe I'll make sure she has a meal too."

"Earth!" Virginia gasped.

I said maybe. Seemed nice enough to me.

"I oughta bust you," Emogen swore, voice full of attitude.

Some threats really weren't even worth acknowledging, so I turned my back on the woman, carrying V the short distance to the car.

Her arms looped back around my neck, her fingertips grazing the skin just under my ear. Chills raced over my scalp, but I refused to acknowledge them.

"I usually transfer myself." Was that shyness I heard in her tone?

My footsteps halted. "I don't have a board in my car, so you're stuck with me today."

Usually when Virginia went anywhere with us, Neo drove one of Ivory's big SUVs where they kept a long board that could act as almost a bridge between her wheelchair and the seat of the car. I'd only seen V transfer herself a couple times from chair to car, but she did it efficiently, even if it did look difficult.

"Watch your head," I said softly, reaching up to block her head with my leather-covered arm even as I leaned down to put her in the car. When she was seated, I pulled back, a long strand of her yellow hair clinging to my forearm. The enclosed space of the car seemed much smaller when I plucked it away carefully to tuck it behind her ear.

Our eyes met and held as I pulled back a fraction, still close enough to see all the different shades of brown in the depths of her stare.

"Thank you." Her voice was soft. Breathless.

"No problem," I said, wrenching back to grab the seat belt and pull it partway across her chest. "Here."

She took it, tugging it the rest of the way around her. The sharp click of it locking in place seemed loud.

Crouching again, this time in the open door, my gaze ran over her. "You comfortable? Need adjusting?"

The way she tugged at the long length of her dress, making sure it was covering all of her legs, made my heart pinch a little.

"I'm good." She assured me, smiling again.

Seriously, how does she smile so much?

"Watch yourself," I warned before shutting the door between us. If I slammed the metal a little harder than usual, it was because I wanted to make sure the door was thoroughly closed.

Back on the sidewalk, I grabbed the wheelchair and took it to the trunk. After a few fumbles, I managed to remember how it folded up and then stowed it away.

Slipping into the driver's seat and pulling out the keys, I started up the ignition, feeling deep satisfaction at the way the engine purred aggressively. I put my seatbelt on, then snatched the black aviators off my visor and slipped them over my eyes.

Only then did I notice the charged silence.

My head rotated.

Virginia sat, arms crossed over her chest, glaring at me.

"What?" I barked.

She didn't even flinch. Unfolding her arms, she flung one out toward the windshield, pointing accusingly. "I can't see over the dashboard!"

The force of my laugh was so strong the back of my head hit the headrest behind me. "Shrimp."

"I am not a shrimp!" she declared, smacking at the dash, which she couldn't reach. "Ugh. The one time I get to ride in this gorgeous car and I can't even see out the window!" Crossing her arms, she turned her head away to mutter, "Stupid bucket seats."

I was about to laugh again, but then I saw her shoulders rise and fall, and a bit of darker emotion clouded around. I was pretty good at reading people. At sensing things they didn't say.

It was why I was a good killer. Observation was key to making a successful kill.

Also, I was around a lot of different people every night at the bar.

But you know, mostly, it was because I was a huntsman.

I never thought of myself as that before... until Ivory. Until I heard her refer to me that way. It seemed fitting. I was a huntsman. Of people.

Excitement had exploded around V when she saw this beast at the curb. I guess she was used to that boring SUV or yellow taxis. Hell, she seemed pretty annoyed when I showed up at all. Clearly, she'd thought she was getting to venture out on her own for once.

I never really thought about the fact she was always with Neo whenever she left the Tower. It pinched my cold heart to think that perhaps going out today with me seemed like an adventure.

Reaching into the back seat, I grabbed the pillow I'd tossed there and dragged it up front. A passing car laid on their horn when I flung my door open.

I wasn't even out when the clearly offended driver slammed on their brakes, making their back end fishtail and the smell of burned rubber fill the street. As I unfolded more, they squealed into reverse, flying backward to stop right beside the Charger.

I don't know what the driver expected, but it wasn't me striding right up to the passenger window to rap on the glass.

A second of hesitation and then the glass rolled down. I took a second, casually resting my forearm on the window frame to lean in. The young driver's eyes were sharp with attitude, but the way his Adam's apple bobbed when he stared made me chuckle viciously.

Tugging the shades away from my eyes, I hit him with the vacant, unblinking stare that was as natural as breathing to me. "You got a problem?"

"U-uh. N-"

"Run along now. I ain't got time for this."

His eyes flickered, and the arrogant toughness that caused him to back up rose again. His fingers barely shifted around the steering wheel.

"You could reach for the knife you have in your boot, but by the time you even thought about using it, I'd already have it in my possession and inside that meaty part of your thigh. And I wouldn't just slip it in. I'd twist.

That way, the wound wouldn't heal, and you'd lose twice as much blood. Think you could make it to the hospital like that in time?"

Color drained from his face. His eyes flickered in disbelief and then fear.

His tires left skid marks on the street as he peeled away, nearly drifting around the corner at the end.

"Fucking kid," I muttered as I went to the sidewalk. "Gonna rip the transmission right outta that car."

Virginia's eyes were wide when I opened her door. "What was that?" she asked.

I leaned back. "You scared?"

"Why would I be scared? I felt like I was watching *The Fast and the Furious* live!"

"TV rots your brain."

"So does beer," she retorted.

"Touché." I snatched the pillow. "Lift up."

Realization bloomed in her eyes, and she quickly used her arms to push her body up. I stuffed the pillow under her butt, making sure it was secure and fluffed up.

"Better?" I asked when we were done.

"It's perfect!" she exclaimed, gazing out over the dashboard. The way she stretched her neck made me wonder how good the view was, but she didn't complain. All she did was smile.

I grunted and pulled back, but when her fingers fluttered like the brush of delicate butterfly wings over the back of my hand, I paused. Stiffening, I glanced back, seeing her bright yellow nails resting there.

"Thank you," she said, sincerity heavy in her voice.

I stared at where she touched me a moment longer before shifting up to look at her face. For someone so small, she was so very bright. Her excitement and curiosity seemed limitless. Her emotions shifted so easily.

If she had wings, she'd zoom all over the place, embracing everything she found.

"You're welcome, sprite."

Her fingers jolted just barely on the back of my hand. My eyes narrowed.

"No one's called me that in a long time."

"Sprite?"

Her head bobbed.

"Your parents?" I practically demanded.

"Oh, no!" she quickly refuted. "No. It was actually a physical therapist that used to work here."

My upper lip curled. "What happened to him?"

"Oh." The down sweep of her lashes was alluring, as was the need to see whatever her hidden gaze might reveal. Seconds later, they lifted, but I knew whatever had been there was safely tucked away. "He went to work somewhere else."

"Good."

She gasped.

Guess I said that out loud. I didn't apologize. Why should I? She knew I was an asshole. Instead, I said, "I won't call you that. Must be a bad memory."

"I actually like it," she rushed out.

My stare settled back on her, a little bit of surprise in my stare. Her cheeks pinkened, blooming a rosy shade. The ice block frozen solidly around my heart began to sweat. It was uncomfortable, and it pissed me off.

"Well, I don't," I declared, slamming the door between us.

"Earth?" she asked when I was finally back in the driver's seat.

I groaned. *Dear God, does this woman ever stop talking? And isn't she offended I just yelled at her?* "What now?"

"Will you drive fast?" The hopeful excitement in her voice made me tired.

"No."

"Pleeease?"

I grunted. "Fine, but don't tell your brother."

The skid marks I left on the road as I peeled away were much bigger than the loser who left them before.

Virginia

"Faster!" I yelled over the deafening sound of the wind rushing in from my open window.

Earth didn't say a word, but the purr of the engine rumbled louder, and the black car shot past the one in the lane alongside us.

I laughed, reaching out over the partially lowered glass. I trailed my fingers to feel the wind rush around them as the bright rays of sun warmed my skin.

"Hey." His voice was gruff, not loud at all but still easily heard over the rumbling engine and the wind. "What did I say?"

I made a face, tugging my hand back inside the car. I missed the warmth of the sunlight on them already. "Keep your hands inside the car," I mocked in a deep, grumpy voice.

The corner of his lips twitched as he stared straight ahead out the windshield.

He thought I'd obey that dumb announcement if he only opened my window halfway. He was lame, and since he wasn't watching...

"Hey!" he growled, reaching across the seat to snatch my hand and pull it back. Instead of letting it go, he kept his much larger one wrapped around it, basically pinning it into my lap.

"You weren't even looking at me!" I complained, trying to wriggle free.

His grip tightened a little, and a prickle of awareness shot through my upper body.

"I don't have to be looking at you to know you're up to no good."

"Fine. I'll keep my hands in the car."

He grunted, still keeping hold of my hand. "I don't believe you."

He must have eased off the gas a bit because the wind rushing in quieted and the loose strand of my hair fluttered down to rest on my shoulder.

My eyes kept straying to where his fingers wrapped around my hand. No matter how many times I looked away, my stare would go back.

His hand was really big. Warm. Calloused. The contrast between our skin tones was fascinating but lovely. Swallowing thickly, I forced my gaze away once more, turning my head to stare out the window as the city flew by. My ears felt warm, the burning sensation not uncomfortable but not something I could ignore.

The urge to turn my hand over so it was palm up beneath his was sort of like a heartbeat, insistent and steady. I fought it back, feeling like I was basically denying my life force and it was wholly consuming.

"What's wrong with you?" he barked.

My shoulders jolted back, pressing into the bucket seats. "What? Nothing."

"You haven't been this quiet or still all day," he remarked.

Before I could even answer, he was pulling his hand away, those black eyes of his finally glancing from the road to me. It was the briefest gaze, so why did it feel like he saw everything?

His palm brushed against my forehead, and the back of my head hit the seat just like my shoulders did seconds ago. "Are you car sick?"

"Yes!" I exclaimed, pushing his hand away. "You're a terrible driver!"

"If you're gonna puke, put your head out the window."

I screwed up my face. "I thought you said I wasn't allowed to stick things out the window."

"Puke is an exception."

He downshifted, the car slowing further as he took an exit that would lead us toward the large hospital looming in the distance.

Tension tied a knot in the muscles of my neck, and I let out a slow breath. *Another day, another doctor.* But hey, at least I got to ride in this cool car and feel the freedom of speed carrying me down the highway.

"Do you know which way to go?" he asked, turning into the massive lot with about a hundred different signs.

I directed him the correct way and sat quietly as he steered down a long row of parking and pulled in. When he cut the engine, I turned to him. "Neo usually drops me off at the entrance and then parks."

Without a word, he reached back toward the ignition.

"Wait!" I insisted, reaching out toward the keys. "I don't want you to."

Letting his hand drop, he turned unreadable eyes back to me.

Nibbling on my lower lip, I confessed, "It makes me feel like such a... patient."

The was a moment of charged silence, and then he

popped open his door. "Well, today, you're just a regular girl going to an appointment like everyone else. No special treatment from me."

I made a small, excited sound under my breath, turning back to the windshield with a wide smile on my lips. *A regular girl.*

Despite the age and heavy body of the car door, it was soundless when it opened. Earth leaned in, his dark head framed with sunlight. "Seat belt."

Realizing I was still buckled in, I undid the clasp.

"I'm gonna pick you up now, okay?"

My lungs froze, and all I could do was nod. He didn't ask last time. He just picked me up. I liked it better like that because those words… they created an odd sense of anticipation I never really felt before.

His hand protected my head again when he pulled me out of the car. I don't know how he managed to bend down, lift me out, and shield my head all at the same time.

He gave my body a little toss upward when he straightened, and I squealed lightly, then giggled. His booted foot kicked the door shut, and every step he took toward the back of the Charger was one I felt. The way his upper body shifted against my side, the way his arms cradled me like I really was so light to him.

My arms automatically clung around his neck, and my fingertips rubbed at the smooth leather of his jacket. He smelled faintly of stale cigarette smoke and… bread?

No, it couldn't be bread.

But it kinda smells like bread.

When he placed me into the familiar chair, his body moved with mine, lowering so he was crouched in front of me again, staying level with me. Grasping the long hem of my dress, he made sure it was tugged down and lifted each foot onto its footrests.

I usually did all of that myself, so fiercely independent with those small things that when Neo tried to help, I would smack his hand away.

But today I sat quietly and watched the calloused hands of a man who was tougher than sandpaper maneuver me so gently that I forgot to be mad.

When he was finished, his chin lifted, dark brows slanting over opaque black eyes that glittered when the sun glinted in their irises. "That okay?"

I wouldn't be able to feel if it wasn't. But oh, how I could feel that it *was*.

The braids curled in my lap swished when I nodded. "Good."

Glossy midnight hair fell into his eyes as both hands reached up, wrapping around each of my wrists. I gasped, the action finally reminding my lungs to do their job. Dividing my stare between my wrists, it dawned on me I was still gripping his shoulders.

Gently, he lifted my arms away, tucking them into my lap as if I needed help with them too. My ears were tingling again when he straightened and stepped around behind the chair.

"I think I'd better drive today. Seeing how you already broke that old man's foot."

It was all I needed to bring me back to life. "His foot is hardly broken!" I exclaimed, glancing up and around. "Such a crabby old man!"

The chair slid forward with ease, and we headed toward the entrance.

"I like being in the sun," I murmured, lifting my face to let the rays caress it. "I wish I could go out more."

"Aren't you always out with your brother?"

I made a sound. "Doctor visit after doctor visit. Inside tinted-window SUVs, dropped off at covered entrances, and then carted straight back to the Tower. This is the most sun I've soaked up in months."

The silence above was like a dark cloud against the sunshine, and I cracked an eye open to glance up. He wasn't looking at me but straight ahead, and from this angle, his jaw was angular and sharp.

Worried I'd made him angry, I pulled my chin down to stare straight ahead. "I'm sorry, that sounded ungrateful. I'm very grateful for everything Neo does for me."

He made a sound. "Not ungrateful, and I know."

"How do you know?" I sniffed, crossing my arms. "I haven't seen you in months!"

"You been counting?"

Startled, I let my arms fall back into my lap. Restless fingers found and plucked at the ends of my braids. "Of course not."

He chuckled, and the sound felt like the finest sandpaper rubbing along my arms. *Rough at first but leaving smoothness in its wake.*

"Earth?" I asked abruptly.

"What?"

"Why haven't you been to see me? What happened between you and Neo?"

The chair jolted just a bit, then kept moving, the sound of his footfalls on the pavement a little heavier than before.

"He didn't tell you?"

"No. And no one else would either. Not even Ivory."

"So that's why you aren't afraid." The whispered words fluttered over my head like a soft summer breeze. Not even the meaning of them caused a chill.

"Afraid?" I scoffed. "Why would I be afraid of you?"

Suddenly, the sun was gone, kept at bay by the large awning stretching toward the wide automatic doors ahead. The world turned a bit dimmer, the air a bit cooler.

"Because I'm poison." The statement was quiet, not at all sarcastic. Not at all a joke.

I wasn't sure if it was his intention to frighten me, but if it was, he failed.

The familiar, unwelcome feel of the hospital wrapped around me as we entered the building. Fluorescent lighting, crackling loudspeakers, and an odd hush to the antiseptic-scented air.

A few nurses looked up from the large check-in desk, but for once, their eyes didn't flicker to me. I didn't have to see the kind smiles that masked their pity or even their sadness.

Instead, all eyes went to the raven-haired, black-eyed leather-wearer who was currently commanding my wheelchair. What a nice break it was to see them openly gawk at him—some with clear intrigue and some with apprehension.

I checked in on the touchscreen kiosk and then swiveled around to head to the bank of elevators down the hall. It wasn't until we were in the elevator and the distraction of people reacting to Earth was gone that the familiar tug of anxiety, exhaustion, and suffocation started to wrap around me.

"Earth?" I asked, wishing my voice didn't seem small inside this enclosed space.

"Hmm?"

"Will you stay with me?"

The shoulder casually leaning against the wall pulled upright, his eyes growing wide.

"I mean during the appointment," I hurried to add.

"Unless you would be more comfortable in the waiting room…"

He dropped down alongside my chair again. Every time he did it, my heart fluttered. Since my hands were clutched together in my lap, he used my armrest to lean on. "Nervous?"

I considered lying for a fraction of a second but decided against it. There was nothing wrong with being nervous. Or even being scared.

Go on strongly despite the fear. That's what Ivory always said.

"Maybe a little," I admitted.

Reaching out, he tugged my braid, making me smile. "Don't be nervous, sprite. I got you."

Not incredibly reassuring words.

But I was incredibly reassured.

Five

"I've had time to compare my own findings with the results of the previous specialists who have also studied your medical history," said the stiff dude in the white jacket, glancing once again in my direction.

I gave him a bored look. It was quite obvious he wasn't particularly thrilled to be discussing this in front of me.

I didn't particularly give a flying fuck. It wasn't his decision, and he could give me all the side-eye he wanted. It wouldn't change the fact I was staying.

She asked me to stay. That alone would make me fight to the death if anyone tried to boot me out.

Sensing my willingness to wage war, the doctor shifted, leveling his steady gaze back on V. "I'm afraid I don't have anything new to add."

The words weren't particularly special, yet they settled heavily in the room, and even though I wasn't looking at her, I saw the way Virginia sort of slumped in on herself.

"I realize this is not at all what you and your brother were hoping for, but it's my professional opinion that the previous three specialists who also ran tests and gave diagnoses are accurate."

Wait. *What?*

I sat up a little straighter. This was the fourth specialist Virginia had seen? For what? To walk again? Neo had made it seem like it was just a matter of time, so why did that suddenly seem like the furthest from the truth?

The office was suffocating with silence. The doctor cleared his throat and clasped his hands. "I wish I had better news. I—"

"I understand, Dr. Marks." V cut him off politely and with a strong, clear voice. She even offered him a smile. "I honestly didn't expect anything else."

"Well, your brother—"

"My brother will understand as well."

"The location of your injury makes it very difficult to correct. The spine has been severely damaged, and while technology has advanced a great deal in the last few years, I can't in good conscience recommend this surgery. The success rate is good, but for someone with your particular injury, I just can't make any guarantees. And the risk of—"

"Me becoming more injured or staying as I am now is high. The recovery time of a surgery of this nature is very long and grueling, and to go through all of that even after a failed attempt to restore my spine seems like a cruel fate." Virginia's voice was clear and matter-of-fact. Almost as if she were reciting something from a text-book she'd been forced to memorize.

The man nodded. "Correct. And you also run the risk of losing some of the muscle you've worked to maintain with such a recovery."

"Doctor Marks," Virginia said, suddenly very intent.

Both her hands steadied on either side of the chair, her upper body leaning toward him. "My brother isn't here. I would appreciate it if you level with me."

He nodded, sliding a quick glance at me.

Suddenly, the fact he found me intrusive oddly bothered me. "V," I spoke quietly. "Should I wait outside?"

Her fingers curled a little tighter. "Please, stay."

The doctor didn't seem placated by her reply, but I wasn't here to placate him, so I got more comfortable in the uncomfortable chair.

"I will never walk again, will I?"

I was a cold, stoic man. I plotted murder like some wrote a grocery list. I killed without blinking. I washed people's lifeblood from my hands like it was just ordinary dirt.

But this... Hearing her boldly ask this with no emotion in her voice, with what seemed like grim acceptance I didn't even know she had inside her... I didn't fucking like it.

The doctor glanced at me for help.

I lifted an eyebrow. "Why do you keep looking over here? I'm not leaving."

"Neo isn't as... blunt as I am," V said to me, but her eyes remained on the doctor.

I grunted, understanding. Then to the doc, I said, "I'm not helping you out. Answer the questions she's asking. It's your job."

"I don't know," he replied. "The odds... are not good."

I was so used to being the one wielding the knife, but suddenly, it felt like someone had turned the blade on me. *The receiving end is much different than the delivery.*

"I see." Her voice was strong, but emotion welled behind those two words regardless.

"As I said earlier, technology advances every day by

leaps and bounds. In five years, there may be a solution to your specific injury, so I cannot say that you will *never* walk again. It's just my opinion that it won't be anytime soon."

Virginia said nothing. I sat there stunned.

I really had no idea things were this grim. Neo never once said there was a possibility V would never walk again. He only said it was a matter of time and that she needed the right doctors, the right specialists, and the money.

Was all of that a lie?

I'd never heard Virginia speak so frankly. Gone was the girl who was usually giggling and smiling wide. In her place sat a woman much older than her age, a woman who had been through hell. *A woman who's been on the receiving end far more than she deserves.*

"Thank you for your honestly today," she said calmly, not even a hint of tears in her eyes or voice.

"My recommendation for you is to stay the course. Continue with all the therapies and current medications you are on. Meet with the advanced PT I've brought with me today. Allow him to evaluate you. He can also offer ideas and therapies that you aren't currently doing that may help improve things."

Improve things. But not make her legs work again. My stare cut to her, and it felt like I was looking at her for the very first time.

What was it like sitting in that chair? Being confined? Never being able to run when you wanted to. When you needed to. What was it like to live in a care facility, to go to doctor after doctor only to hear the same grim reply again and again?

This is the most sun I've soaked up in months.

Yet she bloomed anyway. A flower growing in impossible conditions.

Anger was no stranger to me. It lived inside me all my life, for anger, to me, was like salt to the sea. But what swelled up inside me went beyond that. Beyond the poison contaminating my veins. Those things were almost grounding to me, making me who I was.

But this? This was precarious and wild, threatening to blow the lid off the cool, calculated way I lived my life. This, I did not know how to handle.

Kill it. Remove it. Wipe it from your life.

"I'd like to see you back in a year. We can reevaluate and, if nothing else, keep a steady record of your condition."

"Of course." Her reply was gracious.

The doctor closed the folder before him, folding his hands on top. It was as if he were closing a door so not even the slightest possibility of hope could enter. "There are many paraplegics that live complete, satisfying lives."

I stood. The swift, stiff movement startled the doctor but merely drew Virginia's eye. Usually bubbling with emotion, switching from laughter to sarcasm and then to warmth, now she was still. Nonreactive in a situation in which I found it extremely difficult to be my usual stoic self.

How fucking offensive. *A complete, satisfying life.* She deserved so much more. What about happiness? *What about sunlight?*

"Thank you so much, doctor. I understand how valuable your time is, and I appreciate that you have spent some of it to look over my condition."

"Well, of course. When Ms. White called, I was more than happy to make room in my schedule."

A rude sound reverberated around the room. "Of course," I muttered.

"I beg your pardon?" the doctor quipped, sounding and looking like he had a giant stick shoved up his ass.

He probably wore it there because the New York Elite paid him to.

"Oh, nothing." Virginia was quick to cover.

"Yeah, it's nothing that the only reason you agreed to even treat her is that someone with money and connections called in a favor. Does that make you a doctor or a pimp?"

The doctor's chair hit against the wall with the force of his stand. "How dare you!" He gasped, the tops of his cheekbones turning scarlet. "I'm very respected in my field, and I've helped countless patients to walk again!"

"Right. And you did it all out of the goodness of your heart and not the notoriety it's given you."

"Earth!" Virginia gasped, her face finally, finally flooding with familiar emotion.

I don't know why, but the anger inside me calmed to a simmer.

"I apologize, Dr. Marks. I'm sure this appointment was a shock for… for my brother."

"I'm not your brother," I spat.

"My brother's best friend." She corrected. "He wasn't aware of some aspects of my condition, and this was probably a lot to take in."

"Yes. Well. Next time, bring Neo with you."

"He'd like it better if you brought Ivory," I retorted.

Virginia made a choked sound, rotating her head to give me a full-on death stare.

I wasn't scared.

"I do not have to subject myself to this," Dr. Marks

declared, straightening his lab coat. "I'm very sorry, Miss Virginia, but I won't see you again if *he* is with you."

Doc stormed out of the room, leaving the door wide open. Virginia's arms worked quickly, spinning her chair around to pin me with an incredulous stare.

"I cannot believe you said that!" she hissed.

"What?" I said, mild.

"You called my doctor a pimp."

"He was acting like one."

A giggle bubbled out of her. Her eyes went so wide I saw all the whites around the walnut-colored centers. Offended at her own behavior, she slapped a hand over her mouth. The hand might have covered the sound of her laugh, but it didn't disguise the way her shoulders shook.

"Are you laughing right now?" I wasn't trying to be funny. That man was a pompous asshat.

Her hand lowered, the sparks of humor dimming until they could no longer be seen. "Would you rather I cry?"

My God, this woman would give me whiplash. Yelling one minute. Laughing the next. Then looking at me like... well, *like that.*

"Fuck," I muttered, instantly starting forward. I had no clue why I was going to her. I had no clue what I was going to do.

"Miss Virginia?" The nurse who'd escorted us to this room reappeared in the open doorway. She was wearing hot-pink scrubs with Mickey Mouse all over them. "Philip is ready for you. Can I show you the way?"

"Who's Philip?" I asked, drawing the woman's stare.

Her tongue darted out to wet her lower lip before she answered. "The physical therapist she has an appointment with."

"Please lead the way," V said graciously, rolling her chair forward.

"I'll do that—" I offered, starting toward the wheelchair once more.

Suddenly, heavy pressure rolled over my shoe, pushing my boot down into the bones of my foot.

"Ow!" I hollered while shooting pain sizzled through my toes.

"Oops!" V called as she kept right on going. "I really am not a very good driver."

"You just ran over me," I deadpanned as she continued forward, leaving me in her wake.

In the doorway, her chair stopped, and she gazed over her shoulder, looking very much like the little spirited sprite she was. "And if you speak to any more of my doctors like that, I'll do way worse!"

I laughed. "Is that a threat?"

"Yes."

Cute.

Before I could even reply, she was out of the doorway, rolling herself down the hall after the nurse. I jogged to catch up, reaching out for the back of the chair.

"I can do it myself," she stated before my hands even closed around the handles.

I let her have her way.

Six

VIRGINIA

WHAT IS IT WITH MEN?

Boorish. Empty-headed. Completely ridiculous!

I mean, here I thought I was just going to be a girl today, out on her own, taking care of her own business… *Free.*

Nope. Earth comes in dressed in leather with a car right out of a movie and says he's my ride. I mean, okay, I was excited. What girl always kept in a tower wouldn't be?

Then he went and opened his mouth. *No.* He called my doctor a pimp!

And I thought Neo was bad.

The look on that doctor's face… I suppressed a giggle. And really, everything Earth voiced was thoughts I'd secretly had.

The difference? I had manners and didn't say those things out loud. Besides, it didn't matter if the only reason I was able to see these fancy doctors was Ivory's name. I was grateful just the same.

Earth was lucky I didn't mow him over in my chair and all he got was a wheel over those boots. I suppressed another giggle.

Without any warning at all, the brush of warm, gentle breath tickled my ear, and the scent of stale cigarettes and bread crowded my senses. "You sure are putting in a lot of effort not to laugh."

The whisper coated my ear like thick, sweet molasses. The lowered, slightly arrogant tone created a prickling sensation along my spine and neck. Overwhelmed, I wallowed in silence for a few long moments as I digested some of the sweetness that really should have been sour.

Finally able to shake off the way my nerves tingled, I turned, Earth pulling back so our noses didn't collide. "You have a booger hanging out of your nose," I told him coolly.

Caught completely off guard, his black eyes went wide and his whole upper body jerked back as his hand flew up to his face.

This time, I did laugh. There was no containing the amusement I got out of finally besting big, bad Earth.

"You lying brat," he all but growled, his face screwed up in a scowl as his hand dropped into his lap.

"*Ahh!*" Laughter suddenly quelled, I gasped when my chair went flying forward. Grappling for the armrests for some sort of anchor, my hands fell over Earth's where he had grabbed to yank me close.

The fierceness in his stare was delicious. The narrowed focus all pinned on me would have kept me in this chair even if my legs suddenly began to work again. Awareness unlike anything I'd felt before, unlike anything I'd honestly thought possible, swept through me like a sudden blaze in a dry forest, consuming literally everything in its path.

Instead of pulling away, my hands tightened around his, still gripping for that anchor, finding him perfect for the job.

If he felt my grip, he showed no notice, that forceful opaque stare never once leaving me. My throat worked with the force of my swallow, and heat burned my middle, making me want to squirm.

"You like playing games with me?" he intoned, quiet because we were so close.

Earth intimidated a lot of people. Okay, everyone. And the way he spoke and stared just now... I should have been intimidated too, but I wasn't. His powerful aura and unexpected actions did not push me away. Oddly, they tugged me closer.

Knowing he asked a question, I wanted to answer, but words failed me.

"Miss Virginia?" A man spoke, stepping into the room and carrying a clipboard.

My head whipped around, but I could still feel the burning of Earth's eyes.

"That's me!" My voice was a little high-pitched, and I cleared my throat.

"Nice to meet you," he said, coming farther into the room. He wasn't dressed like Dr. Marks. Instead, he wore athletic pants, sneakers, and a long-sleeved gray sweatshirt. "I'm the physical therapist Dr. Marks works with, Philip Gains. You can just call me Phil."

Stopping close by, he held out his hand, and it made me realize I was still gripping Earth. Jerking my hands away from him, I offered one to the PT along with a smile. "So lovely to meet you. I've heard wonderful things, and I'm grateful you took time out of your busy schedule to meet with me."

"Well, I love my job." Phil smiled.

Earth made a rude sound, and I shot him a warning glare, which he returned.

"And this is your brother? I spoke with you on the

phone, I believe?" Philip said, ignoring our glaring contest to greet Earth.

"I'm not her brother. I'm her guardian."

Guardian?

"Neo wasn't able to make it today. This is, ah, his best friend, Earth."

"Nice to meet you," the PT said politely, offering his hand.

For a brief moment, I worried Earth would refuse the greeting, but thankfully, he shook the man's hand.

"So I've already reviewed your charts and all the notes from your regular physical therapist. I have to say I'm impressed. You do a lot on a weekly basis to maintain the muscle that you have and even build new."

"Well, we thought it might be helpful for when I"—pause—"walk again."

Philip didn't hang on my heavy pause or the way my voice kinda fell at the end. I was sure he'd spoken to Dr. Marks, sure he knew of the many opinions that walking was not in my future.

"Absolutely." He agreed. "How about we go over there and you can show off those muscles?" He pointed toward the mat, bars, and other various therapy equipment I was all very familiar with.

A dark cloud slipped over me, darkening my mood as I moved across the room. It happened occasionally, perhaps more than I wanted to admit, but usually, I was good at shoving it back where it came from.

I struggled quietly for a few moments, feeling swallowed by shadows as my own self-doubt and anxiety grappled for control of my thoughts. *What's the point of even doing this? Why even meet with this man if it's not for coming up with a post-surgery plan? You won't walk again, V. All this physical therapy is a waste of time.*

"Miss Virginia? Is everything okay?"

The unfamiliar voice cut into my thoughts, lifting my chin to focus on the therapist. He was an attractive man, probably around thirty years old with sandy hair and a lean build.

I felt more than saw Earth shift across the room, but I didn't dare look at him. Not in that moment. I had to focus on myself just then.

"Oh yes!" I said, smiling wide. "Sorry about that. I didn't mean to be rude."

Philip knelt in front of my chair. His smile was gentle. "I'm sure the appointment with Dr. Marks was a lot to take in. And perhaps you were hoping for him to say something else."

"Perhaps," I echoed.

"Well, how about a good workout? It does the mind just as much good as the body."

"Sure." I smiled.

We went through several exercises I knew well, and Philip showed me a few techniques that were new to me that I could do on my own to keep up my strength. He praised my abilities, my strength, and even my flexibility.

I admit it was nice to hear some positive encouragement after what felt like another massive letdown. It bothered me that I was so disappointed. I thought I'd been prepared. I even expected what the doctor said today.

So why did it still hurt?

Why did hope still bloom where it should no longer exist?

How am I going to tell Neo?

That thought seemed to be my final blow, robbing me of all my concentration and muscle memory. My body sagged, bowing against the parallel bars I stood between.

"Whoa." Philip reacted quickly, grabbing onto the white belt that had been fastened around my waist. Hoisting me up by it, he helped support my weight as my arms shook and struggled to support the rest of me. "You tired?" he asked.

"I-I'm sorry. I lost focus."

"That's what I'm here for." He reassured me. Releasing the belt, he palmed my waist, guiding my body upright between the two bars. My ankles and lower legs were locked into braces to help offer support, and I had one hand on each bar so I could "walk" between them.

"Find your balance," Philip instructed. "Focus on the Y-ligament."

I did as he instructed, letting my hips bow forward, then catching my weight when they went far enough. My arms still shook, and part of me was still thinking of Neo. Of telling him that I wouldn't walk.

He'd want to call another specialist. He wouldn't take no for an answer.

I was tired.

My arms sagged again, my body falling off-center.

Philip caught me but this time with his body and not by catching the support belt around me. My whole chest collided with his, and my face flamed with embarrassment. My natural instinct was to push away, to scramble back so he wasn't in my personal space.

I couldn't.

My body didn't work like that even when it wanted to. Even when my instincts told my lower half to do something, my body didn't respond. The message receptors—the nerves that carried those messages to and from my brain—didn't work anymore.

They never would again.

So I stood there slumped into a therapist I'd just met,

arms trembling, body and mind exhausted. Tears burned behind my eyes, and I blinked furiously to keep them back. The frustration of being at the will of someone else to give me my personal space back would not make me cry.

I grappled for the bars to try and push up. "I got you," Philip assured me, and the muscles in the back of my neck bunched.

A rumble rolled through the room, and then I was being drawn back, my entire body tensing even more as I moved without any control.

"Getting a little handsy, wouldn't you say, doc?" Earth intoned, his arms wrapping around my waist, drawing me away from the therapist.

"I'm just doing my job," Philip replied. "Unless you would prefer I let her fall?"

My whole body quivered from the effort, a fine sheen of sweat across my forehead. "Give me your weight, sprite." Earth coaxed gently. "I won't let you fall."

"You are not trained in this. Let me do my job." Philip stepped forward.

I released my weight to Earth, my breath catching as I felt myself go boneless. The arms already around me tightened, and my entire back became supported by his front. The instant relief that coursed through me was startling but so welcome. Like a rainbow painting a previously gray sky with color.

I sighed.

"Just relax a second." Earth encouraged.

Above my head, his voice echoed much harder, much grumpier than he'd just spoken to me. "Don't you think you're pushing her too much? What kind of place is this? She almost fell!"

"I can assure you that all we've been doing here today

are things she is capable of. Sometimes these things happen. It's normal."

"Letting a girl fall into your body and holding her there is normal," Earth's voice was low and calm. Deadly.

All the relaxation I'd allowed evaporated, and I straightened my shoulders. "Earth," I warned. "This was all my fault. I wasn't concentrating, and it caused me to fall. Phil didn't do anything that I'm normally able to do without issue."

I could practically hear his teeth grind in his effort not to argue. Against my back, his heart beat uncontrollably.

"I think we should call it a day. You did well. Your body needs a break," Philip suggested. He was much more reasonable and calmer in the face of Earth versus Dr. Marks.

I nodded once.

"I'll assist you in taking off those braces," the man said, taking a tentative step closer.

I nodded again.

"I've got eyes on you," Earth said, his voice creating a chill in the room.

"Go sit down," I told him.

Philip helped me to stand, and Earth moved to the other side of the bars, crossing his arms over his chest to glare at us.

"Just ignore him," I whispered to Philip.

"You sure that's not your bodyguard?"

I laughed lightly.

Once I was back in my chair, braces and belt removed, I sank back gratefully, feeling more exhausted than I liked. "I apologize," I told Philip. "I can usually handle much more."

"It's perfectly normal." He reassured. "Change of location, your appointment with the doctor, travel to get here… all of these things are connected. I can still tell what great shape you are in. Just do those few new things I showed you, and you'll see even more improvement."

I nodded.

"And if you'd like to have another session—"

"No."

Both Philip and I turned to stare at Earth.

"No?" I echoed.

"Thanks, but no thanks, doc."

"I'm offended that you would challenge my integrity and appropriateness with a patient," Philip told him.

"I don't give a damn if you're offended."

"Earth, please," I said, voice weary.

His dark stare shifted to me, the stoniness there crumbling into something a little softer. "You ready to go?"

I nodded.

"Thank you again. I will be sure to tell my brother what a great help you were today."

"My pleasure. If you have any questions or would like to meet again, just call my office and we will set something up."

Thankfully, Earth said nothing as he wrapped his hands around the handles of my wheelchair. My arms still quivered lightly as the therapist left the room, and the second he was gone, I let my core relax to slump even more into the chair.

"You're just as bad as Neo," I muttered, rubbing my forehead with my hand.

He made a rude sound. "Now I know why he warned me about the physical therapists. They all perverts like this?"

I gasped, rotating to stare up at him. "They are not perverts! Is that what Neo said?"

"Sure looked like he was enjoying you pressed up against him," Earth muttered, voice dark.

I felt my cheeks grow hot. "Then what would you have me do, fall on the floor?"

His eyes cut down, searing me with their intensity. "Next time, call for me."

"And if you aren't here?"

His eyes slid away, his jaw like granite. "Let's go."

Settling back in the chair, I didn't argue about letting him push me. Truthfully, I was still exhausted. My arms felt like limp noodles.

Enclosed in the small elevator alone, my leg jolted, shoe smacking against the footrest.

My reaction was more in annoyance than that of surprise. I'd hoped this wouldn't happen, but really, I should have known better.

It jerked up again, and then the other made a similar movement. Panicked, Earth hit the floor in front of me, hands hovering over my legs, eyes wide with worry.

"I-I thought you couldn't move your legs!" he exclaimed. "What's happening? What's wrong. Goddamn that doctor! I knew he was a quack." His head snapped up, eyes narrowing into small crescent moons while menace literally vibrated from his pores. "I'll kill him."

A light shiver ran down my spine, and even though I only felt it halfway, I was sure it continued down into the parts I couldn't feel.

"It's okay." I quickly tried to assure him. He'd never seen this before. He didn't know. Of course he would worry.

He didn't seem to hear, his eyes wild but also focused, lips set in a thin line.

"Earth," I called, voice forceful.

Attention became all mine as I held his dark gaze. "It's just muscle spasms. It's normal."

His brow creased, drawing together his thick dark eyebrows. "Normal?"

His hands still hovered, so I took one, guiding it down just above my knee. He stared down at where I encouraged him to hold, fingers lax until my muscles spasmed again, jerking and shaking.

I saw rather than felt his grip tighten. His sharp intake of breath filled the elevator, and his chin lifted. "Does that hurt?" he demanded, and I couldn't help but wonder…

"What if I said it does?"

An ominous growl rumbled through his chest, and I briefly wondered if he was animal or man.

Leg still jumping, I reached down to cover his hand with mine. Both our arms bobbed up and down as they basically rode the ride my body gave them. "It doesn't hurt."

"Why?" he asked, watching them bounce.

The elevator sprang open, revealing what I just realized to be an intimate moment to the couple standing on the other side of the doors.

Feeling the change in me, Earth spun, his hand pulling from beneath mine as he stood with so much grace that a piece of me ached.

His body was firmly planted in front of me, hiding all of what he could from prying eyes. The doors started to close, but he slapped a hand against them, forcing them back. "What are you looking at?" He challenged.

Did he not know how to have a regular conversation with anyone?

My legs were still shaking, and it took effort for me

to place them back on the footrests. "Earth? Can you help?"

Immediately he came behind me, nudging my chair out into the hallway between the couple who'd parted.

"Have a wonderful day!" I told them as we passed.

Outside, the sun was bright, and I was eager to soak in some of its warmth. "Can we maybe sit over there for a few minutes?" I asked, pointing to a small sitting area with a bench and some potted flowers that were just past the awning so it was in the sun.

He said nothing but directed us there, stopping my chair right in front of the bench, leaving only enough space for him to sit down beside me.

My legs spasmed some more, the steady jolts lessening already. "It usually doesn't last very long," I told him.

"Why?" He echoed the question he'd asked in the elevator.

"I'm paralyzed from the lower waist down," I explained, and he nodded. "So I can't feel or move my legs at all, but they can move themselves."

Earth frowned but nodded as if he wanted to know more.

"The muscles spasm sometimes. Mostly in cases when they are overworked or just tired. Sometimes in cases of stress."

"That doctor overworked you."

I giggled. "Stop blaming it all on the therapist. It just happens. The spasms can actually be good because it's kinda like a workout for the muscles, you know? I just did a lot today, and now my muscles are letting me know."

"Does it happen a lot?"

"Sometimes. I guess not that often."

"I don't like it," he whispered.

My heart pinched at that. There wasn't pity in his voice. There wasn't even disgust or anxiety. It was almost like he just… didn't want me to hurt.

"It really doesn't hurt," I assured him.

"Really?"

I smiled, a small lump forming in my throat. *He really is worried.*

I nodded eagerly. "Every once in a while, I'll get a burning sensation or like a phantom pain and that can be uncomfortable, but this doesn't hurt."

"I didn't know," he muttered, sitting back against the bench, gazing off into the opposite direction.

"There was no reason for you to know about muscle spasms."

He made a noise. After a moment, he turned back to me. "Neo said you would walk again."

Oh. I'd realized and then forgotten what a shock that appointment must have been. Neo likely didn't think Earth would sit in on it. The truth was Neo didn't often think about what I wanted. He thought he knew.

"Neo is very determined."

"What about you?"

I blinked, slightly startled. Suddenly, the sun felt a little warm on my cheeks. Like it was shining a spotlight on me, making it easier for Earth to see. Instead of answering, I let the question soak in. I sort of reveled in it for a bit. Lifting my face toward the sky, I shut my eyes and breathed.

"Virginia."

Keeping my face upturned, eyes closed, I answered, "No one's really ever asked me that before."

"No?"

"No, everyone just assumes they know what I need,

that all I could want is to walk again. That I just want to forget that day."

"But that's not what you want, is it?"

I shook my head.

"Tell me. Tell me what you want."

Tucking my chin, I raised my lashes to regard him. I hadn't seen him in months, and before that, when I did, it was always light and fun. Quick visits in the presence of the rest of the family. It was never just me and Earth. Alone. It was never just the weight of his engulfing stare, the totality of his attention. When he was around, his presence could never be denied, but now... now it was all I felt.

And I found myself wanting to tell him. Wanting to open up in a way I never allowed before. My deepest thoughts and desires were just that—*mine.* They were personal longings I thought no one could understand, that perhaps no one would even want to understand.

I was falling into his eyes. Into the endless black galaxy he offered in just a quiet stare. As if there were enough room in that darkness for not just him but me too.

"I want a life of my own," I confessed, voice cautious.

I'm trusting you with the wishes I hold deepest in my heart.

"It doesn't really matter if it's in this chair or out of it. I just want to have a life that is mine, one that isn't just about trying to walk again. Where I don't have to—" I pressed my lips together. I wouldn't say that out loud. Ever.

"Don't have to what?"

I shook my head. *Some things I'll keep to myself.*

"I just want to stop wishing for a better future. It's okay if I don't walk again, you know? It's not ideal, but I can accept it. I want to stop waiting for my life to start...

I mean, I'm already living, so why does it feel like everything around me moves but I'm stuck on pause?"

I waited, but he said nothing. Surprisingly, his silence felt oddly comfortable. Maybe because he didn't offer fake apologies or try to pretend he could understand. He just listened carefully to the confession I had never voiced out loud without trying to drown out its importance with the sound of his own voice.

I didn't know how badly I needed that. How incredible it was for someone just to *hear*.

And so we sat in the silent sunshine, the spasms in my legs waning, taking with them a little of the heaviness I'd been bravely carrying all alone in my heart.

Seven

EARTH

EVERYONE HAS SECRETS, UNSPOKEN THOUGHTS AND feelings residing inside them. Hell, I had an entire identity no one really knew. From a very early age, I understood that when you looked at a person, what you saw was exactly what they wanted you to see. They used the more harmless parts of themselves to cover up the parts they wanted to remain hidden.

Some were better at this than others. Some were skilled at seeing beneath the façade all people wore to realize there was much more.

I prided myself on that skill. On seeing what wasn't there. At feeling undercurrents buried deep. I observed, watched… learned. And when the information I wanted couldn't be discovered that way, I hunted.

So this was an unexpected uppercut to the chin, snapping all my reflexes back, leaving them stunned.

I didn't know.

How could I not have known?

Because I never doubted Neo. I never looked beneath the obvious love he had for his sister. I never questioned his motives. But now, watching this long-haired beauty sit quietly with her face turned to the sun, I began to question.

Why have I never done this before?

I was selfish. Blinded almost by my own secrets, knowing that if I dug deeper into others around me, they would react the same. How had I put so much effort into knowing my enemies, into knowing my victims, but put so little into my family?

Suddenly, there were so many questions I wanted to ask V. So much I wanted to know. I could ask Neo later. Hell, I definitely would. But it wouldn't be the same.

Never had the saying, "There are two sides to every story," ever strike so profoundly. I'd known Virginia for years now, but today, I realized that she was mostly a stranger. Everything I knew about her was told to me through someone else.

Could you really know a person through someone else's eyes? It would be their version you met, which would be clouded by their own judgments.

While I respected Neo, I didn't want that. Suddenly, knowing Virginia through him wasn't enough. I wanted to know his sister on my own terms.

"Thank you for bringing me today. We should probably get going now so you can get back to whatever it is that you do."

"What about you? What do you do?"

"Me?" Her brown eyes widened. I nodded, and the tip of her pink tongue jutted out to wet her lips. "Well, since therapy and my appointments are done for the day, I'll probably, ah, read or watch Netflix. And play with Zilla." Her eyes brightened. "Oh! I was hoping I could convince you to stop on the way back so I could get some crickets for her."

"Crickets."

Her head bobbed enthusiastically. "Zilla loves crickets."

"Don't most girls have cats?"

"I can't have a cat or dog at the Tower." She scowled. "Besides, what's wrong with a gecko? They make wonderful pets!"

A light breeze kicked up, making a few loose strands of hair blow, and the petals on the flower clips decorating her braids ruffled lightly. *She looks like summer.* "How many?" I barked.

The smile on her lips faltered, shoulders drawing back. "What?"

My voice was strained, patience suddenly very difficult to hold on to. "How many times have you been told you won't walk again?"

Her warm gaze became shuttered, then was taken away completely when she glanced down to her lap.

Anger forced a gruff sound out of my throat. Sliding forward on the bench, I grasped her chin, pushing it back up, forcing her to look at me. "Answer me."

A stubborn glint sparked in the depths of her eyes. "Most people wouldn't be so bold with their rude questions."

"I'm not most people."

"Around six."

My hand fell from her chin, but her gaze stayed leveled on mine. "Is this where you pity me?"

One eyebrow arched. "Do you want my pity?"

"No."

"Good, because I don't pity anyone." I cleared my throat, lapsing into silence.

Gone was the light mood from when we were talking about crickets, instead descending into an awkward silence.

"You like hot chocolate?" I asked abruptly.

"Hot chocolate?" she echoed, curious.

I nodded, flinging my hand out. "You know, like that kind Fletcher is always asking for."

Her eyes lit up. "Oh, you mean Kismet!" She laughed, the sound sort of like the tinkling of bells. "Who doesn't like it? Their frozen hot chocolate is legendary."

"You've had it?"

Her nod was enthusiastic. "Of course. When Fletcher comes to visit, he brings it. And sometimes Neo does too."

"Have you been to the café?"

The excitement in her eyes dimmed just a little as she shook her head. "I don't really get out much. Neo is very overprotective."

I made a rude sound, boots thumping on the pavement when I stood. "Well, Neo is trapped in Texas, and I can protect you no matter where we go."

Craning her neck, she stared up wide-eyed. "You want to go to Kismet?"

"You don't?" I countered.

A light squeal erupted, her hands slapping over the wide smile stretching over the lower part of her face. "Really? Can we?"

Enthusiasm and cheerfulness made me queasy, and I liked beer, not hot chocolate. But damn if I didn't stand on the sidewalk, practically asking for it all. "Sure. Why not?"

"I heard it's so beautiful inside! Very eclectic and fun. I've always wanted to go."

Then why hasn't Neo taken you?

"Keep your hands and feet inside the ride at all times," I said in lieu of a curse toward her brother. Grasping the back of the chair, I pushed her in the direction of the car.

Partway through the parking lot, she gasped, rotating at the waist to look up at me. The sun was glaring harshly down, making her squint. Shifting easily, I used my frame to block the brightest rays. "Earth? I don't think Kismet is wheelchair accessible."

My footsteps stalled. "What?"

"I wasn't thinking at first, but I've looked it up online before. I'm pretty sure you have to go down some stairs to get inside. And it's a fairly narrow building. I don't think they have a ramp."

It never even occurred to me to think of something like that. Never once did I ever wonder if I was able to go somewhere because it wouldn't be accessible.

This is what she lives.

"So, um, as much as I would love to go, I don't think I'll be able. But just you asking me means so much. Thank you anyway." Her smile was genuine, the disappointment in her voice barely there.

How many places has she wanted to go but been unable to?

Bitterness splashed the back of my throat, only to be chased back by anger. That stupid café. I'd never even stepped foot into that God-awful place before, even though it was Fletch's favorite. He had Ethan to drag there, and before Ethan, it was Ivory who indulged him.

But who would indulge Virginia?

"Can't get in, you say?" I scoffed. Leaning down, my lips brushed against her ear. "Oh, sprite, you have no idea who you're dealing with."

Eight

Virginia

It really wasn't a strange thing to be lifted or carried by others when you were paralyzed. As much as I prided myself on transferring my own weight and being as independent as possible, sometimes help was necessary. Or even just nice.

Neo picked me up all the time. Emogen often assisted me. Doctors, physical therapists… it was normal.

But *this*. This was different.

The catch in my throat. The way my fingers curled into the base of his neck, itching to delve inside the collar of the leather jacket for more contact with skin. The automatic relaxation of limbs I usually held tense while being held.

Being cradled in Earth's arms felt like more than just a means to an end. Like he lifted me because he wanted to, not because it was a necessity. All at once, it was thrilling, intimate, and somehow familiar. Focusing on my surroundings or even what I needed to do to make sure I wasn't being a burden didn't seem necessary.

In this moment, I wasn't disabled. I wasn't a patient being cradled in his arms because my legs didn't work. Instead, I was an ordinary girl whose heart pattered wildly because she was being held by someone who not only excited her but brought her to a place she'd desperately wanted to visit for so long.

"Be careful with that," Earth ordered, his voice stern.

Peeking over his shoulder, I saw an employee of Kismet lifting my folded chair to carry it along behind us. The young man caught me watching him, and his cheeks turned pink. I smiled and gave him an approving thumbs-up.

"Stop flirting," Earth said passively, shifting my weight even closer.

I made a face. "I guess you would assume simple kindness as flirting, considering everyone you talk to you insult."

He grunted, starting down the concrete stairs leading to a robin's-egg-blue wooden door with panes of glass in the center.

I gasped when someone from inside opened the door to allow us in. "Wait!"

His boots made a definite thump when he planted them in place. "Something wrong?"

"I didn't get to appreciate the sign or the building before we came in!"

His face was blank. "It's a sign. And a door. The sidewalk is dirty."

"But I've only ever seen pictures online. I want to see it all with my own eyes!" I exclaimed, widening my lashes to prove my point.

I felt a slight rumble against my side, but he didn't laugh or even smile. "What the hell were you doing when we were standing out there? Closing your eyes?"

"It was hard to pay attention," I muttered, feeling a lick of shyness rush up inside me. "Please, Earth?"

He sighed miserably, his boots stomping back up the

stairs. "We'll meet you inside," he told the boy with my wheelchair.

Cars whizzed by, cabbies laid on their horns, and down the block, a large truck beeped as it backed up. Summer air blew down the street, carrying with it the stench of exhaust.

I patted the back of his head in excitement, my upper body bouncing around in excitement.

"This is ridiculous." He glowered.

I ignored him. He had a bad attitude.

The front of the building was charming. It sat in the middle of what looked like a line of row houses. They were all connected, but this one was defined by white-wash brick, robin's-egg-blue window trim, and a wooden door that was slightly off-kilter at the base of the concrete stairs. I was charmed you had to go down a few steps instead of up to get inside.

There was a door on the bell that rang every time it opened, and the sign was oval, cream-colored, and Kismet was written in gold with stars all around it.

"It's so cute," I exclaimed. "Like a real-life dollhouse!"

"It's ugly," Earth declared.

"I like it!"

He pursed his lips. "You wanna go inside now?"

"Yes, please!"

The bell chimed when the door opened once more, and the scent of rich chocolate and pastry floated out, swirling around my head. Earth had to duck a bit to get past the doorframe, which was also adorably charming.

"Stupid place probably isn't even up to code," he muttered as his hand came up to shield my head as if he worried I might bump it.

"It's a historic building preserved by the city," announced a woman standing at a nearby podium.

"Oh, how wonderful!" I said, smiling. "Whoa! Just look how gorgeous!" My eyes roamed everywhere in the tiny entrance, which was long and narrow and lined with people waiting to be seated. I didn't even have time to be self-conscious of them staring because there were so many other worthwhile things to give attention.

Each side of the narrow space held colorfully painted hutches that were filled with antique-looking teacups, saucers, and dessert plates. Along with the china were vintage toys and games from many years ago. Stuffed toys lined one shelf, as did old books.

Running down the center of the aisle was a carpet that looked antique but capable of withstanding the traffic this popular place knew.

An old golden glass chandelier hung in the center just high enough for Earth not to hit his head on his way past the line.

"Earth," I whispered, tugging on his jacket.

"What?"

"You're cutting the line."

Suddenly, I heard my name being called by a familiar enthusiastic voice. "Virginia! Virginia!"

My head popped up, eyes looking past the woman at the podium and into the interior of the café.

Fletcher waved wildly, a smile on his lips and his floppy hair nearly covering his eyes.

"Fletch!" I called back, happiness blossoming in the center of my chest. On the other side of the table, Ethan stood, adjusting the hot-pink tie under his black sports jacket.

"We're with them," Earth told the hostess as he stepped by on the way to our friends.

"Did you invite them?" I asked, shifting my stare to

him. His skin was incredibly smooth even this close, his black eyes focused straight ahead.

He cleared his throat. "I needed the address of the place. Ethan said they would meet us here. Figured you'd like to see them."

Without thinking, I tightened my arms around his neck, pressing my face closer against him for a hug. "Thank you. Thank you so much."

His muscles tensed slightly, but then he relaxed again. "Don't be too thankful. Fletch will probably try and eat everything you order."

The second we approached the round white table, Fletcher launched himself at us, throwing his arms around Earth and me both. "Hi, guys!" His voice was muffled against my shoulder.

Earth grunted but didn't protest Fletcher's public display of affection. "Hey, kid."

We all knew that Earth had a soft spot for Fletch.

I patted his fluffy hair and laughed. "Fletcher! It feels like I haven't seen you in forever."

He pulled away, a small pout on his lips. "Sorry I haven't been by. I've had so many shows lately."

"I know! Ethan sent me some recordings, and you sound so good! I think you keep getting better."

Fletcher's honey eyes widened, and he rotated toward Ethan. "You've been sending her my music?"

Ethan smiled. "Of course. We're gonna get you to an actual show soon," he told me.

I sighed. "I can't wait. I haven't seen Fletcher play violin since that fashion show of Ivory's way back when she first met Neo!"

Earth shifted, going around the table to where my wheelchair was waiting. It was against the wall, so when

I sat down, I would be able to look around the café and see everything.

"Here, let me help you," Ethan offered, grabbing the chair to make sure it was steady.

Earth put me in the chair gently, making sure my dress was pulled down as he shifted back. Before pulling away completely, I felt a light tug on the end of my braid. "See, who needs a ramp?"

My heart fluttered lightly, and tears rushed to my eyes.

Seeing the sudden sheen, Earth frowned. "Did I hurt you?"

"No. Everything is perfect." I assured him, waving off his concern to sniffle lightly.

He would have no idea how much such a simple thing as bringing me here could mean. How something that everyone else did on the daily was special and so meaningful to me. And he did it so effortlessly as if it was no big deal to just carry me inside. Like the prying eyes, pitying stares, or even sighs of annoyance from the employees were nothing.

And with Earth... maybe they were. Because you know what? I didn't notice any of that not even once since we'd gotten out of his car.

"I'm starving!" Fletcher declared, chair legs scraping along the wooden floor as he dragged his chair to the table.

"When aren't you?" Earth retorted, sitting down beside me.

"Get whatever you want, puppy," Ethan told his boyfriend.

Earth snorted. "Spoiled."

Fletcher beamed at Ethan, looping his arm around his before staring down at the menu.

Ethan gave me a wink, smiling. "So, Virginia, what do you think of Kismet?"

"Oh, it's better than I hoped!" I declared, gazing around at the random chandeliers hanging from the ceiling. The walls were all whitewashed brick, covered in old art, mirrors with gaudy gold frames, and the occasional star painted on the wall.

The sound of water made me turn toward the back of the room. "Is that a real fountain?" I exclaimed.

Earth followed my gaze as Ethan laughed. "Sure is. Many decades ago, there was a small garden behind the building. Almost like a courtyard. When the owners bought this place and made it into a café, they wanted to keep the courtyard, but it was quite impractical because of all the cold months we get here in the city. So they extended the building but kept the centerpiece, which was that fountain."

Now that he explained, I could see how the building was basically extended, and to get to the fountain, you had to cross under a large archway. The sounds of falling water echoed through the place.

"Before we leave, you should throw a penny in the fountain and make a wish!" Fletcher said.

"That's a wishing fountain?" I said, awed.

"Of course it is," Earth muttered, turning back to the table.

"How do you know so much about this place?" I asked Ethan.

"I know the owner."

"Ethan knows everyone," Fletcher announced.

"Good afternoon." A friendly waitress greeted us, stepping up to the table. She was holding a small notepad and a pen with a big, fluffy pink ball at the end. "Are you ready to order?"

Fletcher rattled off a list of things right away, making it clear he knew the menu by heart. When he was done, Ethan ordered an iced coffee with cream, and then all eyes turned to me.

Flustered, I grabbed the menu and gazed down at it. "Well, I don't know…" I worried, feeling all the stares.

"Take your time, sprite. She'll wait," Earth offered, which I found oddly reassuring.

After a moment, I ordered a classic frozen hot chocolate.

"Get a muffin. The muffins are so good." Fletcher encouraged.

Naturally, I ordered a muffin.

Everyone turned to Earth. "I'm good," he told the waitress.

My mouth fell open.

Fletcher gasped. "Earth! You have to get something! We finally got you here. You have to."

Earth sighed and hitched his chin at Fletcher. "You order for me, then."

"Give him the peanut butter frozen hot chocolate and a croissant."

Immediately, Earth looked like he regretted letting Fletcher order for him, but he didn't refuse.

When the waitress was gone, his leather-clad elbows leaned on the table so he could look over Fletcher. "Ethan treating you okay? Do I need to kick his ass?"

Ethan rolled his eyes but otherwise didn't even seem offended.

Fletcher's cheeks turned pink, and his body seemed to tuck closer into Ethan's side. "You know I'm fine, Earth."

"We miss you at the bar," he said, gruff.

Fletcher sat up. "You do? I'll come by tomorrow!" The

second the words were out of his mouth, he glanced at Ethan. "Is that okay?"

Earth scowled. "You don't need his permission."

"But I want it," Fletcher retorted, voice shy.

Ethan's face went soft, his hand reaching up to ruffle Fletcher's hair. "Of course it's okay."

Fletcher beamed, and my eyes went back to wandering around the eclectic café. It was smaller inside than I expected, the tables close together, every single one filled. There was even a metal spiral staircase off to the side of the room where the servers were leading customers upstairs.

"How did you get a table so fast?" I wondered, staring at the long line that was now out the door.

"When Earth called me for directions, I called and told them we were coming in," Ethan replied simply.

Sometimes I forgot that Ethan and Ivory were very well-known here in New York City. I only remembered when their social status in some way benefited me and my friends.

Like getting you fancy doctor appointments. But even knowing New York Elite can't make you walk again.

I don't know how, but Earth seemed to sense my thoughts, his body shifting slightly toward me. His eyes asked if I was okay while his lips stayed closed.

I nodded, then turned back to the room. Fletcher talked about a mile a minute until the waitress appeared with a huge tray filled with our order.

"That's bigger than my head!" I laughed as she slid the frozen hot chocolate onto the table in front of me.

The glass it was in looked like a bowl on a crystal pedestal that sat on a small white plate in case the massive amounts of whipped cream piled on the top began to melt. There was a straw and spoon sticking up from the side and chocolate shavings decorating the white cream.

An equal-sized drink was placed in front of Fletcher and Earth. Earth's had a giant peanut butter cup sticking out.

Along with Fletcher's drink, he also had a giant blueberry muffin, some type of grilled sandwich, and a mountain of fries.

The table in front of Ethan would have looked bare with just his iced coffee if it weren't for all the plates Fletcher spread out everywhere.

I smiled as the server slid a strawberry muffin near my elbow, and then she took her leave.

"Try it!" Fletcher exclaimed, already biting into his muffin. "It tastes even better here than when it's takeout!"

Everyone watched as I leaned in to get a mouthful from the straw. Smooth, rich chocolate the temperature of ice cream burst across my tongue, bringing my senses alive, and I felt my eyes widen.

"This is amazing!" Leaning forward, I licked the mountain of whipped cream, sighing when a few chocolate curls melted against my tongue.

"You're as bad as Fletch," Earth grumped, leaning over to swipe whipped cream off the tip of my nose. "It's all over your face."

My tongue darted out to lick the cream still on my lip, and I couldn't help but notice the way Earth's eyes followed the movement.

A paper napkin was shoved under my nose. "Clean yourself up."

"Thank you," I said politely, taking the offer.

"Aren't you gonna try yours?" Fletcher asked, pointing to Earth's untouched treat.

Dutifully, he leaned forward to take a pull on the straw. "It's too sweet," he declared.

Fletcher beamed. "That means he likes it."

I went back to eating, alternating between the straw and the spoon, listening with one ear to Earth and Fletcher bickering while listening to everything else going on in the room around us. I couldn't remember the last time I was out like this. People watching, feeling excitement buzz in the air. Small string lights twinkled around the ceiling, and the old floor creaked when the servers walked by.

I was making a mental note to look up some old movie that was on a poster hanging across the room when Earth's voice pulled me back. "You're cold."

"What?" I echoed.

He made a rude sound, gesturing to my arms, which were raised with goose bumps.

"Oh." I noticed. "I'm fine. It's probably this giant frozen drink." I felt like I'd been drinking it for a long time, but there was barely a dent in it. How did they expect people to finish all this?

"You should stop drinking it. I'll get you something hot."

I made a face. "No! I like this." I turned sheepish. "Besides, there is no way I will be able to drink all this."

The sound of a straw slurping up the last bit cut through our conversation. Glancing over, I burst out laughing because Fletcher had indeed done the impossible.

"Done!" he declared, sitting back and patting his still-thin stomach.

My laughter cut off when the warm weight of something settled around me. Glancing down, I watched

Earth draping his jacket around my shoulders. "Lean up," he said quietly.

I listened, upper body leaning forward to allow room for the jacket behind me.

"Arms."

"This really isn't necessary. I'm not that cold—"

"Arms," he repeated, this time more firmly.

I slid my arms into the sleeves. The weight of the jacket was surprising. It seemed so light when he moved around wearing it.

"Thank you," I said as he tugged it closer around me.

"Neo would kill me if I got you sick."

Right. My brother.

"So how was your appointment today, Virginia?" Ethan asked, drawing me from the sudden thoughts.

"Oh. Thank you for asking," I said, pausing while I decided how much to say. In truth, I didn't really want to talk about it. I wanted to enjoy being out with friends. For a while, I wanted to not feel like the girl trapped in a wheelchair and living in a tower. "Ah…"

"Fletcher, do you want this?" Earth interrupted, pushing his PB hot chocolate toward his brother.

"You don't?" Fletcher exclaimed.

"If I drink any more, I might go into sugar shock."

"Wow, thanks, Earth!" Fletcher tucked into the drink, oohing and aahing over the flavor.

Ethan smiled fondly. Then his eyes drifted back to me. Waiting.

"Is there a place around here we can get crickets?" Earth asked him.

Forgetting he was waiting on an answer, he turned back to Earth. "Crickets?"

I nodded, feeling a rush of warmth that Earth hadn't

forgotten about Zilla. "For Zilla. I promised to bring her some!"

"Ah, yes. Your gecko." Ethan recalled. After a moment of thought, he began telling Earth about a place a few blocks over and how to get there.

After that, Ethan seemed to forget he'd asked me about my appointment at all, and our conversation turned other places. But even as we laughed and joked, I remembered.

I remembered how Earth directed the subject away from something I did not want to talk about, and he did it not once, but twice.

I wondered if he did that because of my brother too.

Nine

Swallowed up by leather. That's how she looked sitting there with a giant dessert in front of her, whipped cream on her nose, and my jacket literally concealing her frame.

She looked ridiculous, especially with all those flowers in her hair.

Flowers and leather do not go together.

"Earth?" Virginia asked suddenly, words punctuated by leaning over the arm of her chair toward me. Long lashes fluttered, brown eyes tugging on my attention. "Do you have a penny?"

"A what?"

"A penny," she repeated, pointing back toward the fountain.

"You seriously want to make a wish?" I deadpanned.

"If I don't make one, then how will it come true?"

"Wishes don't come true."

She gasped, sitting back as though my words shoved her. She was so ridiculously animated. Practically a girl version of Fletcher except… *prettier.* "I object!"

"You aren't a lawyer," I quipped.

"I have some," Ethan offered, reaching into the pocket of his trousers. "I carry them around for Fletch."

"Really?" She beamed, sitting up straighter, away from me.

How annoying. "Give them to Fletcher, then," I told him, reaching into my jeans. "I have some too."

"But you said you didn't!"

"No, I said wishes are stupid."

"I don't think I can make a wish with that penny," she replied, staring at the grubby-looking coin I'd produced.

"Why not?" I demanded. My penny was just as good as Ethan's.

"It's cursed by your negative attitude."

I sighed loudly.

"Curses are real," Fletcher added, his voice low and sage.

Everyone glanced at him, and any smart remark I would have made died on my tongue. He'd been through a lot, that kid who really wasn't a kid.

"Curses can be broken." Ethan reminded him, palming the back of his neck.

Smiling, Fletcher snatched the penny out of Ethan's palm and headed toward the fountain. "C'mon, V!"

Virginia pursed her lips, looking dubiously at the penny. "Make a wish with me."

"No."

"I will, V. Come on." Ethan stood, coming around the table like he was going to lift her out of the chair.

My hand slapped onto his arm before I realized I'd moved. "What the hell are you doing?"

"It's too narrow between the tables for her chair."

The legs of my chair scraped against the floor when I stood, lifting V with me. "I'll take her." The automatic way her arms looped around my neck sent a rumble of satisfaction through me.

"Doesn't it bother you?" Her voice was so quiet when she spoke I might not have heard her if she wasn't in my arms.

"What?" I questioned, gazing down.

Her cheeks were pink, the tip of her nose still smeared with whipped cream.

"The staring," she whispered, refusing to meet my eyes.

I always made it a point to be hyperaware of my surroundings and the people in my space. I worked to make it seem like I wasn't paying attention, but in reality, I scoped out an entire room every time I stepped inside. So of course I'd noticed. The sidelong glances, the lingering stares. The way people would smile when caught as if they were friendly and not nosy.

Truthfully, I didn't give a damn. People in general meant very little to me, so why would I give a flying fuck what they thought?

But it was different for her. Coming to a new place after a day of disappointing news, the prying eyes probably felt more invasive.

"Nah," I told her, leaning in. "They're just jealous I get to hold such a beautiful girl."

She giggled, her cheek tucking into my chest.

"Come on, then," I said, stopping in front of the fountain, which was giving off a fine mist and making me feel sticky. Opening my hand, I showed her the penny.

Her fingertips felt like butterfly wings when they dipped down to take the coin. "What should I wish for?"

Before I could answer, she gasped, squeezed her eyes closed, and clutched the penny against her chest. Her breathing was even, and a small smile curved her lips.

Seconds later, those brunet eyes popped open, glimmering with whatever unspoken thing she'd come up with. Pressing a quick kiss to the penny, she tossed it out.

It landed with an audible plop and then fluttered to the bottom, where it winked up at us through the rippling water.

"It's done!" she announced.

"Is everything you do such an ordeal?" I wondered.

"I bet everyone thinks I wished to walk again."

"But you didn't."

She shook her head. "No. I wished for something better."

I raised my eyebrow. "And what is that?"

"I'll tell you *after* it comes true."

"Good thing I'm not that curious, or else I'd die waiting."

Back at the table, our foursome finished up, Fletcher and V talking endlessly until Ethan bustled my brother into the passenger seat of his white Mercedes.

"Bye! Let's do this again!" Fletch called, rolling the window down to talk more.

V waved frantically, smiling wide. But she didn't agree, and even though I'd spent many minutes wondering when she'd shut up, her silence now irritated me.

Fletcher was still waving out the window as Ethan pulled away from the curb.

"Why didn't you agree?" I asked, voice gruff.

Her stare left the retreating car, lifting to me. "I only make promises I can keep."

"And you don't think you'll be able to come back?"

One slim shoulder shrugged. "It took me this long to get here."

Anger at Neo burned hot and bright in my gut, making my fingertips burn. *Why doesn't he bring her out more? Why does he keep her locked up in that tower? Why does she listen to him?*

Dropping down in front of her chair, I hooked my hands around the sides, pulling her closer. "Anytime you want to come back, you call me. I'll bring you. I'll take you anywhere you want to visit."

Hope bloomed in her eyes, creating a warm glow. "Really?"

What the hell did you just promise? Neo is going to be so pissed.

But for the first time in my life, my dark warning thoughts were no match for her sunlight. "Yes."

Take it back before it's too late!

I nearly lost balance, tipping to the side when her arms flung around my neck and squeezed. I recovered, steadying us both, my hands flexing against the chair, not understanding the urge I suddenly felt to hug her back.

She didn't say a word, just nearly choked the life out of me, which I strangely sat and allowed. When she pulled back, it was only enough so our stares could collide, the tips of our noses nearly bumping together. The ring of golden yellow around her irises reminded me once more of the sun.

Like a private sun just for me.

"Tell me what happened between you and my brother."

I was a quick guy. My mind sharp, reflexes honed. But those words took longer to sink in than they should have, and when they did, they stuck like chewed gum to the bottom of a shoe.

The sun I'd been so mesmerized by was instantly

swallowed whole by my darkness. I'd always been secre-tive about who I really was, but even in secret, I'd never been ashamed.

Why should I be? I made those choices, and so I would own them.

But now, suddenly, standing here looking into her innocent, curious eyes, I faltered. For once, I felt a tinge of shame for who I was.

I couldn't tell her.

I couldn't tell her the man who just took her out for hot chocolate was actually a killer.

Ten

Virginia

"Why did you say that if you weren't going to actually do it?" I grumbled, tightening the arms I had crossed over my chest, so tight they pinched and tugged on my braids, but I wasn't about to move.

"I said I would take you anywhere you wanted to go. I did not say I would answer nosy questions." He spoke mildly, not even looking at me.

Fine, he was driving. And I knew all too well what happened if a driver took his eyes off the road for just a split second, but he needed to see how mad I was!

"If I could kick you, I would," I muttered, staring out the passenger window at the city.

He laughed. Threw his head back and laughed.

"Are you laughing at me?" I demanded.

His chuckle still rumbled through the car, creating goose bumps on the back of my neck and irritation everywhere else.

"You are aware there are many ways to cause damage without using your legs, aren't you?"

My arms dropped into my lap. Why did that sound so menacing? *And exciting.*

"I do think it's cute you're sitting over there pouting."

"I'm not pouting!"

"Pouting," he reiterated.

"No one tells me anything," I said in a most definitely non-pouting way, rotating away from him. It was irritating and honestly a bit of a letdown that everyone treated me like I was so fragile all the time.

I wasn't. My legs didn't work, but the rest of me did. My heart and mind were just as strong as everyone else's. No! Stronger. Stronger because of what I'd lost.

The sudden, ear-piercing screech of thick rubber against the pavement accompanied by the way the car lurched as Earth laid on the brake practically caused a panic attack.

Even though the seat belt locked tight across my chest, it was almost like an afterthought because Earth's arm locked in front of my body, a steel, unbending rod bracketing me between it and the seat, creating a shield that maybe shouldn't have been so imposing... but, *oh*, was it.

Chest rising and falling with surprise, I glanced down at the tense, locked muscles keeping me in place.

"What are you doing?" I exclaimed, but it came out more as a breathless squeak.

The car was at a standstill in the middle of the street, and the smell of burnt rubber made my nose wrinkle.

From behind, car horns blared. My neck craned to glance out the back window, but a hand grasped my chin, keeping me from looking.

"I do not think you're weak."

I felt my eyes flare as they jumped to his ridiculously dark, unflinching gaze. "What?" I whispered, a little lost.

His fingers tightened a bit, biting into my jaw, but not enough to cause pain. Giving me a little shake, he made an irritated noise. "That's not why I won't answer."

My lips parted. Realization caused heat to burst in my cheeks. "Did I say all that out loud?"

No way. I couldn't have. I wouldn't have! I'd never say that for anyone to hear!

The honking grew more impatient and frantic, and behind us, someone started to yell. Reaching up, I patted insistently on his wrist. "Earth! You're holding up traffic. People are getting upset!"

His fingers remained on my skin, his impenetrable gaze not even flickering with a hint of worry. "Let them."

Hooonk! Hooonk! Yell!

"I don't like it," I confessed, hands bunching in my dress.

Dropping my chin, he moved the car forward again, turning at the corner and parking at the curb.

An angry driver whizzed by, waving his arm out the window as he sped on.

"He just gave you the finger," I informed Earth.

"How ever will I sleep tonight?" he asked, knowing he would sleep just fine.

I pressed my lips together to hold in my giggle.

"Look at me." His voice was quiet and unheated, yet it commanded me.

Breath stalled in my lungs. The giggle I'd been suppressing vanished as if it hadn't been there at all. Swallowing thickly, I focused on Earth, the tug he created making it easy to do.

"Things with me and Neo are... complicated. Telling you something he clearly didn't want you to know would just make things worse."

"And that's why you won't tell me. Because of my brother." I searched his eyes, asking for the truth and finding nothing but.

Out of nowhere, hurt pierced me, pricking my heart

like the sharpest of daggers. All day, he'd been reminding me that everything he did was because of Neo.

Not because of me.

Was I even living my own life, or was I just an extension of his?

A tidal wave of emotion rose within me, threatening to pull me under like the rip currents I read about in the sea. I pulled away from the truth in his eyes, trying also to pull away from how badly it hurt.

It surprised me how much I wanted to be seen as more than Neo's sister in those obscure eyes. I ached because I would never be.

Confined to a wheelchair. Locked in a tower. Thought of only as a sister and never as a woman. Seemed this small taste of freedom I'd had today only served to remind me of how much of a prisoner I truly was.

"I want to go home now," I said, not allowing an ounce of the weariness I felt to shine through my request. "Please."

"No."

My back straightened, shoulders going tense. One of the flowers in my braid fell into my lap with the force in which my head whipped around. "What?"

"I said no."

"Listen here," I intoned, jabbing a finger in his direction. The tears I'd been pushing away now glimmered with anger. "I might put up with my brother's overbearing and bossy ways, but I will *not* put up with it from you too. I asked to go home, and I even said please. And you have the nerve to say *no*."

"I thought you wanted crickets," he said, the hint of amusement pulsing around him.

Following his finger, I glanced up the block to the pet

store Ethan had told him about. When I said nothing, he palmed the keys still hanging from the ignition. "Did you change your mind?"

"No!" I quickly said, stopping him from turning on the car. "I promised Zilla."

Yanking the keys from the ignition, he tucked them in his pocket.

"Can I come in too?" I asked, hopeful. The ache in my heart was definitely still there, and sure, this little taste of freedom reminded me a bit too much of how confined I really was… but I wouldn't let that stop me.

"You're the one who's touching those bugs," he told me, throwing open his car door and going around to begin the process of pulling out my chair, opening it up, and placing it on the curb.

It made me feel a little guilty because it was so much work. It would have been a lot easier and faster if he'd just walked in and gotten some himself. A simple task to most people was a task that took double the time for me, sometimes more.

When he opened the door, I expected some kind of impatience. Perhaps even a little resentment. I definitely did not expect his leather-clad upper half to lower into the doorframe as he crouched down to my level.

Long fingers reached into my lap, plucking up the fallen daisy clip. The white petals seemed so flimsy against his sturdy, calloused hand. He spun it between his fingers, watching the petals flutter lightly, leaning forward, and then reaching up.

I bit down on the inside of my cheek, wanting to look away but absolutely unable to avert my stare. He seemed to concentrate hard, frowning a bit as he clipped the flower back into my hair. The whisper of his fingertips at my cheekbone created a shivering sensation across my skin.

A few beats of silence seemed thunderously loud and could only be drowned out by the sound of his voice. "You'll think bad of me." His gruff, almost angry tone registered before the actual words.

"What?"

He kept his face downturned. All I could see was the top of his black head and how his knuckles turned white when they gripped the edge of the passenger seat. "It shouldn't bother me. But goddamn, it does," he muttered to himself, the words filled with self-loathing and angst.

I still didn't understand what he was talking about, but my heart raced as fast as my mind as I tried desperately to figure it out.

"I don't want to tell you what I did because then you won't want me around either."

I sucked in a breath. Was he…? Was he saying that he didn't want to tell me not because of my brother but because of *me*?

Because he was afraid I wouldn't want to see him?

Everything under my ribcage fluttered like a million flower petals being blown around in the summer breeze. It made me jittery and kinda giddy, maybe a little nauseous.

I really like it so much.

"So you did something that made Neo mad, and that's why you fought? Why you haven't been around?"

He gave a curt nod.

Without thinking too much, I rested my fingers over his knuckles, which were still white against the edge of the seat. "Is it something you regret?"

Earth's head lifted then, his bottomless, cool stare

swallowing me up. His hand pulled away, leaving the tips of my fingers to tingle. "No."

My eyebrows lifted with mild surprise. So he did something that made Neo almost kick him out of his life, yet it's not something he regrets?

"Okay."

Surprise sparked across his features. "Okay?"

I shrugged one shoulder. "Regret doesn't change anything. Just makes it harder to accept the present."

Something shifted behind his eyes, but then he blinked, and whatever it was disappeared.

"Come on." I patted his arm expectantly. "Let's get Zilla some crickets."

We went together down the sidewalk toward the pet shop, him walking alongside my wheelchair.

All the hurt I'd felt just moments before was forgotten.

Eleven

EARTH

WHAT IN THE EVER-LOVING HELL WAS WRONG WITH ME?

Was I going into sugar shock because of that massive, overly sweet drink Fletcher insisted I have?

Since when did I give a good goddamn what anyone thought? Since when was I worried that my actions might keep someone away? Usually, I was glad people stayed away.

Not Virginia.

The thought of letting her down, of doing anything at all to cause her pain, made me want to rip apart the city and pull out the knife I loved so much.

It was a conundrum, this war of chaos inside me. I wanted to protect her by any means necessary, even if that meant those means of protection made me less in her eyes.

I couldn't have both. I couldn't remain a hero in her eyes if, in reality, everything I did was that of a villain.

But I *was* a villain. A villain standing inside a pet store, pretending to be a hero. Disgust flung up the back of my throat, threatening to choke me. A hero I was not. A hero I would never be.

Why pretend? Why perpetuate some stupid falsehood of a man I didn't even want to be?

I should tell her. Open my trap and blurt out I killed people. That the body toll I left in my wake was impressive and the pile of money in my bank accounts was bathed in blood.

It would be the fastest, most efficient way of killing this. Whatever this was. V had enough hell in her life without hanging out with the devil himself.

My lips parted, the truth rolling across my tongue, ready to meet air.

"*Eww!*" she screeched, jolting back against her chair. A small hand shot out, grasping the hem of my leather jacket. The one that now smelled faintly of her.

Maybe that's what is wrong with me. Maybe her light floral scent cast some kind of spell, making me momentarily forget who I was.

She clung on, gripping my coat and staring up my body with a wrinkled nose. "One of them is missing a leg," she whispered loudly before sticking out her tongue to make a retching sound.

So fucking cute.

"It won't have any legs when Zilla gets ahold of it," I deadpanned.

"I'm not touching them," she announced. "You do it."

"Me?" I scoffed. Who did she think she was, ordering me around?

She nodded sagely. "Put them in that container there and then put the lid on."

"Why me?"

In response, she widened her eyes, offering up a pleading look as she tugged on my jacket some more. "Please, Earth?"

"Fine," I muttered, stepping toward the tank. I would do it because then she would shut up.

"Not that one, though." She was suddenly no longer frightened as she pointed out a big, fat insect.

"What's wrong with that one?" I demanded.

"It's too big. They should be no bigger than the space between Zilla's eyes."

"You'll touch a lizard but not these things," I pointed out, turning back to my task, making sure to avoid the "too big" one. "How do you even feed her, then?"

"She's not a lizard. She's a gecko. And I use big tweezer things," she explained. "Ooh! Can we get some mealworms too?" she asked, pointing to another tank.

"Guess you want me to get those too." I assumed, not bothering to hide my annoyance.

She said nothing, just batted her eyes.

I went to get the worms, and she rolled off down the aisle, blabbering on about decorations for Zilla's tank.

"At least you're quiet," I told the worms as I scooped some out.

The bell on the door at the front of the shop jingled loudly, and with it, a familiar tingling sensation prickled the back of my neck.

Keeping my stance casual, my movements unhurried, I finished as awareness pounded between my ears. The inclination of being watched, the unmistakable tinge to the air of wicked vibes was very familiar to me, so recognizable it was like a sixth sense.

Why shouldn't I know it? It was exactly what I was made of.

I didn't panic, though, or even become overly suspicious because there were bad apples all over this city, so encountering one wasn't exactly rare.

But then I noticed the quiet. Something I normally

appreciated now sent tendrils of ice rushing through my venomous veins.

All of her incessant chattering had stopped.

And for the first time in forever, the presence of a bad apple actually pierced me with fear. Gripping the containers tightly, I spun, the insects flinging around inside. My jaw clacked together upon seeing she wasn't there. Boots pounding, I rushed around the corner and into the next aisle.

My heart beat so hard my veins trembled under the force of the heavily pumping blood and adrenaline. Transferring the bugs into one hand, my other slid up under my jacket, reaching for the holster I always had strapped beneath.

Only it wasn't there. I didn't wear it because I was with her.

Which is exactly why you should have!

"Virginia," I yelled, the sound husky and harsh as I burst forward.

Her golden head popped up, eyes lighting up at the sight of me. "I can't decide which one is prettier. Come help me!" she called, turning back to whatever in the hell she was holding.

Completely clueless to all the blackhearted things that lurked.

Hot anger swept through me, burning up the adrenaline that previously had been taking over. I stalked down the aisle, eyes sweeping everything for any signs of danger.

She was alone here... but that feeling... It still sat like a rock in my gut.

A guy like me never ignored his gut.

"What the hell do you think you're doing wandering off like that?" I demanded.

Her shoulders tensed, inching up toward her ears. Lowering the packages in her hands, she glanced up. "I'm not a toddler."

Dropping the bugs in her lap, I braced my hands on her chair, leaning in so she could see the angry fire burning in my eyes. "Don't you know how dangerous this city is?"

"I'm in a pet store, not the ghetto."

I laughed, but it was not humorous. "Trouble can walk in here just as easily as we did."

I expected an argument. Hell, I hoped for it. I hoped for her sharp tongue, sarcasm, and jabbing finger. I couldn't wait to dish it all back, to make her understand just how—

"Were you worried about me?"

My mind went blank.

Reaching up, she patted the side of my face, her palm cupping my jaw just slightly. My mouth ran dry. All the fight left me like it was water down a drain.

Her soft smile further discombobulated my brain. "I'm sorry I wandered off and scared you. I'm fine, though." Her voice was as soft as her smile and soothing like a warm blanket on the coldest night.

She turned back to the things she held, completely oblivious to the complete wipeout she created within me. "Here, I can't decide between these. A mossy cave or a coconut hideaway. What do you think?"

I barely glanced at those things before focusing back on her.

Up ahead, a figure passed by the aisle, a mere shadow as the person moved to the next. My instincts went wild, my gut screaming that there was something sinister close.

"Earth? Which one?"

"Get them both," I said, moving around the back of her chair to take control and push her toward the checkout counter located at the back of the store.

I almost tossed everything on the floor and headed for the door. Going deeper into this shop defied every sense beneath my skin, but if I did that, I would scare her.

Apparently, the idea of scaring the sprite in front of me was far worse than any poison lurking in here with us.

Come closer. I mentally taunted. *I might not have my blade, but my hands will do just fine.*

I felt indirect attention the entire time the cashier rang up our stuff. The man worked painfully slow, and it was making me crazy.

Out of patience, I dug into my pocket and pulled out enough cash that would more than cover the cost. "Here. Just take it." I grunted, tossing it down while basically throwing everything back in V's lap.

"Don't you want a bag?" the man yelled after us as I wheeled her toward the door.

"Earth!" Virginia gasped, grappling at the pile on her lap as I sped to the door.

If it was just me, I'd seek out whatever the hell was lurking and give it a swift demise. But I couldn't do that. Not with V.

"What has gotten into you?"

The bell jingled when I shoved it open and maneuvered us both out onto the sidewalk. The second the city-heavy air hit me, my lungs loosened just a little. About halfway to the car, V let loose an exasperated noise and slammed her hand down on the top of one wheel.

I stopped immediately, heart lurching into my throat in fear her fingers would get tangled up.

"What the hell are you doing?" I hollered, reaching down to snatch her hand off the wheel.

Her palm rotated, fingers clasping around mine with a strong grip. "What is the matter with you? Did something happen back there?"

The feel of her palm against mine somehow grounded me. The worry in the depths of her beguiling eyes made me refocus.

"Nothing. I'm tired." My voice was gruff.

The hint of suspicion gave way to guilt, and she nodded. "Of course. I've asked a lot of you today. We should go." She tugged her hand free, leaving mine to clench around nothing at all.

I opened my mouth to tell her my asshole behavior wasn't her fault and that being around her wasn't making me tired. But the words were cut off by the jingle of that goddamn bell, and I was reminded.

As she started off toward the car, I glanced back where we'd just been, seeing nothing but the melting of two shadows into one. I watched a few seconds longer, but whoever was there remained hidden with me unable to give chase.

And so I let Virginia believe I just wanted away from her because it was easier than explaining that wherever I went, trouble constantly followed.

Twelve

Virginia

THE ONLY SOUND THAT COULD BE HEARD OVER THE aggressive purr of the car's engine was the occasional scuffling of the bugs in their respective containers.

Truth was I thought it was a little gross that Zilla ate live mealworms and crickets, but what was a girl to do? I couldn't exactly blame her for her biology. Besides, when you loved someone, you accepted their faults.

Bug eating probably wasn't a fault to Zilla, but to me, it was a little questionable. She was a good friend. Always there, perching on my shoulder and sometimes hiding in my hair. The leopard gecko was a good listener and never complained about my Netflix choices.

Earth's aura was moody and dark, which wasn't exactly anything new. But underneath those steady currents, there was something a little more unstable. Irritation.

Like he couldn't wait to get rid of me.

Being a burden was something I didn't think I'd ever feel at peace with and something I would always struggle against.

Maybe I should see another specialist... I shook my head at the thought. I was exhausted, and when that happened, sadness tried to overcome my usual fighting spirit.

The Tower came into view. Even though the brick building was kinda shabby, nothing special, and at times felt more like a cage than a home, I breathed a sigh of relief. But instead of making me feel relaxed, the sensation of anxiety grew.

Earth parked right at the curb, shutting off the engine and climbing out without a word.

By the time he had my chair out and ready to go, there was a fine sheen of sweat dotting my hairline, and my breathing was coming in quicker gasps. My neck felt warm, and I closed my eyes, wondering how much time I had.

When the door opened, the early evening air felt cool against my flushed skin but would do nothing to calm the storm building inside me.

Schooling my features, I ignored the rapid pounding of my heart and tried to cover the way my chest rose and fell a little more aggressively with my bounty from the pet shop.

Too perceptive, Earth was barely leaning in before his nostrils flared. "What's wrong?"

"N-nothing. I'm just ready to go inside."

Glancing down at my lap, I was glad to see my legs were not shaking.

Yet.

With an impatient noise, he ripped everything I was using as a shield out of my arms, tossing it onto the floorboard. If any of it hit my feet, I wouldn't know.

His cool palms wrapped easily around my upper arms as he drew my upper body up a bit so he could dagger me with his hard stare. "Are you sick? Did I upset you that much?"

I never thought black could be a soft color until suddenly something in his expression seemed to mute and melt, the coal-black stare turning into something warmer.

My breath caught again, but this time, it wasn't because of my body.

"This is my fault," he said, fingers tightening around my arms.

"It's not your fault. I'm just ready to go inside." I could barely process this conversation or decipher his new mood. I really needed to get inside.

Nodding once, he went to pick me up.

"No!" I cried, voice sharp and panicked. "Don't touch me."

He stopped immediately, entire body going rigid, jaw like granite, hands curling into fists, and one dark brow arching over tumultuous eyes. "No?" he echoed.

Swallowing thickly, I felt a bead of sweat run between my shoulder blades. "You've done enough for me already. I know I've been a burden. If you ring for Emogen, she can—"

The sound he made was more animal than man, an aggressive growl that caused shivers to run across every nerve ending I could feel.

When the tingling finally allowed for awareness, I was already out of the car, cradled in his arms.

"Put me down!" I shrieked, squeezing my eyes closed and fighting tears.

He was so rigid I could feel every cord of muscle in his upper body and the intensity of his hard stare, which I refused to meet.

"You're sweating, and your neck is splotchy," he growled, almost as if he dared me to have another symptom he didn't like.

"Please," I whispered, the plea watery.

The second he put me down, I patted myself down, quickly touching my lap and legs, and let out a relieved sigh. "Thank God," I whispered to myself.

"What is—"

The familiar sound of the door to the Tower opening had me looking around.

"About time you got back," Emogen fussed. "I was so worried I extended my shift to wait for you!"

"Emogen," I squeaked, wringing my hands in my skirt.

A knowing look widened her eyes, her unhurried pace quickening. Her eyes slid toward Earth, then back to me, and I gave a small, curt shake of my head.

Her lips pursed disapprovingly, but I didn't have time to fret about that. My goodness, everyone was getting upset with me today.

"Thank you for escorting Virginia today," Emogen told Earth as she grabbed the back of my chair to push me toward the building. "I've got her from here."

"What's wrong with her?" Earth ignored his clear dismissal, and I wanted to cry.

Please just go. I'm already embarrassed enough.

"Nothing for you to worry about," Emogen chirped.

A hand locked on the side of the chair, preventing me from going through the open door into my safe haven. So close but so far away.

I fought down the urge to wheeze.

"You're not going anywhere until I get an answer." Earth's voice was deadly calm, utterly quiet, and my legs started to tremor.

"Please, Earth," I burst out. "Please let me go. I need the bathroom!"

He let go immediately, posture shooting up straight.

"The bathroom?" he echoed, but I was already wheeling toward the elevator, staring down at my lap as tears dripped over my cheeks.

Emogen rushed in behind me, hitting the button about a thousand times to close the doors. When they finally started to shut, I took a chance, glancing up through tear-blurry vision to see him standing on the other side, a look of confusion on his face.

The second the doors hid me away, I let out the sob I'd been holding in.

Emogen remained quiet at my side, quickly helping me into the private bathroom. "Do you want my help?"

"No. Thank you," I said, already getting what I needed.

The door shut quietly behind her, and I did what I needed to do, unable to stop more tears from falling. A short while later, I washed my hands and my tear-stained face. The blotches on my neck would fade now that I was calm and my breathing had returned to normal.

I wanted to cry all over again when I thought of how I ruined a perfectly fun afternoon with my behavior. Shame burned the back of my neck, making my shoulders want to bunch up to my ears and my eyes to duck even though I sat there alone.

I knew, rationally, I had nothing to be embarrassed about, but being rational wasn't possible when I kept picturing those dark eyes drilling a hole in me as the space between the elevator doors grew smaller and smaller.

Neo would say I told you so.

Maybe Neo is right.

I don't know how long I stayed in the small bathroom, but my eyes were dry, and weariness cloaked me when I finally tugged open the door. Immediately, I sensed I was not alone.

Expecting to see Emogen, my mouth dropped open when it was Earth's dark, towering frame I laid eyes on.

Emotion I thought I'd wrung out immediately welled up inside me again. "What are you doing here?"

"I brought up your stuff," he said, cocking his head toward the pile of purchases lying on my bed.

"You could have just given them to Emogen."

The arms that were folded across his chest dropped as he stalked slowly toward me. "You trying to get rid of me?"

"Weren't you the one trying to get rid of me?" I tried to imitate his lazy but somehow threatening vibe.

His jaw worked, eyes glimmered, but then suddenly, everything about him softened, transforming him into someone not threatening at all but someone capable of protection and comfort.

The kind of comfort I'd never really had before.

Sinking down in front of me, Earth didn't touch me at all, but somehow his very presence and calm stare felt like an embrace. "Are you okay?"

The question lacked his usual sarcastic, bored tone. My lower lip wobbled, and I pulled the betraying flesh between my teeth. "I'm fine."

His hand extended, and I thought he might reach into my lap for mine, but then he pulled back, offering only the comfort of his presence.

It's better this way.

"Did I... did I do that to you?"

I sucked in a breath, eyes going wide. "What? No!" I insisted instantly before it even fully registered.

Realization dawned.

"Is that why you're still here? You felt guilty? You

didn't do anything, okay?" Placing my hands on the wheels, I backed out of his space to pivot away. "I won't tell Neo, and he won't be mad at you."

"I'm not worried about Neo," he insisted, shooting up from his stance. Making a frustrated sound, he jammed his hands through his hair. "I'm worried about you."

I stopped rolling away, my back falling deeper into the chair. "What?"

"I need to know if it's something I did, V. I need to know so I don't ever do it again."

A sudden thick lump lodged in my throat, and heavy pressure sat on my chest. I cleared my throat, but my voice was still hoarse. "It's not like I even see you much anyway."

"Just tell me. Is it because of what happened at the pet shop? Did you have some kind of… panic attack?"

I didn't answer. I didn't want to.

He didn't take the hint. I was beginning to think this man was just as stubborn—if not more—than my brother.

"I'm not leaving until you tell me."

"Visiting hours are almost over."

He raised a brow and smirked. "Do I look like someone who gives a damn about the rules?"

The banter I usually loved to exchange with him suddenly just felt like so much work. "I'm tired, Earth."

I don't know what possessed me to come out with that. It was like the filter I had and operated quite well completely forgot it existed in his presence. That just a certain look or even closeness to him made everything inside me short-circuit.

Perhaps it would chase him away, though. Perhaps he'd finally feel guilty and leave.

Nope.

Instead, I found him hovering over me, glaring down until I lifted my eyes to meet his. "I'm gonna lift you out of that chair."

"Why?" I exclaimed, immediately gripping the armrests.

"Because you'll be more comfortable on the bed."

"No, I won't," I retorted.

"Liar."

He scooped me up, placing me in the center of the bed so my back could lean against the pillows. I let out a sigh, adjusting my legs so they were stretched out.

The bed dipped when he sat down, making my body tilt toward his. With his position mirroring mine, his back against the pillows and headboard, he, too, stretched out his legs. The combat-style boots on his feet looked massive at the end of the mattress, my feet not nearly reaching to his and looking sorely small and weak without shoes.

I was about to ask him what he thought he was doing when his hand came around to cup the left side of my head, gently pushing so my right cheek met his shoulder.

Under my cheek, the leather of his jacket was soft, and his scent swirled beneath my nose. He was sturdy and warm pressed against my side, so when his hand pulled back, my cheek stayed pillowed where he'd pushed it.

"Tell me."

"I had to go to the bathroom."

Pause.

"Like you had to piss?"

I slapped him in the chest. "Earth!"

"What?" he muttered, rubbing where I hit.

"Girls do not piss."

He made a rude noise, holding up his hands. "Okay, so you had to tinkle."

I laughed.

He didn't make a sound, but with my cheek still pressed into his shoulder, I felt him vibrate with silent laughter.

I like this. The thought was sobering because I had no business thinking such things.

"I'm paralyzed from the lower waist down, and that means I can't control my bladder. I don't just... feel when I have to go. So my body has to tell me in other ways."

"All that because you had to pee?" He glanced down at me. "That was like a damn panic attack."

"Well, my body has to get my attention somehow. And since I pretty much had been ignoring the clock..."

He jolted enough that my cheek was no longer against him, so I sat up, staring straight ahead.

"You mean to tell me you ignored the fact you had to... and I kept you out too long."

"No!" I insisted. Grasping his arm, my fingers tightened, pleading with him to understand. "It's not that. I just..." My explanation fell short.

He made a noise. "It is that."

"It's my fault," I whispered. "I was just having a wonderful time with you. I felt normal for the first time in so long."

He sighed, pushing my head back into his shoulder.

"I should have paid better attention to the clock. I have a pretty set schedule. I just... I didn't want to be a bother, and then it hit me kinda fast and I almost—"

"You almost what?"

I remained quiet. He reached down to grasp my chin to tilt my head up.

"It's embarrassing," I confessed, feeling the oncoming tears.

The back of his knuckles brushed across my cheekbone, his black eyes turning into liquid silk, that stare enveloping me in some kind of protective shield.

"Don't be embarrassed, sprite. Not with me. You don't have to be ashamed that your body might not work the same as most."

"I was so worried I was going to pee myself," I rushed out, squeezing my eyes shut so I didn't have to see his reaction. "And I wouldn't have been able to stop it. You picked me up, and I—"

"Shh." He soothed me, leaning down and pressing his lips to my hairline.

I stopped breathing, but my body melted farther into his side.

"It's okay. I understand now," he whispered.

"You can't possibly," I informed him, still practically buried into his side. I wanted so badly to wrap my arms around his, to hug it into my chest, but I resisted. This would be enough. It would have to be.

"You're right. I guess I can't. But I can tell you that even if you went all over me, I wouldn't be mad."

I snorted. "Yeah, right."

"I've had a lot worse things on me than pee."

Intrigued, I lifted my face. "Like what?"

"Forget it," he said, pressing his lips in a thin line.

"I just confessed I almost peed on you, and you won't tell me?"

"Want me to almost pee on you? Then we'll be even."

I squealed a little, and he laughed. A warm feeling bloomed inside me. Without thinking much, I snuggled back against his shoulder. "You should laugh more. It suits you."

He didn't say anything, and I didn't either. When the silence stretched enough that I was sure he was about to leave, he spoke. "Can I ask you something?"

"Sure."

"If you can't tell when you need to go… then how do you?"

I wasn't really surprised by the question. It was something I thought everyone probably wondered about. And given what just happened, it seemed normal for him to want to know. It was embarrassing to talk about, honestly, embarrassing to live, but when he told me I didn't have to be embarrassed, I believed him.

I stared down at his feet while I answered, still slightly shy. "I use a compact intermittent catheter," I explained. "It's basically a bag with a long tube on the end, and I just throw it away when I am done."

He was quiet a moment. "So the tube—"

I nodded. "It gets inserted into the urethra, and that's how I empty my bladder." I finished for him. Then, so he didn't have to ask, I just continued. "It doesn't hurt. I can't feel it. I really only need to do it a few times a day, and I usually just do it around the same schedule. Usually, I don't react like I did earlier, but like I said, I kinda just ignored my body."

"You shouldn't have done that," he scolded.

"It was nice to be normal for a while."

He pulled back, robbing my cheek of the warmth of this shoulder. "You're normal all the time, V. Don't let anyone tell you differently. You might have different needs, but you're always normal. And the next time I take you out, you tell me when you need a bathroom, and I'll find you one. Don't do that to yourself again."

I didn't technically do that to myself. I mean, it sometimes happened, but I wasn't going to argue because it clearly really upset him to see me like that and to think it was his fault.

But then I thought of what else he said. "Next time?"

He made a humming noise in the back of his throat.

"But I thought—"

"Forget what I said, sprite. I'm a bastard."

"That's not true," I scolded.

"I think we both know that it is," he said without heat. "And it would probably be smart if we both kept that in mind."

Thirteen

THE HEADLIGHTS OF MY CAR LIT UP THE END OF THE alley, sort of like shining a spotlight on the place I liked to keep private. It couldn't be helped, though, as I needed the light to manhandle the dumpster out the way to reveal the hidden garage door in the side of a building.

A building I actually owned but no one knew about. It was a shitty, rundown structure just like every other here in the Grimms, but I bought it because there was this garage tucked into the back. Drug dealers used it as a den before I owned the place. I couldn't blame them for choosing it because it was private, out of the way, and well-protected.

But as soon as the ink was dry on this purchase, I showed their small-time criminal asses the door and hadn't seen them since. Most people around here didn't challenge me much, but I wasn't so arrogant and stupid to think they wouldn't. I upgraded the small garage with a security system and a door only I knew the code to. And yeah, I parked a heavy dumpster in front of it to keep it out of sight.

The bottom floor of the building used to be some kind of business that had since gone bust. It needed a lot of work now to even be usable. There were a couple apartments on the upper floors. Those needed work too. So mostly, the building sat unoccupied, rotting away not only with age but also lack of use.

I thought about fixing it up and renting out the spaces, but that was as far as I got.

Once the car was parked in its spot, I turned off the headlights but stayed put behind the wheel. Eventually, the crappy automatic light that came with the automatic door flicked off, saturating everything in complete blackness.

I wasn't afraid of the dark. In fact, I was most comfortable here. I knew the dark far better than I would ever know the light.

One day—no. *Half* a day. That's all it took to churn up my insides, to make me feel like I was living in some foreign place instead of my own damn head.

My response to her was so... not who I was. Not who I wanted to be. Thoughts and waves of emotions I didn't even think I was capable of slapped me around all day.

I hadn't felt this confused since... well...

Shut. It. Down.

And what in the ever-loving hell was I thinking telling her we could hang out again? We couldn't. I wouldn't. There were so many reasons to stay away.

But you want to go back.

With a slew of dirty curse words, I slammed out of the car, moving around in the dark with genuine ease. Because the door was still open, I left all the lights out, going to the back wall to pull a familiar lever.

Confident, I reached in, grabbing the item I felt bare without, not needing light to find the extension of myself. The handle was weighty, cold against my palm, but a perfect fit. The long blade glinted even in the dark, its edge sharp enough to kill.

And kill it had. Many times.

Reaching up, I sheathed it in the holster against my back, then closed up my place. Once the dumpster concealed the door, I moved down the alley toward the street, which was dimly lit with the occasional streetlamp.

The Rotten Apple would be filling up by now. It was rare I wasn't behind the bar, and Beau was probably watching the door, waiting for me to get there and relieve him.

At the juncture of the alley and the street, I peered right toward my bar where the light from the place spilled out across the sidewalk. Then my boots pivoted left as I turned my back.

Too unsettled to go home. My dark mood would only draw attention. Everyone knew I wasn't someone to piss off, someone to challenge or cross. But downright scaring customers was bad for business, and the way I felt right now, I'd definitely scare some off.

It had been a while since I'd accepted a job. Since I'd taken a life for profit. The last job was Ivory... the only failed assassination gig I'd ever had. My spotless, perfect kill record was suddenly marred by my inability to perform.

And it wasn't because I couldn't. I'd had plenty of opportunities to kill that princess. Opportunity hadn't been the problem.

The problem had been me. *Never make it personal.*

The most important rule in my line of work, a rule I never even blinked at until that raven-haired, ocean-eyed beauty stumbled into the Grimms.

I told my family I wouldn't do it again, and I kept that promise.

But here I was slinking through the dirty streets of the Grimms, melting in with the shadows, slipping into my alter ego of being a ghost as if I were ready to break that promise.

As if I craved a kill.

And oddly, the main reason I stopped killing was also the reason I wanted to experience it again.

Emotion.

I quit because I broke my own set of standards, because I compromised who I was as an assassin. I was the best at what I did because I did it with clean precision. No hesitation, void of emotion, not one ounce of regret.

It was a job, pure and simple. A contract ordered, a contract fulfilled.

The control of that lit up my veins and gave me bone-deep satisfaction. I did what I wanted on my own terms. No one told me when or how. No one told me why. I was in control. Always.

Until Ivory. Until my brother went and fell in love with my target and, worse, dragged her home to sleep on my couch. Then my dog fell in love with her, and I... I started to *feel*.

That emotion was far different than the flat existence I knew.

It fucked me over, and it fucked up my family. I cared about that more than I expected too.

So I stopped. Not because they asked me to but because I didn't trust myself anymore.

Although, I didn't think I'd be able to tolerate the look of disappointment in Fletcher's eyes if I started killing again and the kid found out.

Don't tell anyone I admitted that.

Letting it get personal, allowing wild emotion to eat me up, put an end to my sordid career, but now those exact things were making me want it back.

How I craved the precision, the control... the flat-lined sentiment taking jobs gave me. Right now, I felt churned up like sediment that usually lay undisturbed on the deep ocean floor was somehow being dragged to the surface.

Half a day with Neo's little sister, with her mood swings, confessions, and those damn flowers in her hair, and I felt more out of control than I ever had before.

Kill. Kill. Put everything back in order.

Several blocks over from the Rotten Apple, I knew I was being followed. The same ominous energy that stepped into the pet shop now plagued the dark streets. I didn't bother to turn and look over my shoulder. I wouldn't see whoever it was, but I didn't need my eyes to feel their intent.

I chose to ignore them, wondering how long they would shadow me, what they hoped to see. Part of me hoped they attacked and gave me a reason to defend myself. I was already in a very dark mood, and I would welcome to excuse to spill blood.

My pursuer still followed as I turned into another seedy alley, this one just as dark as the rest. Even though I couldn't hear the music that blasted inside the building, the pavement underfoot vibrated with its intensity.

After a quick succession of knocks on the black-painted door, a small rectangular window slid open, revealing the glow of neon lights, which was almost instantly blocked by a large head and a pair of flat eyes.

"Password," he said, his voice deep but somehow still heard over the music rushing out through the opening.

I stepped closer and gave him the finger.

The window slammed shut, and then the door pulled open. I moved inside past the giant manning the door. His head was bald and round, his body massive, and his height much greater than mine.

"Sorry, I didn't know it was you at first," he said when my eyes met his.

I grunted, not accepting his apology, and turned my back.

"Hey!" he yelled, likely annoyed I didn't give him a pass.

Halting, I rotated my head, leaving my back to him to pierce him with just one of my black eyes. I might be chaos inside, but on the outside, I would be in control.

"Nice seeing ya," the doorman said after a beat of nothing at all.

I hitched my chin in acknowledgment and then moved into the exclusive club. The Grimms was the ghetto—actually, the slums of the ghetto—but it was also home to Blacklight, a private club where people here blew off steam. Hard to believe a place like this could stay afloat where most people were poor as dirt.

But no, Blacklight thrived because people came to forget. They came to live beyond their shitty circumstances, and they came to connect.

A lot of the same reasons the Rotten Apple was usually full, except with this place, you had to have a password. You had to have more than just cash to get in the door.

And because of this, I paused just around the corner, lying in wait to see if anyone else came in behind me.

No one did, and it proved my suspicion that whoever was tailing me probably wasn't from around here. *So where are you from?*

Shoving off the wall, I moved deeper into the club. This building had been hollowed out and soundproofed, then redecorated with a high stage to the left and a full bar to the right. The brick walls were all painted black with light colors splashed randomly around. Spotlights hit the stage with colored lights, and the rest of the place, including the bar, only glowed under blacklights.

People wore body paint and clothes that lit them up. Bodies gyrated on the dance floor, and two strippers worked on their poles. Near the bar, a cage hung from the ceiling, inside it another scantily clad woman wearing a mask and dancing like her body was an invitation.

The loud music vibrated my eardrums and made my chest feel like it was shaking. The crowd parted as I walked, my mood preceding me and clearing a path. People stared, but when I returned the gaze, their eyes dropped instantly.

The weight of my blade under my leather jacket waited with anticipation, almost whispering it wanted blood.

The bartender appeared in front of me almost at the same time I stopped in front of the high wooden bar. A tall shot glass was produced, and I picked it up, throwing back the contents, feeling the spicy burn of straight Hennessy down my throat.

Another appeared, and I took that too, no hesitation.

The bartender waited, giving me a look when I set down the empty glass. Crowds of people yelled for him, demanding drinks, but he stood in front of me, silently asking if I wanted another.

I did.

Fuck, I wanted to take that entire bottle out of his grip and chug it. I wouldn't because that would mean relinquishing the control I was already grappling to maintain. I shook my head once.

"Beer," I said, and the bartender moved off to do his job.

The music changed to something that sounded almost identical to the song playing before, but the lights aimed toward the stage shifted from red to purple, and the bottom of the cage hanging overhead swung out.

Leaning an elbow on the bar, I lounged back, watching the dancer basically swing out of the open bottom, landing in the center of a crowd. Men closed in, for obvious reasons, but the sharp crack of a whip had them all scattering back.

The woman emerged from the group—black stilettos, black leather bikini bottoms, and a black lace top that was completely see-through—and made her way toward me. The long whip coiled around her wrist like a slumbering snake was so long it dragged on the floor behind her like a tail.

Miles of skin glistened with body oil, but her face was masked, only revealing red-painted lips and eyes lined with smokey shadow and gleaming silver gems.

The person standing closest to me shifted back, allowing her to shimmy in, her claw-like red nails climbing up my chest. "Been a while since you've come."

"I'm not here for you," I said, feeling nothing as her nails continued to climb.

"That never stopped you before."

For the briefest of moments, I thought about giving her what she wanted. About pinning her against a wall and taking some control by taking her.

Her hand cupped the side of my jaw, and all of those meanderings shut down. Her eyes widened in surprise and, yes, a glimmer of fear when my hand shot up, clasping around her wrist and tugging enough so that her hand could not touch me there.

A flashback from earlier today assaulted me. The feel of another palm gently cupping my cheek tingled my memory.

I'm sorry I wandered off and scared you. I'm fine, though.

A sharp cry snapped me back, the woman struggling against the hard grip I was forcing on her wrist. I threw her arm away, watching her tuck it into her chest.

"You're in a mood tonight," she purred.

I felt my jaw flex. "Get the hell out of my sight."

Red lips parted with surprise, but then her eyes narrowed in challenge. Now was not the time to challenge me. *Especially after you soiled such an innocent touch with your filth.*

Sensing movement behind me, I reacted, catching the arm reaching out for me before I'd even fully turned around. A forceful yank slammed the body into the bar top with a pained grunt.

Pinning him down, I spun, hand closing around his neck as I bent him over the edge of the bar, head hanging off the wood.

The man wheezed, his sneakers grappling for something but only catching air. Everyone around us paused to watch. But I remained focused on the threat that tried to sneak up from behind.

Seeing it was the bartender, I loosened the hold on his neck.

"B—beer," he rasped.

I glanced at the bottle resting atop a napkin just to my left.

Instead of shoving him back across the bar, I pulled, bringing him over to my side. He landed in a heap at my feet, scrambling up almost instantly. Eyes wide, he gulped as he stared.

"Don't touch me," I warned.

Nodding, he scrambled off.

The cage dancer watched him go. I could practically smell her arousal, and frankly, it was making me sick.

When she turned back to me, I slapped her with my stare. "Get lost. I don't want you."

Fury radiated from her, and I caught the whip as she brought it up. With one jerk, she lost balance on those stilettos, plummeting forward. I didn't bother to catch her. I already told her not to touch me. She landed at my feet just like the bartender had seconds before.

Bending down, I dropped the end of the whip beside her. "You should know better than that."

I turned my back before she'd even gotten up. Life around me started back up, and I snatched the beer to take a long draw.

The Hennessy had relaxed some of my limbs, made my brain feel a little fuzzier than normal but not enough to mute my senses.

Lowering the beer from my lips, I grimaced because it was a shitty brew, oxidized long ago and tasting flatter than an old woman's ass. Not that I knew what that tasted like. The napkin sitting there had a damp ring in the shape of the bottle, the dampness allowing me to see the hint of ink underneath.

Setting the beer aside, I lifted the corner of the paper square, finding a message left in black ink.

Answer your phone.

I glanced around, but no one was looking, and the back of my neck did not prickle at all like it had in the alley.

My contact knew I was out. So why the message?

Crumpling the napkin in my fist, I sneered at the piss-poor beer and left. The outside air felt cooler than what was inside, but I barely registered the change, shoving my hands along with that note into the pockets of my jacket.

Maybe my contact knew what I'd been trying to deny. Once a killer, always a killer, and there was no quitting when venom ran through your veins.

The reasons for the note became merely a second thought because, almost immediately, I realized they'd waited.

Whoever had been tailing me picked up right where they left off the second I turned out of the alley, slinking along with conceited confidence, believing I didn't know they were there.

Frankly, it was insulting, and it only fueled the anger and unrest already boiling inside me.

I went another block, then slipped into an alley, fusing with the dark without a single sound. Moments later, they followed, confused and worried they'd lost me.

My hand clamped around the back of their neck before they even saw me move, their body slammed face first into the wall. He struggled, actually seemed to have some moves.

The low vibration of my blade as it whizzed through the dark made him pause. His sharp intake of breath when the tip pricked into the vulnerable flesh of his neck fed something hungry inside me.

"Who the fuck are you?"

Silence.

I pressed the knife a little deeper, hoping the spilling of blood would loosen his tongue. He whimpered, but that wasn't the answer I wanted.

Pressing my knee harder, I pinned him more cruelly into the brick. I leaned in, hoping the pungent smell of the Cognac I'd ingested burned his nose.

"Last time. Who are you and why the fuck have you been trailing behind me like an untrained dog?"

"Just getting to know you."

"I'm not very interesting."

He shifted a bit, turning his head, though it caused my blade to puncture his skin even deeper. His stare connected with mine, that single eye holding more than its share of nasty.

"That's an awfully pretty girlfriend you got. Never woulda pegged you as the type for a wheelchair kink—"

His words were interrupted by the sound of a garbled gurgle, and then he sprawled at my feet. I swiped the soiled blade along his jeans, ridding it of his blood. More gurgling sounds erupted as his wide, glassy eyes stared up.

"As a rule, I only ever kill for hire," I told him, squatting by his head. "But it seems I'm not too good at following rules."

He reached out, limp fingers grabbing onto the leather of my jacket.

"You never should have mentioned her," I told him, angry all over again that this was the piece of shit who made V think it was her fault I wanted away from her.

His lips moved, but no sound came out.

Shrugging off his hand, I stood, sheathing my knife. "If you make it to the hospital within thirty minutes, you might live."

I walked away and left him there to bleed.

Fourteen

I BEGAN MY DAY AS I ALWAYS DID, WITH SOME LIGHT stretching to work out as much of the cramps in my muscles (from sleeping in the same position the entire night) as I was able. Then I maneuvered into the bathroom, did, you know, bathroom things, and then made a coffee with the one-cup machine I had in my room. After adding some creamer, I settled on the bed with Zilla and ate my breakfast while watching Netflix.

Today's episode wasn't new. It was a rerun of a show I loved, *Strong Girl Bong-Soon.* It was a Korean drama about a girl who was born with incredible strength, and in a lot of ways, that strength made her weak. She had to hide the real her a lot, couldn't be herself. It was hard to get a job, hard to have relationships. Not many people saw the real her, only who they thought she was. She was small like me, and I felt some kind of affinity for her character.

Breakfast was always oatmeal and fruit because, you know, fiber. But sometimes I pretended it was blueberry pancakes dripping with maple syrup and drenched in butter. I also imagined fat, greasy slices of bacon alongside that would slide into the pool of syrup on my plate.

Then it was more bathroom things and getting dressed for the day. Since I had PT later, I chose a pair of black leggings and a simple lavender T-shirt with a pocket on the left. By the time I began brushing the knots out of my hair, a few hours had already passed, but it was still fairly early in the morning. I was an early riser, not really because I was a morning person but because I needed the extra time to prepare for the day.

Even if my day was mundane and predictable.

Someday, it might not be, and I would thank myself for already having this routine well-practiced and in place. Before I could start daydreaming about what that life might look like, there was a swift, familiar knock on the doorframe.

Squealing, I glanced up. "Neo!"

"There's my princess!" he exclaimed, smiling wide and sweeping in to likely lift me up.

"Wait!" I cautioned, lifting a wave of hair to reveal Zilla chilling on my shoulder.

"Godzilla." He pretended to roar, leaning in to stroke her head.

"I told you not to call her that." I laughed.

"She likes it," he insisted, lifting her off my shoulder to place her gently into her enclosure.

When he was done, he swept me out of my chair, legs dangling over the floor, and spun me around. "I missed you!"

"You were only gone two days."

Halting his turn, he lifted one dark brow over his very dark eye. "You saying you didn't miss me?"

Smacking his shoulder with the brush, I laughed. "Of course I did."

He finished twirling me and sat me back in the chair.

"Here, let me brush your hair."

A look of horror came over him as he dodged the brush and my hand, stepping back. "I already brushed it."

"It doesn't look like it."

"The last time I let you brush my hair, I ended up with about fifty flowers in it and glitter that fell every-where for days."

"I won't use glitter today," I vowed.

His eyes narrowed, and his lips pursed. "I see you crossing your fingers, Virginia Ann."

"You're no fun." I pouted.

"You have enough hair on your own head to brush."

He was right, so I went back to brushing. "How was California?"

"It had palm trees."

"Really, Neo? That's all you have to say? You flew all the way to the other side of the country. A place with endless sunshine, celebrities, and beaches, and all you have to say is *there were palm trees?*"

"We went there so Ivory could work. It wasn't a vacation."

"Still better than being here," I muttered.

His palm pushed under my nose, and in the center sat a big pale-pink seashell. Dropping the brush into my lap, I scooped it up, running my ringers over all the identical ridges stretching across the top, then flipped it over to feel its silky-smooth underside.

"Oh my gosh, this is beautiful."

"I found it on the beach and saved it for you."

I clutched it against my chest, both palms cupping around it protectively. "This was on the beach? Like in the sand? Washed up from the ocean?"

His eyes softened a bit when he nodded. "Sure was. I rinsed the sand off in the waves."

Pulling it upward, I studied it again. Oh, how I longed

to go to the beach, to hear the ocean waves, to push my fingers into the sand. "It was really there?"

"Cross my heart," he said, making an X over his chest.

"I thought you said you only went for work."

"Our hotel was oceanfront," he said, his voice a little sheepish.

Longing and jealousy were like a tidal wave inside me, pulling me under and spinning me around. There was happiness too. Genuine happiness that my brother finally got out of here even for just a little while and got to experience something else. I might always think of myself as a prisoner, but in many ways, he was one too.

At least one of us got out. At least one of us lived.

"Thank you," I whispered, running my finger over the textured top of the shell. This had once been lying in the sun, covered in sand, and kissed by salty waves. And now it was here, a part of my world. "It's perfect, and I love it so much."

"Ivory took pictures. She said she would email them to you. She also said she would come visit tomorrow."

"I can't wait!" Tucking the shell into my lap, I gazed at it as I continued to brush. "So when did you make it back to New York?"

"Late last night. It was too late to call."

"As you can see, I'm perfectly fine."

"How was it?" he asked, his tone shifting just slightly, and that minor change caused my back muscles to tense and a hard knot of dread to form inside me.

"Well, it was quite a surprise when Earth showed up," I answered. "I thought you two were in a fight."

"We're not in a fight."

"Well, up until yesterday, he was banned from seeing me."

"He's still banned. I was stuck in Texas. I had no choice."

I didn't bother to point out he could have called Beau, Fletcher, or even Ethan.

"I asked him what happened between you."

Neo stiffened. "And what did he say?"

"He wouldn't tell me either."

My brother's posture relaxed again.

"Did you know he has a gorgeous black sports car? It's just like the kind they drive in the movies. I wanted to drive so badly." I sighed longingly. "But of course, he said no."

"Virginia." There was that tone again.

I knew I couldn't avoid it forever. My hands fell to my lap, long waves of golden hair cascading around me.

"How was the appointment? What did the doctor say?"

"It was the same as always," I told him.

He was quiet for a few beats, and then he paced away. "He was supposed to be better than the others. More innovative. More experienced." When he stopped in front of me, his tone turned harsh. "Are you sure? What did he say exactly?"

I sighed. "He said what they all say. That it's too risky. That the damage is too great."

Neo's jaw worked, and then he spun away once more. "He's wrong. Clearly, he just doesn't have the skill set. I'll make some calls. There's this doctor I read about in Sweden—"

"Neo."

"It might be hard to convince him to travel here, but he will. I'll—"

"Neo!" My raised tone brought him around. I hardly ever yelled, hardly ever argued. But for some reason, this morning, it was a lot harder to just go along. "Stop. Just stop."

"Stop what?"

"Stop trying to force something that isn't going to happen."

I saw the argument form on his tongue. I saw that familiar stubborn glint in his eyes.

Holding up my hand, I plowed on, letting loose so many of the things I'd always wanted to say but never did. "How many more doctors, Neo? How many more tests and X-rays and scans? How many more physical therapists and experimental drugs will satisfy you?"

He turned a little incredulous. "Me? This isn't about me. This is about you."

I shook my head sadly. "I don't think it is. Have you ever really asked me if I wanted to do all this? Sure, maybe in the beginning, this was what I wanted. But how long? How many more times am I going to listen to an expert tell me I won't walk again? That my crushed spine is irreparable? How much longer will I have to wait to live? It's been over seven years, Neo. Countless doctors. I'm tired."

His expression softened as he knelt in front of me, hands brushing through the wheat-colored hair to reach for mine. "I'm sorry I wasn't here yesterday. Hearing that by yourself was probably very difficult and scary."

"I wasn't alone. Earth was with me."

Neo's fingers lurched against mine. "He was in the room with you?"

I nodded. "Yes. I asked him to stay."

"So he knows…" His words trailed off.

"He was pretty surprised. He was under the impression I was about to walk again."

"You will." He tugged away to stand. "As soon as I call that doctor in Sweden."

"Are you not listening?"

"You're scared. Frustrated. And yes, tired. But it will all be worth it in the end."

I pressed a hand to my forehead. "Says who? You?"

"You just said you were waiting to live. As soon as you can walk again, you won't have to wait anymore."

I swallowed past the huge lump in my throat. The pressure on my chest was so heavy I worried my ribs might collapse, and it was this pressure that also fired words straight off my tongue. "It isn't walking that's holding me back from living, Neo. It's you."

He flinched like I'd smacked him, and I immediately pressed my fingers to my lips, wishing I could take back those words. They might have been true, but it was a truth perhaps better left unspoken. He was my brother, the only family I had left. The last thing on earth I wanted to do was cause him pain.

"I'm holding you back?" he croaked. "I'm not the one giving up. I'm out there calling doctors, reading research, doing everything I can to fix what—" He stopped abruptly, pressing his mouth together.

"To fix what you did?" I asked gently.

A stricken look crossed his features, and a dark, cloudy aura enveloped him. It was a mood I was well acquainted with. One that had only gotten better when Ivory came into his life. Perhaps that was why I was suddenly courageous enough to bring this up, because I thought he might be more receptive.

"I don't blame you, Neo. I never have. What happened to me is not your fault. It was an accident, a horrible, tragic accident. Maybe we should stop trying to undo it and focus instead on moving on."

"And how are we going to do that if you can't even take care of yourself?" he spat.

It was my turn to flinch. His words made me feel small and pathetic, completely dependent on everyone else. I sniffled. "Maybe I could if someone believed in me a little more."

"V." The regret was evident in his tone when he stepped forward.

Fighting tears, I raised my chin and lifted my hand to stop him from coming closer. "It's okay, Neo. Maybe we should talk about this later."

He hesitated for long moments, and the silent tension crowding the room was almost too much to bear. Finally, my brother relented, sighing deeply before turning toward the door.

Just when I thought he would disappear, he stopped, broad shoulders filling the doorway. "You're my sister, and I love you. I only want what's best for you."

But what's best for me and what you want are not the same.

Even though he wasn't looking at me, I turned my face toward the opposite side of the room. My chin trembled, lips quivered. "I love you too."

Then he left me alone in my tower, a place I might never escape.

Fifteen

"What's wrong with you?"

I glanced up, startled to see Beau gazing over his computer monitors, green eyes studying me intently.

How long has he been staring?

"Nothing." I rebuked his concern. Dude barely ever looked up from his screens, so I don't know why he felt the sudden need to do it now.

"Usually, by now, you're down at the bar cleaning up."

"I did it last night after I closed up. Couldn't just leave it the way you left it."

Pushing out of his chair, Beau tugged at the beanie on his head, rolling his eyes. "You're welcome for covering the bar for you."

"You could have at least restocked. Everything was empty!" I yelled after him as he disappeared into the kitchen.

Truth was the bar wasn't in bad shape. No more out of order than it would have been had I been there. Except maybe the coolers wouldn't have been so low. I just used it as an excuse to stay late, working until I was so tired I knew I wouldn't be able to lie awake and think.

To wonder who that shadow was following me. To wonder what he wanted and who sent him.

He mentioned Virginia. His filthy stare had laid upon her innocence.

The hand not holding the mug slapped onto the arm of the leather sofa, my fingers digging in aggressively. I definitely hadn't planned to slice him open. But I wasn't the type who could let him walk with any vision of her in his corrupted thoughts.

Snort lifted his head off my jean-clad thigh when Beau sat in the chair nearby, holding his own mug of coffee and propping his feet up on the table. After a sip, he smirked, glancing at the way we sat.

"Ivory would kill us if she saw our feet on the coffee table."

I made a sound. "Ivory ain't here."

"Something happen with Neo?"

I glanced up, then away, my hand absentmindedly rubbing Snort's belly. "Didn't see him. Not even sure if they're back from Texas yet."

"Then Virginia? How was the appointment?"

I opened my mouth to tell him to mind his own fucking business but bit back the words when I saw the concern in his face. Telling him to butt out of my business was a lot different than telling him not to care about her.

"You know, Neo made her condition seem a lot better than it is."

"What do you mean?"

"I mean that fucking pimp of a doctor told her she wouldn't walk again."

He sat up a little straighter, feet dropping off the table. Both hands wrapped around the mug when he leaned forward. "But Neo said—"

"Apparently, Neo is living in a dream world," I spat, then paused to toss some of the black coffee down my throat. "Every doctor says the same thing, and he just keeps dragging her to another one, hoping to hear something different."

Beau seemed shell-shocked for a moment, and it made me relive the first moments after I'd heard that quack tell her. "And V?"

"Virginia just goes along with him, acting like every time someone else tells her she won't walk again doesn't kill her inside."

"Well, maybe she's hoping someone will say something different too."

"She's not," I snapped.

It is just like she said. Everyone just assumed all she could want was to walk again.

"She's more than a wheelchair," I muttered, picturing her smile when I drove too fast down the highway as I stared down into the last sip of the black brew.

There was a pregnant pause, and then Beau said, "Of course she is."

I don't know what it was—the tone of his voice, the fact I couldn't get her out of my head, or lack of sleep—but I heard myself say, "He just keeps her locked up there."

"And that bothers you," Beau stated. For someone who lived in front of a computer, he sometimes was too good at reading people.

Realizing I'd voiced something I should have kept inside, I made a rude sound and brushed him off. "Whatever. It's not my business."

Snort's nails clip-clapping along the scuffed-up wood floor as he followed me to the kitchen was the only sound in the apartment.

"He made it your business."

My retreat halted, shoulders and spine stiff as I lingered in the opening between the kitchen and living room. I didn't turn back, and though I wanted to keep going, my feet remained rooted in place.

Beau's voice was a little louder, almost as if he was speaking up because he realized he had my attention. "Neo made it your business when he called you. Besides, we're family. If we can't be all up in each other's business, then what's the point?"

There was no point. To any of this. So I continued into the kitchen to set my mug in the sink.

"I'm going to the bar," I informed Beau on my way to the door.

"It's okay to be worried about her, you know."

"I'm not." I rebuffed, practically slamming the door when I left.

Snort stared up at me from the floor, his bottom row of teeth sticking out along with his smooshed nose made him look like he was in a permanent bad mood.

"I'm not worried about her," I repeated.

He made a sound, a cross between a sneeze and a snort, and followed me downstairs. Since the place was already prepped for opening, I went into my office to do some paperwork. My leather jacket was hanging on the hook where I'd tossed it the night before, so I reached in to pull out the napkin.

After glancing at the note one more time, I fished out a Zippo and lit the corner. The flames creeped up slowly, curling the thin napkin in on itself as it slowly ate it away. After a few moments, the flame grew, and it scorched faster. I held it until the fire licked my fingers, then dropped the small piece into an ashtray on my desk where it burned the rest of the way.

Dropping into the chair, I pulled out a desk drawer, opening a false bottom no one knew about but me. The phone I was requested to answer sat there silent, screen dark.

A few taps on the screen lit it up, revealing a notification of twenty-one missed calls. Before curiosity got the better of me, I hid the phone away once more, turning my back only to have my gaze land on the cabinet where I stored my blade.

Thoughts of last night pricked the back of my mind, and I flipped on a small flatscreen that was mounted to the opposite wall.

I let the local news play in the background while I pretended to work on purchase orders and inventory when, really, I was waiting for the discovery of a dead body to be reported.

None came.

I refused to search the internet, knowing damn well that kind of stuff left a trail. Hell, normally, I wouldn't give a damn at all, but this was different.

He mentioned her.

The news went off without a single mention of the man in the alley, and I could only assume two things:

1. He hadn't been found yet.
2. He actually made it to a hospital in under thirty minutes.

Why hadn't I just made it a clean kill?
Holy shit. *He mentioned her.*

The realization had me on my feet in seconds, the blade and holster in my grasp before I even knew I'd reached for it.

The odds that douchebag was alive were slim. Slim

wasn't zero. The worry I denied so heartily before roared inside me, so aggressive there was no way I could fool myself into thinking I wasn't suddenly bone cold with fear.

He'd seen me with Virginia. Whoever he worked for could know about her now too.

The second my hand closed around the leather jacket, Snort was up on his feet, staring expectantly at me.

"C'mon, boy. Let's take a ride."

Sixteen

Virginia

Tears slipped across my forearms, saturating the colorful quilt spread across my bed. I lay facedown, my hair creating a barrier between my sadness and the rest of the world, further hiding me as if I weren't already nearly invisible.

I couldn't regret the things I'd said because they were things I truly felt. But I did not want to fight with my brother.

And so I cried. Cried for the carefree teenagers we used to be. Cried for my parents who tragically died too young. For Neo who carried around suffocating guilt that trapped him nearly as bad as my paralyzed lower half did me.

Seven years had passed, but in many ways, we still lived on the day a freak car accident altered everything forever. I couldn't blame Neo solely for where we were today. It wasn't fair to feel that he locked me up in here like a villain.

My older brother sacrificed so much for me. Giving up dreams of college, travel, and a life well spent all for petty theft, living in the Grimms, and using every dime he had to make sure I had the best care he could give.

I might not have a state-of-the-art wheelchair or reside in some fancy facility with the best equipment, but what I did have was wonderful and more than some people could wish for.

I'd probably sounded ungrateful to him. Selfish. As if I weren't thankful for all the doctors and research, for the hope that he'd sometimes shouldered on his own that I would walk again.

That doesn't mean letting go of your own wants so he can have his.

My thoughts were an endless tug-of-war drenched in tears that wouldn't stop.

Probably why I didn't notice the extra weight suddenly on my bed. It wasn't until the strands of hair clinging to my tears blew back with a very loud snort that I did.

Jolting up onto my forearm, I blinked wide, damp-lashed eyes at the intruder. "Snort!"

The English bulldog wiggled his entire body upon hearing his name, a few more loud snuffs and snorts breaking past his exaggerated underbite and smooshed nose.

A fat, wet tongue slurped up my cheek, and I giggled. The dog's hair was super short but silky soft, and his head was wide as it pushed against my palm while I scratched him.

"I haven't seen you in so long," I told him, rubbing his ear. He licked me again, and I squealed.

"Give me a name," a gruff, dark voice demanded.

Oh, that was right. Snort couldn't have come on his own.

"Earth," I announced as if we all didn't know the dark-headed, glowering man standing there at the side of the mattress.

Impatient, he crossed his arms over his chest, expression growing even more threatening. "Give me the name."

"The name?" I asked, swiping some of the hair away from my face. My back was getting a cramp from being twisted around in this position.

"Who made you cry?"

Oh. I guess he'd noticed. "No one."

"Was someone here?" he demanded. "What kind of security does this place have? If you won't tell me, I'll go find the head of staff—"

He started away, and I struggled to sit up and rotate my lower body. "Wait!" I yelled, dropping back onto my side. Snort pawed at me as if he was trying to help.

I grunted in irritation, pushing up to try again. Suddenly, my whole body flipped, and I hit my back with a rush of air bursting from my lungs.

A stare ripe with intensity loomed down, my body bracketed by leather-covered arms, caged in by a power that left me breathless but the opposite of trapped. "W-what are you doing?"

"Helping you sit up."

"I can't sit up with you… hovering."

"Who was here?"

"What makes you think someone was here?"

His tongue seemed very pink against the white lines of his teeth as it dragged across. "Maybe it was the fact that the sound of your sobs was torturing my eardrums when I walked in."

I felt my face flush, heat rushing to my cheeks. "Well, no one invited you!" I snapped. *How embarrassing.*

"Fine." He started to draw away, and just the withdrawal of his overwhelming intensity left me feeling panicked.

"It was Neo!" I rushed to say, reaching out to grasp his forearm.

He paused, eyes narrowing on my face.

"Neo was here," I admitted in a much softer tone. I felt my lower lip quiver, emotion coming over me once again. "We got into a fight."

Releasing his arm, I pushed up onto my elbows, preparing to push myself up the rest of the way. I didn't have to, though, because his arm slid around, warm palm splaying across my back to lift.

I wouldn't say I was touch-deprived, but somehow, that single touch made me feel I was. A thousand little tingles raced along my body, drawing out sensations I didn't know. Part of me always worried that since part of my body couldn't feel, I'd somehow be… muted. As if the ability to be affected by simple touch would somehow become void.

But in this moment, I was not muted. I was alive and on fire, burning from the inside out with tingles that echoed throughout me, creating wants and needs I worried I might never know.

Oh, but to know them. To discover that part of me was indeed working felt like a wish I'd unknowingly made in my heart had suddenly come true.

His tug was a little more zealous than it needed to be, and with me sitting there all stirred up with unexpected feelings, I had no guard to catch myself. So I fell into him, my upper body colliding with his, my forehead bumping along his collarbone.

He stiffened, clearly overshooting his intent, and began to shift back. I threw my arms up, wrapping them around his neck and sliding my face to press into the side of his neck. Earth froze, clearly caught off guard by the sudden hug I'd claimed.

His arms fell to his sides, hands resting on the mattress as he supported both his weight and mine. I sniffled just slightly against him, overcome by more emotion, sensitivity vibrating my nerves. Even in the midst of my sudden awakening, I felt comforted and somehow protected. The raw hurt of my fight with Neo ebbed a little, muffled by this man who smelled of bread and cigarettes.

The skin on his neck was smooth. It felt warm against the tip of my nose. His stillness only amplified everything I felt being this close to him. This touch was far different than that of my brother, doctors, and friends.

The tears on my face dried themselves against the warm cocoon of his body, and my heart beat steady with a relaxing rhythm. I knew I should pull away. I worried that he was completely offended I would dare latch on like this even as he didn't hug me back.

I pulled back ever so slightly, my nose nudging against the underside of his jaw. "Earth?" I whispered, feeling exposed. "Do you want me to let go now?"

He was quiet for a few minutes. The entire time he thought, I kept myself tucked in. I worried perhaps he did want me there but didn't know how to say it.

His voice stopped me. Gruff and low like sandpaper going against the grain. "You're fine, sprite. Just take what you need."

Those words almost ripped a squeal out of me as millions of big-winged butterflies took flight in my belly. But I held the sound in, instead tightening my arms around his neck to press my face in anew.

He still didn't hug me back. In fact, his body stayed rigid almost as though this kind of touch were just as new to him as it was to me.

But it didn't matter because he gave everything without having to move.

Seventeen

AN ANGRY HUNTSMAN WITH A BLOOD-STAINED BLADE stormed into a building, scanning every nook and cranny for any faceless threat.

Willing to burn the world down over the slightest disturbance, I stalked down the hall, only to be met with an enemy I didn't know.

Tears. Sobs painful enough to pull on even the blackest of hearts.

All I wanted was a name. Someone tangible I could slay. I growled and grumbled, threatened and snapped. Arms slid around me anyway. A cold nose pressed against my throat.

All I knew was retaliation, blood, and antipathy. She didn't ask for any of these things. What she seemed to want was solace.

I did not know solace.

But it seemed not to matter because somehow she found it in me anyway.

Eighteen

Virginia

"WHAT ARE YOU DOING HERE?" I WONDERED, HOPING THE reluctance I felt to pull away did not show on my face.

He cleared his throat, shifting to reach into his pocket. "You left this in my car."

One of the small daisies I pinned in my braids yesterday lay in his palm.

"Oh. Thank you," I said, taking the flower. "You didn't have to bring it all the way here."

Snort flopped down in my lap, nudging my belly with his nose. I laughed, not feeling his weight on my legs but being tickled by his breath.

"Snort," Earth grumped. "Move. You're heavy." He started to push the dog away, but I stopped him, wrapping an arm around the bulldog. "He's fine! Let him be."

He made a face like he smelled something rotten, and I smiled. "Good boy," I told the dog, patting his head.

"You wanna get out of here?"

The unexpected words made my head pop up. "Me?"

Earth nodded, dark hair falling into his eyes. His open jacket revealed a faded black T-shirt with a beer label across the front. The label featured a rotting apple, so I knew it was likely the beer that he served at his bar.

A bar I'd never been to.

Neo said I was too good for it.

"Where to?" I asked.

"Does it matter?" he countered.

I pursed my lips. "Can Snort come?"

"He's driving."

"You let your dog drive but not me?" I demanded.

His lips twitched, opaque eyes glimmering with mischief. "He's a better driver than you."

Unable to help it, I laughed. It was a complete contrast to the grainy feeling crying had left in my eyes. "I'm insulted, but I also can't pass up the chance to get out of here for a while."

Earth pushed up off the bed, gazing around. "Get your stuff."

"My stuff?"

He blanched. "Don't girls need like a bunch of stuff?"

"Did I need a bunch of stuff yesterday when we went to the hospital?"

"No. But look how that turned out." He glowered.

I flushed a little, remembering the little bathroom emergency.

"Do you have a backpack?" He still gazed around my room.

He was serious.

"Are you planning to, like, keep me out all night?"

"No. I have to work tonight."

"Everything I need is in the back pocket of my chair," I said, pointing to the black pouch that hung off the wheelchair.

"Backpack," he repeated. He was stubborn and unrelenting. Bossy.

"There." I pointed, giving in.

He glanced where I pointed, then back at me, clearly unamused.

"What?" My voice was innocent as I batted my eyes. "That's what I have."

"It's purple."

"Oh, I'm sorry. Does it clash with your black-leather, bad-boy vibe you love so much?"

Pinching the bridge of his nose, he sighed dramatically, and my lips rolled in on each other. "I told you everything is in the pouch. I don't need a bag."

Scowling, he grabbed the purple backpack and opened it up. "Put it all in here. Add extra."

"Extra?"

"I'm a man of little patience, sprite."

How rude. "I already said I didn't need a bag."

"And I am not taking you out of here and having a repeat of yesterday. I like to be prepared at all times. Your well-being is my responsibility."

I took the bag. He pushed the wheelchair close enough for me to transfer the items out of the pouch. Then I transferred myself into the chair and went through the room, adding a few other things I probably didn't need, but he seemed much calmer the more I tossed into the bag.

"Acting like I'm a baby and need a diaper bag," I muttered as I wheeled out of the bathroom, bag in my lap.

A big black boot came out, jamming against one of the wheels on my chair, stopping my forward progress.

I scowled, but he seemed completely unbothered, squatting in front of me, placing a hand over my knee.

I stared at his hand, feeling insanely robbed. He was touching me, and I couldn't feel it. The warmth of his palm, the tingle of nerves he always ignited. I could see that his hand engulfed my knee, but I couldn't *feel* that protective sensation. I couldn't revel in it.

Instead, I felt like an outsider in my own body. Seeing but not experiencing.

You know, on most days, I accepted my condition. I'd learned to live with it and see it as just who I was. But in this moment? In this moment, who I was just wasn't good enough.

"I know you aren't a baby. Having stuff you might need, it makes me feel better. I..." His throat worked, and this almost pained expression shone in his surprisingly earnest stare. "I care."

Suddenly, it didn't matter I couldn't feel that hand on my knee because those two simple words that seemed so difficult for him to say made me feel ten times more than that one touch could.

He cares. My stomach dipped, heart fluttered, and breath quickened. "I feel that," I whispered.

Brow furrowing, his almond-shaped eyes wrinkled at the corners. "What?"

I didn't realize I spoke out loud, but I wouldn't take it back. His admission seemed to cost him something, so it didn't seem like much to spend a little on my end too.

"I can't feel your touch," I said, gesturing to where his hand still covered my knee. "But what you just said, I felt that."

He drew his hand back, and even though I felt nothing, it still disappointed me. I guess just knowing he touched me was better than nothing at all.

He surprised me, though. Instead of dropping his hand, he pushed it between me and the arm of the wheelchair to grasp around my elbow. "Better?" he whispered.

His hands were warm, skin slightly rough against

mine. My arm was even smaller than my knee, so his palm engulfed it completely. The pad of his thumb moved lazily, caressing the inside of my arm. Those tingles of awareness I could only long for moments ago rushed over me, prickling my skin with goose bumps and creating a light shiver.

People had no idea the kind of deprivation that came with the inability to feel the sensation of touch. To understand without words what someone wanted to say. To be unable to interpret the physical vibes that could often be transmitted through the skin.

My eyes fluttered closed as his thumb continued to lazily stroke. His words were gruff and impatient, his tone bossy and rude.

But his touch... *Oh, his touch.* It whispered I was precious and how unbearable it would be for him to see me in any kind of distress. It asked for understanding and maybe even a hint of forgiveness.

"Better," I whispered back.

"When did you sneak in here?" Emogen's voice seemed so loud from the doorway, her sudden presence startling me like the popping of a balloon.

Earth's hold on my arm tightened a bit with my startle, but then he stood smoothly, releasing me to look at my nurse and friend. "I didn't sneak. I walked past the front desk."

"Two days in a row, that's more than we've seen of you this whole year," she commented, coming farther into the room. Her eyes glanced at the bag in my lap, then back at Earth. "To what do we owe this pleasure?"

"I'm going out with Earth this afternoon!" I exclaimed.

There was a short but poignant pause. Emogen glanced at me with gleeful eyes.

I gasped. "Not like a date!" I hurried to say, feeling completely ridiculous and knowing my face was beet red. "I just meant, like, out."

"Mm-hmm," Emogen practically sang.

"You got a problem with that?" Earth quipped, tilting his head at the curly-haired woman.

"As a matter of fact, I do."

"I'm not a prisoner here." *Even though it feels like it.* "I'm allowed to come and go as I please." I was twenty-one years old, for crying out loud. An adult.

"You have PT at two." Emogen reminded me.

I cringed, feeling Earth's stare and single raised eyebrow.

"I forgot," I told him. Turning to Emogen, I said, "I haven't missed a single appointment in seven years. Can't you cover for me just this once?"

Her red-painted lips pursed.

"Pleeeaase?" I asked, folding my hands in front of me like a beggar.

"This have anything to do with that argument I heard between you and Neo?" Leave it to Emogen to cut right to it.

"How is that your business?" Earth barked, clearly offended she would talk to me like that.

"She's my friend!" I declared.

He made a rude noise.

"You heard that?" I asked her, ignoring him.

"Half the floor heard it."

I grimaced.

"Relax." She went on. "We couldn't hear what you were saying, just that your voices were raised, and then Neo stormed out with a black cloud over his head."

"Sounds like Neo," Earth muttered.

Emogen turned chestnut eyes to me, waiting for an answer to her previous question.

I sighed. "Can't I just get out for a little while?"

Appraising my face, which likely still had red-rimmed, puffy eyes, she debated, then sighed. "Fine. I can move PT to six. But you have to be back in time."

I glanced at Earth. He nodded.

With a light squeal, I clapped. Snort leaped off the bed and put his two front paws on my lap.

"You know he's not allowed in here," Emogen said.

"We were just leaving." I promised, scratching behind his ear.

Earth reached into my lap, grabbing the bag to zip it closed and sling it over his shoulder.

"That purple really brings out your eyes," Emogen noted.

He glowered as I giggled endlessly.

"I'm leaving. You better hurry up. I won't wait." He went without looking back, the purple bag still resting against his shoulder.

Snort started to run after but stopped to look back at me.

"Let's go, boy," I said, pushing the chair forward.

Emogen stood watching the three of us parade out the door. "Where are you going?"

"I have no idea," I called back, some of my hair floating around me as I moved forward.

"And what if Neo calls?"

I paused at the door, heaviness weighing on my heart. "He won't call," I told her. "At least not today."

"You gonna tell me what went down between you two?"

I swallowed. "Later."

She made a sound. "All right. Get out of here. Don't do anything I wouldn't do."

That made me laugh because Emogen wasn't the type to back down from anything.

The hallway was already empty when I wheeled down the corridor. I started to worry that Earth really wouldn't wait for me and that my chance to be free for a little while was lost.

But then I rounded the nurses' station and saw him standing in the middle of the open elevator, arm thrown against the doors to keep them from closing.

Snort was already sitting inside, tongue lolling out the side of his mouth, the sound of his heavy breathing echoing in the enclosed space. The second Earth saw me, he scowled.

"You waited!" I said brightly, trying to hurry forward.

"Snort wouldn't get in the elevator until he heard you coming." He shifted back to let me wheel in.

The second I did, Snort had his front paws in my lap again.

"Were you waiting for me?" I cooed. "Who's a good boy?" Snort's fat tongue licked up the side of my cheek, and I squealed.

Earth huffed in irritation, stepping back so the doors could close.

Still patting Snort, I lifted my face. "Earth?"

He grunted, refusing to look at me.

"That purple really does bring out your eyes."

His lips twitched, then again. In the reflection of the elevator door, I was pretty sure I saw him smile.

Nineteen

EARTH

THIS WAS NOT IN THE PLAN.

The plan was to stop by, snoop around, get a feel for the energy around here, and see if anyone was watching the place—watching V.

Then I heard her crying.

Great deep sobs that lunged into the venomous heart beating haphazardly inside my chest. Even muffled in her blankets, they still resonated with an ache not many people could know.

But she did.

This small sprite that was like the sun.

This small sprite that knew darkness.

We both knew darkness, but the difference between us was that she lit hers up. And me? I embraced mine.

So when I heard those muted but loud-to-me cries, the worry and anger driving me here grew tenfold. Red spots swam before my eyes, demanding I exact revenge for whoever dimmed her natural light.

The temperature in my already cold bones dropped to negative numbers, and the amount of self-deprecation I felt for not severing that shadow's head last night could have brought me down. It was only countered by her need, the need to make right whatever it was she deemed wrong.

The frigid temps within me heated to just above freezing when she told me it was just Neo. The urge to seek justice for those tears became hardly a demand, but I found I still hated them.

The sound echoed off the inside of my head, bouncing around all the hollow places in my body like a symphony of moans haunting an ancient castle.

I could live with pain. Ghosts. Blood spill and even hate. I could live with anything. But in that moment, I learned of one exception. Her tears.

Virginia's misery was something I could not stand. Its very presence caused a reaction within me strong enough to war with chaos. Strong enough to make a man who lacked compassion overwhelmed with empathy.

So here we were, the rubber tires eating up the road as I whisked her out of the city on what she probably thought of as an adventure but something I was beginning to think of as a necessity. I needed to see her smile again. I needed to see her light shine as brightly as before.

As noted, I didn't mind the dark, but V didn't belong there, and I refused to let her wallow in it because it made me comfortable. In fact, it seemed Virginia being lost in shadows did not make me comfortable at all but instead urged me to wail against the very thing I loved to be enveloped by.

"Where are we going?" she asked, breaking what I thought was probably a record of quietness for her.

Those ten minutes must have been so hard for her.

Sliding a glance in her direction, I noted how the long, wheat-colored strands of her hair twirled around her hands until they weren't even visible. She had so much hair. It probably was half her weight.

It looks like sunlight you can touch. Suddenly, I was jealous of her swallowed-up hands, wanting to bury mine too.

"Why? You nervous?"

"Of course not. You'd never take Snort somewhere unsavory."

"*Unsavory*," I mocked. "You've been hanging out with Ivory and Ethan too much."

"Well, *they* come to visit. Unlike some people."

My hands tightened around the steering wheel. "I had my reasons."

"Yeah, reasons no one will tell me."

"I thought you wanted to know where we were going." My voice was gruff, this conversation irritating me.

"I've never been in this part of the city before," she commented, gazing out the window. "It's less crowded."

"We're outside the city limits, but I still consider it the city, just less busy." And just because it was outside the city limits didn't mean it was nicer. It was still basically an abandoned ghetto.

"You've been out here before, then?"

I nodded once, keeping my eyes trained ahead. "A few times a week."

"Something else no one tells me about," she commented, still looking out the window curiously.

"No one else knows about it either."

Head whipping around, her eyes glowed with curiosity. "Why?" She leaned closer, widening her eyes. "Is this where you hide the bodies?"

"You don't hide bodies. You let them be found so it's less suspicious." The very second the words were out, I regretted them. What the hell was I doing telling her that? Not only that, but the way she was, she would want to know how I knew that.

Oddly, she was nonplussed, going right along. "True. And if you really needed to get rid of it, why hide it? Just, like, dissolve it in acid or something."

My neck craned in her direction, dazed. *And frankly impressed.* "What did you just say?"

She shrugged. "I watch a lot of crime shows."

"Well, you shouldn't." She didn't need to be filling her head with that kind of crap.

"The show I'm watching now has this crazy serial killer in it. He's hoarding brides."

"Brides," I echoed. *What the fuck?*

She made a noise, which I assumed was a confirmation, and then chattered on. "Yeah, he's obsessed with some play. Anyway, he's kidnapping these women and putting them in cages and making them all his brides. Dude is totally whack. And he wears this mask." She motioned to her face and shuddered. "It's like totally creepy and—"

"What in the hell kinda crap are you watching?" I demanded.

"It's Korean."

I barked a laugh. Then I laughed again. "Is that supposed to make me think it's okay?"

"It's a comedy romance story anyway," she explained.

"With a serial killer who is hoarding brides."

"Well, all romantic dramas need a plot."

"This conversation is ridiculous," I announced.

She was silent for maybe thirty seconds.

"You're Korean, right?" she asked, curious.

"Yes. But that doesn't mean I'm okay with you watching Korean serial killer shows."

But it's okay for her to sit in the car with one? Minus the serial part.

"So does that mean you can speak Korean?"

"Mmm." I agreed, feeling a prickle of unease. That prickle kinda pissed me off. Why the hell would I be uneasy about being Korean? I mean, it was what it was. And the memories of it... Well, that's all they were. Memories.

Memories I don't want her around.

"You probably wouldn't even need subtitles to watch that drama!" she exclaimed, completely awed.

"Why the hell would I want to watch it? It sounds horrible."

"It's my favorite," she said, her voice kind of pouty as if the fact I insulted her weird show hurt her feelings.

"A show you have to read to watch," I muttered, this time with less heat.

"Well, you wouldn't have to read it," she retorted.

I pursed my lips. "If I'm ever *really* bored, maybe I'll give it a try," I muttered.

V brightened, her full lips pulling into a big smile. "Really? Thanks, Earth!"

Why was she acting like I'd just given her some fancy present? *Why do I like it?*

"We're here," I announced, turning toward a rundown building that had been abandoned years ago. When I found the place, it was in shitty condition, and honestly, the outside still reflected that.

The old warehouse wasn't as big as the title suggested, which was probably why it was abandoned long ago. Weeds grew around it, poking through cracks in the sidewalk and pavement on the side of the building. Some places were worn so thin they were permanent puddles, and when bone dry, they looked like the parking lot had just caved in on itself.

The brick was faded from what was probably once a bright red to a dirty rust color, some of it slightly crumbling. A lot of the windows had been busted and broken. All of them, I replaced. The doors were all replaced with steel because, like I said, this was basically an abandoned ghetto.

"Are you in a gang?" she questioned as though the very thought excited her.

I scoffed. "Hell no. I work alone."

"So what are we doing here?"

I tapped my chest, and she frowned. In the back seat, Snort gave a bark, ready to go baptize all the weeds he could. Probably why those stubborn things kept growing 'cause he was watering them.

I got out, and he rushed out behind me, hurrying toward a big dandelion. By the time I had V's chair out of the back, he'd already pissed on three plants.

"The ground is uneven out here," I told her as I reached in to pick her up. The long silky strands waterfalling down her back whispered against my fingers. "So be careful."

"Okay." Her voice seemed slightly breathless, and when I glanced down, our eyes collided. Both of us had what most might consider standard "brown" irises, but though it was the same color, they couldn't be more different.

The very light she radiated was there, giving a warm hue to her stare. Gilded flecks shone like undiscovered gold. But it wasn't the contrast of how her eyes looked alive and mine looked dead that made me fall into their depths.

It was the *way* she held my stare. Not once did her

eyes shift away. Not once did she pull back or shutter her gaze. Virginia looked at me—*into me*—like she was searching for all the things most people were intimidated by, as if the dark, flat depths were not scary but something to be curious of.

I was a villain in most stories. Hell, even my own.

But the way this woman was looking at me whispered I wasn't a villain in hers.

How I want to be her hero.

The thought slapped me across the face, bringing with it harsh reality and making my entire body jolt.

She made a sound, her arms tightening around my neck.

"Stop looking at me like that," I spat, pissed off with my head and pissed off I'd scared her.

"Like what?" She wondered as I gingerly sat her in the chair.

I grunted, quickly pulling away. But the damnable woman caught the collar of my jacket, curling her small hands into the leather to tug, stopping me from going any farther.

Truth was I could have wrenched back, loosened her grip.

I didn't.

Instead, our eyes clashed again, and I let my stare go cold, hoping to make her see what she clearly hadn't before.

"Like what?" she repeated, hands not even trembling where they clutched.

How dare she? How dare she grab on to me and demand an answer? How dare she not be intimidated?

"Like you like me." The words sounded like they scraped over gravel on their way out of my throat. Gruff, irritated, and hopefully scary.

"I do like you," she said without any hesitation at all.

This was why Neo locked her up. Because she was too pure and big-hearted for the world. Because she liked people she really shouldn't. Because there was something about her that could soften even the hardest of hearts.

Unbeknownst to my internal colloquy, she went on as if her life wasn't altered at all. "So I really hope you didn't bring me to this gangster pad to off me because then I'd have to change my mind."

I blinked. A smile cracked my face, probably making it look like this fractured pavement we were standing on. *Thank God.* Those sardonic words somehow put us back on level playing ground. It righted the world that was oddly starting to tip.

"If I wanted to kill you, you'd already be dead," I said, snatching the damn purple backpack out of the car before taking my place behind her chair.

"I can do it." She fussed, trying to shoo me away.

"I told you this pavement is uneven." My hands closed around the handles. "I should have it repaved."

"What for? You're the only one who comes out here."

"Snort!" I bellowed. "Get over here!"

"Could you yell any louder?" V complained, covering her ears. "That poor dog."

Snort came barreling over, his breathing even harder than usual.

I started pushing her toward the large side door a short distance away. It was painted an ugly shade of brown and had some scuff marks along the bottom.

I liked it that way. If I let it look too new and replaced, then people rolling around these parts would know I had something valuable inside.

"Earth?"

Every time she said my name, my heart stuttered just a little. Like an engine that was about to putter out but then suddenly found the energy to run again.

"What?"

"I really want to know why we're here."

I laughed. Everything that came out of her mouth was a surprise. "It's my brewery."

I enjoyed being the one to surprise her for once.

"A brewery?" she echoed, watching me unlock the door.

I nodded.

"Like to make beer?"

"Do breweries make anything else?"

She glanced at my chest to the Rotten Apple logo. Her eyes widened. "You make your own beer!"

"Poisoning guaranteed," I quipped, throwing open the door.

"It's times like this I wish I could run."

I stilled. Rotated. "If you don't want to be here, I'll take you away."

"Don't be an idiot! I meant so I could run inside. I've never been to a brewery before." She gasped. "I've never even had beer!"

"No," I deadpanned, knowing where this was going.

"But, Eaarrrth," she whined, and goddamn it if my heart didn't pinch with the urge to give in. "I'm twenty-one."

"I saw all those pills you put in this bag." I tossed a thumb toward the backpack.

Her eyes rolled so hard I thought they might fall onto the pavement.

"If your eyes fall out and Snort eats them, I won't be responsible."

She laughed. The kind of laugh that made her bend in

her chair, press her hand to her belly, and a curtain of hair hide her features.

The sound bloomed in my chest, creating an odd sense of peace. It made me uncomfortable. Peace was new to me. I only operated on chaos.

She was wiping the tears from her eyes as I pushed her inside. The open room was too dark to see anything, but I knew this place like the back of my hand and parked her chair before hitting the light switch on the wall.

She gasped when the brick walls, concrete floor, and hanging lights appeared. Her eyes didn't stop moving, touching on everything: the steel tables, brewing kettles, fermenters, bottles, and all the other items I needed to brew the house label beer I served at my bar.

You're surprised, right?

Did you think killing was my only hobby?

It ain't.

"This is amazing!" V exclaimed, rotating to look at me.

A little pride swelled in my chest. My arms crossed as I regarded her. "I'm still not giving you beer."

Her lower lip jutted out. The bottom of my stomach exited my body. I was afraid if I looked down, I'd see it at my feet.

"Don't you want your beer to be my first?"

"If I catch you drinking beer anyone else gives you, I'll kill them."

She laughed.

She thought I was kidding.

I was not.

"So I can have some?"

I pursed my lips and walked away to check on my latest batch. "Maybe just a sip," I called to her.

She clapped. "I'm exploring!"

"Don't touch anything!" I demanded.

"Okay." She agreed readily, but we both knew she'd be touching everything she could reach. Just like we both knew I wouldn't yell at her when she did.

Twenty

I wanted to like it. I really did.

How fascinating it was to listen as Earth explained the steps in brewing his own beer, seeing all the different equipment and even getting to see the beer in different stages.

I loved the way he transformed this old building everyone thought was useless into something capable of producing something for people to enjoy. He was so smart and capable, so much more than he let on.

Even though he scowled and put on a big fuss, he still poured some of the brew that had been resting at room temperature for a little over two weeks—so it could carbonate—into a glass so I could try my very first taste of beer.

It was a big moment, and I felt his keen stare as I lifted the brew to my lips.

It was warm, bubbly, and kind of tasted like stale bread. It wasn't… terrible.

Fine, I'll say it. It was how I imagined pee would taste.

Beer tasted like pee.

I swallowed, feeling the warm liquid prickle down

my throat. Tilting the glass, I studied the amber liquid, wondering if perhaps the second sip would taste better.

Earth's laugh rumbled up to the high ceiling, creating a buzzing sensation in my ears. "You hate it."

"I do not!" How offensive!

Stifling his laugh, he crossed his arms over his chest. He did that a lot, a gesture probably meant to make him look closed-off and intimidating. All it did, though, was make his T-shirt stretch over his biceps when they flexed. It was distracting and created a flavor in my mouth that was far better than beer.

"Don't lie." He admonished me.

"I'm not. I could never hate something you made."

His arms slackened a bit, the hard edge to his eyes giving way to something more tenuous, something, for a few silent seconds, he wasn't able to bury behind that opaque glare.

Although we said nothing, the energy around us became electric. Butterflies knocked together beneath my ribcage, and for a moment, it was a little harder to breathe. I wasn't sure what was happening, but I knew whatever it was, he felt it too.

There was no way he couldn't. And for those brief minutes, that charged energy stripped us bare, leaving behind naked emotion that neither of us ran from or acknowledged.

As much as it intrigued me, as adventurous as I was, it was also frightening. The one and only time I'd felt the stirrings of something like this, it did not go well, and the letdown had hurt.

With Earth, it was even stronger than before. It made me... want. It made me... ache.

It made me wonder why Neo didn't want him around me.

Thoughts of my brother were sobering. We'd just gotten in a fight, and I knew deep in my gut this would only make it worse. I loved my brother. I didn't want to fight with him.

So I pulled back from the enticing current between us, just enough so I could breathe again. Just enough to restore the balance we seemed most comfortable in. Even so, it was still there. It pulsed in the air as if it waited for the opportunity to strike again.

"Is this what it's supposed to taste like?" I asked.

Pushing away from the steel table he leaned against, Earth hooked a long finger inside the rim of the glass, lifting it out of my grasp. I didn't know why the action was so mesmerizing, but I watched him sip the same liquid I just had, unabashedly watching the way his Adam's apple bobbed.

His lips were slightly glossy when he pulled the glass down, his eyes thoughtful as he swallowed. "It's a good batch," he announced, setting aside the glass. "Once it's cold, it will be even better."

"Does all beer taste like pee?" I wondered.

A choked sound ripped from his throat. "And how do you know what pee tastes like?"

"That beer just told me!"

He laughed.

"Maybe you should add sugar," I suggested.

"Maybe you should stick to water."

"Earth?"

Another current of that charged energy cracked through the room like lightning just before a thunderstorm.

"What, sprite?" The sound of his voice did nothing to quell that energy.

"It kinda tasted like bread." I realized something.

"Actually, you always smell faintly of bread. This must be why."

Thick, dark eyebrows arched up his forehead. "You think I smell like bread?"

"And stale cigarettes."

He blinked, then scowled. "What are you smelling me for?"

"Well, it's kinda hard not to when you pick me up," I replied, feeling self-conscious.

He grunted. "It's the hops. It's like yeast. You use it to brew beer."

His dark eyes strayed to where his leather jacket lay across a table. There was a hint of vulnerability to that look, and I found it endearing.

"It's actually kinda comforting," I said.

His eyes snapped back, and I smiled.

His movements were controlled and slightly stiff as he moved about, cleaning up the glass and putting some of the ready beer into cases to bring back to the Rotten Apple.

"Now that you've had it, don't let me catch you drinking it anywhere." His voice was gruff as he worked.

"As if I'd want to," I muttered.

He chuckled. "It's an acquired taste."

Not one I'd be acquiring.

"After I pack some of this up, we'll go," he said, still moving around.

His aloofness was not something that ever bothered me. It was just how he was. But the more the silence stretched on, the more worry began to prickle me. Maybe it was because of what happened earlier with Neo. Maybe it wasn't.

"Did I hurt your feelings?" The words rushed out, practically chasing him around the room.

His entire presence stilled, but even as he stood unmoving, I felt dark chaos. "I don't have feelings."

Turn and look at me.

"Now who's lying?" I challenged.

"And what makes you think that's a lie?"

Nerves coiled in my middle. I felt shy, but I wanted to be bold. "Because if you really had no feelings, I wouldn't be here right now."

He finally turned, the weight of his stare settling on me. It was a delicious weight, one that oddly soothed some of the tension in me.

"You heard me crying, and you wanted to distract me, right? You didn't want me to be upset and alone at the Tower." The more I spoke, the softer my voice became, but it didn't matter because I was still bold enough to speak.

The same charged mood lying in wait started to move, curling around our feet and beginning to swell.

The nerves I felt shifted to something more, fluttering lightly at first sort of like I was being flirted with but quickly turning much more aggressive as his stare narrowed into crescent moons and the black began to glitter.

Unable to sit still under that intense, simmering gaze, my hands gripped each other, wringing nervously in my lap.

"So did I?" I asked, feeling breathless. "Because the thought of hurting your feelings after you were so thoughtful really isn't something I can bear. At least let me apologize."

He moved suddenly, but despite the burst of movement, Earth was graceful and stealthy, soundless even under speed. The distance between us shrank, but the thickness in the air grew.

Crouching before me, he settled his hands over my anxious ones, quieting the fidgeting with a single touch. I was afraid to meet his eyes. Afraid to peer up from beneath the lashes offering some semblance of a shield. My stomach was full-on tumbling now as if someone pushed my wheelchair down a hill and it was racing out of control, taking me on the ride of my life.

In an effort to ground myself, I reached out. The closest thing my grip found was him. The second my hands clung desperately to his, two things happened:

1. The party in my stomach spread into my chest, making my heart jitter instead of beat.
2. His hands curled around mine tighter, as if accepting the death grip and returning it.

My heart galloped beneath my ribs so forcefully I could hear it echo in my ears. Pulling in a shuddering breath, my lungs vibrated on the exhale, making me feel all shaky and unstable.

Why was I like this? What was it about him that made me react this way? I wanted to push him away, but even as I thought that, my hands seized his tighter.

"You'd have to try a hell of a lot harder than that to piss me off."

As he spoke, I still didn't look up. Instead, I turned, captivated by how swallowed-up my hands were in his and the contrast between my pale coloring to his olive tone. We couldn't have differed more, but somehow that very stark contrast was reassuring.

"I hadn't planned on bringing you here. But you're right. I couldn't stand the thought of leaving you behind."

His words beckoned, forcing my eyes up. I felt fragile

and weak, my body still trembling under the strange assault of his closeness. But still...

I wanted more.

More breathlessness. More weakness. More erratic heartbeats.

His thumb stroked over the joint where my thumb met my hand, causing a burning sensation to swell in my middle.

His stare was wolfish yet guarded as though he were trying to hold back.

All the times I had held back or been held back by things out of my own control surged forward, crashing over me like a tsunami, threatening to fill my lungs with water and swallow up all my air.

I was weary of holding back. Weary of so many things.

In a war against that tsunami within in me, my hands ripped free of his. His face was warm under my palms, the chiseled angles of his jaw like smooth granite. A question poised in his eyes but never met his lips.

"Earth?"

He answered not in words but in the shifting of his gaze. Recognition and something more possessive sparked in its depths the moment I whispered his name.

"No one has ever kissed me."

His nostrils flared, the irises of his eyes expanding. His tone did not match the unspoken reaction. "Why would you tell me that?" The words ripped out aggressively, almost as if he were angry with what was transpiring between us.

"Because I thought..." *Be brave.* "Maybe you would?"

The fingers curled so protectively around mine tightened almost painfully, and the guarded glint in his stare turned predatory. I couldn't even feel shy or proud at my own boldness because the currents racing between us were too strong to allow anything else in.

He wanted to kiss me. I could see it on his face. I could practically smell it on his skin.

Yet he still sat there, unmoving, nearly hypnotizing me with those black eyes.

"I shouldn't," he finally said, his voice sounding foreign to my ears.

Disappointment stabbed me. The only thing keeping me from doubling over from the pain of his rejection was my pride. But even my pride wavered; even my pride began to bleed.

"But that's exactly why I'm going to." The self-loathing in his voice was secondary to the absolute desire firing in his eyes.

Before I could even make out what he'd said, his hands hooked under my arms, lifting me out of the chair like it took no effort at all.

My lower body hung inert but, for once, not feeling as lifeless as it was. I felt the way his arms flexed, the slight quiver in his muscles as he held me up so I was slightly suspended above the floor.

The length of my hair fell down my back and over my shoulders. Even though I was completely dependent on him to keep me upright, I wasn't scared.

All I could do was anticipate, held captive by the entrancing, hungry eyes that looked like they wanted to make a meal of me.

All at once, he pulled back, and the sound of my gasp echoed around the room. I slipped down maybe an inch before he caught me again, pressing our chests together, my entire upper body now in contact with his.

I was breathless. Tingling.

He whispered my name. "Sprite."

The second my chin lifted, he bumped his nose gently against mine, extending the contact by dragging his upward, the tip of his nose caressing the way mine slightly sloped. A kiss without meeting the lips. A kiss of emotion.

Lips parted as I sought for air.

The air I found was him.

He wasn't cautious or even gentle. He claimed and owned the instant we met. The rumble deep in his throat vibrated between us like a lion finally taking down his kill.

A heavy veil fell over me, blanketing every thought my brain might have. Sensation took over, and literally, all I could do was feel.

For a girl who spent most of her life only half feeling, I was totally overwhelmed.

His lips were thick and warm, slanting over mine with abandon as if it didn't matter part of me couldn't participate because the part of me that could was more than enough.

The friction of our lips rubbing together generated electricity that stood the hair on my neck on its ends, shivers of intense delight raced over me, and a storm of desire waged on.

Something about this kiss felt dangerous, like I was teetering on the edge of something sinister, but it promised so much sinful delight I was incapable of resisting.

Releasing his biceps, I slid my palms up his arms, dragging over his shoulders to grasp his neck. I held on tight, the pads of my thumbs digging into the underside of his jaw. He growled in what I assumed was approval and adjusted the angle of the kiss, slamming me with desire all over again.

I tried to give as good as I got, but he kissed with experience I didn't know. He attacked as the predator I was not.

Our lips were slick when he nudged back just slightly. The huffing breaths he pulled in puffed against my wet lips, making me shiver. The arms around me were tight like vises, though he'd been holding me up for an undefined amount of time.

A few steps forward and he sat me on one of the steel-topped tables.

Holding my waist, he pulled back enough for our eyes to meet, silently asking if I could sit here without his help. I nodded once, and both hands moved to my knees, eyes never once straying from mine as he pushed my legs open enough to step between.

Both hands grasped my neck, palming the sides, wide fingers caressing the base of my skull. I shivered, my upper body quivering visibly, my eyes lowering halfway. His thumb caressed the corner of my mouth, and the sound of his heavy breathing was making it impossible to think.

Suddenly, my head was tilted upward, forcing my half-shut eyes to his attention. His were dark and ominous, clouded with something I didn't recognize but had definitely put there.

His head lowered, making the space between our mouths just enough to keep us separate. "This okay?"

All I could do was make a sound, and it was all he cared to hear.

He claimed me again. The sound of us fusing filled the room, and the way he seemed to suck in air as he kissed me without pulling away made my hands fist in the front of his T-shirt.

He still kissed with ownership, but this time, he also

explored. Almost as if he were satisfied he'd already made his claim, so now he could play.

Dear God, I didn't know what was more deadly: his ownership or his playfulness. Perhaps they were equal.

All of that became an afterthought when his thick tongue dragged across my lower lip. My lips parted, gasping at the new sensation, but he didn't pause. That wicked tongue slipped inside me, twisting and twirling around mine.

My fingers fisted in the hair at the back of his neck, and he kissed deeper, going so far as to lick along the roof of my mouth.

My ears turned hot, cheeks tingled, and heart slowed to a thump. Every part of me was taken over. Every part of me hummed just for him.

I'd asked for a first kiss, but Earth... he'd given me something far more than that. Something I would never be able to even define.

Retreating a little, his lips and tongue gentled, and when he nibbled on my lower lip, I pressed a hand to my stomach and sighed.

I didn't know how long that kiss lasted, but when he finally lifted his head, he did that thing again with the tip of his nose, caressing mine tenderly—the ultimate act of affection.

My body started to slump and might have fallen over, but his arm curled around my waist to cradle my lower back, keeping me upright as I stayed suspended between wherever that kiss just took me and the reality of being right there with him.

His lips were an ultimate destination. When he'd kissed me just then, I wasn't a girl in a wheelchair who could only feel half. I wasn't a girl trapped in a tower, feeling like she needed permission for even her own life.

Instead, I was brimming with emotion, free from all confines, and flying high.

There once was a girl who was told she'd never walk again... but a girl doesn't need legs to fly.

"Your lips are swollen." The pad of his thumb pressed lightly against my bottom lip.

"They are?" I sounded drunk. Who needed beer when this man was walking around with that mouth?

That little gem of realization made me straighten, the hand against my back no longer necessary to hold me up. The idea of him kissing anyone else like that was like being tossed into a pool filled with ice.

"Did I go too far?"

My gaze flickered up, our stares like Velcro. Once meeting, they stuck and held. His eyes were fuzzy, warmer than I'd ever seen them. There was something soft in their depths, something akin to satisfaction, which made me wonder if he normally walked around unsatisfied.

There was a sheen on his lips, a lustrous gloss I knew was from me. I wasn't nearly as skilled with my tongue as this man, but I responded to his devilish call.

I knew—*I felt*—that he'd been the one doing the claiming, but just then, I knew I'd left my mark.

"No," I answered, that previous icy thought literally melting to a puddle just from his stare. "I liked it."

"We should go." His voice was gruff.

My arms looped around his neck when he lifted me off the table. The shyness that couldn't break through before suddenly came rushing in, squeezing my heart and making my face feel hot. Dropping my cheek to his shoulder, I did my best to hide my face.

My first kiss. And my stars, it was amazing!

"Did you like it?" I asked even though I was embarrassed and afraid of his reply. Look, I learned a long time ago a girl like me had to act when she could, because if she didn't, she'd find herself shut away in her tower, wondering about the things she should have done when she had the chance.

His footsteps didn't even pause. "I'm not doing it again. So don't ask."

I made a face. "I wasn't going to."

"Well, why not?" he bellowed, irritation loud and clear.

I pressed my face into his shoulder, hiding my smile. *Maybe he liked it after all.*

He grunted when I didn't answer but was gentle when placing me back in my chair. Before he could pull back completely, I pressed my palms against his cheeks, smooshing his lips together just slightly.

A confused look flashed in his eyes, but he didn't pull away.

I felt his jolt of surprise when I leaned up, pressing my mouth fully against his. Opening one eye, I noted both of his were wide with shock, watching aptly as I kissed.

It definitely wasn't the kind of kiss he gave. Just a quick, firm meeting of our mouths with maybe a little smile thrown in. But it was enough to make my pulse pound.

Feeling pretty accomplished, I sat back, released his face, and gave him a cheeky smile. "Why ask when I can just do it myself?"

Still rooted in place, Earth rolled his lips inward as if he still couldn't believe I'd just kissed him.

"You're really not scared of me. Not at all."

I puzzled, feeling my nose crinkle. "Should I be?"

"Yes."

No hesitation. No hint of doubt. Just clear, unadulterated honesty. He really seemed to believe he was dangerous, but to me, he was anything but.

"If you really wanted me to be scared of you, then you shouldn't have kissed me that way."

He drew back, a mix of emotions flitting over his face the way fireworks burst then disappeared in the night sky. He turned away, gathering up everything we needed to leave.

When he spoke, his voice wasn't loud but still echoed ominously around the room.

"I never said I wanted you to be afraid, just that you should be."

EARTH

YOU KNOW WHAT MY PROBLEM IS? I DO WHAT I WANT.

I never really thought this was a problem until five minutes ago. Until the beauty currently riding shotgun asked me to kiss her.

I mean, who even does that?

Not even the ho-bags who dangled in cages at that hole-in-the-wall club I frequented were that bold.

Guess they didn't need to be when their titties were hanging out and they were in actual cages.

But you know what? Those mask-wearing maneaters were no match for V. Not even on their best night, wearing their sexiest getup.

Her innocent curiosity and easy acceptance of the fucking chest of chemistry we seemed to stand on took them all down without spilling any blood. Hell, I was impressed.

I was also fucking out of my mind.

The last thing on this planet I should have done was kiss her.

But how could I deny that request? I should have. I didn't want to. I wanted to kiss her with more ferocity than I'd probably ever wanted anything.

The need intoxicated me, bubbling over in my blood.

Laying my lips upon hers only made it worse. She tasted untainted, a woman without a drop of poison in her blood. Like unfiltered sunshine on a summer day, the kind of warmth that caressed your skin and spread, seeping deep to warm cold bones.

I forgot what innocence tasted like, the flavor of only pure desire. She didn't try to take anything or battle against what I tried to claim. Instead, she melted into it as if it were me who was the sun and not her.

I'd set out to kiss her gently, perhaps just satisfying her request for another first like I had with the beer. But the second my nose brushed along hers, I knew I'd burn the whole world down around us if she disliked my kiss even a fraction as much as she disliked my beer.

I kissed the way I lived: aggressive, all-in, and selfish. I thought—*no*—I hoped I might scare her. Frighten her enough to never ask for another kiss again.

Because that was the thing. I did whatever the hell I wanted, but she seemed to be my limit. If she said no, I'd deprive myself to satisfy her wishes.

She was not afraid. She did not draw away. Her sweet mouth was so pliant and willing. The way she anchored herself against me to weather the storm I created only made me want to claim her more.

The poison in my veins likes her.

I felt it awaken, incensed by the raw passion only she had ever made me feel. But its fondness wouldn't matter because even if the venom sought to embrace her, its embrace was deadly just the same.

The sharp claws of fear punctured deep, claiming me instead of her.

Fear was not something I often met because, in order

to be afraid, you had to give a damn. I mostly did not give a single one.

Still, its stickiness coated the back of my throat, defiantly swimming up my esophagus like a tenacious disease seeking to taint our kiss.

I was tenacious too, though, and denied fear the pleasure. I should have also denied myself because now her unique flavor called to me like a craving. It hammered the back of my consciousness, begging for more.

"Does the reason you think I should be afraid of you have anything to do with what happened between you and my brother?" Her question filled the interior of the car, which, up until this point, had only been filled with the sounds of Snort's heavy breathing.

"Yes."

"But you still won't tell me?" She pressed.

"No."

My God, why did she ask so much of me? *Why do I want to give it?*

"Well, if you won't tell me, then you can't possibly use it to intimidate me."

"Isn't it enough already?" I suddenly bellowed, hands tightening to a bone-aching degree. "I got you out of there. I gave you beer, and I even gave you your first kiss! What else do you want from me?" My chest was heaving with angry gulps as I sucked in air. *Goddammit!*

Her silence was poignant, swollen with shock and tight with hurt.

A pang of conscience hit me, but the poison stirred up in my blood tried to dissolve it away. I knew I should apologize, but I couldn't get out the words. I couldn't do anything but sit there and brood hotly, staring at the road as it carried us closer to the crowded city.

Instead of saying anything, she leaned forward and turned on the radio.

The CD I had in (no Bluetooth in this old girl) roared to life, and I almost laughed at the absurdity.

I felt rather than saw her pause in surprise, her hand hovering over the volume knob before pulling back.

I counted down in my head. *Three, two, one...*

"You listen to K-pop," she remarked.

I wanted to laugh because there was no way in hell this girl would not comment about this.

"It keeps me fluent in Korean," I mumbled as the heavy beat of Monsta X filled the speakers.

Instead of telling me I was ridiculous, she started to sing along.

I probably looked like an owl as my head rotated on my shoulders, gaping at her with wonder.

She saw and shrugged. "You think I watch all those K-drama shows on Netflix and don't listen to K-pop?" she reasoned before going back to singing.

We spent the rest of the ride back to the Tower saying nothing to each other, but her constant singing filled the silence.

It was annoying.

Annoyingly endearing.

I would bring her home. Drive away. Never come back.

The moment the car shut off, an awkward silence descended. Intent on ignoring it, I snatched the keys out of the ignition, fully intending on getting the fuck out of this car as fast as possible.

I needed space. I needed to simmer down. I needed to get my head on straight.

"First Neo and now you."

As urgent as my previous thoughts had been, it

turned out they were incredibly fragile, for they vanished the second her solemn words touched my ears.

"What?" My voice was gruff.

"People always say you won't regret being brave and bold, but how can I not when it ends like this?"

The keys fell out of my hand. The leather of my jacket made a sharp sound against the seat when I rotated all the way to face her.

"Tell me what you mean."

"It doesn't matter," she said, reaching for the door handle like she wished she could get out and run away.

I felt her frustration and even understood it. Still, I used the fact she couldn't run against her. "You aren't getting out of the car until you tell me."

She half smiled, kind of bitter, kind of like she expected that reply. "Always at the mercy of someone else." She spoke those words purely to herself.

"You aren't at my mercy."

Flashing eyes ripped up to mine, burning with intensity I didn't often see in her. I realized then it was always there; she just kept it hidden well. "No? Is that why you *gave* me two firsts today? Is that why you gracefully *allowed* me out of my cage?"

My lips started to open, but she threw up her small hand.

"Is that why you only give what you choose and withhold the same? Believe it or not, Earth, I am at your mercy. At everyone's. The minute I speak out or ask for something someone doesn't want to give, I'm left behind. Banished into my tower and punished until I come around to whatever it is they think is best."

And there it was. The darkness I knew she harbored. The darkness she usually lit up. Oh, darkness did not become her. In fact, it made me exceedingly uncomfortable to watch it close in.

Guilt, swift and sharp, shackled my chest, and a feeling of contriteness stabbed my normally unfeeling heart. I was selfish—something that never bothered me until she looked at me like this.

"What happened with Neo, sprite?" I thought the soft tone and nickname she seemed to like would take the edge off my question, make it seem more like a request.

But her eyes shot daggers as if she knew I was trying to manipulate her.

Perhaps I was.

Holding up my hands in surrender, I backed down without a fight. As loath as I was to leave things this way, it seemed trying to smooth them over would only make it worse.

The sound of my doorjamb releasing was masked by her voice.

"I said awful things to him." The change in her tone, the quiet sorrow, made my fist tighten around the door handle. Even though I itched with the desire to turn toward her, I stayed still, keeping my back turned, keeping my hand on the handle but not pushing the door ajar.

"You can tell me about it. But only if you want." Really, I wanted to demand. Everything inside me screamed with it. But not with V. I wouldn't do that with her.

"I told him it was him who held me back. I threw his worst insecurities and guilt right in his face." She sniffled.

My throat tightened painfully with that small sound.

"Can I turn around, V? Please let me turn around."

"I wish you would."

I spun, eyes desperate to search out every inch of her. I didn't know what to do or how to do it, but I wanted to figure it out. She looked so small and lost sitting there in the black interior of my car. Her eyes were sad, not bright the way they should be, and shadows seemed to reach out their wicked talons, trying to engulf her.

The enclosed interior of this car was stifling, keeping me from indulging the sudden urge to pull her into my lap. If I could, I would wrap myself around her because my darkness would keep hers at bay.

Unable to do as I wanted, I shrugged off the leather and draped my jacket around her back, pulling the front closed beneath her chin. Just seeing her swallowed up by it, even all that glorious hair protected by the leather, settled some primal instinct inside me.

I didn't push. I waited even though I was not a patient man. I would burn with impatience, allow it to eat me alive, before I demanded more explanation and made her feel as if she couldn't make her own decision.

"I'm grateful I didn't die that day because, if I had died, then Neo would have been alone. His survivor's guilt is wretched, and if I hadn't been here to give him a purpose and something to focus on, I don't know what would have become of him. And then Ivory came along, and I'm so grateful. She gave him love he truly needed, showed him he could love again. Maybe that's why I thought I could tell him. I thought maybe now he would understand."

And what about you, Virginia? Who gives you the love you need? I didn't say those things out loud because, frankly, I was shocked I even thought them.

"Understand what?" was all I said.

"I've told him a thousand times I don't blame him for the accident that paralyzed me, even if he was the one driving the car. It was a terrible accident. I truly believe it." She shook her head forlornly. "But my forgiveness doesn't matter because he blames himself. I want to embrace my life, but I can't do that because he won't let me. He's obsessed with finding a way to fix me because, if he fixes me, then he will finally be free. I just wish he saw I wasn't broken."

The jacket I'd placed around her wasn't enough after all. There was still too much distance between us. When my palm cupped her cheek, she nuzzled deeper, eyes drifting closed for a few quiet moments.

It only happened a few times, when she took something from me instead of gave it. It was the only time in my entire life I was willing to be taken from, the only time I wanted to give.

The unsteady, heavy beat to my heart pounded against my ribs, acting as if it were trapped in a cell and begging desperately to be set free. Beneath that war, butterflies erupted, their damnable fluttering making me feel sick.

I endured it all. Hell, I reveled in it.

"He wants to send me to Sweden. A new doctor. A new surgery."

He wants to send her away. Over my dead body.

"You told him no." I guessed, reining in my true reaction and swallowing down the urge to yell.

"He was mad."

He has no right. How dare he does this to her?

"Tell me what you want. What does life look like outside this tower?" I cajoled.

She nuzzled against my palm again, a soft, dreamy smile warming her face. "A small apartment with lots of windows. A cat. And a dog. And Zilla of course. A kitchen where I can try my hand at cooking, even though I'll be terrible at it. A big TV to watch all my favorite shows and a door that locks so people can't just barge in whenever they feel like it."

"Your door doesn't have a lock?" I growled just thinking of people having such easy access to her.

"Flowers everywhere. Independence. And…"

Her teeth sank into her lower lip, stopping whatever else she would wish for. Using my thumb, I tugged the flesh free, suddenly desperate to kiss her.

"And?"

She whispered the rest as though it were too impossible to even say out loud. "And a flower shop downstairs where I could make colorful arrangements that would spill out onto the sidewalk."

"That's all you want?" I asked, thinking that it was really nothing at all.

I'll give it to you. Every last piece of it. And if anyone dares to get in the way, I'll kill them.

She pulled away. "It may not seem like much to you, but to me, it's everything."

She thought I was ridiculing her when, in actuality, I was in awe of how she could make something so simple and boring sound like heaven on earth.

"What about love?"

Both of us paused, but there was no way she could ever be as shocked by my words as I was.

Love? My inner voice mocked. *Love?* The venom in my veins laughed. It was preposterous I would even think of it, let alone allow such stupidity to come out of my own mouth.

I endured the ridicule I rained onto myself because, sure, a man like me would never know love. But Virginia? It seemed so wrong for her to not have it.

"I think I've dreamed enough already." Eyes

ambiguous and gaze shuttered, she stared down into her lap.

The sparks of rage that always lived inside me lit up, roaring to life in a great fire. I didn't know what made me more pissed off: the fact that she seemed to think no one would love her or the fact I knew someone would.

They wouldn't be good enough. No one will ever be good enough for her.

"Tell him," I demanded, throwing my anger at Neo instead. "Tell Neo this is what you want."

"I can't." She refused. "He's sacrificed so much for me. I won't ask for more."

"You haven't asked for anything!" I yelled.

"That's not what you said before." She didn't have to raise her voice for her words to hit their mark.

Sagging back into my seat, I could only mourn the distance between us and sulk because I was the one who insisted it be there.

Grabbing my jacket from the inside, she tugged it off, gently draping it over the center console. "I should go in. I have PT. And you have a life."

I banged out of the car, boots stomping on the pavement, doors slamming as I got her chair. How dare she just dismiss me like that? How dare she make me feel?

She sat calmly in the passenger seat even after I wrenched open her door. Despite my ire, I leaned in gently to unclasp the seatbelt I knew she was perfectly able to release herself.

My knuckles grazed over her middle and then across her collarbone as I retracted the belt. I heard her low intake of breath, and something hot blazed within.

I reached for the closest patch of skin I could, dragging my knuckles lightly over her forearm all the way to the inside of her elbow.

Chest heaving, her brown eyes fell to where I grazed. "Please don't make me want more things I can't have," she whispered.

I couldn't breathe, but who needed air?

I couldn't think, but thoughts were overrated.

Lifting my hand from her skin, I pushed her chin up so she had to meet my eyes. "What things?"

"Things you told me not to ask for again."

"Ask anyway," I beckoned.

"No."

Her refusal only made it sweeter, only made the need gnawing at my insides that much greater. I smiled, liking the way she declined to give in. Loving the way she refused to be afraid.

I leaned in slowly, like a predator stalking prey. I moved with intention, allowing her to see exactly what I planned to do. If she wanted away, I would let her escape, but if she wanted to be caught… My lips covered hers, my hand spreading out to cup her chin, keeping it in place.

Her soft sound was like a satisfied whimper, lips parting to let me swallow that beautiful sound. Blood roared in my ears, satisfaction seeped out of my pores, and my tongue hunted for hers.

I loved the way her fingers encircled my wrist, holding on to me as I held on to her. Our lips clung together, moving without parting as a feeling I'd never known until we kissed took root inside me and a piece of me howled to never let it go.

Something hard and heavy slammed against me, fisting into the T-shirt stretched over my back. Usually quick to react, this time I was slow, my lips clinging to hers even as I was wrenched back.

Her soft sound of alarm brought me to my senses,

and the roaring, overwhelming sense to protect took over.

Even in my natural violence, I used a steady hand to make sure whatever force grabbed me did not affect her, and only then did I spin, dislodging the grip.

Planting myself between the open car door and whatever threat had arrived, I readied myself for a fight.

"What the fuck is this?" a deep, angry snarl burst out. A flash of red plaid was a mere blur as a fist plowed into my jaw. I rocked back but held my ground, the sound of Virginia yelling from inside the car the only thing I heard.

I didn't think. I didn't see. All I did was hear her scream and feel a threat.

I had him pinned to the dirty, uneven pavement before I even blinked. The blade usually at my back had been put in the trunk because I didn't want to scare Virginia.

Instead, I reached into my boot, drawing out another blade, its sharpened silver glinting in the sun. The man below me fought and struggled, but I was incensed and brought the blade whistling down.

"Earth! No!" Virginia wailed, her panic breaking through.

I slowed enough for a hand to stop my wrist, keeping the blade from nicking flesh and giving me a moment to actually see.

Neo.

Feeling my eyes widen, I glanced down to where I had the knife at his throat and he had his hand blocking me from opening him up.

"Earth, please!" Virginia cried. The pure terror in her tone brought everything else I'd been missing crashing back.

I blinked, pulled the knife away, and sat back.

Underneath me, Neo glowered, eyes blazing like he wanted to murder. "You pulled a knife on me!"

"You snuck up on me."

"You were kissing my sister!"

V was still crying, and the sound was all I could really hear. Shoving off him, I sheathed the knife back in my boot and went toward V.

"It's okay," I told her. "He's fine."

She looked like she was about to give me a piece of her mind, but then Neo was there, shoving me back and stepping between us.

"Don't even think about touching her," he spat, turning his back on me completely.

Teeth gritted, I watched as he reached in and lifted her out of my car, cradling her in his arms.

"I still have that knife," I said darkly.

Neo started to say something, but V cut him off. "Would you two knock it off? Honestly! We're in the street!"

We both shut up, breathing heavily, refusing to break the stare first.

Between us, Virginia sighed dramatically. "What are you doing here, Neo? I thought you were mad?"

"You're upset with me?" he snapped. "I'm not the one who took advantage of you and then pulled a knife on your brother!"

"I didn't know it was you," I snarled, thinking about maybe pulling the knife out again.

Neo snorted like he knew what I was thinking.

Asshole.

"He didn't take advantage of me." Virginia's quiet voice was like some kind of nuclear bomb silencing our fight.

Neo's eyes ripped from mine, his mouth turning down and brow puzzling. "What?"

Virginia glanced at me. I shook my head, telling her not to say it. I'd take the blame. I'd let him hate me for it and not even think twice. I'd rather Neo fight with me than with her.

She smiled softly as if she understood all of that from just a shake of my head, but then she turned her gaze back up to her brother and it took on a different note.

"I said he didn't take advantage of me. I asked him to kiss me."

Neo reacted physically, stepping back, his arms slackening just a little.

I lurched forward. "Be careful!"

That brought his back up. "Don't you tell me how to treat her! I've been taking care of her all her life!"

"Yeah!" I burst out. "How the hell is that going?"

Silence.

Actual dead silence in the center of the city. In the middle of this just-a-step-above-ghetto neighborhood.

I took the moment to rush in, pulling her out of Neo's arms and into mine. Her upper body was rigid. Her arms didn't wrap around my neck like always.

I told myself I didn't give a damn and gently put her in the wheelchair.

"You should go," she told me, voice quiet but not unkind.

"I'm not leaving you here with him." I didn't keep my voice quiet.

Neo made a rude sound and then said some even ruder words.

Virginia laid her hand on my forearm, brown eyes pleading. "I need some time alone with my brother."

"Fine." I straightened away, giving her what she asked for.

"Earth?" she called out when I was a few steps away.

I turned back.

"You'll come back, right?" The soft vulnerability in her voice made me want to kiss it away.

"Hell no, he won't!" Neo fumed.

I spared him a mild glance and then returned my stare to V. "If *you* want me to come back, I will."

She nodded once, and it was all she had to say.

"This isn't over." Neo spat the words at my feet.

"I know."

I drove away pondering the fact that what started out as a favor to help out my brother and hopefully get him to trust me again turned into something that could very well rip apart the tenuous bond that had been holding us together.

Twenty-Two

"NEO," EMOGEN SAID AS WE CAME AROUND THE CORNER just after a stonily silent elevator ride. The surprise in her voice was punctuated by the way her eyes widened. "I wasn't expecting to see you."

I cleared my throat. Emogen's stare cut to me, and her very full cherry-painted lips pressed together.

Neo glowered. "You knew about this and didn't call me?"

Emogen snapped upright. "Since when is it my job to report to you?"

His arms crossed over his chest. "Since when is it not?"

Emogen's springy curls bounced with sass. "It's true I work here. It's true I'm Virginia's nurse. It's even true you're her guardian. But the last time I checked, she was well over the age of eighteen, and going out with a friend is *not* a medical emergency."

Neo's expression pinched. "Friend, my ass."

Emogen arched a questioning eyebrow at me, and I sighed. "I have PT in an hour, so let's go talk."

"I thought you had PT earlier today," Neo said, following along behind me.

"I had it changed. It's not like my day was so full I couldn't."

"V." It was one letter. One syllable. One sound. But the way he said it made my shoulders slump and a whole slew of emotion crash over me.

"I didn't think you would come back today," I said quietly, wheeling into my familiar room and expertly maneuvering the chair around to face him.

Neo shut the door softly and turned. "I guess you were counting on it."

"Don't be like that," I chided, my chest aching a bit. "You know that's not what I meant."

His demeanor softened. The anger and fight drained away. "I don't like fighting with you. I didn't want to leave things like that."

Feeling my lower lip wobble, I bobbed my head, afraid to speak.

The next thing I knew, his plaid-covered arms were wrapping around me, tugging me into a fierce hug.

I clung to his shoulders, fighting tears. "I'm sorry."

"Me too. It's not fair of me." He sat back a little, crouching in front of my chair. "It's not fair to keep making appointments and expecting you to go along. I should have asked first. I just..." His dark stare slipped away, jaw clenching.

There was a bit of stubble shadowing his face, a stark contrast to the smoothness of Earth's jaw.

"It's really hard to see you like this." He finally finished, rushing the words out as though he'd just admitted some horrid secret. Reluctantly, his eyes met mine. "It's even worse knowing I'm the one who did this to you."

"Neo," I said, his words shoving away all thought of

Earth. Placing my palm against his face, I brought it around so I could meet his shadowed gaze head on.

Definitely feels so much different than Earth.

Stop thinking about him right now!

The little war going on inside my brain must have lasted a little longer than I realized because Neo pulled my hand from his face, linking our fingers and resting them in my lap.

"It's really hard to see me like what? In a wheelchair? Unable to walk?"

He gave a curt nod.

I kept my words gentle. "Is that all you see?"

A new expression came into his eyes. It started out like confusion and then morphed into something else. "What?"

"Is that all you see when you look at me? A disabled woman? A woman incapable of everything because her legs don't work?"

He released my hand roughly and stood as if the very words repelled him.

I waited him out, wanting it to sink in, everything he felt. Everything I just pointed out. I wanted to know the truth.

It was time. Time we had this conversation. Time we faced the things we never wanted to look at because our relationship was all we had for so long.

But we would still have that relationship. Neo would always be my big brother. My hero. My family.

But it wasn't enough anymore. As loath as I was to even acknowledge that inside me, I felt like I had to. And I felt like he would understand.

He had Ivory now, and they were building a life.

"You know that's not how I see you."

"Then how do you?" I pressed, patient and kind.

"Beyond being your annoying little sister and the one you've had to take care of since Mom and Dad died… how do you see me?"

He shifted uncomfortably. Silence stretched, but I waited until his eyes flicked to mine. "You're my best friend."

My heart clenched and sang at once, almost as if his words were a beautifully painful song. "You're my best friend too," I told him.

"You're also my responsibility," he admitted, guilt leaking into his tone.

"In a lot of ways, I think you're right."

He jolted, clearly not expecting that at all. I smiled a little, glad to have caught him off guard.

"If it wasn't for you, I might not be as strong as I am today. One minute, we were teasing each other over a date at the movies and songs on the radio, and the next…" I took a breath. "The next, you were mom, dad, and caregiver all before the age of eighteen."

"I don't resent you for it."

"I know that. You resent yourself instead. But, Neo, you shouldn't. I cannot imagine how hard it must have been for you. To wake up in that car and see us all like that. Sitting in the hospital for hours and then being told I was paralyzed. You've been through so much, but you never complained."

"I have no right to complain. I walked away. The rest of you didn't."

"Oh, Neo." The sadness in my heart bled out in my words. "You lost just as much as the rest of us. If not more. You gave up your dreams, your friends, your entire life. You practically became a criminal just to make sure I got treatment. Yes, Neo, you might be alive and you might have the use of your legs… but those things don't mean you lost any less."

A soft sound left him, and I watched my big, strong brother drop to his knees in front of me. I lifted my hand, and he laid his head in my lap.

I wished I could feel his cheek against my legs, but I could feel the silky strands of his dark hair cascade against my fingers, and I pushed them through.

"I'm sorry," he whispered. "I'm so fucking sorry, Virginia."

Tears I didn't realize had gathered fell over, rolling down my cheeks with damp trepidation. His pain was palpable, and my heart ached so fiercely I thought it might burst if it tightened any more.

"I know," I said, still sliding my hands through his hair, offering comfort that he usually refused to accept. "I forgive you." True, I could tell him again that I never blamed him, but it wasn't what he needed to hear. He needed to be granted my forgiveness so he could accept it and then maybe forgive himself.

A choked sound throbbed in his throat, and I patted his head lovingly. "Shh," I whispered, rubbing his shoulder with my free hand.

"I took so much from us," he choked out, burying his face in my legs. "So much from you."

More tears fell over, and I let them come. Why had I waited so long to force this issue? Why had we let each other suffer?

"You've given me far more than I ever lost," I vowed. "It's because of you I can even fight with you like this."

My fingers stayed in his hair when his face lifted. His eyelashes were damp, cheeks red. "That supposed to make me feel better?" he quipped.

My heart lightened hearing some of that sarcasm coming back into his tone. *We are going to be okay.*

I pulled the strands I held just enough to make him wince. "Ow!" He complained.

I smiled. "You've taken such good care of me, Neo. You made it possible for me to fight for the independence I know I can have."

His gaze turned shuttered and vulnerable. His instinct would always be to protect me. To shelter me. It must have been incredibly hard to even let go of just a little of something you've been gripping like a lifeline for so long.

"What happens if I let go… and then lose you too?"

A rough sound ripped from my throat. "I'm not asking you to let go, big brother. You will never lose me. I wouldn't even try and get away. You're my favorite person in the whole world."

He snorted, but I saw the darkness swirl in his eyes, and I knew he thought of Earth. I wasn't ready to go there yet, and honestly, this was about way more than whatever was happening between Earth and me.

Is something even happening?

My fingers tightened in his hair again, stopping whatever rude words he was likely to mutter. "You are. And all I'm asking for is for you to listen. To really *hear* what I want. I've had a lot of time to think." He frowned, but I plowed on. "This holding pattern I'm in—that we're in—is not what I want. I don't have to walk again to have the things I want."

He sat back, face thoughtful. "You keep saying that."

"Because it's true. Let me ask you something. If you weren't the one driving that day and the accident was caused by something else, would you still be adamant I walk again?"

His eyes flared, and he paced across the room. "Of course! I want you to walk again!"

"Really?" I pushed. "Do you really think I won't be happy if I can't? Do I seem so miserable to you?"

His movements stilled. His head cocked to the side, and though he was turned away, I could practically see his face furrowed in thought.

"Do you think I'm unhappy, Neo?"

As he rotated slowly, there was a new light in his eye. "I've never asked you that."

I half smiled. "You could ask me now."

His tongue darted out to wet his lips. "Are you happy?"

Emotion jumbled in my chest, and something close to butterflies tickled my stomach. "I am. But honestly? I could be happier."

I watched him fight back the words I knew he wanted to speak, the assumptions he clung to for the last seven years. He won the battle to instead say, "What would make you happy?"

Pride welled up inside me so strong that fresh tears streamed over. I felt them track wet emotion over my cheeks. *He is asking. He is finally asking me what I want.*

"A life that doesn't focus on the fact that I can't walk. I want to define my life, not let my life define me."

His throat worked with the force of his swallow. "How?"

His question wasn't harsh or even mocking. It was genuinely curious, and I knew it was because not walking didn't just currently define my life but his too.

And it hit me that perhaps he pushed for me to walk again not just to assuage his own soul-crushing guilt but because he didn't know how else to not let this accident define us for the rest of forever.

It was up to me to tell him, to let him know that we didn't need to be ruled by my disability.

"I want to be a bigger part of the family. To be able to go and see everyone, not just them come and see me. I'd like my own place, not just a room at a care center. Like a real home that makes me feel settled and not just in waiting."

His face paled slightly. The way his lips pinched told me exactly how much he disliked that idea. And it wasn't that he was trying to hold me back—he was afraid.

I pushed the chair closer toward him. "I'm capable of taking care of myself, Neo. Yes, I'll need some help from time to time. And I'll always need you. But I could manage in a small apartment that was wheelchair friendly. I pretty much do it all for myself here except for cooking."

"Living alone is dangerous, V. You could fall. You could get hurt—"

"It's like that for people who aren't in wheelchairs too."

He fell silent, and I knew it wasn't because he agreed. He was trying to listen.

"I want windows I can open to let in the sunlight and fresh air."

"The air ain't fresh in the city," he deadpanned.

"Well, then I want to breathe in the city air," I quipped. "I want to stroll through the park, down a sidewalk, and into shops I've never explored before."

All his features pinched, and a definite aura of anxiety bloomed around him, polluting the air just like the city streets. "The city ain't that great, V. You aren't missing much."

"I wouldn't know because I haven't been out there much."

"Can't you just take my word for it?"

"Could you?"

His eyes snapped up. Our stares met and held. I saw the answer he didn't want to voice right there in his expression.

"Could you see the city through someone else's eyes? Could you live your life through someone else's experiences?"

He knelt before me, hands resting on my knees. I expected some heartfelt answer to go with this emotional breakthrough we seemed to be sharing.

I should have known better. I mean, this was Neo.

"People are dicks, V."

I blinked. And giggled. "Neo, that is rude."

His eyes rolled. "Rude or not, it's the truth." Clasping my hands, he held them tight. "People aren't as tolerant as I wish they were. People stare and whisper. They get irritated, and they're lazy. The streets get crowded and busy. People push and shove. And I know you want to see many places, but, sweetheart, a lot of them aren't wheelchair friendly."

He was right, but that didn't mean I should let it stop me from living my life. "You can't protect me forever."

"Yes. I can."

"This isn't protection, Neo." I gestured around the room. "Sometimes this feels like jail."

He sucked in a breath.

Guilt assailed me, and when he started to pull away, I clung tightly to his hands, tugging him back. "I appreciate everything you've done, and this room is beautiful. The Tower has been a wonderful place to heal and learn about my body and my limitations. But I've outgrown this place."

He remained silent, so I forged on. "I'd also like to get

a job. I probably won't be able to make a lot or even work full time, but I'll do what I can. I'll cover as much of my own expenses as I can."

"You don't need to worry about money," he said almost off-hand as if he were distracted.

"Well, I certainly don't expect you to support me for the rest of my life!" I refuted, annoyed that he wasn't fully listening.

He stood, a sour expression ruining his usually handsome features. Towering over me, he folded his arms over his chest. "Is this because of *him?*"

I faltered. "Him?"

"That asshole I saw you sucking face with on the sidewalk!"

My mouth fell open. "First of all, how dare you talk to me like that? Second of all, he is not some asshole! He's your brother, your friend, and, up until you met Ivory, your roommate!"

"After everything he's done, he is *not* my family!"

"Then why did you call him to bring me to my appointment?" I shot back, not understanding this insane sort of feud between them.

"Because I thought he would keep people from taking advantage of you." He laughed bitterly and then went on as though he were talking only to himself. "Of all the things he is, I never thought he'd do this."

"I told you he didn't take advantage of me."

Neo looked at me stonily. "You're telling me you asked him to kiss you?"

"Yes."

"Don't lie to me, Virginia." Neo's voice was dangerously cool.

"I'm not lying!" I said, unable to keep the same sort of

calm. Then, because I couldn't lie even when it really wasn't a lie, I said, "Well, I didn't ask that time."

Probably not the best choice of words.

"You're telling me that wasn't the first time he kissed you?" he roared, hands going up in the air, chest heaving, and eyes glittering dangerously.

I spared a glance at the open door. "The entire floor is going to hear you," I hissed.

His response was to stare stonily at me.

"No." I kept my voice strong. "It wasn't. The first time was at the brewery."

His eyes widened. "Brewery?"

"Earth makes his own beer. He took me to the warehouse where he makes it. It's so cool."

"He took you to a warehouse. Where he makes alcohol." His words were like an angry echo. A new wash of anger slid over him. "Did he get you drunk?"

"You are so ridiculous!" I insisted. "Do I seem drunk to you? Besides, that stuff is so gross I'd never be able to drink enough for that."

"So you did drink it?"

"Oh for heaven's sake, Neo. Stop being ridiculous. It was a sip of beer, not a keg. I had to beg him for just a taste. And I liked the brewery." I went on, specifically not calling it a warehouse. "It was so fascinating. He really must put a lot of effort into his beer."

"I always thought he just bought custom labels and slapped it on store-bought bottles," Neo mused, the anger in his face giving way to curiosity.

"Isn't that illegal?" I wondered.

The anger came back. "Yes, and Earth is the kind of guy who wouldn't give a damn."

"Is that supposed to shock me?"

"I wish it did."

"Should I remind you that you are hardly a saint?"

"I'm not as bad as he is," he snapped. "And I will not have my baby sister involved with the likes of him."

"Too late."

The words dropped into the room like a heavy anvil. The silence they brought was deafening and honestly a little disconcerting. Just when I thought I was making headway with my brother, things got heated again. And over what? His best friend he considered family?

I opened my lips to ask again what happened between them, but Neo spoke first.

"I absolutely forbid you seeing Earth again. Whatever happened between you two is over. Do you understand me?"

"No."

A thick, dark brow arched up his forehead.

A knot formed in my stomach. I absolutely detested arguing with my brother. But I refused to back down. "I like spending time with Earth, and I won't stop just because you had some stupid fight with him."

"It wasn't a stupid fight."

"Then what was it?" I pressed.

Neo's lips pressed together, and he averted his gaze.

"Still don't want to tell me, huh? Well, you can't have it both ways, brother. One minute, you trust Earth enough to come here and escort me out, and the next, you're forbidding me to even look at him!"

"I saw you kissing."

"A kiss I asked for." I reminded him. *A kiss I wished to repeat a thousand times.*

"Is this about Jake? Is this some kind of payback?"

I threw my hands up. "First Earth and now Jake." With jerky, angry movements, I started to turn the chair around to move away from him. I was so insulted by his words that I wasn't sure if I wanted to yell or cry. Maybe both.

I had the chair all the way around, about to wheel away, when he caught me. One strong hand on the handle on the back and the other over the wheel.

I tried to roll forward to dislodge his hold, but of course he was stronger.

Instead of crying, I let out a yell. "How dare you?" I rebuffed the second he recoiled from the abrupt cry. Not bothering to turn my chair back around, I glared over my shoulder. "What happened with Jake was like a year ago. And yes, it hurt me—*you* hurt me—but I forgave you. I tried to understand where you were coming from."

"Virginia—"

"No." I cut him off. "I've made allowances, but when have you ever done that for me? Huh? I cannot believe you. I pour my heart out, I tell you how I feel and what I want, and then you act like the only reason I could want anything other than this room is some guy!"

This time I did spin back around, my chair rolling on top of his foot. He blanched and yanked it free, but I didn't apologize. "I want a life for me. A life I choose. I've wanted these things for a while now. I just didn't want to upset you by bringing it up." I took a breath. Blew it out. "You know, maybe some of this was Earth. Maybe he gave me the courage to finally open up to you. Do you know why?"

"Why?"

"Because he listened. He asked me about *me* and what I want. He didn't ask me about this chair. Or make my life seem impossible. He didn't act like I was incapable. He made me feel like I was more than a girl with a disability. When I'm with him, I feel things, Neo. Deep, *whole* things, and for a girl who's only felt half for most of her life… that's pretty freaking amazing."

"Not Earth, Virginia. Just… not him."

"Why?" I pressed again.

He balked again, and I laughed. "You are so ridiculous. If he's so terrible, why not just tell me what he did so I'll stay away on my own?" And then I realized. "You're protecting him."

The look on his face was all the confirmation I needed. "What?" he asked as if his expression didn't give him away.

"He did something that you hate, something that you refuse to forgive, yet you can't seem to cut him out of our lives, can you? You still like him."

"You don't turn your back on family even when they turn their back on you."

Pretty sure I'd heard that in a movie somewhere, but now was not the time to discuss that. Also, I wasn't about to point out that just seconds ago, he was vehemently denying Earth was family. *You can lie to your mind all you want, but the heart is always true.*

"Earth didn't turn his back, Neo. He's still here. I can see how much your anger upsets him."

He scoffed. "He doesn't have a conscience."

"I don't believe that."

His eyes flicked up. "Actions speak louder than words."

"Neo," I implored, asking him for the last time, "tell me."

My brother's nostrils flared as a hefty debate waged in his eyes. I watched every emotion under the sun flicker over his features, and then an eerie sort of calm washed over him, wiping out all the expression and feelings I knew he wrestled.

The muscle at the back of his jaw jumped. Once. Twice. A third time.

Finally, his whispered words dropped like a stone into a pond, creating ripples on the surface.

"He's a killer."

Twenty-Three

THE ROTTEN APPLE WAS BUSY, WHICH SHOULD HAVE BEEN a good distraction.

It wasn't.

My mood was darker than usual, but aside from a few wary sidelong glances, no one said anything.

Although, to be fair, no one would dare challenge me or ask me to talk. I ran a bar, not a therapist's office, and frankly, most everyone was afraid of me. I liked it that way. 'Course, that didn't stop drunk assholes from crying on the bar top after they had one too many. I usually cut them off and sent them packing.

I knew.

I knew how Neo would react to any hint of anything between me and his sister. I'd had a chance to patch up a little of what went wrong between us, and I fucked that up too. Now he was even more pissed off, and I couldn't even fault him. Hell, in his position, I would have reacted the same. I wasn't good enough. I had no business even looking at Virginia. Touching her. I was the one in the wrong.

But still, I fought with him. I challenged him instead of backing down.

I still wanted her anyway.

What the hell was wrong with me? Going around… *feeling* shit. All my life, I prided myself on not feeling. Being detached.

All that started to burn the day Ivory White walked into our lives. The day the hit was ordered on her well-groomed head.

It was like she was the catalyst—the key to opening a floodgate of shit I didn't want.

And now look. Just fucking look. I was fighting with Neo more than before. I was slicing open guys after I said I wouldn't, and I was seriously craving a kill.

But more than that, I was craving something more.

No. Not something. *Someone.*

I could disappear. Get into my car and drive until I didn't even recognize what reflected in the rearview mirror and there was absolutely nothing waiting for me when I stopped. I'd done it before.

I knew how to disappear like smoke. I knew how to exist in the shadows.

All these emotions would die, and I would be left the way I'd always been. Hollow, cold, and precise. I could go back to being a huntsman.

The thought of disappearing didn't offer the relief I thought it would. Instead, it created a heavy knot of something that suspiciously felt like panic.

"Get out!" I roared, my shout punctuated by the slamming of the cooler door. Inside, bottles clanked together from the force. It was late. I was annoyed, and frankly, I was sick of looking at people, even paying customers.

I heard a few heavy sighs, but no one argued. Instead, they all shoved to their feet, a few awfully unsteady, grabbed their bottles, and filed out onto the sidewalk.

The silent solitude settled in, and though it didn't do

much to ease my mood, I was glad to be alone. So of course the door jangled, announcing a new arrival. I all but snarled, straightening from the counter I'd been wiping down to see Officer Fig and his partner, whose name I never cared to remember, make their way toward the bar. They were still in uniform, which made me wonder if they were on duty.

I wasn't much for any police officer, but this guy was my biggest dislike. Fig considered himself the Grimms' finest officer of the law, and I considered him a loser with a badge he used to hide his insecurities.

Maybe I'd respect him more if he didn't have it out for my family, having hauled in Neo and Fletcher more times than I could count. 'Course now with Fletcher's new "identity" and the fact that he was living with New York's favorite prince, his days of hassling him were over. Unless of course he wanted all the top lawyers in the city riding his ass. And Ethan's fist in his jaw.

Look, I gave Ethan a hard time and a glare every time I saw him, but secretly, I was glad Fletch got with a dude like him. Everyone saw Ethan as some proper Upper East Side elitist, but I knew he wouldn't hesitate to toss his manners out the window when it came to protecting Fletcher.

I felt a small smirk curl my lips. That'd be something to see.

And of course, it would be about the same for Neo now too, thanks to Ivory's team of lawyers on standby, so I figured about this time, Fig was starting to get bored. He'd yet to haul me in despite many threats and feeble attempts, but maybe now he'd start putting more effort into it.

Despite the clear dislike he harbored for me and my brothers, he still drank here a lot with his buddies. I mean, this was the neighborhood bar. I didn't give him free beer, though. Cops didn't get perks in my place. Hell, the only reason I let them in was that they paid.

I wasn't in the mood for his shit tonight—especially if he was on duty—and I was about to tell him to see his way out when I noticed the exhaustion and somberness that clung to him and the man trailing behind.

When he noticed my scrutiny, Fig's expression pinched, and the legs of the barstool scraped loudly as he pulled it back. "We just got off," he explained, setting his hat off to the side. "It's been a hell of a day, and we need a drink."

"Was just about to close up."

"Just give me a shot, then," his partner said, raking his hand through his already mussed strands. He looked even worse than Fig.

Reaching under the bar, I pulled out two shot glasses and a bottle of vodka, filling them to the top.

His partner picked his up immediately and downed it all in one go. The second his glass clinked against the wood top, Fig lifted his.

Typically much more boastful, they were unusually stoic, which made me curious. I pulled out two long-necks from the cooler, popped the tops, and set them down.

"Another arrest gone bad?" I needled.

Fig's eyes flashed as he grabbed the beer, tugging it into him. "I came to drink, not put up with your shit."

"We found a body floating in the river." His partner burst out, turning a little green around the edges. Pulling the bottle of beer into his chest, he whispered, "I'd never seen a dead body before."

"Oh for shit's sake, Paul, that's official police busi-ness!" Fig snapped.

His fellow officer lurched up, pressing a hand to his lips, face turning a deeper shade of green as he lunged for the bathroom.

"If you make a mess, you're mopping!" I yelled after him.

"Fucking rookie." Fig grunted, drinking the beer.

I didn't bother to point out he was looking a little green himself.

"A body, huh?"

Fig lowered the bottle, eyeing me suspiciously. I didn't even blink. They brought it up, not me. If he didn't want to chat, I wouldn't make him. I'd find out when the tongues starting wagging. This might be the ghetto, but people still gossiped.

I guess Fig knew this too because he spoke. "Got a call about something down near the river, so we went down… There he was, bobbing by the shore, tangled up in some weeds."

Even though the back of my neck prickled, I remained passive and moved to wash the two shot glasses beneath the bar.

"One of ours?" I asked. We all pretty much knew each other here in the Grimms.

Fig shook his head once. "No ID yet. Won't be long, though. He hadn't been in the water that long."

My hands paused before continuing. Placing the glasses aside to dry, I grabbed up a rag. "Well, it's a rough area. Kid probably got tired of trying to survive and jumped."

Fig made a sound. "This was no suicide. Unless he somehow slashed his own throat."

Never woulda pegged you as the type for a wheelchair kink. The gravelly, sinister words slid over my memory, coating it with the flavor of sulfur and acrimony.

Beneath the rag, my hand fisted as another memory, one much more vivid, played behind my eyes like a private movie screening.

The keen awareness of being followed by someone sloppy and not making an effort to remain hidden. The sound of my blade whistling through the dark night, the way it sliced across flesh like a hot knife on butter, and the gurgling sounds of spluttering blood spilling out, draining life away one splatter at a time.

I'd left that man in the alley to die, encased in shadows, his life expectancy about one hundred to one.

I expected to hear about the discovery of his body on the morning news, even just a mere mention of a mysterious slaying of an unknown man.

None came, and I wondered if perhaps he'd defied the odds and made it to a hospital. If perhaps he'd somehow lived.

He didn't.

He'd ended up in the river… but I knew he didn't get there on his own.

Someone must have put him there.

Whoever hired him to tail me.

I leaned on the bar, giving away none of my actual thoughts. "You saying we got a murderer running around the Grimms?"

"Now I ain't saying that," Fig said like I might fall apart if he said yes. "We don't know where the body came from. Could have floated downstream from any borough. It was probably a gang rivalry gone wrong."

"What makes you say that?" I asked, mildly interested as I went back to some chores behind the bar. Truth was that was the go-to assumption for all the cops around here. Violence? Gang-related. Maybe these uniform-wearing derps really thought gangs were the worst of this city, or maybe they just wanted to believe that so they didn't get caught up in something they definitely could not control.

I wasn't about to argue. Why would I? Blaming gangs kept all the suspicion away from people like me.

"Kid had a bandana tied around his wrist."

I stilled. The shadow in the alley did not have a bandana around his wrist.

That meant one of two things:

1) My tail from the alley and Fig's body in the river were two different people with very similar wounds.

Or…

2) That bandana was put there *after* I left him to die and before his body was dumped.

I didn't believe in coincidences, so that left me with the second option.

I grunted. "Guess that makes it easy to know where to look and tie up the case."

Paul, the green-gilled officer, made his way back from the bathroom, looking less green and whiter than when he'd run off. Gingerly, he sat back on the stool, giving the beer a longing but also wary look.

"You make a mess?" I asked.

"I flushed it."

The worst thing about owning a bar wasn't the drunk people. It was the people who couldn't handle their liquor and puked all over the bathroom, leaving me to clean it up.

Or in this case, a cop who couldn't handle one little floating body. Probably wasn't even bloody. The river would have seen to that.

Amateur.

"C'mon, we should go. Tomorrow's gonna be another

long one," Fig told his partner. He grabbed up the bottle. "I'm taking this with me."

I arched an eyebrow. "Why, officer, I can't allow you to take an open container out of my establishment and into the city."

"Shut it, Earth. You think I don't see everyone tripping down the street at closing time, toting bottles with your logo on it?"

"I don't know what you mean." I lied.

"Hey, we should ask him about the tattoo," Officer Paul suggested.

A heavy sensation of foreboding settled over me. Despite its weight, the hair on the back of my neck stood.

Fig glared at him. "That's twice tonight you've brought up official police business."

"Like you weren't out here talking about it," Paul said around a less-than-demure burp. Part of me wondered if he would go running back to the bathroom. "I heard you when I came out."

Fig didn't even pause. "I was just reassuring a citizen of our jurisdiction that he didn't need to worry about murderers running around."

Paul snorted. "Like anyone would fuck with Earth."

Fig looked as if he'd swallowed a hive of bees, and I couldn't help it. I grinned.

Guess I'd need to file away ol' officer Paul's name for future reference.

"Let's go," Fig hissed.

Paul turned back to me, his red-rimmed eyes focusing a little more than they had since he stepped in. Some of the color returned to his cheeks, making them look ruddy.

"You know pretty much everyone around here

because of this place. You probably hear all kinds of talk too."

I shrugged. "Doesn't mean I'm a nark."

"See! Absolutely pointless to even talk to him." Fig fumed.

"Not asking you to nark. Just wondering if you knew of a new gang forming around here. The tattoo on the victim, it wasn't one we recognized."

Oh, I was definitely interested. I wanted every detail about that tattoo… and at the same time, I didn't.

Faint flashes from long ago assaulted me, almost blinding me with the way they flickered behind my eyes in rapid succession. My left hip tingled, the skin there turning hot.

I blinked, shoving away the bad memories and urge to rub at the burning spot, and forced myself back into the present.

"Do you have a picture?" I asked.

Fig sputtered, but Paul pulled out his phone, tapping at the screen.

"That's official!" Fig protested.

"Then consider this an official question for the investigation," Paul told me.

I inclined my head, not really agreeing but not disagreeing either.

He pushed the phone toward me, and I looked down.

Ice ran through my veins, so frigid that hypothermia was not just hypothetical but an actual danger. I looked a few seconds longer, pretending to really concentrate on the crude yet unmistakable mark marring the dead man's wrist.

In reality, I couldn't concentrate at all.

"Tattoos don't smear like that," I pointed out, the edges of my vision slightly blurred.

"Well, it ain't really a tattoo. It was drawn there with marker. Figured it might be the gang's way of marking their kill."

The nosey tail in the alley didn't have this mark. I would have noticed this. I would have noticed it as if it had been drawn with glow-in-the-dark ink.

That means he definitely didn't die in that alley. And if he did, someone found him first. Someone wanted credit for this kill.

Or…

A message was being sent.

Message received.

Clearing my throat, I looked up at Paul. "Sorry, that's new to me too. Haven't seen anyone with this mark."

"You're sure?"

I glanced down again, not because I needed to but because it seemed like the thing to do. "I'm sure." I confirmed. "Sorry I couldn't be more help."

Paul shrugged and shoved the phone in his pocket. "It's no problem. Thank you for your time."

"Let's go," Fig called, and this time, his partner followed him to the door.

The second the men were gone, having walked down the block and not even visible in the windows, I sagged against the bar top, drawing in a breath.

It couldn't be. Not after all these years.

The faint yet distinct ringing of a phone interrupted my jumbled thoughts. The bar phone remained silent, and the cellphone in my pocket was definitely not the culprit.

My eyes hastened in the direction of the office.

The crudely scrawled note on the napkin at the club flashed into my brain. *Answer your phone.*

I took off into the back. The door to my office

banging against the wall with a loud crack and the sound of a drawer being yanked free of the desk fought to see which was louder. Everything inside scattered at my feet, but I ignored it, ripping open the false bottom of the drawer to grab the ringing phone.

Without a second of hesitation, I flipped it open, pressing it against my ear.

Silence greeted me.

The caller paused.

As did I.

We both waited soundlessly to see who would speak first.

Twenty-Four

REASON NUMBER FIVE HUNDRED AND TWELVE ON THE LIST of why I need my own place: so physical therapists can't walk into my room unannounced and declare it's time for therapy, giving the perfect excuse for my thick-headed brother to hightail it out of the room like his backend was on fire without explaining why he suddenly announced the man who'd given me my very first kiss was a killer.

That was one hell of a sentence.

Imagine how my brain must have felt.

A first kiss. A sip of beer. Not one but *two* fights with my brother and the proclamation that a killer was among us all in a single day.

Look, I said I wanted some excitement in my life, but this was taking things a bit too far.

PT seemed harder than normal, probably because I was distracted, agitated, and mad my brother would make some sort of declaration like that and then leave.

Why would he call Earth a killer? What could he possibly mean by that? He didn't mean like an actual killer?

Actions speak louder than words. My brother's words

stuck inside my brain as if he'd glued them there, and I couldn't stop hearing them.

If I went by those words, then... actions... No. *No.* It couldn't be. Earth, a killer? It was ridiculous. Sure, the guy was grumpy, moody, dark, and scared everyone, but he also listened to Monsta X and had a dog.

He did pull a knife on my brother. A knife from his boot.

And so round and round my thoughts churned all through physical therapy, a late dinner, a halfhearted conversation with Emogen, and a shower.

"What do you think, Zilla?" I asked the gecko who was perched on my right shoulder as I brushed through the length of my hair, which fell over my left. "You've met Earth. What do you think my brother meant by that?"

Zilla tilted her head.

"You're right. I could call Earth and just ask him," I replied. "But how do you just bring that up in a phone conversation? Asking him to kiss me was easier than asking him if he's a killer," I muttered.

Zilla turned around, facing away from me, and I sighed.

"Fine, we don't have to talk about it."

The brush continued gliding through my hair, the tangles having been brushed free long ago. Just the familiar act was grounding somehow.

Finally setting the brush aside, I worked deftly, not even needing the mirror to style my hair into a crown braid that wrapped around my head, securing the rest at the nape of my neck. It was late here, visiting hours long over, and not for the first time, I wished there was a window so I could catch a glimpse of the night city or even the moon.

Instead, I gazed at the giant mural Neo painted, the vivid tall tower rising out of a flower-covered meadow.

But it didn't matter.

Mural, window, or even the moon wouldn't be a good enough distraction for my mind to stray very long from Earth.

I thought about the way he'd reacted when Neo surprised him out on the sidewalk. How deft and graceful his movements were despite the precise way he was able to pin my brother down. I thought about the way the small blade he'd dug from the inside of his boot glinted off the sun.

He'd backed off immediately when he realized it was Neo.

Would he have backed off if it had been anyone else?

Moving to Zilla's habitat, I carefully placed her inside. "Sweet dreams," I told her. Almost immediately, she went into the little tent I'd gotten her at the pet shop I visited with Earth.

Once she was settled for the night, I moved a bottle of water onto my nightstand and switched off the overhead light.

At night, I slept with the bathroom light on, the door pulled around so it wasn't too bright but it was still lit up enough for me to be able to see. I would have preferred a completely dark room, but on occasion, I woke up and needed a drink or the bathroom. After a few times of falling out of bed in the attempt to transfer to my chair in complete darkness, I decided a dim light was best. I could have used the flashlight on my phone, but the battery wasn't always reliable.

There were even a few times when I would settle myself into bed and then realize I'd forgotten to turn off the light at all or pull the bathroom door around. By then, I was usually too tired or too lazy to move, so I'd just have to sleep in a bright room.

Yes, there was night staff here I could call for, but I didn't do that. Not unless I really had to. I tried to be as independent as possible, and I wanted to be able to rely on myself.

The room was dim as I transferred myself onto the bed with the colorful quilt. I lifted one leg and then the next onto the bed. After pulling down the sheet and comforter, I used my upper body to scoot toward the middle of the mattress, then moved my legs, one by one again, beneath the blankets.

After arranging the pillows and covers the way I liked them, I lay back, letting out a long exhale. It always felt good to lie down at first, to feel my tight muscles relax against the cool sheets on the bed. Because of my paralysis, I slept in the same position all night. I couldn't roll over or twist around like most people.

Sometimes I did feel the urge to roll, and I would maneuver myself onto my side, tucking a pillow between my legs. No, I couldn't feel it, but it seemed it would be a more comfortable position for my legs.

Mostly, I just slept on my back, a position that had taken some getting used to, but after seven years, it was just natural now.

Sleeping in the same position for an entire night might seem restful because your body is completely still, but in truth, I often woke up with muscle cramps and spasms, and those sometimes hurt.

Upon waking every day, I would do a routine of stretches to help work out some of the stiffness that a night's sleep always gave.

A slim ray of light stretched across the ceiling from the ajar bathroom door, and I gazed at it, imagining instead I was under a sky filled with luminous stars. I envisioned a velvet sky so black I would marvel at how it didn't swallow up the glittering stars that were so small in comparison but still so brilliantly bright.

My lashes began to flutter, sweeping across my cheeks. My palms, which rested on my abdomen, rose and fell rhythmically with every breath I took.

Warmth tingled my lips, making them curl in on themselves, and then I was tumbling into a dreamlike sensation, floating in the vivid memory of what it had been like beneath Earth's kiss. Impossibly, I felt weightless, recalling how he claimed me without a single word, how he licked into my mouth, tangling our tongues as though they were two halves of a whole.

I'd requested a first kiss, an experience I didn't have.

He set an expectation. A standard by which every kiss I might ever have would have to live up to. It was unfair really because, even with my inexperience, I understood something very profoundly.

No one else could ever compare.

The harsh realization caused my eyes to fly open. It took a moment to focus, but when I was able, I was back to staring at the light stretching across the ceiling, consumed with the hollow feeling of loneliness.

Blowing out a shuddering breath, my mind started to race once more.

A killer? He couldn't be. No one who kissed with that much emotion could be that devoid of life.

"When I see Neo tomorrow, I'm going to kick him," I vowed, knowing full well I'd have to hit him instead. "How dare he leave me to wonder all night long?"

Turning my head, I glanced at my cell lying facedown on the nightstand and debated calling him. "He deserves to get woken up! If I can't sleep, then he shouldn't either," I muttered darkly.

Thud!

My head lifted from the pillow, looking at the closed door of my room.

Crash!

Shatter!

Pushing up into a sitting position, I stared at the door, alarmed by the violent sounds beyond it.

More shattering glass echoed in the hall, and my fingers twisted in the sheet. What was going on out there?

"*Ahh!*" A deep, angry roar echoed through the Tower, and my stomach dropped.

The sudden twisting of the handle of my door made panic seize my throat. Lifting a hand to press against my neck, I stared in horror as the handle without a lock turned and the door pushed in.

"*Ahh!*" *Crash! Thud!*

"Please, no," I whimpered, terrified in a way I'd never been before.

I glanced around for something, anything I could use as a weapon, seeing very little. Suddenly, the fact I had no lock on that door wasn't just an intrusion of privacy but a genuine threat to my safety.

Flinging my upper body forward, I was able to grab my phone. The charger clattered against the floor with the force of my grab, but I didn't stop to worry about the sound. Instead, I threw myself back into the corner of the bed, sitting up against the wall.

Another shout. More sounds of things breaking.

The handle turned again, this time with more force.

Despite the tremor in my hands and the unsteady

breath filling my lungs, I tapped the screen on my phone, wincing at the way it illuminated as I used it.

The door unlatched, pushing in not enough to open but enough to make a strangled sound rip from my throat.

A voice on the other end of the line yelled something, but the sound of my own heartbeat in my ears made it hard to make out the words.

Or maybe it was the sound of someone still screaming.

"H-h-*help*." I wheezed into the line, praying he could hear me. Praying he would come.

I heard him call my name.

But then the door to my room pushed in, and whatever/whoever was in the Tower invited itself in.

Twenty-Five

"PEOPLE ARE LOOKING FOR YOU." THE RUSHED, WHISPERED words practically hissed through the phone into my ear.

"Who?" I demanded.

"There's been some quiet inquiries, strange eyes on the street."

"Who?" I demanded again, my voice harsh but low.

"I don't know."

"Lies will get you killed."

"This call could get me killed too."

I paused. "Then why make it?"

"These are our streets."

He was scared.

"You should probably disappear for a while."

"Okay."

I started to pull the phone away from my ear, but he spoke again. "They're like you."

A chill crept down my spine, but I said nothing.

"Did you hear me?" he whispered, anxiety hanging off every word.

I made a sound.

The call disconnected.

The sound of my phone snapping shut was like a gunshot in the silence.

I covered my tracks. Vanished to the other side of the world. I told myself that they'd likely given up, but it was a lie, and deep down, I knew that all too well.

I could escape, but I would never be free. The only freedom I would get from my past was death.

Some weird Freudian thought penetrated the shit I really needed to think about to whisper, *Perhaps that's why you really kill, searching for the freedom you will never be allowed.*

"Or maybe I'm just an asshole," I said out loud.

What difference did it make anyway? Choices had already been made. And now, potentially, I was found.

I started to put the cell back into the drawer, pausing halfway. I knew I should destroy it, but a piece of me hesitated, a piece of myself I didn't recognize. How odd. I still wanted to listen.

I debated for long moments. My sigh echoed around the room when I pulled on my leather jacket and stuffed the dinosaur of a phone in the inside pocket. I'd give the kid a few to get out of town before I cut off all communication.

I felt like I owed him because he called to warn me even though he shouldn't have.

Stepping over the mess still literally all over the office floor, I stepped out into the bar, boots freezing when I saw I wasn't alone.

Our eyes locked and held. A brief, odd sensation of weariness stole over me, but it was quickly vanquished by the fist ramming into my jaw.

Head snapping back, I felt my teeth gnash as red tinged the corners of my vision.

Upper lip curling, I slowly turned toward Neo. "That's the last hit you're gonna get for free."

His fist came hurling at me again, but I caught it with one hand and used the other to deliver a punch of my own.

He staggered back a couple paces, glittering eyes narrowing into slits. "You put your hands on my sister." A growl rumbled deep in his chest, and then he rushed me.

Arms locked, feet planted like trees in soil, we clashed, bending and swaying against the wind of our grudges. I understood why he was pissed, but I was pissed too.

He was pissed I dared enter his sister's tower, and I was pissed he dared to lock her up there.

Neo made a move, pivoting out of the way we were deadlocked, twisting as if he might come up behind me, but I anticipated his move and countered it with my own.

Dropping down, I rammed into his middle, lifting him off his feet and using the force of our momentum to drop him on the bar top and pin him there.

Breath whooshed out of his lungs the second his body slammed into the wood. My palm was heavy against the center of his chest, and I ignored the spastic way his heart raced.

Leaning over him, I taunted. "If you didn't want me near her, you shouldn't have invited me into the cage you keep her locked in."

"You son of a bitch," he intoned. "I trusted you to keep her safe."

"The one hurting her right now is you."

He shoved me back and leaped off the bar, straightening to meet my steady gaze. "You putting that kinda shit in her head?"

"Her legs might be out of order, but her mind works just fine."

Neo's fists balled at his sides. My back muscles tensed as if readying for another punch. "The fuck you just say?"

"Come off it already, asshole. You know I'm not insulting your sister. I'm speaking the truth, and that's what pisses you off, isn't it? I can accept that her legs don't work, but you… you can't stand it."

He charged me, and I let him. I took another hit, not bothering to stop it. It wasn't me he was hitting anyway. It was himself. All these years of guilt had done nothing but fester. So he put it all on me. He could hit me. He could rage and blame.

I would give him a few more free hits after all.

They weren't really for him anyway. They were for Virginia. She was just as trapped by Neo's anger as he.

I felt blood trickle from my lip down the center of my chin. The side of my jaw ached, and my eye socket felt like it was on fire.

Inside me, the huntsman roared to retaliate, but the brother in me? He understood.

Neo drew back his arm again, fist so tight his knuckles were stretched taut over bone. There was blood smeared across his fingers. I braced for another punch, but his arm dropped like it was too heavy to swing anymore.

"Why aren't you hitting back?" He launched forward and shoved me off balance. "Hit me back, you son of a bitch!"

"No."

His eyes flared, stubborn indignation lighting their depths. "I told her you're a killer."

And just like that, all the breath in my body was siphoned out, the little bit of light she'd lit my darkness with snuffed out as if it hadn't been there at all.

The all-encompassing darkness was startling despite its familiarity.

"She'll never want to lay eyes on you again." Neo sneered.

My knuckles split with the force of the blow, the newly torn flesh stinging with the same ferocity I'd thrown into the punch. Neo was bent over a nearby table, and when he stood, a rivulet of blood dripped down his cheek, a bruise already forming at his eye.

I shook out my hand, not even remembering the burst of movement, but the aftermath made it crystal clear.

"Does that make you feel better?" I spoke, deadly calm and words like ice. "Knowing that I'm far worse than you will ever be? Knowing you took away something—" I stopped. "Proving to her you're the hero and I'm just a villain."

"That's not what—"

My rude sound cut him off. "It is, and we both know it. But it's not a lie, and I'm not denying it."

Neo took a step forward, his face flickering with more than just anger for the first time since he'd walked in. "Earth…"

"Don't," I said, stopping whatever he was about to feel guilty about. "You have them both, Ivory and Virginia. We don't have to keep doing this. You told her the truth, and now it's over, whatever it was. I hoped maybe we could work things out, you and me. But it's obvious some betrayals are too deep."

I righted a barstool as I walked by, continuing my way behind the bar.

Maybe it was time for me to cut ties and go. The past was getting dangerously close, and the present was too complicated to fix.

I had a fleeting thought of Fletcher, and my heart lurched a little. Maybe I could keep in touch with him.

Maybe he can keep me updated on Virginia after I'm gone.

I felt Neo still standing there even as I worked behind the bar. Finally, I turned, taking in his rumpled flannel, bloodied face, and scraped knuckles. I chose to not see the grief in his expression.

"It's fine. Don't add this to the list of shit you heap blame on yourself for. This is all me. I made my choices, and you're right to protect your sister." My heart constricted at her mention, and I tried not to think about her face when Neo told her what kind of man I really was.

She probably regrets that kiss.

I never will.

Clearing my throat, I had one last thing to say. "Ease up on her a bit, though. She has too much light to be locked up in the dark all the time."

Neo shifted like he was about to speak, but I thought of something else to say.

"And just because she's partially paralyzed doesn't mean she isn't all woman. Someone will love her... if you let them."

"Earth."

"Get out."

I felt him hesitate, but I'd had enough.

"Out!" I roared, the demand punctuated by the sound of a glass hurtling through the air and bursting on impact as it hit the wall.

Pop! Shards of glass splintered everywhere, raining down onto the floor and scattering across a nearby table.

"Family doesn't turn their back on family even when they turn their back on you."

Snort, who'd been by the bar this whole time, scurried out, and then there were footfalls on the stairs.

Beau burst into the room. "Did a fight break out?" His green eyes widened when he saw the empty bar with just me and Neo. "I take it things aren't going well."

"He kissed my sister," Neo informed him.

My hackles rose.

"She could do worse," Beau retorted.

I glanced over my shoulder at my last remaining roommate. He shrugged.

It's okay to be worried about her, you know. His words echoed in the recesses of my mind. He knew. Somehow he knew how I felt about Virginia, and he was the only one who didn't care.

"You're taking his side?" Neo was incredulous.

"Family doesn't have sides."

Beau must have felt my stare drilling a hole in the side of his head because he half smiled, glancing in my direction. "I might sit behind a computer all day, but I'm not blind and I'm not stupid." He glanced at Neo. "And you aren't either."

The room fell quiet, but the silence wasn't long. The ringing of a phone cut through, making my entire body tense.

Concentrating on the weight of the secret phone tucked inside my jacket, I expected to feel it vibrate with the ring.

The second I realized it was not that phone, some of my tension ebbed away.

"It's not me," Neo said, glancing up from the phone in his hand.

"Mine's upstairs," Beau said.

I reached into the back pocket of my jeans, pulling out the ringing device.

Neo turned to finally leave.

I glanced down at the caller ID.

"Wait," I demanded, accepting the call.

"Virginia?" I asked into the line, heart pounding with wonder she would even call.

Heavy breathing and nervous tension filled my ear. I straightened. "V? What's wrong?"

Nearby, Neo and Beau straightened in attention.

A low, plaintive whimper was her reply.

Flashes of that crudely drawn mark and the recollection of the ominous call I'd had just minutes ago slammed into me, and I reached out blindly, closing my hand over the edge of the bar.

"Virginia!" I demanded. "Virginia, what's happening?"

I could barely hear over the thundering of my pulse and the rush of blood in my ears. Adrenaline spiked so fast inside me that my head swam as I clutched the phone, practically screaming for a reply.

"H-h-*help*." Her call was ragged, breathless, and filled with fear.

"Is that screaming?" I yelled. "Who's screaming?"

I didn't notice Neo so close until he tried to snatch the phone out of my hand.

I reacted as if he were the threat, grabbing his hand and twisting his arm at an awkward angle behind his back.

"Virginia!" I hollered again.

The line went dead.

I pulled the phone away from my ear to look at the flashing screen.

"What is it?" Neo demanded, still hunched over from the way I had him pinned.

I let go of him, rushing toward the door. "We have to go. They found her!"

Neither of the men questioned my words as we rushed into the night because the urgency there was all they needed to hear.

Twenty-Six

THE DOOR SWUNG OPEN, AND I DISCONNECTED THE CALL, dropping my phone facedown in my lap to hide the light.

Clinging to the covers, I thought again about what I could use to brain whoever it was when they got close.

"Miss Virginia," a familiar voice hissed.

"Patrick!" I whisper-yelled, staring at one of the night nurses as he slipped into my room, pushing the door around immediately after entering. His uniform made him glow in the dark, and frankly, it was not comforting. "What is going on?"

"I came to tell you to be calm and please don't leave your room right now."

"*Agh!*" Another scream echoed down the hall.

"How am I supposed to be calm when it sounds like this place is being attacked by a heinous beast?"

"Well, beast wouldn't be far off," he muttered but then seemed to realize he was speaking with a patient. Straightening, he smoothed his features. "A new resident has come to stay with us here at the Tower, and his transition isn't going smoothly."

My mouth fell open as more sounds of things shattering echoed toward my room. "You're telling me that's a new patient?" My hands trembled as if my body couldn't stop being afraid. I glanced down very briefly at my phone, the small pang of guilt for calling Earth taken over by a much stronger sensation of longing.

I want Earth.

"How is a patient in this place even able to make that much noise and destruction?" I asked, worried.

"He's not elderly like everyone else here." Realizing what he said, he rushed to add, "And you, of course. You aren't old."

The fact that I was in a home where ninety-nine percent of the residents were far older than me was not something new. And neither was being lumped in with them.

"But what about his condition?" I wondered.

"His condition," Patrick echoed. "Well, he's much more capable physically than all our other residents."

Then why is he here?

More screaming. More thuds.

I slid a glance at the door. "He must be very afraid," I whispered.

"Him!" Patrick exclaimed quietly. "I think I almost peed my pants!"

"You should go sit with some of the elderly patients. They're probably confused."

"You're going to be okay?"

I pressed my lips together and nodded.

"Stay in your room, okay? No sense in provoking him."

Fear slithered down my spine.

"We called in some extra help, so we should have him calmed down as soon as we can get close enough to give him some medication."

They were going to sedate him like he was a wild animal on a rampage.

But really, what else could they do?

"I won't go anywhere." I promised.

"You probably wouldn't get far anyway," Patrick said flippantly on his way back to the door.

His words pierced my heart with accurate precision, creating an instant hurt.

Realizing he'd spoken out loud, he stopped and turned, shock and guilt so evident on his face I could see it even in the dim light.

"It's okay," I told him. "Go be with the others."

He slipped out of the room just the way he'd come, and I sat there listening to the ruckus the new patient created. My new housemate.

"Get away from me!" I heard a strangely deep voice roar.

Slam! Crash!

I wondered if they were going to have to call the police. I also was curious about his condition. Most people in this place were incapacitated in some way, but from the sounds of things, he was clearly able to move around and move *other* things around.

The trembling in my hands did not stop even after knowing what was happening. If anything, it only made me more alert. Knowing something volatile was happening, that I could very well be in danger, made it all the more upsetting that I really couldn't protect myself.

Patrick, while rude, was right. Even if I tried to run, I probably wouldn't get very far. It left me with a very real feeling of helplessness. It was a feeling I hated, a feeling I often told myself to either ignore or learn to live with.

I didn't know how to do either.

A sudden eruption of chaos had all my thoughts

fleeing and my pulse spiking anew. Through the chaos, I heard Emogen's voice, and I sat up straighter.

What was Emogen doing here? Was she part of the staff they called in as reinforcement? That was ridiculous! What if she got hurt? My goodness, that man out there sounded like a savage beast!

"I'll be fine!" Emogen insisted almost as if she could hear my thoughts.

Argh!

Was she going to try and calm him down?

"Emogen!" I called, the name sounding more like a hoarse whisper than anything.

I couldn't just sit here and do nothing. I couldn't just listen to my friend try and deal with a crazed person!

Reaching toward the end of the bed, I grappled for the board I used to help transfer myself to my chair. It seemed heavier than usual, probably because my arms were weak with fear. But I pushed on, dragging it to the side of the bed and pushing it toward my chair.

The edge of the board hit the seat and pushed the chair away from the bed. A sound of frustration vibrated my throat as I inwardly scolded myself for forgetting to lock the wheels in place.

I tossed the board at it again, the edge catching as I tugged, half falling backward as I tried to drag the chair back.

My efforts only resulted in pushing the chair sideways.

Tears built up in my eyes, frustration and fear spilling over.

If I can't get the chair to come to me, I will have to go to the chair!

Positioning the board one end on the floor and one

on the mattress, I maneuvered at the top, legs off to the side, and pushed off to hopefully slide down.

The board was slightly short, and my weight made it slip away from the bed, sending me and the wood crashing to the floor.

A sob wrenched out of me the same moment the door to my room burst in and light flooded the room.

My head shot up as two bodies fought to fit through the door at the same time, resulting in them practically falling over the threshold.

"Virginia!" Neo bellowed, eyes going to the bed. "She's not here!" he declared merely one second after seeing my empty mattress.

"I'm down here," I announced, pushing myself up into a sitting position.

Earth lurched around Neo, black eyes widening the second he saw me.

"Virginia," Neo rushed out, stumbling forward.

I couldn't tear my eyes away from Earth. *He came. I called him, and he came.*

My lower lip wobbled. "Earth."

Neo paused in the middle of reaching for me. I could feel his probing stare, but I was still unable to rip mine from the intense gaze roaming over me, taking stock of my well-being.

Without thinking, I lifted my arms for him, silently asking.

A rough sound ripped from his throat, and then I was being lifted, swung up into safety as the scent of bread and cigarettes curled around my senses.

"What are you doing on the floor, sprite?" His voice was gentle and attentive, making my eyes fill with waterworks once more.

"I fell," I admitted.

A frown creased his forehead, and one of his hands stroked a strand of hair off my forehead. "Are you hurt?"

I shook my head. I wasn't, but the gentleness in his voice made me feel bruised. "You came."

"Always," he whispered.

A loud shout and the slamming of something seemed to shake the walls. I ducked into Earth's neck, trying to control my quivers.

"What the hell was that?" Beau demanded.

Hearing his voice, I remembered that it was not just Earth here. Peeking up, I saw my brother and Beau standing inside the room.

Crash! Shatter!

"We're gonna have to call the cops," someone out the hall said.

"No!" Emogen called out. "Give me a few more minutes."

I made a worried sound.

"Did someone hurt you?" Earth asked, all trace of gentleness gone. Then over my head, he spoke. "Go see what's going on."

"No!" I exclaimed, straightening in his hold. "Don't go!"

Beau and Neo seemed conflicted, hesitating in the doorway.

"We need to know what the hell is going on," Earth told them.

"It's a new patient. He's having trouble adjusting to this place."

"So he's trashing it!" Neo spat.

"Patrick said they called in extra help to settle him down." I chewed my lower lip. "But I'm worried about Emogen."

"Who the hell is Patrick?" Earth demanded.

"He's one of the night nurses," I explained. "I was scared because I thought whoever was out there was breaking into my room. That's why I called you. But it turns out it was just Patrick coming to tell me what was happening."

"A male nurse coming into your unlocked room at night." Earth's voice was deadly calm, eerily controlled, but promised so much hell. I wasn't afraid. Strangely, his ire made me feel so safe.

He turned toward Neo. "And you think I'm the problem?"

Neo had the decency to flush. Wait. No. He wasn't flushed. He was bruised and bloodied!

"Have you two been fighting?" I exclaimed.

"We're fine, sprite." Earth tried to soothe me, but I saw the blood and bruises on him too.

Gasping, I grabbed Earth's chin to study his split lip. "*Neo Florian,* did you do this to him?" I demanded.

My brother's head shot up, and his eyes went round. "*Veee,*" he whined.

"Florian?" Beau repeated. "Is that your middle name?" He began snickering with glee.

"And you!" I said, turning my gaze on him. "What were you doing while your brothers were beating each other to a pulp?"

"They were down at the bar." He defended himself, no longer snickering.

Rooaarr!

I snuggled back into Earth's chest.

"Don't be afraid." He soothed, arms tightening around me. "He's not going to hurt you."

"Emogen is out there." I worried.

"I'll go check on her," he offered, crossing the room to my brother.

"No!" I refused, tightening my arms around his neck when he moved to hand me over.

More flurry of activity burst in through the door as Ethan, Fletcher, and Ivory rushed into my room.

"We're here! What's going on? Virginia, are you okay?" Fletcher exclaimed.

"What are you doing here?" I asked, surprised. The last thing I expected was my entire family filling up my small room in the middle of the night.

"We called them from the car," Beau explained.

"Why would you bring Ivory?" Neo exclaimed, pinning Ethan with a look. "We had no idea what kind of danger we were walking into!"

"Don't be a caveman, Neo! Honestly, the entire family is here, but you wanted me to stay home? I've survived much worse than this!"

Earth's body went taut against mine, his muscles nearly vibrating with tension.

I looked up, questions filling my gaze.

He avoided my stare and handed me to my brother.

"I'll be right back," Earth told me.

I caught his arm as he turned away. "Earth, no. You might get hurt. That man sounds dangerous."

To punctuate my worries, there was another loud thump.

"What in great gods was that?" Ethan wondered.

"Some crazy new patient," Beau informed him.

Gently tugging his arm from my grasp, Earth leaned in to kiss my temple. Tingles of awareness brushed across my scalp and down my neck. "No one is more dangerous than I am."

I frowned, wanting to ask so many things but realizing now was not the time.

"Go with him." I turned pleading eyes on Ethan and then Beau.

The two men moved to follow, as did Fletcher.

"Hell no, puppy. Stay here," Ethan told Fletch, stopping him with a hand on his shoulder.

"I'm just as capable as you are," Fletcher argued.

"I know that." Ethan acknowledged. "But Neo might need backup here."

"And what are we?" Ivory retorted. "Helpless women?"

"We don't have time for this," Earth snapped, his voice cold. "Fletcher. Stay," he ordered and then stomped out into the hall.

Fletcher scowled but stayed behind as the three men disappeared into the hall.

"You okay, princess?" Neo asked Ivory, stepping closer to her.

"What happened to your face?" she exclaimed, reaching out to cup it gently. "What is going on?"

Feeling like a definite third wheel literally wedged between my brother and his lover, I cleared my throat. "Could you please put me down?"

"Oh." Ivory drew her arm back. "I'm so sorry, Virginia. I just saw his bruises and reacted."

"I understand," I told her sincerely. "You have every reason to be worried." I looked at my brother. "Put me down now."

The second I was on the bed, Ivory was in my brother's arms and making tsking sounds over his battered face. He scolded her for not staying home. They were so in love, and usually, it made me warm all over, but tonight, it just made me stare anxiously at the door.

"It's very quiet out there," I murmured.

Fletcher climbed onto the bed beside me, one of his hands wrapping around mine. "They're okay."

"You really think so?" I asked, squeezing his fingers.

"Of course. I trust Ethan." His eyes widened. "My brothers too, of course!"

"Of course," I echoed.

"What's going on anyway?"

I briefly explained to Fletch and Ivory, all the while watching the door.

"You sure you're okay?" Neo asked me. "What were you doing on the floor?"

"My goodness!" Ivory worried, turning her vivid blue eyes to me. "Did you fall out of bed?"

"Kinda," I muttered, embarrassed. Thankfully, I was saved from having to recount my own stupidity because Beau and Ethan walked back in. Anxiously, I gazed past them, waiting for Earth to appear. When he did, I felt my shoulders relax.

"How is Emogen?" I worried.

"Girl, you know I'm fine. Takes more than some pissed-off patient to bring me down." Her voice floated in behind Earth, and then she stepped into the room.

Her eyes went wide, seeing the entire family here. Hands planting on her hips, she shook her head. "It ain't visiting hours. What in the world are you all doing here?"

"We were worried about V," Fletcher said, still holding my hand.

"Everything's fine now," Emogen announced. "The new patient is sleeping. There's no cause for concern."

"Until he wakes up," Earth muttered darkly.

He was standing across the room, and it was too far away. I felt needy and scared, feelings I really hated but feelings I had just the same.

"Maybe you should come stay with us for a while," Ivory suggested. "At least until we know that this new patient is not a danger."

"I don't think he is." Emogen spoke up.

"Can you guarantee it?" Earth challenged.

She fell silent.

"I don't know," I murmured, glancing at my brother. Things between us were kinda precarious right now. If I went to stay with them, would we just keep arguing? Would he make it even harder than he already did for me to see Earth?

He's a killer.

Did I want to see Earth?

Yes. Yes, I did.

"Y'all can discuss this tomorrow. During visiting hours," Emogen emphasized. She wasn't even dressed in her usual scrubs and had on not one stitch of makeup. Instead, she was wearing a pair of loose sweatpants and a T-shirt, likely because she rushed here straight from bed when they called her in.

"I'm not leaving her here," Neo announced, stubborn.

"The patient is sedated. He will not be awake anytime soon. You can come back in the morning," Emogen told him. "And what in the world is wrong with your face?"

As if she knew, Emogen turned to Earth, taking in his busted lip and bruised eye. Her *tsk, tsk* filled the room. "Saw that coming," she said to no one in particular.

"What?" Fletcher wondered.

"Beau, could you get me the first aid kit from the bathroom, please?" I asked.

"Earth and Neo were fighting?" Fletcher surmised. "But I thought you made up already?"

No one answered as Beau handed me the small white and red kit.

"Oh, no. They can clean up their mule-headed behinds by themselves. At home. Everyone out," Emogen declared, her voice taking on a *don't even try me* tone.

"Do you want to come home with us?" Fletcher asked, tugging on my hand.

I smiled. "Thank you for the offer, but it's late. I'll just stay here."

"If you change your mind, call. We'll come right back." He glanced at Ethan. "Right?"

"Of course." Ethan agreed. "Just call if you need anything at all. And we will call you tomorrow to check in."

"Thank you," I whispered, tears filling my eyes.

Fletcher hugged me, and I returned the embrace. Sometimes I felt so alone even though I knew I wasn't. But then other times—like tonight—I was reminded of just how lucky I was to have this family.

"Let's go for hot chocolate again soon. Okay? And then you can come visit Gwennie!"

"I'd like that," I said, thinking fondly of the cat Fletcher had found in a subway.

"I'm glad you're okay," Beau told me, still close by. "Call me if you need anything."

I nodded, giving him a watery smile. He patted me on the head, which made me giggle, and then he moved to the door, following Ethan and Fletcher.

Neo was standing there stubbornly, his feet planted like there would be hell to pay if we told him to leave.

"Go with Ivory," I told him. "Let her clean up your face. You look like dog meat."

He pursed his lips, shaking his head. "I can't do that."

"You can. I'm just going back to sleep. I'm exhausted." It wasn't entirely a lie. I was exhausted, but I doubted I would be able to sleep.

Then to everyone, I said, "I'm so sorry to worry you all like this. But thank you for coming. I appreciate you all."

My eyes slipped to Earth, who was still too far away, still avoiding my gaze.

Yeah, I definitely wouldn't be able to sleep tonight.

"We'll come back in the morning, talk more about you coming to stay with us," Ivory suggested.

I nodded.

She gave me a warm hug. She smelled of lavender, and even in the middle of the night, her midnight hair was glossy and her fair skin flawless.

Everyone started toward the door, Neo trudging along as though his feet weighed a hundred pounds. "You too," he intoned, stopping beside Earth to glare.

I looked at the man I wanted to leave least of all, wanting him to stay, knowing he could not. His eyes narrowed into half-moon shapes when my brother tried to kick him out. Then instead of heading for the door, he moved deeper into the room.

My heart somersaulted, and a light feeling crowded my stomach.

Earth stepped to my wheelchair to gently push it right up to the bed and then locked the wheels in place.

The board still lay on the floor. He picked it up and laid it on the seat of the chair.

The second he was done, he turned to leave. He hadn't even looked at me once.

My lower lip quivered, so I sank my teeth into it, trying to make it stop. "Thank you," I said, voice small.

He stopped, his head turning like he might glance over his shoulder.

I anticipated his eyes. I wanted whatever expression

he would show me. I was so hungry for him, so hungry I was starved.

Neo made a rude sound, and Earth's head whipped back around.

Anguish cut through me, lancing me with pain. I thought about arguing and calling my brother out.

I was tired.

And then my family was gone. I was alone in my tower once more.

Twenty-Seven

DULL SHOUTS COULD BE HEARD EVEN FROM OUT ON THE street.

Glass shattering made my blood run cold.

She was in there. A girl no bigger than a sprite, a soul gentler than a lamb.

Her whimper for help still burned my eardrum. It pounded at my temple as if any part of me needed a reminder.

It was me she called. My phone that rang.

She could have called her brother. She *should* have.

She didn't.

And then she reached for me. Lifted her arms, seeking solace I didn't have but she always managed to find regardless.

Neo and I both stood in front of her, but it was me she looked at. Me she chose.

In that moment, I felt the heavy weight of an invisible collar shackle itself around my neck. The key wasn't mine to wield, but even if it was, I wouldn't have used it.

She owned me now. Despite my busted lip and thoughts of disappearing. Despite the fact I was not nor would ever be good enough.

I belonged to Virginia, and the rest of the world could go straight to hell.

"We aren't done talking," Neo informed me after we'd all been kicked out and the doors to the Tower locked behind us.

"Talking involves words, not fists," Ivory stated coolly.

We both glanced at her, then back at each other.

"I thought things were getting better between you two. What happened?" Ivory asked.

I glanced at my brother—funny how I still thought of him that way—and quirked an eyebrow.

He made a face. "I saw them kissing."

Ivory's brow creased, but then realization dawned. Her eyes blew wide, and her naturally red lips pulled into a smile. Her arms grasped my forearm to tug in excitement. "You and V?" she exclaimed. "Oh goodness, this is wonderful!"

I glanced down to where her manicured hand lay on my arm, then up, and our eyes collided.

Nothing.

I felt nothing.

"It is not." Neo glowered.

Ivory turned to him to demand, "Why not?"

"You know why."

Her lips pursed, and she turned back to me. "You would never hurt Virginia, would you?"

"I would rather die."

Her eyes turned warm as if I'd recited some romantic poem. She was a weird woman.

"See!" she told Neo.

"And so I'm supposed to take his word?" Neo bit out. "He tried to kill you, Ivory. More than once. He—"

"But he didn't." Her quiet words cut off Neo's tirade and drew my eyes once more.

Hers were gentle and forgiving when they touched on mine, and she smiled. "If it weren't for Earth, I really would be dead and it was all because of my wretched stepmother."

"Don't make excuses for me," I told her.

"I'm not. But I have forgiven you. You're my family now."

A lump formed in my throat. My eyes drilled holes in hers as I thought so many things I would never say. Things I wouldn't even know how to voice. How it had been her who woke up the change inside me, how her annoying, screeching presence in my life had somehow cracked open the door to the humanity I'd managed to suppress.

"Family," was all I said.

"She called you instead of me."

I looked away from Ivory to acknowledge Neo's words. "Yeah."

"You could have rushed out without telling me she was in trouble."

I could have.

"You care about her."

"No," I said immediately, feeling my upper lip curl. I could have just agreed, but I didn't just care. "I love her."

Neo rocked back on his heels, and Ivory made some kind of low squealing sound.

I stood there stoic because that declaration wasn't all hearts and rainbows. Not all love was like that. Some love was dangerous and slightly obsessive. Some love was capable of living in the dark. Some love was capable of burning the world down around the one you gave it to.

That was my kind of love. The kind of love that consumed and was loyal to a fault.

Neo grabbed the collar of my jacket. "Don't you play games. That girl up there ain't strong enough for games."

I shrugged him off. "She's stronger than you think. But that won't matter because, with me, once you're in, you're in. I'll do anything for the people I love." I flicked a glance at Ivory. "Including turning my back on my own set of rules."

A jealous growl ripped out of him. "My sister is not a consolation prize. She isn't a placeholder for—"

Slam!

My fist cut off his words instantly, the force of the blow knocking him back onto his ass. I stood over him nearly vibrating, his words angering me like nothing else.

Ivory moved as if she would rush to Neo, but I pinned her in place with one cold, hard stare.

Knuckles stinging from where they'd plowed his face, I dropped onto my haunches, squatting in front of him. His lip curled when I dropped a hand onto his shoulder, a light snarl forming on his bloodied lip. I didn't back off, instead squeezing the tense muscle there.

"V is not a consolation prize, and not even you are allowed to suggest it. All your girl did was show me I could feel more than I thought. And *all* those newfound feelings are directed at one girl... a girl who isn't yours."

I stood and stepped back, aware of Ivory staring between me and Neo like she wasn't sure what she should do. It was the closest we'd ever come to talking about the elephant in the room, and I hoped he understood. There was no need for his jealousy because I wasn't looking at his princess. I had my own.

Neo jumped to his feet, swiping at his lip, all the heat and anger gone from his tone. "But she *is* my sister."

I realized then that this conversation was likely pointless, and I wasn't into pointless things. "It doesn't matter anyway," I said, straightening. "You told her who I really am."

"Neo!" Ivory exclaimed, horrified.

Neo winced. "She has a right to know."

"You could have let Earth tell her!" she scolded.

But would I have? Would I have told the one person who might look at me like a hero that I was actually a villain?

Probably not. Villain, remember?

"Let's go," Ivory insisted, pushing Neo toward a big black SUV at the curb. Ethan, Fletcher, and Beau were long gone. "I'm tired, and you're bleeding."

"You just want to lecture me more," Neo complained.

"You deserve it," Ivory informed him, that haughty NYC elitist air coming over her. She gave him another shove toward the SUV but then turned back to me.

Before I knew what was happening, she stretched up on tiptoes to wrap her thin arms around me.

I stood there frozen, shocked she would hug me like this. I cut a glance at Neo and saw him staring at us, frowning, and started to push her away.

"He's fine." She promised. "I've wanted to do this a really long time, but I think now it's okay."

"Because now you know I'm not harboring some mega crush for you?" I deadpanned.

Her giggle against my ear made my lips lift just a fraction.

"Because sometimes sisters want to hug their brothers."

I lifted my arms to hug her back but put them down again.

She pulled back, a strand of black hair blowing across her cheek. Reaching up, she pushed it away and smiled. "Maybe next time."

Neo materialized beside her, tucking her possessively against his side. "She called you, E. Not me." He reminded me.

Then he was bundling Ivory into the SUV and they were driving off before he could even make sure I left first.

Maybe because he knew I wasn't leaving and maybe because this was his way of saying it was okay.

Twenty-Eight

Virginia

I was bundled into the corner of my bed, sitting up against the wall.

I didn't see or hear the door open even though I wasn't watching the drama playing on the screen in my lap.

Instead, I stared down at the moving people and scenes, vision slightly blurred, looking without seeing. The earbuds jammed into my ears made it easy to hear the music and dialogue. Still, I wasn't listening.

I was lost inside my own head, replaying the few brief moments I'd had with Earth before he left without a good-bye. He rushed in so fast but rushed out at the same pace. I'd barely had time to feel his presence despite the way he overwhelmed me.

I had no idea what there was between us or even if there was anything at all, but I craved him unlike anything before. He was the one who left me unsettled, but he was also the one who could put me at ease.

Lost in my own world consisting only of him, it took a moment to notice the long fingers snake across the top of my screen. When at last the movement registered, I jolted farther back into the corner, a small shriek befalling my lips.

The iPad was wrenched out of my lap, the earbuds popped out of my ears, and both were tossed aside. Pressing a hand to my pounding heart, I looked into the shadows, recognizing him immediately.

"Earth!"

"You called me." Oh, his voice was deep and rough, the words ripping out with intensity that made me shiver.

My answer was breathless. "Yes."

"After what he said, you called me anyway."

"Yes."

I didn't know it was possible for black eyes to glimmer this way in the dark. Almost like there was fire within them, lighting up their darkest depths with the sole purpose of letting me see just how dangerous this man truly was. "Why?"

"Because I wanted you."

He growled, rumbly and deep, and pounced. Jean-clad legs straddled mine, and his hands slammed into the wall on either side of my head.

The second our lips locked, he inhaled deep as if he could fuse us tighter together, as if the only air he needed was me. Surrendering wholeheartedly, I turned boneless against the wall, lifting my chin to offer full access to everything he might want.

One of his hands cupped the back of my head, supporting it as he ravaged my mouth, kissing so deep all I could do was moan.

The thickness of his tongue moving against mine created this looseness in my middle, and when he sucked my upper lip between his to tug and pull, I arched up.

My skin was hot, heart erratic, and my lungs burned

for air he refused to let me have. Reaching up, my hands delved beneath the leather jacket, smoothing across the fabric of his T-shirt before shoving at the coat, trying to get it away.

Our ragged breathing filled the room when he finally pulled free. His chest heaved as he rose above me, knees on either side of my legs. The jacket disappeared, and I barely had time to register the holster-like straps at his shoulders before they were gone and so was his shirt.

Nervous excitement skittered along my nerves. I was inexperienced and unsure, but I was also filled with want. The shoulders I'd clung to many times before looked as strong as they'd always felt, and his chest was smooth and defined. Earth wasn't overly muscular, but he radiated the kind of energy that declared it didn't matter. His natural strength was commanding and deliciously ominous, making me forget my nerves to stretch out my hand. Before I could make contact, he gently pushed my hand away to crawl down my legs, moving farther out of reach.

I made a sound of protest, which turned into a gasp when he grabbed my ankles and pulled, my entire body going flat against the bed.

My stomach dipped and tumbled when he rose over me again, lips descending once more onto mine.

I kissed him back, effort slipping when my palms finally slid over the warm, smooth skin along his sides, fingertips exploring the surface of his back. Vivid sensations stole over me, and I marveled at the way he felt above me, how the pads of my fingers and the palms of my hands tingled from just touching his skin.

My head fell to the side, and he dragged his lips across my jaw, nose nudging at my ear before his lips closed around my lobe. I gasped, eyes flying open as chills raced over my body. Suddenly, I felt like an exposed wire, overcome by electricity and heat.

The air felt cold against my damp earlobe when he released it, adding another layer of awareness as he nudged behind my ear before diving into the side of my neck.

My body went taut and then melted into the mattress. Sounds I'd never made before echoed off my lips, making me sound wanton and offering enough awareness to prick me with embarrassment.

I was reluctant to pull one hand away from him, but I did so I could cover my mouth just in time to moan into the palm as his teeth dragged over that same spot.

I shuddered and wiggled insatiably. If my lower half worked, I probably would have managed to wiggle away. But from my lower trunk down, I remained still, which oddly added a layer of allure because I couldn't get away. I was almost trapped here underneath his ministrations, a willing victim to every ounce of pleasure he decided to give.

His hand covered mine, gently tugging it away from my mouth. "Don't you dare keep those sounds from me."

"E-Earth." My voice shuddered around his name.

He groaned and licked across my neck, making me arch up into him again.

"Fuck," he ground out, pulling back and leaving my skin shivering from the loss of his heat.

My finger hooked through a belt loop on his jeans, curling around the strip of fabric "Don't stop," I whispered, giving a small tug.

And then we were kissing again, one of his hands curling around the side of my waist, pushing between my body and the mattress, holding me against him as the kiss ravaged us both.

The faint flavor of metal bloomed across my tongue, and I realized his split lip was bleeding again, his blood swirling between us. A sense of rightness tightened my chest, perhaps an odd reaction to the taste of someone's blood, but it was my reaction all the same.

It seemed completely fitting to have his blood across my tongue. I didn't know the details, but I knew enough to understand that Earth was not a gentle man, that any kind of life with him might always be tinged with blood.

He pulled back just enough to disconnect our lips, and when I followed him blindly, he made a sound. "I'm getting blood on you."

His voice was hoarse, as though he hadn't spoken in months, and the rough, uneven tone made my stomach bottom out.

Catching his face between my palms, I dragged the width of my tongue across his lower lip. *Lick. Lick. Liiick.*

He went still, and the way he froze only accentuated the erratic way he breathed. Onyx eyes stared through slim half-moons, somehow making me feel wholly seen. Latching on to that gaze, I did it again.

Lick. "I like it," I confessed.

Something shifted around us, and a primal light beamed through his slitted stare.

I watched the tip of his tongue slip out, swiping up the newly welling blood from the bottom of his lip. Scarlet smeared across his tongue as he leaned down and kissed me again.

This time, the kiss was deep and slow. The kind that broke me apart and rearranged me according to his law. The blood was salty, but the kiss was sweet, creating an intoxicating combination.

When his hand closed around my chin and jaw, I

sighed deeply, loving how possessive he was, wanting desperately to be possessed.

I was a girl who always thought I was half. A girl who assumed she would likely always be alone. I thought kisses like this were made up in books, watched dreamily on dramas, and yearned for quietly in a lonely heart.

I realized then, as my fingers curled into my palms against his back, that even though I fought for independence, deep down, I still wanted to feel owned.

This was probably the most languid kiss he'd ever given me, and even though it still tasted of metal, the gentleness overruled all.

He kisses me like I am his.

Like even though he owned me, he wanted me too.

The pad of his thumb brushed across my cheek, and he abruptly lifted his head. "You're crying."

I blinked, feeling the wetness on my cheeks for the first time. "I am?"

"Did I hurt you?" he asked, a look pinching his features. He sat back, but I grabbed his belt loop again, keeping him close.

"No!" I quickly swore, shaking my head, realizing I felt dizzy. "I never thought anyone would ever kiss me like that."

He studied me a moment, silently assessing, but what, I wasn't sure. Then he made a gruff sound. "If anyone else ever kisses you like that, I'll kill them."

I used to think he was joking. But now I wasn't so sure.

"I don't want anyone else's kisses," was all I said.

"Stop looking at me like that." He was gruff, averting his gaze. "I can hardly control myself as it is."

This was him in control? Dear heavens, what would it be like when he wasn't? Without thinking, I allowed my eyes to travel lower, across his chest and to his navel where a line of dark hair disappeared into the waistband of his jeans.

It was the only hair on his body, and my finger itched to touch it.

"Earth?" I whispered, still staring.

"No."

My mouth fell open. "You don't even know what I want!"

"The answer is no. I've already given in way too much."

The finger still curled around the beltloop slid free and started reaching for that trail of hair.

A rough sound ripped out of him, and he caught it, giving me a hard look. "I said no."

"I trust you."

A silent exhale moved his shoulders and chest. Watching his body react to my words was satisfying in a way I didn't realize it could be.

The hard light in his eyes gave way to something that honestly looked like wonder, and he pinned me with it as he slowly carried my captured finger up to his lips to press a kiss against the tip.

"You shouldn't."

"I do."

He lowered my finger from his lips. "How much did Neo tell you?"

"Hardly anything at all. He threw out some major accusation and then sent me off to physical therapy." I accused Neo. Then to myself, I muttered, "Big jerk."

The hand holding mine slipped away. "You'll change your mind."

"Hand me the first aid kit. You're still bleeding," I instructed, pushing up into a sitting position.

When he left the bed, a part of me mourned, but I consoled myself by staring at the way the muscles shifted in his back. Then my stare slid down to the way his jeans hugged his butt.

What? I was in a wheelchair, not dead.

"Can you turn on the lamp?"

"So you can get a better view of my ass?"

How'd he know?

"So I can see your lip!" I retorted.

He chuckled like he knew better and turned on the light. After a quick glance to make sure the door to my room was closed, I peeked back at his butt.

It was pretty nice, and I felt sorry I hadn't grabbed it earlier.

With the kit beside me, I tugged my legs in, folding them closer to my body so Earth could sit close.

He watched quietly, and when I looked up, he spoke. "Did I hurt you before?"

"No." I assured him. "I—" My voice faltered. I didn't like this conversation.

"Say it. Say everything to me."

My eyes flashed up to his. "I couldn't feel you straddling me."

His eyes stayed on mine. "I could hurt you without you knowing."

"Sit down," I said, breaking eye contact and patting the mattress.

I worked quietly cleaning up the split in his lip and wiping away the blood. When it was clean, I dabbed on some antiseptic, making him hiss. "Ow!"

I added more.

He growled.

Smiling softly, I leaned in, blowing across the area to soothe it. His eyes went soft again, bestowing upon me a look that I somehow knew was one he didn't share often.

"Poor baby," I murmured, blowing again.

"Baby, my ass," he grumped.

Clearly, pain made him ill-tempered. Ignoring the way he glared and grumbled, I pecked a lingering kiss beneath his lip, just below the injury. I heard his intake of breath, but I didn't acknowledge it, instead turning his head to kiss the forming bruise on his jaw and then another on his cheekbone.

"I really wish you and my brother wouldn't fight."

He stayed silent, but his stare was so loud. Finally, I gave in, tilting my head back to open my stare to him completely.

"Did you not believe what he told you?" His eyes searched mine.

"Part of me didn't want to. But I know my brother wouldn't just lie about something like that."

"Why didn't you demand more explanation?"

"I told you I got called to PT, and he was gone when I came back."

"You could have called him. You could have demanded he stay tonight to tell you."

"I'd rather hear it from you."

"You'll be sorry you let me kiss you like that." As he spoke, his eyes shifted to the bed and the blankets still rumpled from where we lay.

"Are you sorry?"

His eyes flew to my face. "What?"

"Do you regret it?" I forced myself to ask again. *Be brave. The ugly truth is better than a pretty lie.*

"Why would you ask me that?"

"You asked me first!" I exclaimed, completely self-conscious. Then, realizing how loud I'd been, I slapped a hand over my mouth and glanced at the door. I frowned. "How did you get in here anyway?"

"The security in this place sucks. Might as well leave the door wide open and plug in a neon sign."

I rolled my eyes.

"Virginia."

My shoulders slumped. "I'm different from other girls."

"Definitely louder and more annoying."

I gasped.

He chuckled.

"I'm not as responsive," I whispered, glancing at my lap.

His laughter was gone, and pungent silence filled the space for the span of a few heartbeats. He grasped my chin, forcing my face up. As much as I reveled in the same act earlier, now it made me insecure.

"You mean because you can't move or feel your lower half." It wasn't really a question because we both knew what I meant.

I nodded against his palm. "I... I—" Oh, there was a lot that wanted to pour out, but it was so embarrassing and also scary.

What if, after kissing me that way, Earth realized what I might never be able to give him? What if he didn't like me?

"Everything." He reminded me, his voice soft but made of steel.

I pushed his hand away from my chin, lowering my gaze once more. "I've never had sex before, Earth."

"Obviously."

I gasped, face flaming. "That was the meanest thing

you've ever said to me!" I yelled, launching my fist, which he easily caught.

"Easy," he murmured, lifting me into his lap, wrapping me up in his embrace. "I didn't mean it because it wasn't good. I meant because of your condition and because Neo stands over you like a snarling rottweiler."

I half smiled because my brother was totally like that. "So you liked it?" I asked, voice small.

He grabbed my hand and pushed it down between us, tilting his hips up against my palm.

I gasped, snatching my hand back, ears nearly on fire. "Earth!"

"I'm still hard even after you put that burning crap on my face."

"I blew on it," I protested.

"Yeah, another reason I'm still like this."

I made a choked sound.

His lips brushed against my ear. Feeling them against me as his hushed words traveled into my ear made me shiver. "I more than liked, sprite."

Collapsing into his chest, I tucked my head just under his chin to stare across the room. "I can't wrap my legs around you. I can't rotate my hips. I-I..." he stroked my head, and it somehow loosened the rest of my words. "I don't even know if I'll be able to feel it. I mean, I think I might in some way. I mean, everything down there still works." I paused to worry my lip. "At least I think it does. The doctors say it does. I just... The nerves are blocked so I can't feel or move."

He stroked my head again, pushing my cheek a little closer into his chest. I sighed, realizing he still wasn't wearing a shirt and my skin was against his and he was so warm. Lifting my hand, I pressed the pads of my fingers against his chest, feeling the muscle there, feeling the erratic beating of his heart.

He was nervous too.

"No one wants to have sex with half a woman," I whispered.

An angry sound ripped out of him, and then I was on my back again, blinking up at his glittering, ominous expression as he stared down at me without blinking.

"You are not half a woman," he declared. "And don't ever say that again. Don't even think it."

"You can't control my thoughts."

A dark eyebrow quirked. "Is that a challenge?"

I started to answer, but he kissed the words away, tongue slipping inside me easily like it had already memorized the way. Without breaking the kiss, he lowered, this time giving me more of his body weight, pressing against me with his bare chest.

Breath shuddered through me, and beneath my shirt, my nipples hardened instantly. I gasped, feeling the way they puckered tight, shooting little zings of pleasure and pain all through my chest and into my stomach.

He took advantage of my distraction to kiss deeper and delve his hand beneath the hem.

"This okay?" he asked, not even lifting his lips.

I mumbled an agreement, practically vibrating from feeling his fingertips drag over my ribcage toward my chest.

He tugged my lower lip, making it snap back when he released us from the kiss. I had no time at all to think because, at the same time his hand closed over my bare breast, his palm ground down against the hardened center.

I cried out and arched into him, body trying to move closer, but his weight pinned me down.

"Not responsive, you say?" he murmured, his voice sounding drunk.

Or maybe it was me and the buzzing in my ears.

"I think you can feel this." He plucked my nipple, and I gasped, tingles of pleasure racing across my skin.

"And this," he murmured, kissing my lips softly.

"And this." He continued, dragging his mouth over my jaw and making my body go taut as it remembered the way he'd kissed my neck before.

The tip of his tongue swirled inside my ear, his fingers still rolling and playing with my nipple. My stomach felt funny like that time I'd gone on a crazy rollercoaster when I was fourteen.

I shifted subconsciously, trying to get closer, trying to shift away.

Teeth dragged lightly down my neck, the ends of his silky hair tickling my cheek and beneath my jaw.

"E," I gasped out, unable to say the rest of his name. My fingers found the back of his head, burying themselves in his hair.

He continued to work my breast, lips clamping down on that spot on the side of my neck.

I cried out, probably pulling his hair. My heart rate was accelerated, my breathing shallow and quick. My entire head tingled with pleasure, but beneath it all, something inside me throbbed.

He lifted his head, backing off my breast.

"Oh, baby," he murmured. "Don't ever tell me you aren't responsive, because you are."

I was still panting as he shifted, covering my body with his once more, resting his elbows on either side of my head.

He did that thing where he rubbed his nose against mine, and my heart felt like it was going to explode. A small kiss to the corner of my mouth. Another nudge from his nose. A brief kiss to my cheekbone. Another caress with his nose. Kiss. Nudge. Kiss. Nudge.

By the time he pulled back, everything was blurry. My body yearned for something I didn't even know if it could have, and my brain was nothing but empty buzzing.

"There are a thousand places on your body that are capable of knowing my touch," he murmured right beside my ear.

I moaned in response, which would have embarrassed me if I could think at all.

"You have erogenous zones in more places than between your legs." He went on, his voice pure seduction, the promise in his words addictive. "Like here." He licked over that spot on my neck.

I shuddered.

"Maybe here," he said, pinching my nipple.

"Oh, sweetheart." He kept talking, making me feel like maybe just the sound of his voice was enough to make me burn. "I'm going to enjoy mapping out this body, finding every single spot that I can use to wring pleasure out of you until it won't matter at all that you can't feel your legs because everything above them feels double."

A tear slipped free, sliding down the side of my face and disappearing into my hair. I was so overwhelmed by him that the emotion literally had nowhere else to go.

"I'm a greedy, bad man, sweetheart," he confessed. "I want every last ounce of pleasure you have, and I will do anything to get it."

Okay, so maybe the idea that I couldn't orgasm wasn't accurate because if he kept on talking to me like this, I might seriously just come on command.

Pushing up to straddle me, Earth lifted the hem of my

shirt, exposing my waist to his stare. "You are so small. Don't worry. I won't break you."

I had to bite my lip to keep from asking him to. *What the hell is wrong with me?*

His laugh was husky as if he knew exactly. Choosing not to point out that he clearly had me in the palm of his hand, he dragged a single finger down the center of my waist, stopping to circle my belly button.

Gasping, I pushed up on my elbow, staring down at where he touched.

"Can you feel that?"

I nodded. "My paralysis starts below my belly button, my lower waist."

Smirking, he pushed the finger just touching me against my lips. "Suck."

I obeyed instantly, not even knowing why his finger was in my mouth but licking around it anyway. When it was wet, he made a grunting sound and brought it back to my waist. Circling the small hole in my waist once, he delved inside.

I collapsed against the mattress, eyes wide as I stared at the ceiling.

It was just a belly button. It didn't go that deep. But my God, feeling the tip of his finger delve into it, feeling it massage inside, made every single muscle in my body clench.

I made a sound, a cross between fear and pure pleasure. He backed out, easily swirling around it again and then wrapping both hands around my waist to hold.

I shuddered again, the pads of his thumbs playing with the flesh beneath my belly button.

"I think I found another spot you like," he murmured, cocky pride dripping from his tongue.

I panted, and he backed off a little.

Cracking open an eye, I peeked up at him. "My doctor told me once that the skin around the neurological level of where I lost feeling could have heightened sexual response, and some found that area to be extremely erotic and pleasurable."

"I love it when you talk doctor to me."

I laughed, but it sounded more like a breathless whisper. My entire body was still trembling, feeling bereft of something it didn't have. Hungry and somewhat unsatisfied.

"Are you making fun of me?"

"Oh, baby, never." He shifted, moving farther down my legs. Hooking his fingers in the waistband of my shorts, he tugged them down, not all the way but just enough to expose more of my lower stomach. "So… about here?" he asked, caressing my waistline. It was the area above my injury.

I nodded.

In one graceful move, he lowered, trailing kisses along my belly. As he kissed, both hands delved under my shirt again, settling on my breasts.

I could barely believe this was happening. How it seemed like I'd just been resigning myself to a life I would need to fill on my own to lying in this bed with Earth over me, making me feel things that scared and excited me.

It was a brief moment of marveling because his hands started to move, kneading and massaging my breasts, rolling my nipples between his fingers.

I let out a small whine, and his tongue delved into my belly button. I arched up, my breasts flattening against his palms. Earth pressed me back down, holding me gently but with enough force to keep my body flat. He laved and licked at my belly button as I panted and tried to squirm.

He kissed all around my waist, right in the area above my injury. Tension built and built inside me. So did anxiety and the unknown.

I felt like I might snap at any moment, and I didn't know if that was good or bad.

"Earth," I said, putting enough force into my voice to make him pause and look up.

"Too much?"

"I don't know." My eyes filled with unshed tears, making his angular features seem soft.

Gliding up my body, he settled his weight on mine, my exposed stomach meeting the skin of his. He brushed some hair off my face, kissing my forehead gently.

"I'm afraid," I confessed, wrapping my arms around his shoulders to bury my face in his neck.

He let me pull him in, his weight not at all encumbering but somehow reassuring.

"I got you, sweetheart," he whispered. "I'll protect you."

I felt the words against my ear and subconsciously turned, tilting so my neck was exposed.

"I want," I whispered, not sure what to ask for.

He kissed the side of my neck, and I clutched at him for more.

"Tell me stop and I stop," he said and then dove in.

Both his arms slid between my body and the mattress, wrapping me tight against his chest. My head fell back, arching my neck more, and he rumbled low in his chest, latching on almost instantly.

My head swam.

A fine sheen of sweat pebbled my forehead.

Tension strung so tight in me that I dug my nails into his back, practically begging for release.

His nose slid along my neck, and then his lips latched on to that spot.

That perfectly weak spot.

I cried out, and then one of his hands found my waist, dragging lightly across it, a finger dipping into my belly button.

Pleasure rose. From that line of absolute injury, something else was born. Like a beautiful flower blooming impossibly from inside a sunless, wrecked building. My upper body went taut and then melted like hot butter, dripping over the arm still holding me as I literally came undone against him.

I shivered and shook, my lips quivering under the assault.

I thought I might never experience an orgasm. I thought if I did, it might hurt.

Oh, how wrong I was.

It was as if all the denied pleasure that had built up in my body for the last seven years was finally released, and it poured over me endlessly.

My whole body was boneless, my skin sensitive and hot to the touch. My nipples were still erect even though he hadn't touched them for long minutes. My neck felt wet from his mouth, and my stomach trembled.

Earth pulled back, the triumphant smile on his face giving way to worry. "V," he murmured, brushing at my cheeks. "You're crying. Did it hurt? Did I hurt you?"

"I honestly believed that wasn't possible," I whispered. "I was even too afraid to try on my own." More tears fell. My breath hitched.

"Oh, baby," he crooned, pulling me in.

I snuggled so tight against him, squishing in until I

could barely breathe. Earth rolled, pulling me along with him so I was draped over his chest and he was supporting my weight.

I sniffled all over his chest, feeling my tears drip onto his skin.

"I'm so s-sorry." I hiccupped. I was completely overwhelmed and couldn't stop the tears.

"You promise it didn't hurt?" he pressed, worry still edging his tone.

"I swear," I vowed. "That was… It was so good."

His chest expanded with pride, and if I wasn't so overcome, I would have told him not to be so cocky. All I could do was cling tighter, half shocked, half awed… all of me completely sated.

"It's okay, then. Cry all you want. I got you."

I didn't know if he completely understood. As I lay in his embrace, all I could think about was how maybe, just maybe, I wasn't half a woman. And that maybe, just maybe, I was capable of being everything he could need. Obviously, this one time wasn't enough to completely make me believe.

But a flower that bloomed in an impossible place offered hope.

And once there was hope, anything was possible.

Twenty-Nine

"Will you tell me?"

I knew the post-coital bliss would wear off eventually. Hell, I hadn't even planned on any postcoital bliss at all.

But *holy hell.*

My dick stayed in my pants the entire time, but as I lay there, I somehow felt as though I'd just had the fuck of my life.

Bringing her to ecstasy was better than any orgasm I'd had to date. Yeah, I said to date because sometime soon I was gonna get into her body, and then that fact would probably change.

Until then, I wouldn't even be suffering over here because, like I said, *holy hell.*

I don't know how long we lay there. The tears on my chest were long dried, the quivering of her body had ceased, and her sniffles had turned into even breathing. I thought perhaps she'd fallen asleep, but her question hung in the air, proving she was very much awake.

After silence stretched on and I still said nothing, her whisper filled the dimly lit room. "Say everything."

Well, fuck.

"I tried to kill Ivory. More than once."

Her body startled, and I winced as she used my chest to push herself up, planting her elbow practically in my sternum. Her eyes were so wide and round, the whites around the chestnut orbs glowed like stars in the dark. "What?"

"There's bones in here, woman." I grimaced, sliding my hand between her elbow and my chest.

"I need to sit up!" she said, pushing up. "Help me!"

"Give a girl the orgasm of her life, and then she thinks she can boss you all around," I muttered.

Her gasp filled the room. "Forget it!" she declared. "Don't help me." Her hand practically punched into my stomach as she "helped" herself.

"*Oomph!* Now, sweetheart, I was just trying to lighten the mood," I told her, grasping her gently to help her.

"Over there," she instructed, and this time, I just did what she asked, sliding her body over so her back was to the wall and her legs were stretched out in front of her.

With a small sound, she grasped her legs and positioned them so she sat cross-legged, hands in her lap. The second she was settled, her eyes came back to mine, and I knew all distraction was over and now it was time to lay it all out.

"Say that again," she requested.

"The huntsman that was after Ivory? It was me. I'm him—the Huntsman."

"You're the one her stepmother hired to kill her?"

"Yes."

"But… how?"

"I'm a contract killer. I murder for money." No point in making it sound pretty because it wasn't. It was the cold truth, and even though I didn't want to tell her, I would because there was no changing who I was.

Her body leaned heavier into the wall, her head tilting just slightly. Some of the hair in the braid wrapped around her head had come loose. Light-colored strands wisped around her cheeks and ears, making her look exactly like the sprite I had nicknamed her for.

Her eyes dipped to my hands, and I flexed them subconsciously. I knew what she was doing. Looking at the hands that killed men and women. Probably wondering how just a little while ago, she'd let these murderous hands give her pleasure when what they usually brought was pain.

"I don't kill kids." The words rushed out. Random, almost desperate, and completely unnecessary. But as she stared at the hands of a killer, perhaps imaging them covered in blood, I wanted to at least clarify even I had limits and I would never harm a child.

As if that detail made me a better man.

It didn't.

If anything, it showed I had somewhat of a conscience, and that meant I should know better than to kill anyone at all.

"The huntsman Ivory was running from, the one my brother was trying to protect her from… it was you?"

"Yes." I laughed, but it sounded more like a groan. "I told her to run away and never come back. And what did she do? Found her way onto my couch."

"But you didn't kill her."

Ah, so we were going this way, were we? With her reasoning, I must not be bad because I couldn't go through with it. Wrong.

"I've killed others. Many before her."

She leaned forward, pure curiosity in her gaze. "How many?"

Why is she leaning closer instead of away? How unnerving.

"That's a rude question."

"Trying to kill my sister is also rude," she countered. She was completely ridiculous.

"I'm not telling you."

"Why?"

Because I don't want you to know just how terrible I really am.

When it became apparent I wouldn't answer, she changed her question. "So why not Ivory, then?"

"At first, it was because I felt I owed her father."

She gasped. "You knew Ivory's father?"

I nodded. "I met him many years ago when I'd come to this country and was trying to survive. I pickpocketed him, and he caught me." I half smiled, thinking about what an inexperienced punk I was back then, thinking I knew it all.

"He didn't turn me in. Instead, he helped me. Gave me a start. I own the Rotten Apple because of him."

"And you knew Ivory was his daughter?"

"Rule number four: Do your research on your target. Rule number five: Finished your research? Do more."

"There are rules for killing?" she echoed, more inquisitive than anything.

I shrugged. "Every business has standards, and mine is no different."

"Then what happened?"

Why was she so calm? Why wasn't she smacking me and telling me how horrible I was? "You know this isn't some fairy tale, right? This is real, and it all actually happened. Even if it was a fairy tale, I would be the villain. I *am* a villain."

Her nod was sage. "I understand."

I wasn't so sure because she was still sitting here.

"I let her go. Told her to disappear and never come back."

"And you cut off all her hair and ripped her nail off!" she said, reaching up to touch her own beautiful locks.

Why are women so attached to their hair? "I sent that stuff to her stepmother and told her I'd finished the job."

"Ew! You put some hair and a bloody nail in a box and mailed it?"

"Better than a body," I deadpanned.

Her lips pursed. *I want to kiss her again.* "Well. You have a point."

"This conversation is ridiculous."

She ignored my evaluation of this talk and continued as if she thought everything was wonderful. "But then Ivory ended up in the Grimms, at your house, and my brother fell in love with her."

"I broke the rules."

"Which rule?"

My eyes flashed up. "Never make it personal."

Her quick intake of breath was filled with silent realization. The atmosphere around us shifted, the banter we had going disappeared, and the mood turned heavy. "And that's why he can't forgive you."

I wasn't surprised by the churning undercurrents in this room. I was more surprised they hadn't shown up until now. That they blew in with the mention of things becoming personal for me.

Virginia was perceptive, though. Very, *very* perceptive to understand something not even Neo and I could entirely work out after so long. But after earlier, I wouldn't even be able to deny what I knew she was likely about to say, the real reason he struggled to forgive.

Uncomfortable, my jaw tightened as my eyes looked everywhere but at her.

"You love her," she whispered, curling back against the wall, those words somehow much more heinous to her than the fact I was a killer.

If I wasn't so caught off guard, I might have enjoyed her jealousy.

"No!" I refused, eyes flying up to hers. *You should know better.* "I don't. I never did."

"I wouldn't blame you. Ivory is the fairest of them all." Her voice was small.

"She isn't you!" I burst out.

The confession hung between us, thick like humid air.

"Then why does my brother despise you so much?" she asked.

The guttural sound I made reflected how much I hated those words, words I never wanted to say out loud but would just to make this woman understand. "Because she made me feel. Somehow her stupid shrieking and ridiculous haughty behavior got under my skin. I saw the way my brothers fawned over her. I knew Neo was falling deep. And I just... I couldn't do it. I couldn't kill her. For the first time in forever, she made me hesitate to kill."

"Sounds kinda like love." Goddamn that insecurity in her voice, the doubt and hurt in her stare.

I leaned close, ferocious with my words. "Listen here, sprite. I'm a bad guy, but I'm loyal to a fault. If I loved her, there is no way in hell I would have done what I just did with you. Ivory is my family, but you... you have my heart."

"Family doesn't turn their back on family. Even if

they turn their back on you," she murmured almost as though she were coming to a realization.

I glowered. "Now is not the time for movie quotes, sprite. I'm trying to have a conversation."

The room was so dim, but it didn't matter. It didn't conceal the brunet eyes gazing at me like I was some kind of puzzle she'd put together, missing that final piece.

"Neo said that to me. I thought he meant it was you who turned your back on him."

"My whole life blew up because I didn't." I grumped. What an asshole. Couldn't he at least give me *some* credit for not killing his girl?

"He meant him. He was the one who turned his back, but you stayed. You still came when he called. You waited for him to forgive you."

"He still hasn't."

She made a soft sound. "My brother forgave you a long time ago for the lies and even the killing."

"He can barely be in the same room with me."

"But he never turned you in. He helped the rest of the family protect you."

Something inside my gut squirmed. "I don't need protecting."

"Everyone needs protecting sometimes."

That soft-spoken rebuttable sank into me like a pebble thrown into a bottomless sea. I felt it sink, traveling into my deepest depths to my most carefully guarded memories of another time and place.

A time when protection was also betrayal.

Her voice seemed far away at first, but even with the distance, I could hear every word. "Neo's always considered you family, but he thought you were in love with Ivory. With the one woman he's been able to open up to since our parents died. He couldn't give her up, even thinking you wanted her. He was stuck. Looking at you probably made him feel guilty for taking something you wanted, so he blamed you instead. He turned his back, but he wasn't able to cut you out of our lives."

"He cut me out of yours." *I can't even blame him for it.*

"Maybe for a little while, but then he invited you back in. Because he trusts you. Even with me."

A rude noise filled the room. "The bruises on my face say otherwise."

He thought I was going after you because I couldn't have Ivory. That thought—those words Neo gave voice to— burned in the back of my throat like acrid stomach acid, tossing itself up my esophagus, making me feel like my insides were on fire.

I'd never tell her what he said. I'd never put that doubt in her mind. It wasn't true, not even just a little. And to be honest, it still one hundred percent pissed me off Neo would even think that. That he would think V wasn't better than that.

Dude can't see past Ivory.

Everything revolves around her, even his own sister. And that's how I knew what Virginia was saying right now was right. That stone of knowledge V tossed into my sea settled inside me, rippling with truth.

I couldn't even be mad for any of it. I understood. Because now, for me, everything revolved around Virginia.

"He's very protective."

"He's an asshole."

"So are you."

I barked a laugh. "Touché."

"He'll come around. If he really was dead set against us, he would have gotten rid of you already."

I snorted. "Like he could."

"He's done it before."

My spine snapped up, and a cold feeling I recognized well unfurled within me. "What does that mean?"

"Nothing," V murmured, glancing down into her lap.

"*Virginia*," I commanded, absolutely unwilling to let that go.

"We're talking about you."

Despite the murderous way I felt and the fact I wanted answers yesterday, I was still gentle when I pushed her chin up so I could look into her eyes. "What did Neo do, sweetheart?"

The tip of her small pink tongue darted out to wet her lips, a nervous reaction that made my gut tighten and the pads of my fingers jolt lightly against the underside of her jaw.

"There was this physical therapist that used to work here," she said. "Maybe you remember seeing him around. His name was Jake."

I searched my memory, thinking back to the times we'd all be here and how sometimes a nurse would come in to get her for PT. The vague memory of a tall guy in khakis and a polo came to mind, and my eyes narrowed.

"He's the one that called you sprite." My voice was a mere rumble.

She nodded. "We, ah, got close. I liked him, and he liked me. One day after PT, he was going to kiss me."

A low growl vibrated my lips at the idea of anyone touching what was mine.

"Neo walked in and saw us. You can imagine his reaction."

My upper lip curled. "I hope he decked him."

"Not only did he deck him, but he accused him of

sexually harassing a disabled patient, taking advantage of me, *and* he got him fired."

I made a gruff sound. For once, I agreed with Neo on something. "Good."

V gasped, crossing her arms over her chest. "It is not! That man lost his PT license because of my brother's accusations! And no one would listen to me, the girl in the wheelchair. As if my legs not working somehow make it so my brain and heart can't work too."

"You liked him," I observed, keeping my voice neutral even though the idea made the poison in my veins bubble up.

"Yes." Her voice was small. "And I thought he liked me."

"He didn't fight for you, though, did he? He let Neo chase him off, and he never looked back."

Coward.

"Guess I wasn't worth the fight."

Her light squeak was kinda cute when I jolted forward to slide my hands under her arms to drag her forward.

Holding her up like a rag doll, I pinned her with a hard gaze. "He wasn't worthy of you."

Her eyes bounced between mine, her lower lip quivering slightly. "Are you?"

"No," I said immediately because it was the truth.

Her lashes swept downward, fanning across her cheeks and hiding the hurt in her gaze. I wouldn't apologize, though, because it was the truth. Virginia was way too good for me, and it was wrong I was still here. But I wouldn't walk away. I wouldn't leave her behind to sit and think she wasn't worth the fight.

"Help me." I beckoned softly, pulling her into my lap. Her eyes reopened, gaze shuttered. But she helped me settle her, positioning her so she was straddling my lap and I was leaning against the wall.

When both her legs were on either side of me, my hands slipped up to her waist, fingers splaying out high enough so she could feel me holding her.

"Okay?" I asked, making sure the position was comfortable.

She nodded.

"Eyes on me."

She listened immediately, making my chest feel tight with pride.

"I'm not good enough for you, sweetheart. I never will be." Her lips parted, but I placed a finger against them, keeping her quiet. "But I want you anyway, and I'm not honorable enough to let you go. I will fight for you. I will kill for you. I will hurt you. The only person on this planet that could make me walk away from you is you. Tell me to go. Tell me to just love you from afar. It's safer for us both."

One glistening tear fell from her eyelashes to slide gracefully down her cheek. "I don't want you to go. I won't send you away."

"Fifteen."

"What?"

"That's how many people I've killed. And I've hurt and nearly killed many more."

Her eyes widened.

"The kills I've made were not accidents. They were choices I made. I like the control I feel when I make a kill, the freedom that comes after. I like living on my own terms, by my own rules."

"My spine is shattered. I'll never be able to walk. I've been living trapped up in a tower for over seven years. I don't have much self-confidence. I don't have any money, and I don't even know if I can hold down a job. Having a romantic relationship with someone like me might be unsatisfying because I can't feel like a normal woman. Everything takes me twice as long, and I need special equipment and wheelchair-accessible places. Going to the bathroom takes extra time, and to be honest, it's gross the things I have to do. My life will always be filled with doctor visits, therapy, and everywhere I go, someone will stare and might even say something rude."

"I'll kill them," I intoned, deadly calm.

"You can't. I won't let you." She went on. "And then there's my bossy brother. He'll always be a huge part of my life."

"What are you doing right now?" I asked.

"Aren't you trying to scare me off with a list of your bad qualities? I have a list too."

This was absolutely ridiculous. "Being a murderer is a lot different than being paralyzed. They don't compare."

"Well, you can stop, but I can't."

I stilled. "Are you asking me to stop killing?" *Are you saying you would be with me?*

The request was small and timid. "Would you?"

I swallowed. "And if I did that, you could just forget about the fifteen other people I told you about?"

"Maybe not forget them, but I could forgive."

"Why?"

"Because I'd rather love you than hate you."

A broken sound filled the room, and I crushed her to me, merging our lips and refusing to let go. I kissed with a passion greater than the venom in my veins, wishing I could crawl inside her and live beneath her skin.

I was a man who lived and breathed nothing but hate,

a man who, up until recently, didn't understand he could choose something else.

Until her.

Until Virginia smiled in the face of my grumbling, found solace in my cold heart, and looked at me with eyes filled with everything but fear.

She made me feel like it didn't matter I was poison because she could be my antidote. With her, I wanted to be better, but even if I wasn't, she would accept me the way I was.

I pulled back abruptly, but her sound of surprise made me lean back in to kiss her quickly. My fingers tried to bury themselves in her silky hair, but that damn braid was in the way.

Digging in, I loosened the style, pulling out the clips and pins holding it in place and watching it tumble in very long waves over her shoulders to curl into our laps.

"God, you are so fucking beautiful," I swore, pulling my fingers through the freed strands. They clung and curled around my digits, making me feel even more possessive. Golden-hued waves framed her small face, making her eyes seem even larger.

Her cheek nuzzled toward my hand, and I cupped it, caressing her softness with my thumb.

"I stopped taking jobs after Ivory." I spoke quietly, not wanting to ruin the magic swirling around us with a loud voice.

Her perky nose turned up with the news. "Really?"

"Really." I promised. "I would stop if you asked me to, but I already have."

This time, her palms landed on either side of my face, holding me prone so she could kiss me. I could taste the smile on her lips.

"That means so much more because you did it for you and no one else."

I cleared my throat.

She tilted her head. "Someone else asked you to stop?"

"Fletcher was pretty upset…"

She giggled.

"What's so funny?" I demanded, instantly annoyed.

"You really do have such a soft spot for him."

My annoyance faded, and I tugged on a piece of her hair. "Not as soft as the one I have for you."

She snuggled into my chest, curling both arms between us, resting her cheek on my shoulder, and gently rubbing her nose against my throat.

"I knew I was done before anyone asked," I whispered softly, dragging my palm down her back. "I just couldn't stay detached anymore."

"Because of Ivory."

"Because the idea of telling the family who I really was made me ashamed. You know, if Neo hadn't told you… I probably wouldn't have."

"You thought I would hate you?" Her lips tickled against my neck with every word she spoke. It brought on a sense of calm, a sense of rightness.

"I didn't want to be the villain in your story, but lying about it only made me more of the villain I pretended not to be."

"What about our story?"

I stopped stroking her back. Her body rose and fell with the deep breath I took. "*Our* story?"

"What if I don't want to have my own story? What if I want to have one with you?"

As I tugged her away from my chest, cool air whooshed between our bodies, trying to chill the heat between us. Pushing her hair back from her face, I held her head, staring intently into her shy expression.

"You'd really accept me?" I whispered, awe grabbing my heart, squeezing until it could barely beat.

"I already have."

"Be careful what you ask for, sprite. I don't let go, and I don't play fair. Once you're mine, I won't ever let you go."

"Y-you would want someone like me?"

"*You* are the only one I want."

More tears spilled over her cheeks, and I brushed them away. My heart was beating heavily. The urge to claim and own was the rhythm by which it beat. I never thought such darkness could be attracted to such light, but the way I wanted her was completely undeniable.

Her teeth sank into her lower lip, worrying the flesh I'd just loved with my tongue. Reaching up, I tugged it free. "What is it?"

"I really do accept you. It's just—"

"Say everything," I reminded her softly, stroking the length of her hair in hopes of reassuring her.

"You won't take any more jobs like that? I just... I don't..." Her sigh trembled, and it made my heart turn over. It made me want to rip apart the world to give her whatever she asked for. "The thought of you out there doing that. You're so much better, Earth, so much better than death."

She wanted assurance I wouldn't start killing again, but she felt guilty asking for it because she wanted to accept me as I was.

I wasn't offended. How could I be? I knew she accepted me. Hell, I would even go so far as to suspect she loved me. She fell before she knew I stopped. She called me even after Neo told her what I was.

Virginia had every right to ask me to stop. She had every right to help write *our* story. I couldn't even blame her for not wanting it to be a murder book.

I didn't blindly promise. Instead, I took a moment to look deep.

I thought about the craving I still sometimes got to kill. About the way my eyes would sometimes stray to that ringing secret phone. I thought about the pollution in my veins and how running away hadn't kept me from the life I was born into.

"Eyes on me." I beckoned, and hers were there instantly, filled with yearning and apprehension.

I smiled, rubbing my thumb along the underside of her lower lip.

"I swear I won't take any more jobs. I won't kill for money. I'll toss out my contact phone and never get another."

"You have a contact phone?" She wondered.

I shrugged. "How else would I get jobs?"

Her nose wrinkled, and it made my heart turn over. "What kind of people hire someone to kill for them?"

"Cowards."

"You really will stop?"

"I swear."

She smiled, and my heart leaped down into my stomach. *She is saying yes. She is mine.*

Her face leaned in, but I leaned back. Her eyes widened, and then she scowled. "Did you change your mind already?"

I laughed. "Oh no, sprite, I'm forever yours."

She tried to kiss me again.

Again, I fended her off. "I want to make something clear."

She sat back, hands falling between us.

"I won't take any more jobs. I'll keep my hands as clean as I can."

Her eyes narrowed. "But?"

"But I will do anything to protect you. And I mean anything."

She rolled her eyes. "You act like I live some wild, dangerous life."

"Not you. Me."

Her breath caught.

"Being around me comes with a certain kind of risk. I thought about disappearing—"

"No!" She flung herself against my chest, arms winding tightly around my neck. "You can't leave." Her voice cracked, arms quivering. "You can't. Promise me."

Possessiveness swelled along with an amazing sense of satisfaction that the idea of me leaving made her so distraught. I'd never been wanted before. I'd never been needed.

Sure, my brothers relied on me, but this was entirely different.

It felt good. Better than I ever thought it could.

"I'm not leaving, sweetheart. I promise."

She pushed up, her eyelashes damp and strands of hair clinging to her cheeks. "I've lost so many people in my life. My world is very small, Earth. Most of it is just inside this windowless room. You make my world bigger, and I'm already very attached to you. Please don't take that away from me. Please."

My back left the wall, my body pushing into her space, claiming it as my own. When I licked across her lips, she parted with a sigh, and I delved deep into the warm cavern of her mouth, kissing until my lungs nearly collapsed from lack of air.

"Try and get rid of me," I whispered, nudging her nose with mine.

Her hands came up to rest over my ears, her fingers playing in the strands of my hair.

"But just know that when it comes to protecting what's mine, I don't have limits. I will kill, and I won't think twice."

"Okay." She accepted, wrapping her arms around me and pressing close.

"Okay?"

"Mm-hmm." She agreed, tugging on my neck. "Closer, E. I want closer."

Tingles erupted over my scalp. I fucking loved the way she clung to me. I loved that she was mine and mine alone.

Honoring her request, I dragged her closer, making it so our fronts were pressed together. She sighed, resting her chin on my shoulder. Her hair was so long it was like a blanket covering us both.

"Mine," I whispered roughly, taking her with me as I leaned back against the wall.

"Yours," she purred beside my ear, making hot desire nearly dissolve my skin.

I just hoped she didn't regret this when I had to prove just how serious I was about doing anything to protect her.

Thirty

Virginia

I KNEW HIM *BEFORE* I KNEW HIM.

When you first meet a person, you get an unspoken sense of them. Be it the vibes they naturally radiate, the aura blooming around them, or simply an instinct down in your gut. This first impression is often influenced afterward by the way they dress, speak, and behave. And often, people are fooled.

Actions indeed speak louder than words.

But vibes *never* lie.

I'd known Earth for roughly five years now. We spent holidays, birthdays, and more random family visits together than I could count. He was grumpy, short-spoken, and intimidating. He always wore leather or black, always needed a haircut, and was always a breath away from yelling at someone. Except for a certain snorty dog he saved from being euthanized at an over-filled shelter in the ghetto.

He also opened up his home to my brother when he was essentially living on the streets and stealing money to make sure I had care. Neo was in a murky place all those years ago. He tried to hide it from me of course, but as I mentioned, vibes never lie. I could only imagine what it was like to bury our parents, pack up their home, and sell everything off all alone while the only other survivor of a crash he blamed himself for lay paralyzed in a hospital.

He went from a sixteen-year-old kid with a date at the movies to the instant guardian of his newly disabled little sister. All his personal dreams and goals vanished as though they were never even there, but I knew he felt the gaping hole they left behind.

When social services tried to take us, he put up a huge fight and somehow kept us together. I didn't even know all the details of how he managed because he would never tell me, and I'd been too weak back then to argue. Later, when I was stronger, it didn't seem to matter anymore.

I do know it got easier for him when he met Earth. When Earth brought him to his apartment and gave him a home. I knew there were months when Neo couldn't pay rent, but Earth let him stay anyway.

Earth was undoubtedly a grouchy, mean-tempered man. But he also invited three lonely misfits into his one-bedroom apartment in the ghetto and made them a family. A family I was a part of.

All of them were criminals. All of them did what they had to in order to survive. But criminals weren't all they were.

They were my brothers. My family.

They brought me candy and magazines when they came to visit. Made me laugh with dumb jokes, played cards and video games but didn't just let me win. Never once did any of them act like I wasn't good enough because I couldn't walk.

So *yes*. I could forgive Earth for the things I didn't know about him because of all the things I did know.

My mom used to say, *You don't have to like someone to love them.*

She was right.

I didn't like that part of Earth, but I didn't have to like every part of him to love him.

And I did love him.

I tried gallantly to keep my eyes open. Sleep seemed such a waste of time. The excitement and curiosity I felt with Earth were so refreshing to my normally repetitive and boring days. My mind spun with so many questions, so many things I longed to know.

So many feelings to experience.

Alas, sleep was like a seductive siren coaxing me under with the strength of Earth's warm body, the feel of his skin beneath my cheek, and the lullaby of his beating heart. His soft, rumbly promise to stay with me through the night wrapped me in the most comfortable blanket of safety I hadn't realized I lacked.

Oddly, the confession of his savage behavior did not scare me in the least. In fact, it reassured me more, and so I tumbled into slumber, knowing it didn't matter where I landed because he would be there too.

Unfortunately, I did not wake with the same sort of gentle lulling.

"I told you to go home!" The exclamation cut right through my sleep, but it was the stiffening body and quick way it moved that had my eyes shooting open.

It wasn't alarm I felt, though. It was the loss of his heat and closeness.

"Don't you knock?" Earth ground out, no trace of sleep in his voice at all.

Lying on my side, my back was to the room, so I glanced over my shoulder where my sleep-hazy eyes met with the wall of his back, which was tight with tension.

The way he was planted in front of me like a shield made my stomach flip.

"What the hell do I need to knock for?" Emogen sassed.

"Because this ain't your room. Because she could have been undressed—"

Emogen made a scoffing sound. "She ain't got nothing I haven't seen before."

The muscles in his back, which had started to relax, rippled anew, and a low, ferocious growl filled the room. My stomach flipped again.

Earth took a menacing step forward toward my best friend. "The fuck did you just say?"

"You better watch your mouth," Emogen warned, her deep eyes narrowing.

I made a small sound. "Earth."

He spun, eyes landing on me and morphing into something much softer. I loved the possessive way his eyes roamed me. I loved how he seemed to measure every inch to make sure I was unharmed.

It was unnecessary and ridiculous, but it still made my heart flutter.

I reached an arm across the mattress, still feeling his body heat on the sheets where he'd lain. He came back instantly, resting a knee on the bed and leaning over me. "Hey there, sprite." His voice was gravelly and low, just for me. "You need a lock on that door."

"What do I need a lock for when I have you?"

He grunted, eyes dipping toward my mouth to linger there.

"You sleep okay?" he asked, using a finger to brush the hair off my cheek.

"Better than okay," I whispered.

The intensity of his stare increased.

"I wasn't on my side when I fell asleep," I observed, recalling how I'd been draped across his chest.

"I moved us. Are you uncomfortable?" A look of concern draped over his Asian features, and he nudged back, ready to move me.

"How could I be uncomfortable with you beside me?"

He paused, eyes lifting back to mine.

Emogen cleared her throat extra loud. "Did y'all forget you weren't alone? And this ain't some Motel 6 where we welcome random guests. We have rules here, and sleepovers are a no-go."

"You think I'm gonna let my girl sleep here alone with some rabid beast down the hall?"

"He's not—" Emogen stopped whatever she was about to say and leaned around him to raise an eyebrow at me. "Your girl?"

I giggled.

"Mine. Now get out," Earth intoned.

Emogen wasn't one to be bossed around, and it was far too early to listen to them bicker.

"Could we maybe have a few minutes?" I asked her sweetly.

Her eyes rounded, and a look of exasperation clouded her face.

"Please?"

"Girl, you're lucky I love you, because if it was anyone else sneaking a man up in here, I'd already be hauling him out by his ears!"

"Just try me." Earth challenged.

Pushing into a sitting position, I called out for him again.

He was there, the mattress dipping under his weight, all his attention on me.

"Fine." Emogen allowed. "But if anyone else catches you, you're on your own."

Earth made a sound, acknowledging her words. "Shut the door on your way out."

Emogen did, muttering the whole way.

"I'm gonna hear about that from her." I scolded him.

His face darkened. "I don't like people having such easy access to this room."

I shrugged. "It's always been that way."

"I don't like it," he repeated.

"Help me stretch?" I requested, holding out my arms and wiggling my fingers.

When he took hold of me, I leaned back, using him as an anchor to help stretch out some of my upper body. When I released him to lean forward to stretch my legs, he watched quietly.

"Do you do this every morning?"

I nodded, face still near my knees. "I'm usually in the same position all night every night. It causes my muscles to get sore and tense."

He didn't say anything, but I felt his quiet, so I unfolded to smile. "But I'm not as cramped up this morning because someone adjusted me in the middle of the night."

"Consider it done."

I paused, glancing up. "What?"

"I'll adjust you every night from now on."

"Every night?" I echoed as a tingling sensation tickled my stomach.

"Mmm." He slid closer. His hand curled around the back of my neck, pad of his thumb brushing over that very sensitive spot he'd discovered last night.

Shivers of awareness prickled my skin as our lips met

gently, and I found myself waking all over again, this time in a much more pleasant way.

Warmth bloomed through my limbs, spreading down my arms and up to the tips of my ears. Lips nudging, he coaxed mine apart, tangling our tongues together as his fingers did the same in my hair.

The kiss was lazy, and I explored the expanse of his bare chest with my palms, rubbing over him, curling around his back, and trying to draw him closer.

All at once, he moved, still kissing as he crawled up the bed, kneeling on his knees with my legs between them. The second my fingers slipped beneath the gapping waistband of his jeans, he pulled away.

I made a disappointed sound, and he smiled.

It completely distracted me. "You have a beautiful smile."

Surprise and then something akin to embarrassment flashed through his eyes. "You trying to sweet-talk me for more kisses?"

"Is it working?" I was hopeful.

"No."

I pouted, and he climbed off the bed. I noticed the way he reached in front of him slightly, adjusting himself before turning back to the bed.

My eyes dropped right to the front of his jeans.

"Stop it."

Biting my lip, I looked up. "You don't like it?"

"I like it too much, but there's no lock on the door, and that fire-breathing nurse is probably still pacing the hall."

He was clearly going to be salty about the no-lock situation forever.

"Emogen is my best friend. Be nice to her."

He made a face.

I made one back.

"Earth?" He must have heard the hesitation in my voice because, when he replied, he was gentle.

"What, sprite?"

"I have to pee."

He was there instantly, slipping his arms under my body and lifting me like I weighed nothing at all. His strides were quick into the bathroom, but then he halted in the center to look at me questioningly.

"Now what?"

"I just need my wheelchair."

"You don't need that. You have me."

My face burned at what he implied, and I ducked into his chest. "I won't do that in front of you!"

"Why the hell not?" he demanded.

"It's embarrassing!"

"Why would you be embarrassed in front of me?"

"Earth," I whined.

Carrying me to my chair, he placed me in easily, then pushed me back into the bathroom. "Please tell me there's a lock on this door."

My lips folded inward.

Incredulous, he parted his lips. "You've got to be kidding me!"

"If there is an accident or I fall, they need to be able to get to me immediately."

Worry transformed his face. "Is this room not safe enough? What kind of place is this?" he insisted. "I'm not leaving. Just do what you need to do in front of me." He crossed his arms over his chest.

"You are so dramatic," I muttered. "This place is perfectly safe. It's handicap-accessible. But accidents still happen."

He made a face, still unmoving.

"If you don't go, I'll pee myself, and then I'll cry."

His arms dropped. "I'll wait outside."

Finally alone in the bathroom, I blew out a breath and grabbed an intermittent catheter. I went almost on autopilot, doing what I needed to do and emptying my bladder. After disposing of it, I washed my hands at the sink and quickly brushed my teeth.

A glance in the mirror made me draw up short. My eyes were bright, cheeks pink, and there was just this… *glow*. Was this what happiness looked like? But I'd been happy before, hadn't I?

Love.

This is what love looked like.

There was a swift knock on the door. "Sprite?"

I rolled my eyes. "I'm fine. I'll be right there."

Before leaving the bathroom, I applied some lip balm and grabbed my brush. The second I appeared, he appraised me like he was looking for injury.

"I go to the bathroom every day." I admonished.

"You made it in time?" he asked, still concerned. "That didn't happen again, did it?"

Realization dawned on me. The last time he'd seen me when I had to go to the bathroom, I'd been pretty much on the verge of some sort of bodily panic attack.

I held out my hand, and he entwined our fingers instantly, sinking down in front of me. "I guess that scared you last time, huh?"

"I didn't like it."

Seeing a worried Earth was new for me. *Why is he so cute like this?* I smiled. "I'm fine, okay? That doesn't happen very often at all."

He nodded. "Is that why she came in here earlier? Does she usually help you in the morning?"

I nodded. "Emogen helps me get up and moving.

Sometimes she helps me stretch or massages any muscle cramps or spasms I might have." His eyes widened. I squeezed his hand. "I didn't have any this morning, probably because you moved me in the night."

"I'll do it every night," he vowed.

I smiled. I should have told him he didn't have to, but really, I kinda liked he wanted to.

"But after that, she usually goes on with all her other duties. I'm pretty self-reliant. I can do my morning routine myself."

"What else do you need to do?"

I ducked my face, shy.

Using our clasped hands, he pushed my chin up so I was looking at him once more. "I want to know everything," he murmured, voice soft. "I want to know all about you and your daily life. The pretty parts are so easy to see, but I want the not so pretty too. I want to know your challenges, and I want to know how I can make them easier."

"And if you can't make them easier?" I asked, feeling emotion welling tightly in my chest.

"Then I'll just be proud of you for doing the hard stuff."

I sniffled. "Being with someone like me... it's not easy."

"You think I'm an easy guy?"

I giggled. "But I'm embarrassed," I confessed. "If you knew some of the things I had to do, I might not be as pretty to you."

"Oh, sweetheart," he murmured, chest coming up against my knees as he moved closer. His hands delved into my hair, the pads of his fingers massaging against my scalp. I liked that when he touched my lower body, he always seemed to touch higher too so I was never missing the feel of his touch.

And his touch was incredible. So much so that my eyes fluttered closed.

"You will always be the most beautiful to me. Beautiful despite an ugly world. Nothing you could do will ever change that."

I swallowed heavily and then took a breath. "I have to do a saline enema to, you know… clean out my bowels."

"Still beautiful," he whispered.

My head lifted, eyes searching his.

He smiled.

His smile was borderline devastating to me.

"I have to take medication to help relax my bladder so I don't pee myself. And I also take medication in the evenings to help with the other thing I just mentioned."

"It's okay, sweetheart."

"And you know how I mentioned that my insides still worked? Like all my, ah, girl parts?"

He nodded, encouraging me. Some of the tightness in my chest loosened.

"Well, I still get my monthly cycle. Sometimes I make a mess on myself."

"Hmm."

"But not often!" I hurried to add. "I'm usually really good about it. But sometimes if it comes before it's supposed to, I can't always tell right away."

"Does that mean you can get pregnant?"

My eyes went wide. I stared at him, unblinking.

"Well, don't you think I should know?"

Heat curled beneath my skin at the sudden image of my belly swollen with his baby. I'd never in a million years thought I'd ever think about being a mother.

"Yes." The word rushed out breathy. "I can get pregnant."

He frowned. "Wouldn't that be dangerous?"

"No. I could actually carry a healthy baby to term."

His eyes slipped to my middle. "You want kids?"

"I never thought about it," I admitted. "I always just assumed it wouldn't happen."

"I'm not father material."

"I think you'd be a wonderful father."

"I have poison in my veins, and they would have it in theirs too." His voice was hard and sort of angry. But it all seemed to be directed inward.

"Okay," I said easily.

He seemed surprised. "Okay?"

I nodded.

He jumped to his feet, paced away, then turned. "How can you just give up a family so easily like that? And for me!"

Is he mad I agreed with him? "I'm not giving anything up if I have you."

There was a heavy thud when his knees hit the floor in front of me.

"Earth!" I worried. The floor was hard!

His arms stretched around my waist, drawing me away from the back of my chair, hugging my middle tight as his head fell into my lap.

Neo did something similar not long ago, but this was entirely different. Neo's emotions had been heavy and sad. He was a brother seeking solace.

But Earth. Earth was fierce and near desperate, holding on to me as if he dared anyone or anything to try and rip me away. His body was rigid, his hold tight. Underneath it all was an unmistakable softness, a wielding of his usually hardened heart.

"*Salanghae*," he whispered, fingers curling into my back.

Time stopped. Everything did. How powerful he was to be able to suspend me in a place where all that existed was just me and that single whispered word.

Perhaps he thought I wouldn't be able to hear him. Perhaps he figured if I did, I wouldn't understand.

Oh, but I did. I understood the Korean he spoke, not just with my brain but with my heart.

I love you.

My voice was trembling when I found my way back, my heart so overfull that I could scarcely speak. "E-Earth?"

He pushed a little closer, his inky black hair rubbing against my stomach, and being able to feel that as well as see it made it even better.

Suddenly, his head lifted, eyes so shiny that I would have been able to see my reflection if they weren't also bottomless. He looked at me like I was all he saw—no—like I was all that existed and I was all he needed to survive.

Unable to breathe, I stared back at him, unblinking, my arms gripping his biceps.

"Don't ever be embarrassed. Nothing, and I mean absolutely nothing, could ever take away what I feel for you. What you are to me."

It took a moment, but my lungs finally shuddered, and I was able to draw in a breath.

Still transfixed by the galaxy of his stare, I said, "All of this because I agreed not to have kids?"

"No," he rasped, voice ragged and hoarse. "Because you picked me."

My lungs were burning again. Collapsing without

oxygen, but I couldn't seem to care. Tears welled up behind my eyes, forcing wetness into the corners.

"Of course I did," I told him, pushing the hair back from his forehead. "Salanghae."

His pupils blew wide, and his nostrils flared. He surged to his feet, pulling me along with him, holding me high so my feet floated over the floor.

A girl doesn't need legs to fly.

The room seemed to implode the second our lips met, my body lowering just enough to meld against his as we kissed endlessly while the meaning of that whispered word created a bubble around us.

I love you.

Thirty-One

SHE CHOSE ME.

In spite of who I am and the foul deeds I've done.

Even if I never kill again, I will always have the heart of a killer.

She loves me.

And now I wouldn't just kill for her.

I'd die for her too.

Thirty-Two

"TAKE THIS."

I stared at the item he extended between us like it was a three-headed baby alien he'd just pulled out of his belly button.

In reality, it was the small knife he carried around in his boot.

"I appreciate you thinking of me for a gift—" I started.

He made a rude noise. "This is not a gift. It's a weapon."

"Well, I was trying to be polite!" I admonished. "You seem to really like knives, so I thought maybe this was your idea of a gift."

He laughed. "Even I know better than that."

I glanced down at the small blade dubiously. "I don't want it."

"Why?"

"Because you tried to stab my brother with it."

"I did not try and stab your brother. He attacked me, and I protected myself."

"I don't need it."

Pursing his lips, he backed up until he came up against

my dresser. Leaning back against it, he crossed one ankle over the other and stared. "You called me last night when you thought someone was breaking into this room."

"I was scared."

"What if that crazed patient burst in here like a beast and came at you? What were you going to do?"

I glanced at the lamp I'd briefly thought of trying to grab.

Earth's gaze followed mine. "Could you have reached that in time? What if he just took it away from you?"

The rush of helplessness I'd felt last night washed over me again. How I'd felt like a sitting duck, waiting to get picked off. The truth was sometimes I was more vulnerable than most people. I wasn't able to move with the same agility, and protecting myself was harder.

"There's not even a lock on that door," he spat.

"I was thinking of moving out," I blurted.

Straightening away from the dresser, he frowned. "What? Where would you go?"

"Well, I've been talking to Neo. He mentioned maybe me moving in with him and Ivory."

"You want to do that?"

"I think I'm ready to move on from this room. I mentioned getting my own place—"

"No."

My mouth fell open. "Excuse me?"

"You can't just live alone."

"Yes, I can." It would take some adjustments, but I could.

"No."

"Why not?"

"Because I'd worry about you every minute."

I deflated, sinking back into my chair. How could I be

mad that he cared? Oddly, it was much more endearing than Neo telling me no.

"Well, that's why he suggested I move in with him and Ivory, so I wouldn't be alone."

"Her place is nice." He allowed, almost bitterly.

I bit the inside of my cheek to keep from laughing. He was trying, and I wouldn't laugh. "It's very beautiful, but my brother is there."

"What about me?" he demanded.

"Are you jealous?" I couldn't help but tease.

A sour look crossed his features, and he crossed his arms over his chest. "No."

I smiled and turned my voice sweet. "Would you come see me at Ivory's?"

"Neo probably wouldn't let me in the door," he grumped.

I hid a smile. "Well, at least there are locks there."

He was not amused by my observation.

Giggling, I held out my hand, wiggling my fingers at him. He came forward to take them but kept his expression foul.

"I could just stay here."

The grump-tastic expression cleared, and his eyes shot to mine with surprise.

"It's closer to you," I explained.

Emotion passed behind his eyes, but then it was gone. "Ivory's is safer."

"Ivory's house has windows," I recalled wistfully. They looked out over Central Park, and it really was like being perched in your own private tower.

"It's also probably wheelchair accessible," he pointed out.

"Well, it does have an elevator."

"It would be good for you. You deserve better than this place."

"Can I see that knife?" I asked, giving his hand a little tug.

He brought it back out, lying in the center of his palm. It was a smaller knife, one that he kept in his boot. It was much different from the one he used a harness for, which was draped over the foot of my bed.

"I guess I could take it, at least until I move."

He made a low sound. "You don't have to. I'll stay here at night anyway. You won't need it."

"Then why did you try and give it to me before?"

"Because I worry about you when I'm not here."

"I've managed for five years in this place."

"Well, now there's a roaring beast down the hall."

"Did you see him?" I whispered.

"No."

"He must be in a lot of pain."

Earth tilted his head to the side. "Why do you think that?"

"Why else would he be carrying on like that?"

"Because he's an asshole."

I shook my head. "'Anger is never without reason, but seldom with a good one.' Benjamin Franklin said that, and I think it fits here. The man down the hall is definitely angry. He's probably been through something horrible."

Closing the distance between us, Earth kissed me deep and slow.

When he eased back, I slipped the knife from his hand into my lap. "I'll keep it with me, okay?"

He kissed me again. "How about I come back and get you in a couple hours, take you out for a while before I have to work?"

I perked up. "Really?"

I threw myself at him, wrapping my arms around his neck. "I can't wait!"

He pressed a kiss to my forehead before standing. "Think about where you want to go."

"I don't care where we go as long as I'm with you."

He tried to hide it, but I saw the small smile form on his lips. "If anyone comes in here just stab them."

"Earth!" I admonished.

This time, his smile was unmistakable. Crossing the room, he pulled on the harness with the very wicked-looking blade against his back. When he pulled on his leather jacket, all trace of it was gone.

"Do you carry that all the time?" I asked.

He nodded. "In my world, a man doesn't walk around without protection."

"Most people carry guns," I commented.

"Not me."

What kind of world does he live in? Why does it feel like it is different than the one the rest of us know?

"Earth?"

"What, sweetheart?"

"Where are your parents?"

He stilled, the question catching him off guard. I hadn't meant to surprise him so much, but I also couldn't help wondering.

He came to this city as a young kid who had nothing. He ended up an assassin and spoke of living in a world where he needed to protect himself.

"Dead." He said it flat, almost emotionless. But I knew. His emotion was there, just much deeper than most.

"Like mine," I whispered, sympathetic because I also knew what it was like to lose parents too young.

"No." This time, the passion and emotion in his voice were unmistakable, and it brought my head up. "Not like yours. Your parents were good people who died tragically through no fault of their own."

"A-and yours?"

"Mine died because of the way they lived."

"That must be very difficult for you."

"Actually, what's more difficult is the relief I felt when they were gone."

The hurt that statement caused had the breath whooshing out of me. "Oh, babe."

"Babe?" He lifted an eyebrow curiously.

I didn't even realize I'd said it out loud. I nodded, acknowledging that I did indeed call him that.

His eyes softened, lingering on my face the entire time he moved forward to press another kiss against my lips. Before pulling away, he rubbed our noses together, making me giggle.

Another kiss against my temple, a slight brush of his fingertips against that spot on the back of my neck.

"I'll be back in a little while, sprite. Miss me while I'm gone."

I watched him stride out the door, all long legs and black boots. I wanted to tell him I would definitely miss him, but I couldn't seem to get the words out. I was too full of butterflies, skin still tingling from his brief caress.

The tip of my nose felt warm where he'd snuggled it, and so I just watched him go, his presence commanding even as it retreated.

When he was gone, my gaze dropped into my lap, to the knife that was lying on the chair against my outer thigh.

I lifted it, flipped out the blade, and looked at the reflective metal curiously.

Oh, Earth. What kind of life did you survive, and what sent you seeking refuge in the Grimms? And why?

The quote I'd shared with Earth came back to me. *Anger is never without reason, but seldom with a good one.*

It's true everyone thought the Huntsman was a villain, and perhaps he was.

But even villains had their reasons, for weren't villains actually just victims whose stories had never been heard?

Thirty-Three

The door to the Rotten Apple was ajar.

From half a block up the street, I could see it bouncing against the frame every time the wind blew. At first, I thought maybe my eyes were playing tricks on me, but then I heard the jingling of the bell tied to the handle.

We definitely raced out last night without a backward glance, but Beau would have locked up when he came home.

Something is wrong. I broke into a jog.

Yes, the sun was out.

Yes, it was early in the day.

It didn't matter.

Most people thought crimes and horrible deeds only happened beneath the veil of night, that villains only stepped out under the protection of shadows.

No.

Villains walked in the sunlight beside the regulars, the heroes, and even amongst their own kind.

I knew because many of the kills I'd committed had been underneath a bright blue sky and sparkling sun. In fact, those things made the best accomplice. After all, sunlight concealed darkness very well.

The frame of the door was bent, a hole big enough for a hand cut right through the glass. *Shattering the entire door would have drawn too much attention.* In my mind's eye, I visualized someone scoring the thick glass and knocking in the perfectly cut circle so they could reach inside and let themselves in.

As if to prove I was right, the little bit of shattered glass crunched beneath my boots as I stepped into my bar, but I barely heard the sound because everything else completely owned my attention.

The place was ransacked. Ripped apart. *Disrespected.*

Fury lit up inside me, scorching my veins and boiling my tainted blood as I gazed at the overturned tables, broken barstools, and shattered glass. One of the neon signs on the wall was ripped clean off, the tubing shattered across an askew table. The graffiti Neo custom painted across the brick wall was defaced with blood-red paint. It dripped like someone tossed an entire can at the wall, and when it splashed, it splattered everywhere, then bled down the wall like it was an open wound.

Beau!

"Shibal!" *Fuck,* I spat, not even realizing I'd spoken Korean.

Boots pounding over the broken beer bottles, sloshing through the wasted alcohol, and leaping over scattered busted furniture, I ran out of the bar and lunged up the stairs toward our place.

"Beau!" I roared, adrenaline pumping straight to my heart. *Jesus, he was alone here last night! What if they came upstairs too?*

"Beau!" I shouted, beating on the thick wooden door leading into the apartment. The door was locked.

I wasn't sure if that was a good thing or if it was keeping me from helping him.

"Beau!"

Somewhere in the apartment, Snort barked, and fear stabbed my heart. Reaching behind me, I yanked the knife out of the holster and backed up, preparing to throw myself against the door.

Wielding the blade, I backed up and lunged. Just before I collided, it opened, and Beau's green eyes blew wide. I tried to stop, but the momentum and adrenaline had a strong hold. I barreled inside, clipping my brother on the shoulder as he was trying to jump back.

Colliding, we both bounced backward, flying apart to land on the floor. The second I hit, I leaped back up, chest heaving, looking for a threat.

Beau was sprawled on his back on the floor, and I rushed over to stand over his body. "Beau! Jesus, are you hurt? Who did this to you?"

A man never put down his weapon, so I held on to it as I began patting down my brother, looking for injury.

I felt him recoil and look down. "What the hell is that?"

"Protection," I growled, still searching his body.

His hand closed around my wrist, his hold surprisingly strong. "Earth, I'm not hurt."

I paused. "Then why are you on the floor?"

"Because you mowed me down when you burst in here!" He glanced at the blade. "With a knife!"

I practically sagged in relief. "You aren't hurt?"

He seemed confused. The beanie on his head had fallen off, and the headphones usually glued to his ears were also on the ground. "Why would I be?"

"Shit," I spat, pushing away from him. "Snort!"

The dog barreled from around the couch, breathing heavily and, of course, snorting.

His front paws slapped on my legs when he jumped up at me, and I leaned down to scratch behind his ear. "Good boy," I murmured, willing my heart rate to return to normal.

"Everything is okay up here?" I asked, glancing around at Beau who was still on the floor, bewildered.

"What's going on?"

"The bar is trashed. I thought they got you too."

"Who?"

"That's what I wanted to ask you."

"Why would I know anything?" he stuttered, pulling himself to his feet.

"You mean to tell me you didn't hear any of that? The place is completely ransacked."

A guilty look crossed Beau's face, and he glanced down at his headphones.

"Fuck!" I spat.

"I'm sorry, Earth. I—"

"It's fine." I cut him off. "It's better that you didn't hear and go down there. There was definitely more than one guy, considering the mess."

"That bad?"

I grunted. "I'm glad you're okay."

My mind was racing. Now that I knew Beau wasn't lying in here dead, thoughts spiraled to other places. To other people.

"Hey, E?"

I swung around. "What?"

"You know you have keys for those locks, right?"

It took a minute to understand what he was saying. I did have keys. But I'd been in the process of busting down the door. "Not for the chain lock."

"Well, it would have been easier to bust through just that one rather than all of them," he pointed out.

"Fuck you."

He laughed.

I was not amused. "See if I rush up here to save your ass next time."

His eyes strayed to the knife I still clutched. His throat cleared. "You, ah, always carry that?"

I sheathed it back in the holster at my back without replying. "You really didn't hear anything at all?"

"Is it really that bad down there?" he asked.

I motioned for him to followed me down to the bar. His low whistle said it all when we stopped in the doorway leading inside. Snort was dancing around behind me, and I paused to tell him to stay. He sat obediently, tongue lolling out from between his crooked teeth.

"Jesus," Beau swore, stepping over the mess to gaze around. "I'm sorry. I should have heard. I should have been more alert."

"Don't," I told him. "I'm glad you didn't get involved. This bar isn't worth your life."

"Spending the night with V made you soft, E." Beau pressed a hand to his T-shirt-covered chest. "That's the nicest thing you've ever said to me."

I grunted. "Fuck off."

He laughed under his breath. "That's more like it."

Stalking over behind the bar, I stared down at the cash register, which had been forced open. It was empty.

The coolers under the bar were all left wide open, the sound of them running to try and stay cold despite the warm temp of the room was loud. Cussing, I slammed them all shut. What was left of the beer inside them rattled like they were ready to break.

"Who'd you piss off?" Beau asked, picking up a

barstool.

My head whipped up. "What?"

"Well, clearly, this was personal. If they wanted cash, they'd have taken it and gone, but they completely trashed the place too. You don't stick around for that unless you have an ax to grind."

The image of the "tattoo" on the dead body in the river flashed behind my eyes. "Who the fuck knows? I piss everyone off."

Beau made a sound. "True, but usually, you scare everyone too."

They're like you.

The words on the other end of that phone call last night haunted me. It was becoming harder and harder not to believe the far-fetched thoughts in my mind. Beau was right. Everyone here knew not to mess with me. So even if they did want to exact some kind of revenge on me, they wouldn't. I wasn't just talk. I'd proved that time and again. And in much more violent ways than even they knew. *But they sense it. They know the violence of a sleeping tiger.*

That meant that whoever did this wasn't from around here.

And really, that could only mean one thing.

"I'm gonna check the office," I spat, stomping off toward the back before Beau could even reply.

Snort followed along behind me but didn't rush into the small office space when I shoved open the door. The sound of the handle knocking into the drywall was loud as I took stock of the small space.

The stuff I dumped out from the desk drawer still littered the floor. The chair was shoved back away from the desk, and the drawer I'd put back into place was slightly crooked.

Just the way I left it.

Why would those thugs trash the place but leave my personal space untouched?

It didn't make sense.

Until it did.

My eyes latched on to the paperwork haphazardly scattered on the desk. It wasn't the paperwork I saw but what lay on top of it.

Carefully placed, directly in the center of my workspace, was a single long-stemmed rose. It was black.

The Black Rose.

Assaulted, I rocked back on the combat boots strapped on my feet, nearly doubling over from the strength of the sucker punch that was my past.

No longer was Earth standing in this cramped, shitty office. No longer did the scent of warm beer and cigarette smoke blemish the air. The sound of Snort's heavy breathing was silenced along with the faint sounds of Beau cleaning up out in the bar.

Instead, a fifteen-year-old boy named Mal-Chin stood trembling in a narrow, dark alley.

The great puffs of white steam constantly pouring out of the vents in the buildings wafted ominously like fog, coiling around everything it touched like it was malnourished and looking for a meal. The scent of frying meat and fermented cabbage was its weapon, choking the breath out of you in hopes of making it easier to swallow you whole. Up near the main street, shouts in Korean filled the night as men in dark suits followed orders to find and destroy.

Feet slapping against pavement grew closer, and I prayed the smoke would hurry and swallow me whole because being eaten alive in this filthy alleyway would be better than being taken alive.

Sinking deeper into the alley, hiding between smoke and

shadows, my shoulder blades scraped sharply against the rough brick of the building, the stinging sensation causing me to bite my lip.

I don't want this. But I have no choice.

I didn't know how long I hid, but when the footsteps faded away and they called to check the next alley over, I was finally able to let out the breath I'd been holding in.

"Dangsin-eul balgyeon." I found you.

The words were accompanied by a snakelike hand materializing through the fog to shackle itself around my wrist.

I was dragged out of the steam and into the middle of the alley where four men in dark suits stood waiting.

Because I still had my pride, I struggled even though it was pointless. Sweat dripped down my back, causing the metal tucked into the waistband of my black pants to slip a little lower.

"He's been found," the man holding my wrists announced.

The four men standing before us parted like a pair of curtains, and the woman who commanded them all came forward.

"Fighting against who you are is a waste of time," she said, eyes flat and serious. "I admire a man with a sense of persistence, but enough is enough. You will be punished this time."

"I'm not coming with you."

Her whole body stilled. Long, silent moments passed through the alley as more steam rose from around our feet. She turned back, almost robotic, her high heels clicking concisely over the pavement as she stepped closer.

"Oh, Mal-Chin, when will you learn that Mother knows best?"

Almost as if the man were hypnotized, the hands binding my wrists slackened. Seizing the moment, I burst backward, knocking him down and, at the same time, pulling out the gun, which was slick with my own sweat.

Mother paused, glancing between me and the gun with veiled interest and not an ounce of fear.

Oh, I hated that. She thought because she made me, she didn't have to fear me.

The sound of the gun cocking reverberated through the alley. "If Mother really knew best, she wouldn't have followed me here."

The cold look in her eyes that I knew so very well finally surrendered to fear. Her lips parted to speak, but whatever she would say was silenced by the explosion of a gun.

"Earth!" Beau's shout snapped me back, and I spun, heart pounding.

"Beau?"

His messy red head poked into the hallway. "Everything okay back there?"

He's okay.

"Why the hell wouldn't I be?" I snapped, still straddling the line between past and present.

"Just checking," he said, disappearing back out into the bar.

My eyes returned to the black rose on my desk. The thorns were sharp, pricking into my flesh when my hand clenched around the stem. One of the petals came loose to flutter onto the floor.

I stared at it amongst the mess, feeling sick because of how well it fit with the mess I'd dumped there last night.

"Hey! Where are you going?" Beau called out when I was already halfway through the broken door.

"Out," I called over my shoulder, exiting onto the sidewalk, feeling blood smear the stem of the rose I still carried.

Yes, all of this could only mean one thing.

They'd found me.

Thirty-Four

A POLITE KNOCK ON MY DOOR MADE ME SMILE WIDE, BUT then I realized Earth wouldn't knock and, if for some reason he did, it wouldn't be polite.

I grimaced a little thinking perhaps Emogen was back to read me the riot act for having a boy in my room. The thought incited a low giggle from me as I settled Zilla on my shoulder.

"Come in!" I called, still smiling a little because *I had a boy in my room last night!*

Okay. Not boy. Man. Earth was definitely all man.

The door opened, and Ivory walked in, looking every bit New York royalty. Not that she was even trying, but really, she didn't have to.

She truly was the fairest of them all, even dressed down in a pair of black jeans and black suede sneakers. Tucked into the jeans, which were belted with a Chanel belt, was a fitted grey turtleneck sweater. The sleeves were sheer organza with black polka-dots that puffed out at her shoulders and a little over the knit cuffs hugging her wrists.

Her sleek black hair was pulled up into a high pony-tail, and she carried a black bag. Her skin was impeccable, makeup light, but as always, her lips were the natural-to-her shade of red.

"Whoa, look at you!" Ivory exclaimed, setting aside her bag and smiling brightly at me.

I glanced down at myself and the long strapless sundress I'd pulled on after my morning routine. It was a beautiful shade of deep purple. I didn't wear it often because of the strap thing, but since I was going out with Earth a little later, I wanted to look nice. Besides, I did a lot of upper body work in PT, so showing off my toned shoulders and arms was okay once in a while—right?

The jersey material hugged my bodice and waist, all the way down to my hips, and then the material flowed around my legs. Honestly, if I wasn't in this chair, this dress would be too long for my short frame. But since I didn't have to walk around, I didn't worry about tripping over the length.

My hair was done in one massive braid down my head and back, the tail falling over my shoulder and into my lap. I clipped every blossom I had into the plait, making it look like a field of flowers.

"Does my dress look okay?" I asked.

"Beautiful." She confirmed. "But what is really wowing is your glow! You are radiant, Virginia!"

I felt my cheeks warm under her praise. "It's just the same old me."

"Oh, no," Ivory said. "You are always beautiful, but there's something different about you today." Pursing her bow-shaped lips, she studied me, then smiled. "This doesn't have something to do with a certain grumpy bar owner, does it?"

I felt my eyes go wide as I leaned forward in my chair. "Did Neo tell you?"

Ivory laughed and grabbed my hands to swing my

arms along with hers. "Even if he hadn't, it would have been obvious last night."

"I'm so sorry to worry everyone and make you all come running." I apologized.

Ivory waved away the words with her hand as she perched on the edge of my bed. I wheeled around to face her so we could talk.

Zilla tugged a flower clip out of my hair, and it dangled out of her mouth precariously. "Zil, you know these aren't snacks," I told her, laughing. Taking the leopard gecko, I placed her into her habitat, making sure to take back the clip.

Re-pinning it into my braid, I turned back to my guest. I liked girl talk with Ivory. She truly was the sister I never had. I was so glad Neo made her part of this family.

And so glad Earth didn't kill her.

If he had, everything would likely be different right now.

"Don't worry about it. That's what family is for." Her blue eyes twinkled, and she leaned closer to whisper, "Besides, it was kind of exciting, wasn't it?"

Her smile was infectious, and I found myself smiling back as both of us dissolved into giggles.

My laughter didn't last long, though, because I was still plagued by the previous ominous thought. "Thank you," I blurted out.

Her smile slipped a little, and her head tilted. "For what?"

"For so many things." Surprisingly, my eyes filled with tears. This was so unexpected, this welling of emotions.

The rest of my sister's smile faded, and she leaned forward, nearly tumbling off the bed to grasp my hand.

Her skin was cool and milky white, her hands not much bigger than mine. So different from the warm, olive-toned ones I'd felt all night long.

"What's this?" she crooned. "What's wrong?"

"I'm sorry." My voice was wobbly, eyes watery. "I don't mean to—"

She was off the bed and hugging me in an instant. Her light, fresh scent wrapped around me, and the silky strands of her hair brushed my cheek when her arms tightened.

I hugged her back, overcome by emotions I honestly didn't know I'd been feeling. "I feel so stupid," I confessed around a small laugh.

"Never say that," Ivory reproached, pulling back to look into my eyes. "Whatever you feel is okay with me. You can tell me anything."

I nodded, offering a small smile.

I wheeled closer to the bed, and Ivory helped as I transferred myself onto the mattress. When I was settled, Ivory sat beside me. Both our legs hung over the side of the mattress, no feet touching the floor.

My feet weren't even visible because of the afore-mentioned too-long dress.

"I really like having a sister," I confessed, folding my hands in my lap.

"Me too," she replied.

"You changed everything when you came into our lives."

She laughed lightly. "Well, meeting you all was defi-nitely unexpected."

Reaching across, I grabbed her hand, giving it a squeeze. "It was like you woke us up. All of us. Neo was so miserable, trapped in his own guilt, and couldn't see the future at all. We were all stuck in this holding pattern, and it was comfortable but so confining. But now there is happiness in Neo's eyes. He smiles more, and the smiles are genuine. He's... lighter. And though I've been fighting with him a lot lately, I wouldn't even have had the courage to bring up most of what I did if it wasn't for you."

"I didn't encourage you to open up to Neo. I believe that was someone else."

My heart felt newly bruised, the center of my chest oddly sore. Letting go of her hand, I absentmindedly rubbed the spot, wanting to ease the hurt.

"That someone tried to kill you," I whispered, not wanting to even speak the words out loud.

Her lips parted, and realization clouded her sky-blue stare. "Ahh..."

And then even more feelings were tumbling out, nearly tripping off my tongue and fighting to be heard. "If he had succeeded, then my brother would still be a miserable zombie, I would be silently miserable, Fletcher would probably still be under the thumb of that evil woman, and Beau..." I couldn't help but giggle. "Well, Beau would probably still be sitting behind his computers."

We shared a snicker because, really, Beau hadn't changed.

"I wouldn't have a new fashionable brother, and I wouldn't have you."

"Virginia," Ivory sniffled, reaching out her hand. I caught it and held, our attached palms resting on the bed between us.

"And Earth..." I glanced up from beneath my lashes. How could I sit and defend him or even give allowances to a man who literally tried to steal away her life?

But also... how could I not?

A look of understanding passed behind her expression, and she nodded. "I know."

"If he'd gone through with it, he never would have stopped. He never would have fought so horribly with Neo, and I might..." She gave me an encouraging squeeze. "I might never have gotten the chance to peer into his heart."

"I don't blame him. I honestly never did."

"I think you changed him most of all," I confessed, tugging my hand back into my own lap. As grateful as I was for that, I was still the tiniest bit jealous.

It made me feel guilty, but not acknowledging that piece of me didn't mean it wasn't there.

"Me?" Ivory echoed.

I nodded. "I think that's also why Neo had such a fit."

She sighed dramatically, but under her words was the unmistakable tone of fondness. "Neo is ridiculous sometimes."

"You got to him. Somehow got below the cold shell he lived behind. You woke his humanity, showed him that there actually was some living inside him. I think you showed him that he was capable of love."

"I think I just threw him off balance because he tried to kill me and then I ended up sleeping on his couch." Ivory snickered.

"He stopped killing because you made him *feel*." It was hard to say. Even harder to feel.

Ivory considered my words, then said, "I made the other people around him feel, and because he cared about them, he couldn't kill me in the end."

"You don't give yourself enough credit," I told her.

"You don't give yourself enough."

"Do you love him?"

"I do," she admitted. "But as a brother and nothing more."

I knew she would say that, but I wanted to hear it from those rose-red lips just the same. I believed her. I knew the one she truly loved was my brother.

"Do you think he loves you?"

"What do *you* believe?"

Glancing down into my lap, I whispered, "He told me he loved me."

"And do you believe him?"

Thump. Thump. My heart beat slow and steady. "Yes."

"And what about you? Do you love him?"

I lifted my head. "Yes."

Ivory squealed and hugged me fast and tight. "I am so happy for you! I think you make a wonderful couple."

I pulled back. "Do you really think that? Or do you think I'm crazy for loving someone who tried to kill you?"

"I just told you I loved him too."

"But what about your stepmother?"

Ivory's nose wrinkled. "What about that wicked woman?"

"Well… I mean, she's the one who hired Earth, right? So she tried to kill you too. You forgave Earth. Did you forgive her also?"

She thought for a moment before shaking her head slowly. "I don't think I can."

"But why?"

"Because, unlike Earth, there was no slumbering humanity inside her. There is no love waiting to be set free. She succumbed to her hate long ago and killed my mother. She would have killed me if Earth and Neo hadn't stopped her."

"He has killed before," I whispered.

"And we love him anyway."

"And that's okay."

"Let me ask you this," Ivory said, seeming to understand my inner struggle. Leaning in, she looked directly into my eyes. "If I told you I couldn't love him for what he did or that you were wrong for loving him because of it, would that make you stop?"

I gasped, my very breath repelled by the idea. "No!"

She smiled. "Then questioning it is kinda useless, isn't it? Because your love will not change."

She was right. It wouldn't change, and deep down, I'd already known that. I think I just wanted to make sure she knew that, though I loved him so unconditionally, I wasn't okay with what he did. "I am sorry for what he put you through."

"I know that, but you don't have to be sorry because I'm not."

"Really?"

She smiled. "It made us a family."

A family forged by loyalty and held tight by bonds we all refused to untie. Family by choice, which oddly seemed much more powerful than blood.

I hugged her again, feeling relief I didn't even know I needed. "Thank you for coming into our lives."

"Thank you for coming into mine."

"So…" She began, a sparkling glint overtaking her eyes. "Is he a good kisser?"

I felt my face heat. "How do you know we kissed?"

She made a sound. "Because I saw Neo's and Earth's bruises."

I rolled my eyes. "Idiots."

"So?" She pressed, curiosity in her stare. "Was he your first kiss?"

I nodded, shy. "Yes. And he took me to his brewery!"

Ivory gasped. "He has a brewery?"

I felt a little bit of pride that I knew all about it before everyone else, and I launched into some detail about the place Earth made his beer. And then, yeah, maybe I told her about our first kiss.

"He is so…" I sighed dramatically and collapsed back against the mattress, hands over my heart, to stare up at the ceiling. "Dreamy."

"Ah, the power of true love's kiss," Ivory mused.

"Do you have that with my brother?" Then I winced and held up my hand. "But no details please. He *is* my brother, after all."

Ivory's laugh was light and melodious. "We definitely have that."

Pushing up onto my elbows, I gazed at Ivory curiously but also shily. "Can I ask you something?"

"Of course."

"It's, ah, personal."

"You can ask me anything, Virginia. That's what sisters are for."

"What does sex feel like?"

Ivory's expression faltered a bit, but she didn't shy away from the question. "Are you asking me because Earth stayed here last night?"

"No. Well, I mean, yes, but we didn't." I felt my cheeks heat again. "I want to, but I'm worried."

"Worried?"

I nodded. "You know, because of my condition. What if… what if he doesn't like it?"

"What if *you* don't like it?" Ivory added.

"I won't be able to feel it anyway," I confessed.

Ivory made a sound as if she understood. "The thing about sex is… it's about more than just sex. Especially when you're with someone you love."

I nodded.

"Like I can tell you how it feels physically, but every woman likely has a different experience."

"What's it like for you?"

"A feeling of fullness and warmth. The feel of my body stretching around his, something moving inside me, creating a buzz of pleasure that sometimes makes everything condense to that one point where you're both connected."

I wouldn't be able to experience that. I wouldn't feel my body stretching around his. I wouldn't be able to focus on that single point where we were joined.

A sense of loss surged over me, the same kind of feeling I often carried when I'd first lost my legs. I guess I hadn't been able to grieve the loss of this kind of intimacy because I wasn't aware of it yet.

"But that's not all sex is."

I glanced up, noting that she was watching me. "It's not?"

"No. That's honestly just a small part. The thing about sex with someone you love is the emotion behind it. Sharing something with that person that you don't with anyone else. Having them right against you and looking into their eyes. The air in the room feels thick with passion, with intimacy and love. It isn't just about inserting part A into part B."

I laughed.

Her eyes twinkled. "Well, you asked."

I did. I'd had a general women's health talk with my mom when my period started but not much else. She died before we could ever have any sort of sex talk, and then after that, I'd been too busy learning other things about my body—like how to use it and how to be independent—that these things never really came up. Yes, I could ask my doctor, and from time to time, I did ask questions because I was curious about what my body was able to do. But those were clinical answers—nonpersonal. I so appreciated that Ivory would speak to me about this and not make it awkward. I knew I could talk to Earth. He'd proven it last night and then again this morning, but speaking with another woman was different.

"It's a way to be as close as possible to someone you love."

"Do you think he'll like it if I can't… move around like other women?"

Ivory leaned in. "I'll tell you a secret. Men couldn't care less as long as they get it."

I slapped a hand over my mouth to stifle more laughter.

Ivory shrugged. "It's true."

Her eyes turned more serious. "Did your doctor say you were able to have sex?"

I nodded.

"So you're worried you won't be able to have an orgasm and you'll miss out on how it feels."

I ducked my head. "Actually, I'd always thought that, but…"

"But?"

"Last night changed my mind."

Her blue eyes rounded. "You mean last night… Earth…?"

"We didn't have sex, but we did other things, and I… I felt it."

"Did you like it?"

I nodded emphatically. "It was like this building sensation. Tension built and built. Then suddenly, it all burst, and every part of me was suffused with humming warmth."

Ivory nodded enthusiastically. "That's exactly it. Geez, you get that even without A into B. Most women would be envious!"

"No way." I scoffed.

"Yes!" Ivory insisted. "Believe it or not, a lot of women who have fully functioning bodies struggle with having orgasms. It's very common. And you did it on your first try. It's rather impressive." She cocked her head to the side. "It was your first try?"

I was shy, but I answered anyway. "Yes."

"I'd say you have nothing to worry about. But if you ever have any other questions, you can ask me anytime, okay?"

I glanced up from behind my hands, face and ears still flaming. "Thank you," I said sincerely.

"Now I know the real reason behind your glow." She teased. "Guess Earth has many talents."

I was pretty sure my ears were about to catch on fire, and all I could do was giggle more. Earth *was* talented. I fell back into the mattress again, smiling wide at the ceiling.

"Truthfully, I'm glad you finally know the truth. Neo was adamant that we not tell you, but it created a divide in the family. His entire feud with Earth did. I would like very much for us all to have some harmony. For us all to be even closer."

"You know Neo was so jealous. He thought Earth was in love with you."

"I know. But I couldn't tell him it wasn't true because then it would seem like I was defending Earth, which only would have made it worse. This was something they had to work out on their own."

"And you think they will?"

"Yes, I do. Neo loves Earth, even if he is a stubborn pig head about it. They both have so much pride, but I think they'll finally set it aside for you."

"For me?"

Ivory nodded. "You think I'm the one who changed this family, but you're just as much a catalyst. You challenged Neo and Earth. They never could put their pride aside for me, but they already are for you."

"I don't know." I worried. "Have you seen their faces?"

Ivory wrinkled her nose and waved that away. "How do you think I knew Earth stayed here last night?"

I paused. She did mention that, but I'd been too preoccupied to wonder how she knew. "How?"

"Neo and Earth spoke outside. We left first. Neo drove away, leaving Earth on the sidewalk... knowing he would come back up here."

Surprise had me sitting up. Wide-eyed, I stared at Ivory. "Really?"

She smiled. "I even hugged Earth, and Neo didn't get angry."

My mouth fell open. But then it snapped shut. "You hugged Earth?" I never really thought I was a jealous type of girl, but the emotion kept rising from somewhere inside me.

It was senseless, I knew. Ivory was not interested in Earth, and I'd literally just confided in her about our intimate relationship. She was in love with my brother. So why would I even care she hugged him?

"He didn't hug me back."

My eyes lifted to hers. "What?"

"He let me hug him, but he didn't hug me back. I bet he hugs you, doesn't he?"

I thought of how he held me all night in this very bed, and I nodded.

"Maybe someday he will be able to." She sighed wistfully. "Might be nice to have a hug from my brother."

The jealousy I felt cleared away. It wasn't very nice, but I would be a liar if I said hearing Earth didn't hug her back didn't make me feel giddy relief.

I want him to want only me. Just as I only want him.

"You didn't have to tell me that," I whispered.

"I know, but it made you feel better, didn't it?"

Reluctantly, I nodded.

Perfectly sculpted nails painted with the most gorgeous shade of green I'd ever seen slipped over my hand, her fingers clasping my hand. "We all have emotions. We're all human. It's because we're family and we try harder to understand each other. And I would never withhold an honest truth from you, especially if it makes you feel more comfortable."

Her hand pulled back to slide over her sleek ponytail. "Besides, we aren't cavemen like Earth and Neo, and we can actually talk and set aside our pride."

"You're a good sister."

"Be confident in yourself, Virginia. Any man would be lucky to have you. Your pure heart and ability to love unconditionally makes you a very rare flower."

A lot of the worry I'd been holding on to melted away. For the first time in a very long time, I felt like life was moving forward and the burdens of our pasts could finally be left behind.

It was a wonderful feeling.

How unfortunate it only lasted a few fleeting minutes.

Thirty-Five

Earth

Caught between past and present, I moved up the sidewalk, mind reeling.

After all these years, why now? How? Why not just kill me?

I always knew it was a possibility I would be found. Not even a possibility, just really a matter of time. But the timing was… off. I hadn't done anything unusual. If anything, I'd been lying even lower than ever.

Is that why? It didn't make sense.

The sharp, unmistakable pop of a gun ripped through my thoughts, slaughtering them all. My footsteps stuttered as I gazed around. *Flashback or reality?*

Roughly two blocks up, a blur of movement at the corner of a building caught my attention. Even though it was merely a flash and no longer in sight, it was all the answer I needed.

Reality.

I took off, black rose petals fluttering behind me as they ripped from the stem. Breathing heavily, I launched around the corner into the alley but saw no one brandishing a gun.

But there was a body.

Heart and feet pounding, I ran deep into the alley, which wasn't as bright because the buildings blocked the sun. The closer I got, the tighter my chest twisted, and recognition rocked my core.

I didn't feel the hard, rough pavement when my knees hit. The wind-beaten rose flopped against the bloodstained chest of the man lying there gurgling and gasping for what I knew would be his final breaths.

My informant. My accomplice...

Perhaps even my friend.

"Riley." The name ripped out of me as though I'd said it a thousand times. In truth, this was the first I'd ever spoken his name out loud. We never used names when he called me on that secret phone. The phone that now weighed about one thousand pounds inside the pocket of my jacket.

I shouldn't have waited for him to call. I should have called.

"E-E-Earth." He gasped and more blood bubbled out of the gaping chest wound.

I slapped my hands onto the gurgling spot, trying to slow the bleeding, as if that would even help. I'd seen lots of people die in front of me. Hell, I'd been the cause of most.

This is different.

How easy it was to remain impassive when the life leached out of someone you didn't know or ever think about.

How difficult it was to watch when the person dying was someone you knew.

Is this what it was like for the families of all the people I had slain?

"I-it w-wasn't me." He gasped, trying hard to get the words out.

"What wasn't?" I asked, pushing even harder against his wound.

He made a pained sound, and I swore even more color drained from his face. He was young. So goddamn young.

"B-barrr…"

I felt my eyebrows draw together. "My bar?"

He nodded once, then grimaced. His feet moved restlessly on the pavement as though, if he could, he would run from the pain. His lips were starting to turn an unnatural shade, and a helpless feeling overtook my gut.

"I know it wasn't you," I told him, glancing around for the person who'd done this.

The alley was empty, but whoever it was couldn't be far. I thought briefly of running off to catch the bastard to deliver swift revenge, but to do that would leave Riley to lie here and die alone.

Like many of your own victims. My head rocked on my neck. The thought was a swift punch to the jaw.

His hand lay weakly against my wrist. "No use," he said, barely tapping.

"Just hang in there," I ground out, pushing harder.

"Making it hurt worse."

"Fuck!" I yelled, dropping my hands, which were now saturated in blood. "Who did this to you?"

He coughed, a low wheezing that sounded somehow sticky and lurid. Deep-red blood bubbled out as if it were trying to clot, but even the thick clots were being dislodged by the blood pouring out beneath it.

He lifted his hand, moving sluggishly like a zombie. I reached for it, but he shook his head slightly, and I backed off. Fingers fumbled on his chest for a minute before connecting with the rose I'd forgotten lay on his chest.

He tapped it. "Them."

Hatred lit me up inside. I felt my nostrils flare. Jabbing a finger at the rose, I said, "This is who did this to you?"

His head lolled off to the side, and a rough sound ripped from my throat.

Grabbing him by the chest, I wrenched his shoulders off the ground. "Riley!" I yelled. "Riley!"

His head lolled again, and a sob built in my throat.

A low wheeze accompanied the fluttering of his lashes.

Laying him back on the pavement, I leaned over his weak body. "I'm sorry," I said. "You're like this because of me."

"No… On me."

My head knew that this kid had made his own choices, but right now, my head wasn't clear. I leaned down beside his ear. "They're going to pay for this."

A sound that would have been a laugh in another time and place slipped from between his lips, followed by a trail of crimson. "I know."

His feet had long since stopped moving as if he no longer had the energy to run from the pain, as if he'd succumbed to it a long time ago.

If death had a visual, I was sure I would see its sharp talons sank deep into his body, slowly feeding off what was left of his life.

For the first time in my life, death felt like a loss.

For the first time—

Slam!

Whatever hit the middle of my back caused me to lurch forward, nearly falling onto Riley. Bracing my hands on the pavement, I kept myself off the fading man and lurched around just as a fist coldcocked the side of my jaw.

Spots swam before my eyes, and I shook them off, surging to my feet as an Asian man came at me again. When his head snapped to the side from my hit, my eyes landed on his neck, on the top of a tattoo I knew very, very well.

A black rose.

Just like the flower left on my desk.

Just like the one drawn on the dead body in the river.

And just like the one tattooed on my hip.

The man tried to hit me again, but I caught his arm, twisting it around his back and slamming him into the wall. His body slack, I forced him lower so he had to look at the carnage he'd left.

"You do this?" I demanded.

"Stupid kid shouldn't have been following us around."

I told him to leave town. Was he trying to get more information for me? Did he see them trash my bar?

The man twisted free from my grasp, kicking me in the side, sending me spiraling sideways. When I straightened, there was a blade in my hand and a gun in his.

His smile was arrogant. "A bullet is faster than a blade."

He fired as I moved, launching forward instead of to the side. I felt the heat of the metal as it whizzed past my ear, then forgot about it when I tackled him.

"Yes." I agreed. "But you missed your mark."

My blade did not.

It went right through his heart.

Once a huntsman, always a huntsman.

Even though the life drained from his eyes instantly, I twisted the blade to make sure it didn't come back.

Glassy, lifeless eyes that were surprised even in death stared up at the city sky as I stood, yanking my blade out of that blackened, shriveled organ he considered a heart.

I turned back to Riley. He was dead too.

"Earth!" A familiar voice made me look up.

Beau was running down the alley, followed by Fig and friends.

"You called the cops?" I accused Beau, making a face.

"Hell no." Beau grimaced. "Heard the gunshot and saw them rushing up the sidewalk and got worried about you."

"I'm fine, as you can see."

"Can't say the same about everyone else in this alley," Fig announced, standing up from checking the pulse at Riley's neck.

His friend Paul was doing the same to the other body.

"What's going on here, Earth?" Fig asked, puffing up his chest like it made him a better cop.

It didn't. He just looked like a bird with ruffled feathers. Stupid.

"Looks like some people died," I said.

"Well, no shit," Fig spat. "Seeing as how you're the only one left alive, makes me wonder if you were doing the killing."

I didn't even react. Why bother? Fig was a moron, and all he wanted was for me to get all bent out of shape. "That one killed that one," I said, pointing first to the asshole, then to Riley. "Then that one tried to kill me too."

"And you defended yourself?" Paul questioned.

"Was I supposed to let him shoot me?"

Fig glanced down at the knife I still clutched. "That's a pretty big knife. That yours?"

"Yep."

"Where'd you get it?"

"Had it for years." I shrugged.

"And you just happened to be carrying it around today?"

"I carry it around every day."

"Interesting." Fig narrowed his eyes a bit.

"We live in the Grimms. It ain't that interesting," I countered.

Fig turned to Beau. "He carry that knife around every day?"

"Yep." Beau lied.

To my knowledge, Beau didn't even know I wore this thing around. I always kept it hidden beneath my jacket and when I didn't carry it, it was locked up in my bedroom or with my car.

There wasn't an ounce of doubt in his voice, though.

"And you don't find that shady?" Fig pressed.

"I'd find it shadier if a bar owner in the ghetto didn't carry around some kind of protection," Beau refuted.

Fig turned back to me. "You got a permit for that?"

"Wasn't aware I needed one."

"What happened here?" Paul asked, changing the subject.

I experienced death for what felt like the first time.

"Someone broke into the bar and trashed the place," Beau said when I remained quiet.

"And you chased the culprit into this alleyway and killed him?"

"I didn't kill him," I said, glancing at Riley. "I was out on the street, looking for anyone who might have busted up my bar, and I heard the gunshot. I went toward the sound and found this."

"That's a nice and tidy story," Fig observed.

Beau moved a little closer to my side, and I couldn't help but glance down at Riley. He'd been loyal to me too.

"You sure that gun ain't yours?" Fig pressed, hitching his chin toward the black piece lying beside the dead man.

"I don't like guns."

"Probably also don't like getting robbed."

"What are you saying?" Beau challenged, folding his arms over his chest.

Fig didn't answer right away. Instead, he meandered back over to Riley's body, acting like he had all the time in the world, while Paul stood off to the side angled away, probably holding back the urge to hurl.

Guy needed a desk job.

Squatting, Fig reached into the jacket that had fallen open against the pavement, and I bit my lip against telling him to keep his hands off Riley. Seconds later, he made a low sound and pulled back, his hand coming up with a wad of cash, some of which was stained with blood.

"Well, what do we have here?" He stood, holding out the wad as though he'd won the lottery. "How much was stolen from your place?"

I shrugged.

"You mean you were robbed and you didn't even bother to count how much you lost?"

"I was busy."

"How do you even know that's from the bar?" Beau put in.

Fig opened the folded wad, and something fluttered from the middle, falling like a feather toward the blood-stained ground.

The cop whistled between his teeth when he picked up the paper and held it out.

It was a label from one of my beers.

They planted it all on him to make him look guilty.

"You know, chasing robbers out of your place is one thing, but running them down the block and shooting them… that's a whole other."

Beau made a sound, arms dropping to his sides.

"You think I shot that kid?" I said, my voice level and cold. "He was one of ours."

Fig gave me a long-measured stare. I saw the doubt, but it was quickly overcome by his usual arrogance.

"What better way to remind folks here in the Grimms that they shouldn't mess with you?"

It was becoming increasingly hard to remain impassive and cool. This man was a class-A moron, and I'd had enough of his posturing.

"No one was even in the bar when we found it," Beau told him. "Earth couldn't have chased them here."

"Or maybe you're lying for your friend."

The sound of my knuckles bouncing off his face filled me with sweet satisfaction. "You want to come at me…" I spoke low, standing over Fig where he was half lying on the ground. "Come on. But you leave my brother out of it."

"E," Beau called, not really an admonishment but more of a reminder to keep myself in check.

Fig sat back, body bumping into Riley's. Reaching over, he plucked the withered rose off the young body. "Pretty sure you told us you didn't recognize this mark."

Tension knotted in my shoulders, squeezing muscles so tight it radiated dim pain up the back of my skull.

"Ain't that what he said, Paul?" Fig tossed out as he stood, bringing the black rose with him.

"This one has the same mark," he replied, pointing to the side of the Asian man's neck.

Paul glanced at me, resignation in his stare. "Sorry, Earth. But this don't look good."

Reaching behind him, Fig pulled out a pair of hand-cuffs. "We're gonna have to bring you in."

It was ironic really. Of all the people I'd actually killed, I was finally being arrested for the one I didn't.

Thirty-Six

VILLAIN

"A BLACK ROSE HAS WITHERED, BUT IT IS DONE."

"He killed him?"

"Just as I knew he would."

"And now?"

"Now the trap is set, the bait is alone, and reckoning has arrived."

"The bait is not alone. The bait has company, the one who escaped his blade."

"Hm. Perfect. Do what he couldn't."

Silence.

The hand holding the line tightened. "Is there a problem?"

"No."

"No, *what?*"

"Mother knows best."

The line went dead, and soon, many others would too.

Thirty-Seven

THE USUAL HUM OF QUIET IN THE TOWER WAS SUDDENLY disturbed by the piercing, high-pitched wail of the fire alarm.

The sound was near deafening as it bounced off the walls, shattering any and all peace and rippling the very air with invisible anxiety.

We looked up from my iPad, no longer seeing the beautiful photos of California that Ivory had sent. Instead, a look of confusion passed between us.

"Were they running a fire drill today?" Ivory inquired, her small nose wrinkling.

I shook my head. In all the years I'd lived here, we'd never once had a fire drill.

"Maybe the sensor or something is faulty." Ivory tried again. "This is a very old building. Do you think the alarms are up to code?"

Before I could reply, someone out in the hall keened. "Fire!"

Instead of fear spiking my pulse, a peculiar inkling of foreboding slowed it down. Rather than instantly wanting to scramble into my chair and race for the closest exit, I found myself gripping the tablet as a sluggish, slow feeling draped over me.

It was far scarier than the rush of urgent adrenaline could ever be.

Moving to the door, Ivory pulled it open, revealing the hallway where several residents were already loitering, some confused, some clearly afraid.

"The place is on fire, Virginia! I knew there was bad wiring in this place," Mr. Donaldson yelled in the doorway over the ear-piercing alarm. "I tried to tell them!"

"Mr. Donaldson." One of the nurses appeared, taking him by the arm. "We all need to get outside until we know what's going on."

"I'll tell you what's going on! We're all gonna burn!" he broadcasted.

My stomach dropped a little. I knew he was an old man, not always rational and definitely filled with dramatics, but I couldn't help feeling a prickle of distress from his words.

"So there really is a fire?" Ivory asked the nurse.

"We have someone checking, but we are all evacuating for precaution," he answered. "Do you need assistance?" he asked, looking at me where I was still sitting on the bed.

"My cat!" the woman who lived across the hall exclaimed. "I am not leaving my baby behind!"

"It's full of stuffing!" Mr. Donaldson yelled at the woman. "It's not like it's alive!"

Claire gasped. "How dare you talk about my Mittens that way?"

The nurse holding on to the older man visibly held his patience. Clearly, the situation beginning to stress him.

"I can go downstairs on my own. Ivory is here."

Ivory nodded immediately. "Of course. We'll go now."

"Thank you," he said, going to break up the arguing elders.

"I won't go without my cat!" Claire shrieked insistently.

"It's so loud!" another pajama-clad resident complained, walking down the hall with their hands pressed over their ears.

"Everyone make your way to the stairwell!" announced a nurse who was not dealing with the elderly couple arguing. She sounded much calmer and in control.

"Can we take the elevator?" Ivory worried, glancing at me.

"I think it should be fine," I answered, reaching for the board I kept close by so I could transfer from the bed to my wheelchair. "They're probably trying to keep it open for those of us who can't take the stairs."

In truth, there was only one other resident here that couldn't take the stairs if absolutely necessary.

"Let me help you," Ivory offered, moving quickly but not panicked.

When I was settled into my chair, I glanced up. "You're very calm."

"Well, panicking won't do us any good. Besides, we've survived worse."

Those words were all too true. They also made me think of Earth. I glanced at my cell phone lying on the bed and wondered if I should call him.

I decided against it, tucking the phone into the pocket on my chair. Ivory and I were perfectly capable of getting out to the sidewalk.

"Do you need to bring anything else?" Ivory asked, a

little worry flashing in her face for the first time. "What do you need?"

I really didn't think I would need anything. Whatever was going on was probably a false alarm or, at worst, something the firefighters could take care of the minute they arrived. But my gaze landed on the purple backpack Earth had set aside when he brought it back. I hadn't even unpacked it yet.

"Just grab that bag," I told her.

It wouldn't hurt to be cautious.

Ivory slipped it over her shoulders, settling it on her back as though she were a school student, and I smiled.

"Let's go," she said, motioning toward the door.

I started forward, then stopped. "Zilla!"

Ivory turned back, glancing over to the gecko habitat.

"I can't leave her. What if there really is a fire?" I worried. "Unlike Claire's cat, Zilla is actually real."

Ivory nodded. "Should we just carry her?"

I rolled over toward the habitat, reaching behind it to grab a much smaller enclosure. It was a small clear box with a vented purple lid on the top. It already had a couple things inside to make the gecko comfortable, so I reached into the large tank and carefully transferred Zilla into the traveling case.

"We're going on an adventure, Zil!"

A loud crash followed by a deafening roar competed with the whistling alarm. Nearly dropping the case in my lap, I looked up.

Ivory's blue eyes were wide, her red lips parted in shock. "What was that?"

"I-I think it was him."

"Him?"

"That beast who lives at the end of the hall. The one from the other night."

"Oh dear," she replied. "Do you think he's okay?"

He bellowed again. He scared me that first night, but now I wasn't as afraid. Uneasy, yes. He was very loud and sounded very destructive. But I also knew that he was probably scared and that he was a patient here like me.

"I can't leave him behind."

"Let's see if he needs help." Ivory agreed.

I wheeled toward the door where she waited. The lights in the hall flickered a bit like they wanted to stay on but the power was trying to cut off.

The alarm still created a cacophony of noise, making my ears ache and my shoulders tense. I sniffed the air, trying to smell for smoke but could not.

"Everyone downstairs to the sidewalk. Help is on the way!" a nurse yelled from down the hall.

The beast of a man shouted again. The sound of wood splintering made us pause.

"Are you afraid?" I whispered, unable to yell over the alarm.

Even though Ivory looked frightened, she shook her head. "Go on strongly despite the fear."

We started down the hall again. At the end of the corridor, his door flung open, and my breath caught waiting to see whoever created such chaos rush out into the hall.

But it wasn't him.

It was a nurse in pink scrubs. She rushed out, the sound of shattering glass following her. She hurried down the hall, face caught between a grimace and fear.

"Nurse Jackie," I called out, and she glanced up, shocked to see us there.

"What are you doing in the building?" she fussed. "Out. Let's go! This isn't a drill."

"But what about him?" I asked.

"He's refusing to leave. We can't wait. Let's go."

"We can't just leave him!" I worried.

"We have to. It's my job to get everyone to safety but not at the risk of my own safety. I'll have the emergency responders come for him."

I frowned. Did she mean she was risking her safety by staying behind trying to convince him to come out or by being in that room with him?

"Jackie, a hand?" someone at the end of the hall called out.

We all looked to see the only other wheelchair-bound patient sitting under an ominously flickering light. It made her color ashen, her cheekbones hollow, but seemed to highlight the way her frail old limbs visibly shook.

"Could you ride down the elevator with Mrs. Cramb? I need to sweep the stairwell one last time."

"Of course." She glanced at me. "Come on, Virginia. You can ride down with us."

I glanced back down the hall. "Go ahead. Send the elevator right back up for us."

"I don't think—"

Ahhh!

Nurse Jackie's protest was silenced by another scream. Blanching, she rushed off to help Mrs. Cramb.

I glanced at Ivory. She nodded.

Just outside his door, we paused. The room was completely dark, not a single light shining within. If he had a window, it was completely covered by curtains, but maybe his room was windowless like mine.

It was eerily quiet inside, and I wasn't sure which was worse: his complete lack of sound or when he screamed.

"Excuse me, sir?" I called from the doorway.

He didn't answer. It really wasn't shocking.

"Um, sir." I tried again. "There seems to be an emergency, and we need to evacuate the building."

When there was still no sound, I started forward, my wheels gliding across the threshold of his room.

"Get *out*," intoned a low, gravelly voice.

I couldn't tell where it was coming from, and I swallowed cautiously. Ivory's hands fell to the short handles on the back of my chair, and I felt her tug me back.

"You need to come with us. You could be in danger." Ivory tried.

"Get *OUT!*" he roared.

Ivory and I stumbled back with her landing on her butt in the center of the hall.

Gasping, I turned to look at her. "Are you okay?"

"Fine. Just startled." She assured me, standing up to dust off her hands.

"Virginia!" A stern voice punched through all the other noise.

Emogen hurried down the hall toward us, her springy curls bouncing around her face. "What in the hell are you doing in here, girl? Why aren't you outside?"

"We were trying to help."

"You can't help someone who doesn't want to be helped." She pursed her lips and glanced to the room.

"We can't leave him here," Ivory insisted.

"Even scary people get scared too," I added.

"He ain't scary." Emogen scoffed. "He's just a stubborn ass." She yelled the last part toward his open door.

He seems a little scary to me.

"Go on," she insisted. "Both of you, out of here. I'll take care of him."

"Are you sure?" I worried, glancing back at his dark doorway.

"Go."

My head had started to ache with the insistent shrieking alarm, and when I glanced at Ivory, I realized she wouldn't go unless I did. I didn't want to put my sister in danger by staying.

"I'll let the responders know you're here," I told Emogen. She looked calm and cool on the outside, but I knew, deep down, she was likely nervous too.

Reaching out, she squeezed my hand. "You're a good friend, V."

Ivory grabbed the handles on my chair, and we went down the hall at a bustling pace. The lights were still flickering, but the hallway was empty now, everyone else having already left the building. "Why is that horrible alarm still going off?" Ivory fussed as we neared the end of the hall.

The strong, suffocating scent of smoke hit me almost immediately. Recoiling slightly, I looked at the door leading to the stairwell.

Billows of thick gray smoke pushed beneath the door and around the edges.

Ivory's steps faltered, and we both stared for long seconds at the clear evidence of a fire somewhere in this building. So much for thinking it might be a false alarm.

"Emogen, hurry!" I screamed down the hallway, hoping she could hear me over everything else.

Ivory pressed the elevator button more than once, and we both stared at the lit arrow.

"Do you think this elevator is safe to use?" She worried, biting her lower lip.

"I think it might be safer than the stairwell."

But really, it didn't matter because I couldn't go down the stairs. Ivory wasn't big enough to carry me. It was this elevator or nothing.

When the door dinged open and the empty car

appeared, even though it was a welcome sight, it was entirely eerie.

"Why do I feel like I'm in some bad movie?" I wondered.

"I've had quite enough suspense to last me a lifetime," Ivory declared. "Let's go."

I rolled into the car first, maneuvering so my chair faced the doors as Ivory stepped in after me. Reaching over, she pressed the button to take us to the ground floor. It lit up, but the car stubbornly sat there, doors open for a few uncomfortable seconds that seemed to last far longer than that.

We shared a nervous look as the lights out in the hallway continued to flicker. If the alarm wasn't still shrieking, I was sure I'd be able to hear the way they crackled.

Uneasiness tapped me with a cold, boney finger, causing a light shiver to race across my skin. Just as I started fidgeting, the doors made a sound and began closing.

Both of us sighed in relief, trying to smile reassuringly at the other while we secretly prayed we made it down.

Just as the doors were about to seal shut, something stopped them.

No. Not something.

Someone.

Four thick fingers jammed themselves into the small space and spread. Pushing wide, the doors started to open, and another hand joined the first. We watched silently as a large pair of hands, which bulged with veins, pushed, reopening the doors that had almost been closed.

It could have been a firefighter. Emogen. Even the beast she was trying to coerce from his room.

I knew it wasn't.

Hostile intentions slithered between the widening doors, oozing into the small space, rising like the smoke in the stairwell. It had no odor. No color. But oh, how it attacked the lungs, seizing them and making it nearly impossible to breathe.

Almost immediately, my fingers started to tremble, but my stare remained focused on the man slowly revealed to us.

Black clothes. Black hat shielding an unknown face. He stood, head angled down, with both arms out, holding the automatic doors open.

Barring us from getting away.

Slowly, his head lifted, and my insides twisted with something insidious. Scrupulous Asian features were revealed inch by inch until hawklike cold eyes glittered menacingly at us as if a predator had found his prey.

My instincts stopped screaming something was wrong. They didn't need to scream something I could clearly see. Instead, a heavy weight of dread settled upon my shoulders as if it could hold me down and drown me.

He smiled. It was not friendly.

I thought maybe I should have called Earth.

"Pardon me. We need to go down." Ivory attempted. How she made those words sound reasonably polite, I would never know.

"I'd say you've reached your destination." His English was not as good as Earth's, but it was perfectly clear what he meant.

Dropping his arms from the doorway, he sniffed, a low, threatening sound I shouldn't have heard over the alarm—

Wait, the alarm had stopped, and I hadn't noticed until now.

Thoughts of the alarm vanished when he lifted a gun, its black barrel pointing right at me. Swallowing thickly, I shoved my hands under my thighs, trying to calm my thundering heart.

"Who are you?" Ivory demanded, the fear in her voice unmistakable.

His black, soulless eyes never left mine as he answered, his penetrating gaze threatening to swallow me whole. "Just here to collect a life owed." Suddenly, he glanced away to my sister, and a corner of his mouth lifted. "Looks like today I get a two-for-one."

I burst into action, pulling my hands from under my legs, bringing with them the knife Earth insisted I keep. Shoving out with one hand, I threw myself out of the chair. It rolled off behind me, and I dropped to the floor.

I used gravity to my benefit, bringing down the knife into the man's thigh as I fell. He howled in pain, stumbling back, surprise flashing in his eyes.

The second he moved, the doors began to close with me lying in their path. Part of me was in the hall, the other still in the elevator.

"Virginia!" Ivory exclaimed.

I gasped, pushing up onto my forearms, reaching out a hand for Ivory to pull me back inside.

"Ah!" I cried out when a violent hand wrapped around my long braid and pulled. Hard.

"You're gonna pay for that." His voice dripped with menace.

With his fast yank, my eyes prickled with tears as my scalp screamed from the hair being pulled so forcefully. I fell back, my body starting to slide into the hall out of the elevator. Ivory lunged, hands locking around my ankles.

I became the object of a tug-of-war, the doors nearly closing, but once they hit my legs, they sprang back open.

The thunderous sound of a gun exploding made us both scream. Metal groaned, and glass shattered, the light in the elevator instantly going dark. Panicked, I searched inside the car for Ivory, praying she hadn't been shot.

She was crouched in the corner, hands over her head, glass everywhere. I couldn't tell if she was shot, and then she wasn't even in my sight at all.

I cried out, clawing desperately at the hand and arm towing me down the hallway, wanting so desperately to fight.

I felt so helpless. So utterly weak.

Tears streaked down my face, a mix of frustration, fear, and pain. "Run!" I screamed to my sister, hoping she was alive. Hoping she could hear. "Run away, Ivory!"

"You can't run from the Black Rose," the voice intoned as he gave me another vicious yank.

The elevator chimed, but I wasn't able to look back because pain so intense radiated through my scalp. I stared up at the flickering light, praying that meant Ivory was on her way to safety.

"Damn, you're heavy for being so small," the man spat. "Fucking gimp."

The slur was a stinging slap to my face, and it also brought out unbridled rage. *How dare he complain that I'm heavy? I didn't ask for this!*

Through watery eyes, I saw the knife still sticking out of his leg as if my effort to protect myself had been so insignificant he hadn't even bothered to pull it out.

Twisting at my waist, I lunged, ripping it out. The gross sucking sound it made was punctuated by his scream, and then he dropped me. Gasping for breath, I pushed up onto my forearms, still gripping the bloodied blade.

He lunged at me with a loud yell, leaping on top of me and pinning me down with his weight. My brother and Earth had endlessly black eyes, but this man's were different. These were the true eyes of a killer. Flat, lifeless. With no conscience or regard to human life.

For long seconds, time hung suspended, and I was caught in a place with this man where life and death were equal. And sadly, he had the power to decide which I would get.

Despite his hands being slick with blood, they were strong when they wrapped around my neck to squeeze.

A feeling of claustrophobia wrapped around me, and I gasped.

Even though I stared up at the man trying to strangle the life right out of me, I thought of Earth.

Of how he'd hit his knees the last time I'd been with him. How he buried his face in my lap and sounded so broken yet so whole because he'd felt chosen for the first time in his life.

This man was completely capable of stealing away my life, but I couldn't allow it. I couldn't allow anyone to take anything more away from Earth.

Fight.

The world dimmed at the edges of my vision as the man squeezed tighter. Feeling the knife still clutched in my hand, I brought my arm out, stabbing it into the muscle in his arm.

His grip disappeared. Oxygen flooded my deflated lungs, and I began to cough and choke.

"You little bitch!" He fumed.

"Virginia!" Ivory yelled, feet echoing in the hall behind us.

I told her to run.

Like a little hellcat, Ivory launched herself onto his back. All I saw was her feet closing around his waist as she clung to his back like a spider monkey. He shouted, reaching behind her with a hand to flip her off.

The gun went off, and I screamed. Plaster from the walls or maybe ceiling rained down over us as they continued to struggle. I shoved up into a sitting position and tried to think of something more to do.

They struggled for only a minute, and then he got the upper hand, reaching around to flip Ivory over his head, slamming her into the floor. Crying, I pulled myself across the floor toward my sister who was lying on her back, unmoving.

The man trained his gun on her.

"No!" I roared, throwing myself at his legs, still unable to reach.

In that moment, I hated my body. My useless legs. I hated being unable to fight.

"What the hell is going on here?" A new voice came from the end of the hall.

"Help!" I screamed.

Across the distance between us, our stares collided. There was something about him... something that seemed innately familiar.

"Please," I begged. "Please help us."

The man terrorizing us laughed. "He's with me, princess."

The new man was dressed exactly like his friend, except his hair was longer because I could see it sticking out from under the edges of his hat.

"What the fuck are you doing? You were supposed to be in and out."

I couldn't pull my eyes off the man. What was it about him? Even his voice.

"Please," I whispered, dragging myself across the floor toward him. He obviously wasn't here with good intentions, but whatever it was about him appealed to my instinct to survive.

"She stabbed me. Twice!" barked the man I was trying to get away from.

"She wouldn't have if you'd just shot her." The man sighed almost as though he were bored. His words were cold and matter-of-fact.

Just like… "*Earth*," I whimpered.

The man's body went rigid, and I glanced up. He reminded me of Earth.

There was a flash of something in his eyes, but then he looked away, the muscle in his jaw jumping. "If you won't do it, I will."

A gun exactly like the one his friend carried appeared in his hand. Eyes cold, he leveled it on me.

"Please don't kill my sister. My brother will need her," I begged and then closed my eyes and waited to die.

Thirty-Eight

EARTH

THE PHONE INSIDE MY JACKET WAS HEAVY.

The rose tattoo against my hip felt more like a freshly seared brand.

I was not innocent, not even at birth.

I was guilty—guilty by association, guilty by action. But I wouldn't consider myself guilty of offing the man who'd killed Riley.

Some people deserved what they got.

The first thing they did at the station was test my hands for gunpowder residue. It seemed tedious and stupid, but I cooperated. Why wouldn't I? The results would just make Fig look like the asshole he was.

I didn't touch guns.

Not since that night.

Afterward, I thought I'd see the inside of a cell, but since I hadn't been officially booked yet, I was led back out front for questioning. I wouldn't be as forthcoming with the questions as I was for the hand test.

They let me sit for a while on the metal chair, acting as if they had to supervise the transportation of the bodies to the coroner's office. Acting as though letting me sit in the center of a police station would somehow make me nervous and more likely to talk.

They weren't that bright, were they?

Giving me time to sit here just gave me more time to think up some plausible story. Not that I needed one. I'd already told them what happened in the alley, and it was the truth. First time I ever told the cops the truth.

Figures they didn't believe me.

Morons. Especially Fig, who walked around like he'd made a big arrest and was the most important contact on the case. Paul trailed behind him, still a little green from his recent encounters with dead bodies. Occasionally, I'd feel his eyes, but I never looked up. I was back to forgetting his name.

"We're gonna need to search you now." Fig stopped beside my chair, staring down as though he were intimidating.

I cocked my head just slightly to the side, angling my eye to pierce him with a look.

Clearing his throat, he drew back but put his hands on his hips like that somehow made up for the way he faltered.

"No," I said.

His mouth slackened, eyes narrowed. "What do you mean no? I didn't give you a choice."

"You didn't arrest me. You can't just search me without my permission."

"You're refusing?"

"Yep."

"Trying to impede the investigation?"

The ankle I had crossed over my knee slid free, my boot landing on the floor with a stomp. "If I wanted to impede your cop playtime, I wouldn't be here."

Fig's jaw hardened, and his voice dropped low. "Now listen here—"

The glass double doors to the station burst in, rattling against their frames. Everyone in the place stopped what they were doing to stare around at the group stepping in off the street.

Three people strode right inside, but as they walked, more fanned out behind them into the shape of a wide V. An entire team of people moving like they were one. The unmistakable air of confidence, money, and intimidation flooded the room, nearly choking out everything else.

I watched, schooling my face into a bored expression when, in reality, I was not bored at all.

In the center, a tall, blond man, wearing a blazer cut to hug the width of his shoulders and the taper of his waist, set the pace. His tie was straight and glossy. His austere features, which usually looked dopey when staring at my brother, were schooled into granite, daring anyone to challenge.

On either side of him were two shorter men dressed in suits. They wore glasses and carried leather briefcases. They didn't gaze around to assess their situation. They, too, stared straight ahead as if it didn't matter where they were because they'd dominate regardless. Those men were flanked by two more men just like them.

Bringing up the rear of the team were Beau and Neo. Neo was dressed in ripped jeans, boots similar to mine, and a lightweight jacket. Beau was wearing the same casual clothes from earlier, but now he had a beanie pulled over his wayward red hair.

They didn't match the men they flanked, but their aura was just as powerful. *Clothes do not make the man.* His attitude did.

"What the hell is this?" Fig spat.

"You arrested my bro. Did you expect me not to make a call?" Beau said, almost as though he were bored.

"What the hell is going on here?" Neo demanded. Ever the hothead. I didn't find it as annoying when it was aimed at someone else.

"Earth!" Fletcher exclaimed, popping out from behind Ethan to push between him and one of the other men.

I started to get up, but Fig had the nerve to push me back into my chair. I made a growling sound and opened my mouth to yell, but someone beat me to it.

"The officer is abusing his power. Using force when unnecessary," one of the men carrying a briefcase announced.

The other three who looked just like him all hummed in agreement.

Lawyers. Not only did my family come, but they brought lawyers.

Fletcher completely ignored Fig and rushed around him to stand right in front of me. "Earth! Are you okay?"

"Don't I look okay?"

"Beau said someone tried to kill you."

I slid a glance to Beau. He shrugged. "He's family."

Sighing, I looked back at Fletcher. He was just as capable as the rest of us. Hell, he'd never had it easy. But his innate kindness made that difficult to remember sometimes, along with his smaller size and big eyes. It made it really hard to involve him in this shit. But Beau was right. He was family, and that meant I wouldn't leave him out.

"I'm good, Fletch. You know I can take care of myself."

He nodded but said, "You don't have to."

See why I wanted to protect the kid? I half smiled. "That why you got your boyfriend to bring down four lawyers?"

Fletch frowned. "He's not just my boyfriend; he's *your* family."

Ethan stepped forward, palming the back of Fletcher's neck. Fletch looked up at him with a sappy, gaga expression, and I rolled my eyes. "Only two are mine. The other two are Ivory's."

I glanced around again, expecting Ivory to pop out like Fletcher did even though she was never the type to stay hidden.

"She's not here. I brought them," Neo said, realizing who I looked for.

"Where is she?"

"With Virginia."

An odd sense of unease wormed through me at the mention of V.

I'd literally just finished telling her I wouldn't kill any more people, and now look at me in jail for murder.

"I didn't call her, just the lawyers." Neo finished.

I nodded, relief easing a bit of my worry. It was better that way. She didn't belong here any more than V did.

"You're all going to have to leave. This is impeding an investigation," Fig announced.

Clearly, it was his favorite thing to say.

"Actually, we are this man's counsel, and telling us to leave is impeding his rights."

Four lawyers. Not just any lawyers either. The best money could buy. And they were here for me.

Even knowing who I was, even knowing I probably wasn't wholly innocent, my family came immediately, and they brought an entire calvary. Even Neo, who I'd literally been fighting the night before.

If I ever doubted how they all felt about me, it was clear now. We were family. Always.

"What are the charges?" one lawyer asked.

Fig sputtered, and while he did, I answered the question. "They didn't actually arrest me yet. They brought me in for questioning."

"Without a lawyer present?" The counsel eyed Fig.

"They haven't asked me anything yet. Just did a gunpowder test on my hands," I said, showing them my palms. "Right before you came in, he told me he had to search me. I told him no."

"Only people who have something to hide refuse!" Fig bellowed.

"My client is well within his rights to refuse. If you aren't going to press formal charges, then we insist he is let go, and we can schedule a time for questioning tomorrow. With his counsel."

Fig pursed his lips. "Which one of you is his counsel?"

"They all are," Ethan commanded.

Fig paled a bit. Dude was scared of Ethan. I fought the urge to laugh.

"He killed someone! Maybe even both of them!" Fig pointed at me.

"Murder is a hefty accusation. I would assume if you had actual evidence, he would already be booked and in a cell? Since he isn't, I would have to ask you to refrain from accusing my client, or you could find yourself being sued for slander."

Fig turned red and sputtered some more.

"I'm going to piss," I announced, standing from the chair.

"You can't!" Fig demanded.

"Going to the bathroom is a basic human right," someone said.

I kept going, letting myself into the basic room, which was hardly a step up from a gas station bathroom. Still, by Grimms standards, it was decent.

There were three sinks along the wall, and I went to the one in the center to wash off all the remnants of blood and residue from the gunpowder test. The water was tepid at best, nothing I would call warm, but at least it didn't feel like ice.

I stared down at the red-stained water swirling around the drain before being swallowed. As Riley's blood vanished from my hands, I felt a weird sense of sadness. What was left of his life was being washed away, sliding into the underbelly of the city to be diluted even further until not even a hint of his DNA could be recovered.

I didn't kill him, but I was responsible for his death.

As the water cascaded through my fingers and slid over my palms, more and more of him disappeared, and the clear turned a shade of pink. Flashes of him lying there, bleeding out, filled my mind, making it impossible to see anything else.

The sound of the gunshot was still knocking around inside my head. *If he'd just left town like I told him... If he hadn't been snooping around for more info, then he wouldn't be dead.*

"Hoping to run up the station's water bill?"

My head snapped up as I stared into the mirror at Neo standing just inside the door.

I didn't even hear him come in.

"Following me to the bathroom now?" I quipped, pulling my hands free of the water, shaking them, and sending droplets everywhere. But I still left the spigot on.

His boots scuffed over the floor, and the sink beside mine turned on. The sound of rushing water in the small room intensified. "Give it to me," he said, voice low.

I played stupid. "What?"

His head tilted slightly toward the door. "Whatever it is you don't want them to find."

I wasn't a man who was shocked by much. I mean, really, when you lived the way I did, the only surprise was actually being surprised.

Right now, standing in this grim, small bathroom, I was. Maybe I shouldn't be. After all, he had shown up when Beau called, and he'd brought two layers in tow. The rift between us made me doubt that, though. No. It made me want to *challenge* it. Sure, it seemed there might have been a change last night when he left me standing outside the Tower. But still, I wanted to push.

"I killed him," I deadpanned, my voice somehow blending in with the running faucets.

Maybe we were trying to run up their water bill.

Or maybe we used the sound to muffle our low conversation.

Neo showed no visible reaction to my words. "Both of them?"

"The one who trashed my bar and killed Riley."

Recognition and something else sparked in Neo's black eyes. "You knew his name."

Not just his name. He was too young to die.

Neo shifted closer, held my gaze, and nodded solemnly. His hand came up between us. I gazed down at his waiting palm.

"This would make you an accessory," I cautioned, flicking a glance to the door.

"Wouldn't be the first time."

My fingers curled into my palm, a loose fist resting at my side. We were still at odds with each other, yet here he was, palm outstretched, not an ounce of condemnation in his eyes.

You really accept me like this?

"You told me no more." *I promised not to kill again.*

As if either of us needed reminding.

"This was different. The laws of the street. Eye for an eye."

That cliché sent me spiraling back into the past, to a night I couldn't seem to keep my head out of.

The sound of the gun ripping into flesh was distinct. Sort of like a thump, sort of like a thick squelch. It lasted a fraction of a second, but I would always remember that sound.

Time seemed suspended. Everything else went on mute, and I saw the eyes of my target widen, eyes everyone said were similar to mine. Is that what I would look like if someone shot me?

Astonishment was more powerful than the first rush of pain, and it shined so bright I could almost see my equally shocked expression in her eyes. But the band holding time snapped, and we were thrust back into reality where nothing lasted more than a second.

Pain glazed over the astonishment, and her entire face grimaced as she looked down. Dark crimson spread over the fancy silk blouse, dousing the thin fabric and making it stick to her body like a second skin.

Her manicured hand hovered over the wound but didn't touch.

Shouts and pounding feet erupted. Chaos filled the night, and the steam from the vents thickened the air even more. I watched as she bowed toward the ground before dropping into a heap. Her legs were tangled, one high heel askew on the pavement.

I'd just shot my mother.

The only living parent I had left.

There was a time in my life I would never have imagined this, despite being born and bred to kill. I'd fought my own nature. Hell, I'd fought my own nurture, but somehow I still ended up here.

Who was responsible? The woman dying on the ground— the creator? Or the one who pulled the trigger?

The gun slipped from my fingers, landing on the pavement with a dull thud. I stared down at it. A thin trail of smoke wafted up from the barrel.

"Get him!" The command cut through the heavy ocean I seemed to be drowning in.

Adrenaline surged, making me remember how I'd gotten here in the first place. I took off, racing toward the back of the alley, leaping onto the fence creating a dead end.

With the reflexes of a young teen, I scrambled up the wire quickly, ignoring the knicks and cuts it left in me along the way.

Add them to the list of scars I will always carry.

Below me, the fence vibrated as men launched onto it, first trying to shake me free. I swung my leg over the top, and a litany of curses floated up.

The sound of guns cocking made my heart stop. I glanced back just as the first shot went off.

The heat of the bullet was so close it nearly singed my face, and I leaped off the top, throwing myself toward the ground.

More gunfire erupted, but it was secondary to the pain that radiated through my limbs when I hit. I felt my flesh split. The warm rush of sticky blood coated my chin and slipped down my neck.

I tried to scramble up, but the bullets shattering the asphalt around me kept me down.

Covering my head, I closed my eyes and waited for one of them to actually hit their mark. Perhaps running hadn't been the answer at all. Perhaps dying was the only way out.

"Sagyeog-eul meomchuda!" Cease fire!

The shooting stopped immediately, but I still lay on my belly, covering my head.

Heavy footfalls stopped beside me, and a heavy hand slammed into my back. I didn't fight as I was hauled off the ground, dragged up on my wobbly feet.

"I've got this," the man holding me yelled.

"How can we trust you with him?" someone called back.

"Eye for an eye."

"Even if that eye is your brother's?"

"The Black Rose demands it."

I started trembling a bit, the adrenaline melting away even though I'd just been sentenced to death. An odd sense of acceptance, of being indifferent to death, washed over me.

On the other side of the fence, the men turned away. There was more yelling and maybe some crying as they all gathered around the fallen woman.

"You killed our mother," a cold voice yelled as I was tossed into the side of a building.

Smacking hard, I bounced back, legs giving out as I crumpled to the ground.

"Get the hell up, you traitor!"

I got up, standing straight and refusing to look like I regretted what I'd done. The poison in my veins regretted nothing at all. The son inside me mourned a mother.

Lifting my chin, I steadied my gaze on my big brother's. "Annyeonghee gaseyo." Good-bye.

The memory of the gunfire made me jolt.

When something heavy hit against my shoulder and

squeezed, I went on autopilot, grabbing him and forcing him face first against the wall.

"Easy," Neo said, holding his hands up in surrender.

I dropped the hold immediately, stepping back. He turned to face me, not an ounce of anger in his face. "Where'd you go?"

"Nowhere."

Surprisingly, he accepted the non-answer and stepped close as though he wasn't worried I'd slam into him again. "They're going to come looking for us."

Reaching inside my jacket, I palmed the flip phone that wouldn't ring again. But it was still evidence, and if they called the last incoming number, the phone on Riley's dead body would likely ring.

Reluctantly, I handed it to Neo, and it disappeared inside his jacket. He moved away, shutting off the water and turning toward the door.

"Are you doing this for her?" For his sister who would be hurt if I got taken down.

"No. You were my family before this stuff with V, and you still are."

He went out first, leaving me to follow behind.

"Search them!" Fig bellowed the second we both left the bathroom.

Two officers started toward us, but Fletcher rushed in front, tripping over his shoes and falling into Neo.

"Sorry," he said, still holding on to our brother but pulling back to stand. "I was trying to help, and I ended up just falling."

"You need new shoes," Ethan declared, pulling Fletch into his side and locking an arm at his waist.

Fletcher rolled his eyes. "These are new."

"Well, they must be faulty if you're tripping everywhere."

"I'm gonna email Dior and tell them you said that!" He threatened.

Who the fuck was Dior?

Ethan smiled, amused, tucking Fletcher even closer against his side. I swear the guy would carry him around if Fletcher would let him.

"I said search them!" Fig burst into the conversation, motioning for the two officers staring at Fletch and Ethan to get back to work.

"You can't search me. I'm not even here as a witness," Neo said, folding his arms over his chest.

Ivory's two sharks stepped up to his sides as if they were his personal guard dogs.

"He could have passed something to you he didn't want us to see!"

I schooled my face into a bored expression.

Neo sighed dramatically. "Fine. You wanna search me? Go ahead."

Fig eyed him.

Neo made a face. "What, now that I'm agreeing, you suddenly don't think I've done anything wrong?"

Fig gestured toward Neo, and the officers started patting him down, looking inside his jacket.

I was on red alert but kept my uninterested face plastered on. What the fuck was he thinking? Was this a setup? Maybe hadn't been doing it to keep his sister from being hurt but to keep me from his sister.

My tongue slid across my teeth as I seethed in anger and betrayal.

Was this to get back at me for almost killing Ivory?

Eye for an eye.

The words he'd just spoken haunted me along with the memory I'd just relived as though it had been yesterday and not many years before.

I sucked in a breath, realization crashing over me like a tsunami.

"See?" Neo spat, straightening the collar on his jacket. "Nothing. Just me taking a piss."

Even in the chaos happening inside my mind, even with the loud thumping of my heartbeat, I realized what he'd done.

Fletch, the little pickpocket, snatched the phone to make Fig and friends look even more idiotic.

If the back of my neck wasn't tingling and my gut screaming, I would have been impressed by the team-work. And relieved Neo didn't betray me.

I was, but none of that mattered.

I was being set up.

They knew any charges I got hit with wouldn't stick. They knew I'd be hauled in and held here anyway. Hell, they probably even knew what a bumbling moron Fig was.

They were just buying time.

An eye for an eye.

You kill one of ours, we'll kill one of yours.

Riley didn't really count as one of mine. And the guy I'd slashed in the alley wasn't the one they'd come all this way to exact revenge for.

The Black Rose demands it.

How easily they'd isolated my weakness.

"Virginia is alone." The words ripped out from a dark, dangerous place. The poison I tried so hard to keep calm bubbled up as if my veins were a cauldron someone was chanting over.

All the chaos happening around us quieted. Everyone turned to me.

"No, Ivory is with her," Neo said, his voice measured, but I could almost feel his panic rise.

"Christ," I spat, pushing past the cops toward the door. "They're alone!"

I heard my name being called. I heard people insisting I couldn't leave. I only stopped to snatch my blade and harness off Fig's desk before fleeing that shitty station and into the night.

Thirty-Nine

My instincts had been wrong about the man holding a gun on me. It seemed today would be my death day.

What was the point of surviving the car accident and my parent's death? Of fighting for life, of fighting my brother for things I wouldn't have anyway. What was the point of falling in love only to lose it so quickly?

What a pitiful waste.

I made my last request, closed my eyes, and waited for flesh-searing heat that would make me writhe as I free-fell into death.

It didn't come.

Cracking open one eye, I stared at the man still holding the gun. A look I couldn't really decipher swam in his eyes as he stared at me.

But then I understood.

Never make it personal. Earth's words echoed in my head.

A war was waging inside him. He knew what he was here for, yet he hesitated.

"Do you know Earth?" I asked, taking a chance.

Something flickered in that muddy gaze. "No."

"You remind me of him."

The gun wavered and began to lower.

"Agh!"

A dark figure shot out from the opening into the hallway. Like a linebacker, he barreled into the man, sending both of them flying sideways. The sound of the gun clattering against the tile was loud, and I watched the weapon glide over the floor until it smacked against the wall.

I couldn't see the two men any longer, but I heard them fighting. The sound of their grunts and roars echoed through the hall.

Eyeing the gun, I started toward it.

"You'll never make it," a hard voice behind me threatened.

I stopped, resisted the urge to cry. Twisting at the waist, I looked at the man I'd stabbed. Blood smeared his clothes and even his neck. A sadistic smile curved his lips as he held his gun on me.

Despite the sounds of fighting and the thunderous booming of my own heart, Ivory's small sound cut through it all, my eyes flying toward her. She was moving sluggishly like she was coming to.

Tensing, the man between us started to turn.

"Hey!" I yelled, drawing his attention back to me. "If I had a gun, you'd already be dead."

I saw it in his eyes—the total lack of hesitation.

He brought his arm up. I watched with rapt clarity as his finger squeezed the trigger.

Life slowed as if I'd been submerged in the deepest ocean. Sluggishly, I watched what could have been mere seconds play out in so much detail it would be tattooed on my brain for as long as I lived.

Maybe even longer.

"*Noo!*" The loud bellow drowned out the pop of the gun as something big and dark literally appeared in front of me like a shield.

He seemed to float gracefully through the air until the bullet slammed into him, making his body jerk and drop onto the floor with a sharp slap.

I felt my lips move but heard no sound. In fact, I heard nothing as Earth shoved up from the floor the second he hit, scrambling forward to throw his entire body over mine.

Despite the danger and adrenaline, instant relief flooded my system, so powerful a sob ripped out of me. I wanted desperately to wrap my arms around him, but he hunched tighter, tucking me beneath him as if he could make me invisible.

I settled for clutching the front of his shirt, holding the material in my hands so tight that my fingers screamed out in pain.

The slow-motion bubble I'd been in popped, and chaos erupted, but I could only look at him.

His dark head lifted, hair falling over his forehead and into his eyes. "Are you okay?" he asked, pain-glazed eyes scanning my face.

"Y-you got shot." My voice wobbled, panic stuck in my throat.

"Sweetheart, are you hurt? Are you bleeding?"

"I-I—" I gasped, eyes going wide. The fingers gripping his shirt let go as I recalled the way his body jerked against the bullet.

A hand slapped against his back, making him grimace as his body was forced away from mine.

"Well, if it isn't the traitor himself. Your ghost has haunted my home for too long." The man sneered, burying his fist into Earth's middle.

I screamed, shoving up into a sitting position just in time to see the man deliver another blow to Earth's face.

Earth sagged and fell to the floor. A smear of red marred the floor beneath him.

I called out, crawling toward him, but a rough hand fisted around my long braid, giving a fierce yank and reversing the direction my body was headed. I screamed and clawed, trying to get back to Earth, to the man who literally leaped in front of a bullet for me, but it was to no avail.

I was dragged down the hall, unable to acknowledge the pain in my head from the way he pulled my hair like it was a rope and not something attached to my scalp.

I could only stare at Earth as I was pulled farther away. "Help!" I yelled, looking to the back of the hall, wondering where that beast-man went along with the other man he tackled.

Ivory made a sound near the wall, and I glanced over at her unfocused eyes.

The elevator was open, my chair keeping it from closing. The man dragging me laughed maniacally as he towed me closer.

"I was sent to kill you, but after all this, that just isn't good enough," he said, kicking my chair into the car so he could move in.

I planted my hands on the ground and tugged backward, trying to make it harder for him to pull. The force of the tug made tears spill down my cheeks, but despite the pain, I still fought.

"That asshole left a permanent dark cloud over my whole organization, and he's gonna pay. I'd say wondering where you are and what I'm doing to someone as helpless as you is a pretty good mind-fuck. I won't be gentle. Shame you won't feel it. Bet I can make you scream anyway," he taunted, going back into the elevator, dragging me toward the door.

My hair was so long that it stretched out like a cable. The flowers I had pinned in the braid fell out all over, littering the floor with petals and bright color in this grim situation.

I grabbed the length of my hair, trying to tug it away from the gangster. He laughed. I gave a bemoaned yell, frustration welling up inside me.

"Where's your hero now?" he taunted, tugging, towing me even closer.

Heavy footfalls sounded down the hall. The glint of a blade reflected in my peripheral vision.

I leveled my eyes on the man I didn't know but hated with a passion. "I don't have a hero," I replied. "I have a villain."

Earth grunted when he hit the floor like a baseball player sliding into home. He glided through the narrow space left between me and the elevator doors, his gleaming blade slicing seamlessly through my braid.

Freed, my body fell back as the man on the other end of the braid stumbled deeper into the elevator, his body hitting the wall. He stared at the severed hair in his hand, completely stupefied, and then looked up at me as the doors slammed shut between us.

And then Earth was there, scrambling across the floor, folding around me like a blanket. I let out a sob as his hand cupped the back of my head, holding it fiercely against his shoulder.

I could feel the thundering of his heart, feel the heavy way his chest rose and fell.

"Y-you cut my hair." I hiccupped, clinging to him.

"This is my fault," he rasped. "I'm so goddamn sorry."

I knew he wasn't talking about my hair, and it didn't

matter. I didn't care about my hair. I didn't care about almost dying. I didn't care about me at all.

"You got shot. You leaped in front of a bullet for me."

His lips moved in my hair, the words more of a caress than a kiss would ever be. "I'd take a thousand bullets for you."

I gripped him harder, pressing closer, nearly forgetting about the horrible things going on around us because, in that moment, all I wanted was him.

Pounding footsteps burst around the corner, and I shrank down as a low growl rumbled deep in his throat.

"Ivory!" Neo called out, making me stiffen and pull back.

Even so, Earth held on to me as I twisted around to look for Ivory who was leaning up against the wall.

"Here!" I called out, pointing to her.

Neo swore, racing over to drop down in front of her. "What the hell happened?"

"She must have a concussion. He threw her on the ground really hard."

Neo's back muscles rippled, but the gentle tone he used with Ivory didn't carry to my ears.

"What happened?" Beau's familiar voice made me look up again.

The rest of my brothers—Beau, Fletcher, and Ethan—were standing a few feet away, all three of them gazing around, mildly stunned.

"There's still someone here with a gun." I worried. "Be careful!" I gasped. "The beast! He's here too."

"The beast?" Beau wondered.

"That big growly guy that lives down the hall," Fletcher reminded him.

"He actually helped us. He stopped the one man from

shooting me," I confessed, pulling back to look at Earth. "He kinda reminded me of you."

An unreadable look darkened his eyes, but he said nothing.

"Let's sweep the floor," Ethan suggested. "Fletcher—"

"If you tell me to stay here, I'm moving back in with Earth," Fletcher deadpanned.

There was a brief silence. "Fletcher, come with me." Earth concluded. "I'll call for an ambulance."

Earth started to pull back, likely to go and help the others, but I clung to him shamelessly. "Don't leave."

I knew he wanted to go, but he settled back down, pulling me close once more. A moment later, the sound of the elevator arriving and the doors opening made me stiffen.

The man rushed out at the same time Earth shot up and spun. The gun the man was holding clattered against the floor with a single kick from Earth.

"You shouldn't have come back here," he intoned, grabbing him from behind and locking his arms around the man's neck. Keeping the man in a strong hold, Earth flicked his eyes to where I sat watching them. "Close your eyes, sprite."

The snapping sound of the man's neck was definitive. He slumped to the ground the second Earth let go.

Leaving the body where it lay, Earth turned back. When he saw me staring, he frowned. "I told you to close your eyes."

"I don't need to close my eyes to love you."

I can't describe the look that washed over him. No. It was more of a transformation coming over his entire being. His Adam's apple bobbed like it was floating in a sea of emotion there inside his throat.

"What?" he rasped, turning fully to face me.

I smiled gently and repeated the words.

Awe. He was awash with awe. As if he never expected I could see him take a life and then still be able to tell him I loved him.

But I did.

He took a step toward me, but a shadow flickered behind him, and fear gripped my heart.

I started to call out, but he was faster, sensing the threat practically before I saw it. Earth spun and unsheathed his blade at once. Without a shred of hesitation, he dove forward, shoving the man back and driving the blade through his upper arm, anchoring him to the wall.

The man grunted in pain, slumping a little.

"This one tried to kill you too?" Earth asked, voice hard. Aggressively, he grabbed the man by his throat, forcing his head against the wall.

A bolt of silence so charged cut through the room. I felt the hair on my neck stand.

The man stabbed into the wall grunted. "Hey, brat."

Earth's grip went slack. "*Hyung.*"

My lungs seized. I knew that word. They used it in Korean dramas all the time. It meant brother. Realization dawned. The reason he reminded me of Earth hadn't been because I was desperate to live.

No.

It was because they were similar. They were brothers.

EARTH

THE RINGING IN MY EARS WAS DEAFENING. IT FELT AS IF MY ear canals were bleeding out from the close-range deafening sound. Hunching over, I curled into myself, pain almost secondary to that damn high-pitched ringing.

Almost.

Even though I was weak, I pressed my hand against my side as hard as I could. My insides were in danger of spilling out of the hole savagely ripped open by the bullet.

The bullet from my big brother's gun.

All my life, he'd been a constant presence, a protection from the tree from which we grew. I knew he was cold and ruthless. We all were.

But not to me.

I thought we had a bond that couldn't be severed. A bond forged in blood and solidified by survival. Tonight, his gun put an end to that.

Or perhaps it had been my gun.

Another shot popped off, the bullet embedding itself in the brick just above my head. I barely even winced despite the chunks of brick raining down over me in my fetal position.

I hoped death hurried up and claimed me. Perhaps death

would be better than life. Sometimes it seemed a hell of a lot kinder.

Warm liquid oozed between my fingers. The pressure I applied seemed to be waning. His knees dropped in front of me, the gun in his hand placed on the pavement near my glassy stare.

I hated guns.

His arm shot out, fingers resting against my neck. "Play dead," he whispered harshly.

My brain struggled to understand because I didn't have to play. The pain ripping through me was proof.

"I'm getting rid of the trash," Daeshim spat, jamming the gun in the waistband of his jeans.

My body was that of a rag doll, pliable and completely boneless. Extreme pain radiated when he tossed me over his shoulder, his bone digging into my rib, his fingers jabbing into the bullet hole.

My world dimmed around the edges until I was entirely numb. I vaguely wondered where he was going to dispose of my body, but as consciousness ebbed, I realized it didn't matter because I wouldn't be there anyway.

He was the same. But different. Maybe a bit larger than I remembered, more filled out. But his eyes were as they had always been: black ice. Upon first glance, you might not realize just how dangerous he was, unable to see the depth of the coldness he embodied because it was well hidden in those opaque chocolate eyes.

But it was there. I knew.

I didn't think I'd ever see him again, but here he was, looking roughed up and pinned to the wall by my blade.

He stared at me with crimson smearing his lips and a bit of a wheeze in every breath. "Glad to see you haven't let yourself go."

Pride. Was that pride shining deep in his gaze?

Unexpected emotion crashed over me again and again like waves gobbling up a beach during high tide.

Recollections flickered, my mind a faulty video player skimming rapidly between memories but fully replaying that final night.

The night my brother killed me.

"I didn't think I'd see you again," was all I said.

"We both knew I couldn't protect you forever."

We stared at each other, saying so much without saying anything at all. I wanted to ask him why he did it. I wanted to ask him why he stayed. I also wanted to know...

"Did you take her place?" *Did you carry on her legacy of venom and chaos? Daeshim, her namesake. Daeshim, heir of the Black Rose.*

Confusion spilled out from beneath the bill of his hat, but then it cleared when something else dawned. "You don't know."

An inkling of something tingled at the base of my spine, and it was something I didn't like. Lashing out, I grabbed the handle of my blade, twisting it just a little.

Daeshim grunted in pain, his mouth grimacing into a straight line.

"Know what?" I intoned.

"She's alive."

I drew back as if his words were a raging fire. *Alive?* She couldn't be. *I shot her. I watched her die.*

"No." I was lost in that night once more, replaying the sound of the bullet ripping into her flesh. The look of shock in her eyes and the way she folded to the pavement in that grim, dark alley. Men had cried over her body. "It's impossible."

"You, of all people, know it's not."

My eyes shot up to his. His stare was steady, eyes clear.

I staggered back. Me. The Huntsman. A man who literally lived by death. So why did finding out my very first kill was not actually a kill shock me so violently? It never once in all these years ever occurred to me that she might still be alive.

I had run without looking back, and I always just assumed.

Yes, I know. Assuming makes an ass out of you and me.

I'd based so much on that one assumption.

A humorless laugh echoed in the hall, mixing with the buzzy, flickering overhead lights.

I ran away, but I could never escape.

"Mal-Chin."

My eyes snapped up. No one had called me that in so long. That boy was not who I was. "It's Earth now."

He inclined his head. "She's never forgotten. Not even for a single minute. When she found out…" His jaw jumped, and he glanced away. When his chin lifted again, the black ice of his stare glimmered with frost. Then his eyes slowly shifted toward Virginia. "It would have been a kindness to let me kill her."

I all but roared, throwing myself at him. As I wrenched the knife out of his arm, he moaned and slumped to the floor, a trail of scarlet dripping down the wall behind him.

"Mianhae Hyung." *I'm sorry, brother,* I told him, roughly grabbing the collar of his shirt. "But when it comes to her, my kills aren't pretend."

I raised the blade above my head, squeezing the handle.

"Earth!" Virginia called, her voice breaking through

the fog draping over my mind. "He hesitated!" She gasped, nearly falling over toward us. "Please, stop! He hesitated."

The blade lowered a bit. "What?"

"He wasn't going to do it. I saw it in his face. He couldn't. He couldn't do it to you." Her eyes were honest and pleading, not at all as they'd been when I'd ended the man who'd tried to haul her into the elevator.

I don't have to close my eyes to love you.

Those words lived in me now. Every breath I took whispered them. My heart beat to their cadence. This woman had just been through hell and watched me kill a man… *But she loves me still.*

Despite the way my shoulder screamed, the way flesh tore, causing a warm gush of blood, I lifted my brother a little anyway. "That true?"

Even if it wasn't, it wouldn't matter. Virginia said it, and even if it was actually a lie, I would believe her if that's what she wanted.

"You love her."

I dropped him onto the floor.

The sound of heels clicking steadily across tile echoed down the hall, even from around the corner.

Daeshim stiffened before pushing to his feet.

An ominous, unstable feeling rippled through the atmosphere. A rush of power and subtle arrogance reached out sharpened claws as though it were testing the waiting enemies, wondering how strong of a fight there would be.

A hard knot settled in my stomach as I turned toward the end of the hall as the click-clacking of the heels grew ever closer.

Off to my right, I sensed Neo stand from Ivory to also rotate toward the incoming presence. There were more footfalls accompanying those powerful, sharp ones, but they were secondary in sound and in thought.

She rounded the corner a moment later, her entourage fanning out behind her. They were all in black, but her?

The Black Rose didn't need to wear the dark shade because everything else about her was black as night.

Her red heels were impressively high, adding height to her embarrassingly short frame. The nude dress she wore hugged a body she likely ate very little to maintain. Instead of a coat, she wore a cloak—leopard print and made of fur. It likely was not faux, for that meant she would have to give a damn.

The buttons down the front were bright-red leather, as was the clasp that held the fabric together beneath her chin.

Her face was likely done up in whatever Korean makeup trend was hot right now, and her black hair fell in a sleek bob to her shoulders. She'd aged, of course, but quite well. It was to be expected, as she had enough money to buy a new face if needed.

Despite her standing there in living color, practically killing me with her ruthless, piercing stare, it felt as though I'd seen a ghost. As if I were being haunted at last by a kill.

But she wasn't dead. The single kill, which had shaped the very foundation of the Huntsman I was today, had been nothing but a farce.

All these years, I thought she was nothing but a rotting corpse, but in reality, she'd been living. Wreaking havoc and likely searching for me while planning my demise.

I couldn't say I was happy to see her breathing. But the smallest part of me felt somewhat relieved my bullet had failed.

One less death to live with.

The unexpected thought was startling. Since when did I ever have to live with the guilt of my kills?

"Look at that," she mused, her tone level without a single drop of affection. It was almost as if she spoke to hear herself talk. "My sons in the same room at last."

Behind me, Virginia drew in a breath, and I shifted slightly, trying to block her with my frame. To my surprise, Daeshim shifted too, the pair of us creating somewhat of a wall.

Mother's eyes flicked over our shoulders and then went back to pierce my brother with a pointed, cold look. "I see you hesitated *again*."

If I hadn't been shoulder to shoulder with him, I wouldn't have known his reaction. His skin practically vibrated with anger and something else.

Fear.

He is scared of her.

My world rocked for a moment because Daeshim Hyung had never been scared of anything.

Movement caused ripples in the tense stillness, and I looked past the she-devil as my three brothers rounded the corner.

"We can't find the—" Fletcher called but stopped the second all the men trailing my mother turned, lifting their guns.

My fist tightened around the blade as ice water flowed through my veins. Ethan moved quickly, shoving Fletcher behind him, rising to his full, impressive size. Seeming to understand the seriousness of this situation, Fletcher didn't argue about being protected.

Beau straightened too, his eyes narrowing on the

group of people between us, his gaze more assessing and alert than I probably had ever seen.

Mother was the only one who did not turn around. I felt her hawklike stare focused on me as if I were somehow a mirror and she could see my family in my reflection.

Forcing my eyes away from my brothers, I met her level gaze. "You came for me. Here I am."

"It's true. I did come for you. But the more I've watched, the clearer it's become that the best revenge against you is to make everyone around you suffer."

"I can assure you that this time I'll make sure you're dead." It was not an idle threat. I'd lived with her death nearly half my life. I knew I could continue doing so.

She laughed, almost as if she were fond of my threat. "It's really quite a shame you turned on me. You're everything I'd hoped you'd be. Unlike my namesake who is nothing but a disappointment."

Daeshim didn't react. It was as though he'd heard those words so many times that they fell on deaf ears.

"I see you still never figured it out," I said, drawing her attention from him.

Her lips pursed.

"I never turned on you. You can't turn on someone who never had your loyalty to begin with."

The temperature of her stare dropped, and cold fury rolled off her in waves. The only other indication I'd hit a nerve was the slight curl of her upper lip. "Your loyalty was owed to me by birth!"

"Loyalty is earned," I said, bored. "But poison seems to be hereditary." I took a step closer, and the wariness I saw slip into her gaze was so satisfying. What was even more satisfying was that every gun in the room redirected onto me. "Be careful, Mother. This poison apple didn't fall far from its tree."

Her dark eyes glittered as one arm came out from the cape, palm up, silently probing. The man closest to her side stepped forward, placing his gun in her waiting hand.

She moved swiftly, raising the gun and squeezing off a shot.

"No!" Daeshim shouted and threw himself in front of me.

The bullet slammed into him, knocking him back, and both of us went down.

Chaos erupted around us. Outside sirens from emergency responders grew loud. The flickering overhead lights chose that moment to blink out. The only light now came from a single window behind us at the dead-end of the hall on the other side of the elevator.

Outside, the sky was grim. I didn't know if it was because dusk was approaching or because the air was filled with smoke from the fire somewhere in this building.

Daeshim grunted in pain as I slid out from beneath his body. The bullet had ripped into his shoulder not far from where I'd stabbed him. Blood stained his clothes. His skin was unnaturally pale. The baseball hat on his head had fallen aside, and sweat beaded his forehead, making his longish black hair cling there.

"Hyung," I said, leaning over him. "Hyung."

"You stupid boy!" Mother yelled. "I forbid you to die! Your life is mine!"

Daeshim's eyes lifted to mine, bleak and tired. "Let me die," he whispered. "I can't go back."

Pure hatred unlike anything I'd ever felt before burst

inside me, crippling all the indifference I'd lived with most of my life.

Adrenaline gave me a burst of energy, and I forgot about the bullet wound in my back. Jumping up, I leaped over my brother and charged.

Pure panic widened my mother's eyes, and she lifted the gun again.

"No!" Virginia screamed, and there was scuffling all around. I stayed focused with single-minded precision, not even blinking at the threat of the gun.

Go ahead and shoot me. Just piss me off even more.

But she didn't shoot. She stood stunned by my pure hatred, and I kicked the gun out of her hand, sending it flying. I leaped on her, tackling her small frame to the ground, and wrapped a hand around her throat.

Stunned, she lay there gasping for breath as I leaned in so she could feel the hot breath of every word I spoke. "You should have stayed away."

"I wonder what matters to you more, Mal-Chin. Revenge on your mother or the life of the woman you love?"

I glanced up at the oddly familiar voice.

The man—Kwan, my father's best friend—stood behind me. His arm pinned Virginia against his chest, her legs dangling toward the floor… a gun pressed to her head.

"You would do this to your best friend's son?"

"Why not? I already took his wife." His eyes were flat, the curve of his lips amused. The gun pressed a little harder into her temple, and V winced in pain.

"You son of a bitch," Neo roared, and there was a scuffle and a grunt off to the side. He and Ivory were also being held at gunpoint.

I leaped up, dragging my mother with me, holding

her hostage the way that asshole held V. But instead of a gun, I let the tip of my blade pierce her throat, making it clear I could slice her open in an instant.

I didn't have to look behind me to know that my other brothers were probably also being held at gunpoint. My scalp prickled as I fought the urge to turn and check. Instead, I remained focused on the man holding what was mine.

"Let them go, or her head will roll." To prove my words, I pressed harder, making Mother gasp and bleed more.

"We seem to be at an impasse," Kwan mused. "Maybe I'll just let you kill her. Then I'll take over the entire organization."

Mother gasped.

I chuckled, then put my lips against her ear. "There's no loyalty among villains."

Virginia whimpered, and my eyes flew up. His hand was around her neck now, and he held her out like she was a rag doll. Her dress was so long it hid her feet and pooled against the floor.

"Pretty little thing. I might be tempted to keep you, but I have no interest in only half a woman."

I shoved Mother away from me so fast and hard I heard her smack into the wall. Lunging forward, I threw myself at Kwan, body slamming into him, the three of us falling into a mass on the floor.

Above me, he went slack, his eyes glazing over with pain. I shoved him off, rolling him onto his back. My blade stuck out from his side, and he gazed at me with shock.

"Don't ever touch her again," I spat, yanking the blade free, the sucking sound it made echoing down the hall.

Kwan rolled into a fetal position, curling around the wound in his side.

Virginia lay close, and I went to her, kneeling at her side. "Are you hurt?"

"We found another one," declared someone I didn't know. He stepped into the hall, carrying a clearly unconscious Emogen.

Virginia gasped as the man all but dumped her unresponsive friend on the floor.

Red, blue, and white lights flashed through the window, making the walls flicker with color. Any minute now, this building would be flooded with firefighters and cops.

"Is she dead?" Virginia sobbed, still staring at her friend.

Red heels appeared next to where V sat, making me stiffen and pull her into my body.

Blood smeared her neck, and her eyes were slightly glassy. She flicked a glance at Kwan and then dismissed him as though he was now her enemy. "Time is out. You and yours are outnumbered. That blade, no matter how sharp, is no match for all of these guns."

"I won't let you hurt my family."

"You could save a few, I'm sure, but not all. Are you prepared to choose?"

My arms tightened around Virginia, but my sprite lifted her chin to stare up at the woman threatening her life. "Why are you so hateful?"

My mother regarded her coolly, then replied, "Hate is easier than love."

"Hate is for cowards."

Mother's eyes narrowed, then flicked to me. "Come with me, and I'll let them all live."

Virginia stiffened, her body cringing back into mine.

I tucked an arm around her, trying to ignore the way her body shook.

"What?"

"Come home where you belong." She flicked a glance at my unmoving brother and then back to me. "Take your brother's place. It's the only way all these misfits will live."

"No," Virginia whimpered.

"Your life in exchange for theirs."

Over my shoulder, Neo stood in front of Ivory, trying to block her from the three guns pointed at them both. Down the hall, Ethan and Beau tried to block Fletcher from the barrels trained on them. Billows of thick smoke carrying bits of floating ash were making their way into this dim, congested hallway. From behind his shields, Fletcher coughed, and Ethan stiffened, proof that time had indeed run out.

My brother lay lifeless on the floor. The bullet in him had been meant for me.

And this venomous woman stood, albeit bleeding but unwavering, in the center of it all, every thorn making up her black rose on full display.

"Let them go."

Satisfaction whipped into her eyes, and she smiled. "Welcome home, *Adeul*." Son.

"No!" Virginia clung to me, wrapping both arms around my neck.

Reaching up, I tried to pry her away, but it was a weak, half-hearted attempt. "Let go, sprite."

"I won't! You promised not to leave." Her eyes were bloodshot, her nose red. Her long hair was now severed and uneven, flower petals littering the strands. Wet cheeks from all her tears, a red lip from being hit, and the bruises forming around her neck—this was what my love looked like on her.

Poisoning guaranteed.

She was better off without me.

"I also told you I would do anything to keep you safe." I reminded her.

"She'll kill you as soon as you go with her!" Virginia sobbed, collapsing into my chest. "You can't go. I won't let you."

"It's better this way. I can't run from what I really am."

She pulled back with a gasp, eyes fierce. Her hands held my face, fingertips digging into my skin. "You are *nothing* like her."

Mother laughed, a cruel, knowing sound. "Oh, dear, he is exactly like me."

"No," Virginia whispered, eyes still clinging to mine.

I reached up to tug her hands away.

"You were my dream," she whispered, fingers curling around mine.

Deep hurt unlike anything I'd ever felt before carved out a hole inside me, and I knew it would be there forever. This was an ache I would live with. This was an ache that would never go away.

The lump in my throat was so swollen it took effort to swallow.

"You were my dream too," I answered, hoarse.

"Let's go," Mother snapped. Her hand shot out toward V, but I caught her wrist without even having to look.

I squeezed until I knew there would be a bruise and then shoved her wrist away.

On the floors below us, I heard emergency responders yelling and sweeping the building. The noise was deafening, but the pounding of my heart was worse.

"Take care of yourself," I whispered, leaning in to drag my nose along the tip of hers.

She cried.

Avoiding her clutching fingers, I stood, knowing she wasn't able to follow.

I glanced at Neo. The look on his face was indescribable. "Please take care of her."

"Come now, Mal-Chin. Let's go home." Her red heels clacked across the floor as she moved along, confident I would follow behind.

I would. My family depended on it.

"Let's go!" she ordered, and all the guns in the room dropped.

Big mistake.

The drop ceiling overhead rumbled like thunder, and then a few tiles crashed in as a body shrouded in dark clothing and a black hoodie literally plummeted from above. He landed like a cat flat on his feet with knees bent. One hand braced on the floor and pushed up, his whole body bursting forward.

Shock rendered everyone still for long moments, but it was all we needed.

"Aghhh!" he roared, running forward and slamming into Mother with surprising intensity. She stumbled back, one red heel flinging off her foot, which only created more of an imbalance. As she flailed, she reached out for me.

I denied the wicked woman help, and she collided with Virginia's wheelchair.

She gasped as she tripped, her body falling against the sole window in the hall, the old glass giving away under pressure.

Her body disappeared, plummeting out of the building, her deafening scream rising as she fell.

I went to the window, watching the cape flap around her and her arms and legs flail.

When she hit the pavement, her scream and movement ceased.

Turning from the window, I was met with many eyes, silent faces, and shock.

"She's dead," I announced, eyes going straight to the man who'd fallen out of the ceiling and given us all an opportunity to take control.

The oversized hood and the way he stood hunched over, chin down, made it impossible to see his face, but I knew who he was.

The man living down the hall from Virginia. The patient everyone referred to as Beast.

Without a word, he turned, rushing over to where Emogen lay unconscious and lifting her into his arms without hesitation. No one protested, not even V, when he fled the hall, taking the nurse with him.

A broken sound ripped from Virginia's throat, shattering the charged stillness, compelling us all into action. I rushed her, tucking away my blade and cradling her into my arms, as my brothers commandeered the firepower, turning it against what was left of the Black Rose.

Before anything else could happen, emergency responders flooded the floor, and I stood in the center of chaos, wondering how in the hell I was going to explain this.

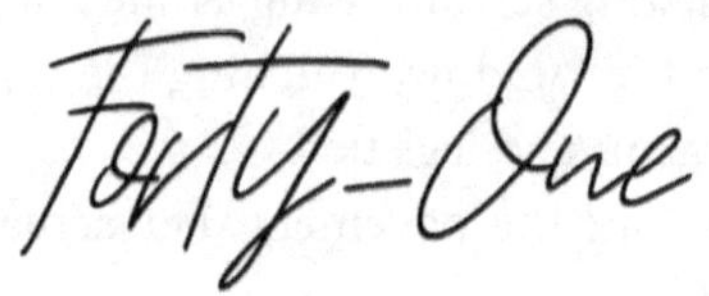

Virginia

LOVING A VILLAIN IS NOT EASY.
But you know what would be harder?
Not loving him at all.

Forty-Two

CONSCIOUSNESS CRASHED IN LIKE A BAD DREAM. THE PEACE of nothingness ruined by the confusion of reality. The room was bright, but everything was blurred. Eventually, my eyesight cleared, and my tongue darted out to wet, rough, cracked lips.

The room was small, sparse, and smelled like antiseptic.

Not at all how I imagined death to be.

"You're awake."

Startled, I glanced up at an unknown man who used an unknown voice. I wasn't afraid, though, because, really, what was left to be afraid of?

"Who are you?"

"No one important."

"Where am I?"

"You're just here until you're strong enough to go."

My brow creased, confusion mudding my mind. It seemed the answers I wanted would only be found within me, for this person would be of no help. Dull pain in my side made me lift the threadbare blanket and gaze down at the large white bandage.

Everything that happened replayed on fast-forward inside

my brain. Shooting Mother. Being chased. Being shot by Hyung and then carried away to be discarded.

"I'm not dead," I murmured.

"No. You are very much alive."

Play dead. *The words Daeshim whispered echoed in the back of my brain.*

The man nearby cleared his throat, and I glanced up. "But no one is to know."

I frowned.

"You cannot go home. Mal-Chin no longer exists. You must disappear and never return."

Reaching down, I palmed the wound in my side.

"It's not a serious wound. He avoided all the organs, just hit you where it would bleed."

He didn't want to kill me. He only made it look like he did.

"Everyone assumes you're dead." The man held up a yellow envelope. "A passport. A new ID. There's money but not much. You need to go."

"How long have I been here?"

"Three days."

I reached for the envelope, and he let me take it. "Did he...? Did Da—"

"Yes. He risked a lot, so don't betray him."

I couldn't say his name anymore. He wasn't my brother any longer. I was alone. Set free. I thought he betrayed me, but he didn't.

"There's clothes. A meal. Don't ever come back."

I killed our mother, and he set me free. Did that mean he forgave me? Or did he just not want my blood on his hands?

Either way, I guessed it didn't matter because I'd never see him again.

Consciousness came to me slowly but then all at once. I jolted awake, ignoring the pain in my shoulder to sit up, looking around wildly.

Where is she? Virginia!

"You're awake!"

Her voice called to me like a siren in the middle of a stormy sea. I rotated toward her, world condensing into a singular person.

Perched in her chair beside my bed, she was rumpled and looked as if she'd been through hell, but the smile on her lips negated it all.

"Sprite." I breathed out, everything inside me relaxing.

"How are you feeling?"

Wait a minute. Where were we? The last thing I remembered was Mother falling out of the Tower to her death and the building filling with cops.

I glanced around at the sterile room and then down at the IV in my hand. "What the fuck is this?"

"You're in the hospital. You passed out."

"I did not," I argued.

"Did too."

"One bullet ain't enough to bring me down." I scoffed.

"You lost a lot of blood." Her lower lip wobbled.

Shit.

"All right now, sprite. It's okay. I'm fine." I pushed up, ignoring the pain in my shoulder and the tug of the IV in the back of my hand so I could put her in the bed with me.

My legs were barely over the side of the bed when a hand fell onto my arm. I glanced up. Neo's impenetrable dark gaze met mine.

He pushed a little on my arm, then picked Virginia up and motioned for me to move back onto the mattress. I did, and to my surprise, Neo placed her gingerly beside me.

Lifting my arm, Virginia burrowed beneath it, forearm wrapping across my chest, which was covered in an ugly-ass hospital gown.

"Where the hell are my clothes?" I glowered.

"Ruined from all the blood," Ivory replied.

I glanced up. Across the room sat my entire family: Beau, Ethan, Fletcher, and Ivory. As I stared, Neo returned to where he'd likely been before, and Ivory plopped down in his lap.

"You're all here," I said, dumb.

"Where else would we be?" Fletcher asked.

My eyes moved back to Ivory. "How's your head?"

"She has a concussion." Neo glowered. He had a new shiner on his eye that was not courtesy of me.

"Why aren't you in bed?" I demanded.

"Because I'm in here instead," she retorted.

Virginia stole all my attention when her chin tipped up and those gold-flecked brown eyes focused on me. "Does it hurt very bad?"

"Feels much better now," I whispered, pressing a kiss to her forehead. The moment of relief I felt holding her was short-lived.

Pulling back, I stared down at her, scrutinizing her from every angle. "Are you hurt? How long have I been in here? *Why are you covered in blood?*"

"Told you to clean up," Neo muttered.

Virginia made a face. "It's only been a couple hours. I haven't had time to clean up."

"She refused to leave your side," Fletcher put in.

"You haven't even been looked at by a doctor?" I bellowed.

"Ethan called one in here so she didn't have to leave." Fletcher volunteered more information.

"And?" I worried, grasping her chin lightly to take in her swollen lower lip and neck filled with purple splotches. Rage swept through me all over again. "Did I kill him?" I asked the room.

Everyone knew I meant the man who put those marks on V.

"Yes," Beau replied.

"Good," I muttered, lightly fingering the blemishes. Feeling Virginia's eyes, I met them. "You saw that too?"

"My eyes were open the whole time," she confirmed.

"You're still here," I murmured, leaning in to kiss the tip of her nose.

I have a thing for her nose.

Tell no one.

"Where else would I be?" she whispered, her hand grasping my wrist.

"It wouldn't matter. I'd find you."

"I know."

"You sure you're okay?" I slid my hand over the back of her head, trailing my fingers through her hair, and then felt a ripple of surprise when my fingers met air too soon.

Oh, right. I'd kinda chopped it all off.

"Besides that hack job of a haircut, she's fine," Ivory informed me. "What is it with you and cutting hair?"

I ignored her.

"Sweetheart?"

She nuzzled into my chest. "I'm okay."

"I didn't put her in bed with you to become nauseated." Neo glowered. "Stop being so gross."

"At least me and Ethan do that in private." Fletcher agreed.

"You do not," literally everyone replied.

Fletcher blushed.

Tucking V a little closer against my side, I asked, "What happened?"

"The police and firefighters came, arrested the guys with the guns, and brought everyone else to the hospital."

"And… *her?*"

"She's dead." Beau confirmed.

"Why aren't the police here? Why hasn't Fig handcuffed me to this bed?"

"He would not!" Virginia declared.

I patted her head and pushed her back into my chest. She was cute.

"We told them what happened," Fletcher explained.

I glanced at Ethan, lifting a brow.

"The police questioned us. We told them what we could, that we were attacked and held at gunpoint and the woman attacked us before falling out a window."

Still, the police should be in here demanding answers.

Beau cleared his throat. "The Black Rose is a new Asian gang recently formed in the city and trying to gain a foothold. They've been committing crimes and making a name for themselves by leaving a black rose everywhere. When they got wind that the cops questioned you about the tattoo on the dead guy, they came looking for you. Figured since you were Asian with a bad reputation, they could pin a lot of their crimes on you. So they trashed your bar, luring you into that alley where you were attacked. When you killed one of their guys, they decided to get some revenge."

Beau looked at Virginia still curled into my side.

"Hey," I whispered in her hair. "You comfortable? You need me to adjust you?"

She shook her head against me.

I felt Neo's stare, and I briefly met it before Beau started talking again.

"So they lit the Tower on fire to empty out the building and went after Virginia and Ivory. They didn't plan on all of us showing up to fight back."

They didn't think I'd have a new family.

I was quiet a long while. It was a neat and tidy story. So clean it almost seemed believable. But everyone in this room knew better.

"And the men I killed?" I finally asked.

"Self-defense," Ethan replied easily.

"How is pushing a woman out a window self-defense?"

"You didn't push her. The beast did," Neo stated. "We all saw him. Some men brought in Emogen and dumped her on the floor. It clearly set him off, and he reacted."

"Where are they?" I asked.

"Down the hall," Virginia told me. "Emogen has a concussion and a few stitches in her head. Those men must have hit her hard. The beast wasn't hurt, but he needed oxygen from smoke inhalation. They are both going to be staying the night."

"In the same room?"

"That dude is wild when she's not in his sight," Beau said. "He wouldn't calm down unless they put them together."

Interesting.

Virginia tapped on my chest, and I glanced down. Her eyes were wide and clear despite the dark circles beneath them. "Do you think Emogen is safe with him? That man is kind of scary."

"He's no scarier than I am." I tucked a strand of hair behind her ear. "She'll be fine."

"The cops had no issue believing he's the one who shoved her after the way he acted earlier," Beau said of the man we only knew as Beast.

"Will he get in trouble?" Virginia worried.

"Considering they were there because they started a fire and tried to kill us? It will likely be considered self-defense as well," Beau told her.

"You sure have all this worked out," I observed.

"Not all of us needed a nap," he retorted.

Gasping, Virginia pushed up on my chest to glare at Beau. "He was shot! He jumped in front of a bullet for me! It was hardly a nap!"

Beau held up his hands in surrender. "Yes, ma'am."

"You're covering for me," I said at last, eyes sweeping the room. "All of you."

"You took a bullet for my sister," Neo said.

"Nobody would have been shooting at her if it weren't for me."

Offended, Virginia glanced up. "You are hardly responsible for other people's foul deeds."

I made a face. "Which one of you taught her to talk like a richie?" I said, dividing my gaze between Ivory and Ethan.

Ethan beamed with pride.

Figures.

"But I am responsible." I reminded the room. "And everyone knows it."

"You're our family," Fletcher said.

"Even after everything you all saw today?" I pressed. It was scary how much I wanted them to accept me, foul deeds and all.

"Well, it would really be nice if you stopped killing people. I mean, eventually, we will run out of plausible alibis for you," Fletcher said almost cheerfully.

Muffled laughter across the room made me stiffen.

Holding on to V protectively, I glanced at the curtain dividing the room. A curtain I hadn't even noticed. Grim, I looked at my family across the room, partly incredulous they would have a conversation, knowing we weren't alone.

Before I could do anything, a hand closed around the edge of the curtain and yanked it back.

Daeshim stood there wearing a set of blue scrub pants but no shirt. Behind him was the bed he'd clearly been occupying.

"Hyung," I said, emotion welling in my chest. All this emotion stuff was hella annoying. "I thought you…"

"I'm harder to kill than that."

His arm was in a sling, his entire shoulder and upper arm bandaged. There were cuts and bruises on his face, a scrape on his forehead, and what looked like a bite mark on his collarbone.

"Did someone bite you?" I wondered.

He grimaced. "That guy really is a beast."

There was an IV in the back of his hand, and his black hair was wild around his face and neck. The black rose tattoo on his chest made me suddenly very aware of the same tattoo I had on my hip. *The doctors probably saw it.* Without thinking, my hand slid toward the area, wanting to rub it like I could make it disappear.

Beau cleared his throat, and I glanced up. A very slight shake of his head stopped my progress. My arm went back around V.

I shared a look with Beau for long seconds, but then Daeshim spoke again.

"Thanks, ah, for getting me to the hospital."

"You're Earth's brother! Of course we would,"

Fletcher declared. Then he turned to me. "How come you never told us you had a brother?"

"It's complicated," I murmured.

"Don't you think we've earned the right to your secrets?" A slight edge crept into Neo's voice. "Haven't we earned your trust?"

He glanced pointedly at my sister before his eyes settled back on mine.

He was right. The entire family deserved an explanation. They covered for me. Protected me. Became accomplices for me. They'd even run into danger for me.

Running a hand over Virginia's head, I gazed down at her. "What do you think, sprite? You wanna know too?"

She nodded.

And so I told them. I told them a tale that was actually the truth about a boy who was born into a powerful and iconic Korean mafia, the second-born son of a man who was brutally murdered when people turned against him. About my mother who stepped up to the helm and ended up far more ruthless and colder than my father ever was.

I was expected to kill. I was expected to steal, threaten, and intimidate. Drugs, money laundering... human trafficking. I was expected to embrace it all and then eventually rule under Daeshim, our mother's namesake.

I learned to fight the moment I learned to walk. I learned to never trust, and I was taught how to lie.

It grew too much, because long before I became the Huntsman, I'd been a boy. A boy who was too soft for drugs and killing. Who stumbled into a shed where sex slaves were chained up and had nightmares for weeks. A boy who'd seen photos of his father's dismembered body and a boy who was only bred by his mother to be the head of an army and never a son.

Daeshim had been the only thing to stand between me and being broken. A boy five years my senior who took on far more than he had to because I was too weak.

"One night, I snapped," I said, voice hoarse from talking for so long. It felt good, though, to pour all this out. I'd never known how hard it was, how much energy it took to keep it all in.

"I snuck into Mother's office and saw a folder of pictures. Girls and boys I went to school with, people I thought of as friends. They were listed to be taken, drugged, and sold to the highest bidder."

I still remember the sick feeling that twisted my gut when I saw those photos of smiling young students and envisioned them chained up in the shed like those others I'd seen before.

"I'd had enough. I was young and stupid... ruled by emotion. Without thinking, I confronted her, the almighty Black Rose. I gave her an ultimatum: to stop or I'd tell. She locked me in a cell for three days until I attacked a guard and escaped. They chased. I shot her. I thought she was dead."

My voice fell quiet. The emotion from all those years ago resurfaced inside me like the swell of an overfull sea.

"The Black Rose demands an eye for an eye," I heard Daeshim explain, picking up where I left off, perhaps sensing I couldn't keep going. "So as heir to the organization, I said I would remove him. No one questioned my loyalty. I'd already proved it many times. So I shot him and took his body to dump it... except I made sure he wasn't dead. I took him to a friend who cared for him until he was able to flee the country."

"Why didn't you just kill me?" I asked, unable to keep the question in.

"Because you're my brother and because you were the only one strong enough to try and stop her."

"But I couldn't."

"No, but you got out, and that was enough for me," Daeshim replied quietly.

But he didn't. I could only imagine the things he had to say and do.

"But she came here. She knew where you were," Virginia said. "How did she know you were alive?"

I glanced at Daeshim, wondering if he knew the answer.

He shrugged. "An anonymous call came in. It was a woman. She gave Mother your name and location. Mother had it checked out, and then she knew."

He fell silent, but it was a charged silence, a silence filled with truth.

"She punished you for not killing me."

"Yes."

Before I could ask more, he continued. "She was haunted by that night. After you shot her and she almost died, she was never quite the same. Some say she suffered PTSD. Some say she just went nuts. Maybe it was a little of both. She would wake up screaming. She had panic attacks during the day. She hated guns, but she continued to use them anyway because she refused to admit weakness."

"And Kwan?"

Daeshim snorted. "They got together after she woke from her coma. I don't know if he cared about her or just her power, but he did help keep her calm."

"She was calm when we saw her?" Fletcher wondered, awe in his tone.

Daeshim chuckled. "You're kinda cute."

A hard look crossed Ethan's face, and he reached for Fletcher, pulling him into his lap. "He's mine. Don't even think about it."

Daeshim rolled his eyes.

"Are you gay?" I asked, shock rippling through me.

"Of course not," he said. "Mother would never allow that."

"So you escaped from your family and came here, lived on the street as a pickpocket until my father helped you," Ivory surmised, glancing at me.

"Yes."

Fletcher frowned. "You escaped because you didn't want to be a killer... but then you became one anyway."

Wasn't that just the crux of it all?

Was I a villain by birth or by my own making?

Perhaps both.

Either way, it was irrefutable proof that there was nowhere a man can go if it wasn't meant to be. It didn't really matter how I got here because the destination was the same.

Forty-Three

VILLAINS ARE NOT BORN. THEY ARE MADE. THROUGH circumstance, mistreatment, trauma. I don't really know every way a villain is made, but now I know how the Huntsman was born.

Earth would hate it if he knew, as I lay here up against his side, I felt sorry. Sorry he believed his villainous characteristics were a result of his blood. Sorry he believed he was trapped by his own breeding.

Live what you know. Think what you're taught. Become a product of your environment.

We faulted people for these things every single day. Acceptance was fickle. Acceptance was really no better than fault because we based both on our personal beliefs and experiences.

I read this quote once: "I stopped explaining myself to people when I realized they only understood from their level of perception."

This explained the man I loved. He didn't bother to defend how he came to be because he knew people wouldn't understand anyway. How could they?

Yes, Earth considered himself a villain. Many people would agree.

But to me, he was a victim. A victim of his childhood, a victim of the Black Rose. A man who survived the best way he knew how.

It didn't excuse his violence or the crimes he committed, but now I could understand.

Or maybe I was making excuses for him because I loved him regardless of his foul deeds. We all did.

Maybe loving him made me a villain too.

Maybe I didn't care.

No. Not maybe.

I didn't.

"I don't expect any of you to do this," Earth told the room.

"Do what?" Neo asked.

"To cover for me. To be here." The power of his midnight stare beckoned me, and I looked up. His opaque gaze caressed my face almost as if he were memorizing it. His hand was strong and steady as it ran over the back of my head. "I put all of you in danger. You're better off without me."

He included everyone in his words, but those eyes never left me.

Beneath my ribs, my heart fluttered, making me feel slightly lightheaded. But then his words penetrated the spell he cast over my mind, and I jolted.

He grimaced slightly when my hand slapped the center of his chest, and I pushed into a sitting position.

"You!" I accused.

One eyebrow quirked.

"You were going to leave here and go back with her!" I practically yelled. My goodness, just recalling that heart-wrenching moment at the Tower when he traded his freedom from the Black Rose for all of us made me want to cry all over again. "How could you?"

"Just once, I wanted to be your hero instead of the bad guy," he whispered, dragging the pad of his thumb along my lower lip.

Everything inside me trembled, but I refused to give in. "I don't want a hero," I said fiercely. "I want *you*."

Impossibly, his already black eyes turned darker. I forgot I was mad he would make such a deal. I forgot everything in that moment. All that existed was him and me.

Somewhere far away, Neo cleared his throat.

"When did they fall in love?" I heard Fletcher ask.

"That explains the bruises he and Neo have been sporting," Ethan mused.

"It was the peanut butter hot chocolate at Kismet," Fletcher declared. "That stuff is magic."

"You're ridiculous," Beau told him.

"Am not!"

"I'm happy for them." Ivory's voice was wistful.

"They aren't in love," Neo announced.

"He jumped in front of a bullet for her." Ivory admonished him.

"Give it up, man. Just look at them," Ethan said.

"We should give them a few moments alone," Ivory suggested.

"Like hell," Neo grumped.

"My head hurts," Ivory whimpered.

I heard Neo jump up. "Come on. Let's go find the doctor."

I smiled a little, and Earth smiled back.

"Come on, puppy. Let's get some food for everyone," Ethan said, following Neo and Ivory from the room.

When they were gone, Beau cleared his throat. "Well, don't I feel like the third wheel."

"You're not," Earth said, pulling his eyes from me and

giving the first indication he'd been listening to the charades of our family. "I appreciate everything you've done."

Beau's green eyes widened. "I didn't do anything."

"We both know that's not true," Earth said. "Thank you."

Beau nodded, cheekbones turning as red as his hair. "I'll be in the hall," he muttered and hightailed it out.

When he was gone, Daeshim grabbed the curtain, swiftly pulling it closed. "Don't mind me. I'm going to sleep."

And then we were alone.

Our eyes were like magnets, the pull just too intense to ignore. "You really would have left."

"Yes."

"But not anymore. She's gone."

His expression was unreadable, his watchfulness intent. "You saw me kill more than one person tonight."

"I watched you save many more."

Perspective. That's all this was. He looked on the dark side while I looked to the light.

"Why aren't you afraid of me?"

"I've spent the last seven years trying to be capable and strong. Trying not to be helpless and weak. But I am."

Nostrils flaring, he sat up, both hands grasping my shoulders. "You are not."

I smiled at his ferocity, my heart turning over. "Maybe not in spirit." I allowed. "But physically? Yes, I am. I fought against that man tonight, but truthfully, if you hadn't come, I wouldn't have won."

He cupped the side of my head. "I'm sorry I was late."

Pushing farther into the touch, I smiled. "Your savageness doesn't scare me, Earth. If anything, it makes me feel safe. It seems we're both opposite ends of the spectrum, one too weak and one too, ah, wild. Perhaps there is balance somewhere between us."

"I'm a villain," he whispered, pressing his forehead against mine. I could practically feel his resolve crumbling.

I whispered, "Not in my story."

"After everything…" His voice fell away, but it didn't matter because I knew what to say.

"I still love you."

He drew back, seeking, dissecting… *hoping.* "Even knowing where I've come from?"

"I love you."

Whatever resolve he clung to tumbled away, revealing the most beautiful unguarded expression I'd ever seen. And then he was holding my face, pulling me up until our lips fused around his low growl.

The sound vibrated my lips, creating a tingling sensation down my throat. I parted, welcoming him deeper, my insides turning to liquid as he claimed, owned, and caressed everything his tongue could reach.

I loved that he wasn't gentle, how he sought to devour and possess. He kissed without holding back, unafraid to hurt me, unafraid to delve too deep.

Curling my fingers into the hospital gown covering his chest, I anchored myself as our lips slid together, slick and warm with passion. At some point, the kiss changed direction, a feat he managed without lifting his head. New possessive growls rose above us, and I mewled into his mouth, letting him feast on the sound.

A quivering sensation bloomed low my belly, tickling that invisible line that divided my body into the parts that felt and the parts that could not. Without thought, I slid a hand over my navel, pressing against my tummy where sensation sparked.

Abruptly, Earth pulled his lips from mine, the sound of our gasps beating out the loud pulse thrumming in my ears. His lips were slick and plump as they dragged across my jaw toward my neck, leaving a line of our mixed saliva trailing over my skin.

Shivering lightly, I pressed closer, the hand against my stomach trapped between our bodies as his tongue lapped over my neck, his lips latching on to that sensitive spot he seemed to have memorized.

I moaned, the sound wanton and surprising. Gasping, I started to pull away, but he wouldn't let me. His fingers tightened in my scalp. His thumb applied pressure, keeping my head tilted enough that he could continue his assault on that secret spot.

My nipples puckered so tight that sparks of pleasure tinged with pain electrified my entire upper body and my fingers began to shake.

"Earth," I whispered, voice wobbly and nearly unrecognizable.

"Sprite," he rumbled, breath brushing over the wet spot against my neck.

I shuddered, fingers delving into his hair to tug.

At last, he lifted his face, eyes hooded, lips red, and a warring smirk of satisfaction and hunger playing on his lips. "Salanghae." *I love you.*

Leaning in, I pecked a brief kiss against his lips, gobbling up those sweet words.

"You know a villain's love is infallible." He smiled. It was a soft smile that transformed his angular face into gentle curves.

"Is it?" I was partly breathless and completely entranced.

"Mmm," he rumbled. "Because it blooms in the most unfavorable conditions, growing in darkness and surviving on hate. Nothing can destroy it, not even death."

I didn't bother to tell him again that, to me, he wasn't a villain. Probably because his kind of love was exactly what I wanted.

Forty-Four

EARTH

"Visiting hours are ending." A nurse dressed in all white standing in the doorway of the room spoke to all the people sitting around.

"Thank you for letting us know," Ivory said politely, smiling at the woman.

"Are you sure you wouldn't prefer to spend the night as well, Miss White? We could get you into a room—"

Ivory held up her hand. "No, but I truly do appreciate your concern. Your staff has been wonderful. Thank you for taking care of our family."

The nurse seemed surprised but pleased with Ivory's kind words. From the bed, I rolled my eyes.

"It's a pleasure. As I said, visiting hours are over, but a few moments longer will be fine." She left, and I rolled my eyes again.

"Money talks," I muttered.

"No. Kindness does," Ivory argued.

Kindness was overrated. It gave people the idea that they could walk all over you.

Everyone started moving around, getting ready to head out for the night. Neo stepped toward the bed, eyes on V. "Come on. I'll help you."

"No!" She gasped, offended. "I'm staying!"

"No," Neo deadpanned.

"Don't you pull that overbearing big brother crap on me right now, Neo. Earth was shot! I'm staying."

His lips thinned. "That bed is not big enough for the both of you. You'll be full of cramps if you sleep here. And what about all the stuff you need? Don't you want to change out of that bloody dress?"

Virginia glanced down at herself. "It's only one night. I'll be fine."

I wanted her to stay, but Neo was right. "Go with your brother, sweetheart."

She gasped again, head whipping around so hard a lost flower tumbled onto my chest. Noticing it, she frowned, picking it up between her fingers. "My poor hair."

"It'll grow back," I told her.

She turned incredulous. "Don't you even feel bad you hacked it off like this?" Using two fingers, she chose one particularly hacked-up strand to hold it out.

"No."

She huffed.

"It was your hair or your life. It was hardly even a choice."

Her entire face softened. "Well, when you say it like that…"

"Maybe you can wear a hat," Fletcher offered.

Ethan stifled a laugh.

"I'll call my stylist. He'll fix it. He has experience fixing Earth's haircuts," Ivory informed the entire room.

She is going to be salty about that forever. You'd think she'd be grateful I didn't kill her.

Women.

I glanced over her head at Neo. "You're taking her to your place, right? She can't stay at the Tower anymore."

He nodded. "They aren't even letting people back into the building. They have to assess the damage first."

"Those poor people," Virginia murmured, thinking of her "roommates."

"Even then, she can't stay there anymore. That place is a security joke," I said, thinking only of her.

Neo nodded. "She has a room at our place already anyway. She can just move in."

"I don't want to be a burden."

"You aren't," everyone in the room said in tandem.

"Well, Neo and Ivory are the ones having to live with me." Virginia practically pouted. It was adorable and endearing, and a wave of want washed over me.

The kiss from earlier still thrummed through my veins, desire coursing through my entire body, and below the blankets, my cock was still half hard.

It was probably better she went with her brother tonight anyway, or else I might try and jump her. Self-control was certainly not something I had much of where she was concerned.

"Well, you can stay with us if you don't want to stay with Neo," Fletcher offered.

Ethan nodded immediately. "Of course." He agreed. "We have plenty of room."

"Why wouldn't she want to stay with me?" Neo fumed.

"You're bossy, and she probably wants to kiss Earth," Fletcher informed him.

More muffled laughter rang out from behind the curtain. Big brother was still awake.

Ethan glowered at the sound and pulled Fletch into his side. "Come on, puppy. We should go."

Seeing his jealousy was amusing.

Even though he clearly wanted to get Fletcher away from charming Daeshim, he still turned to V. "Would you like to come with us?"

Neo looked as though his head might explode, but Ivory slipped her hand into his and he moved down to a simmer.

"Thank you so much," Virginia told them, "but I already have everything I need at Neo and Ivory's."

Fletcher came forward and hugged her, his golden mop of hair everywhere. Once he was done, he threw himself at me.

"*Oomph.*" The sound escaped, and I grimaced. "Watch the bullet hole," I muttered.

"Bye, Earth. I'm so glad you're okay."

Forgetting about the pain in my shoulder, I patted his back and grunted. "Sure."

He pulled back just a little to whisper, "Are you done killing people now?"

Virginia giggled, making me glance at her.

"No," I declared.

Both Virginia and Fletcher drew back, crestfallen.

"What?" Fletcher said, eyes wide. "But I thought the danger was over."

"Me too," Virginia said, eyes concerned.

Goddammit. Both of them were practically in my lap, and both of them looked as if I'd kicked their puppy.

Not even I could withstand that.

"I'm done," I muttered beneath my breath.

"What?" Virginia asked, resting a palm on my chest to lean in. Fletcher leaned in too.

"I'm done!" I burst out. "Okay? No more."

"Promise?" Virginia asked, her voice tentative.

Her wide brown eyes were trusting and slightly

vulnerable. I could almost hear her heart telling me that she would love me no matter what but at the same time asking me not to put her in that position.

"Yes, sweetheart," I said, leaning up to cup her face. "I promise. I won't put you in danger like this ever again."

"Don't make promises you can't keep," Neo barked.

"Could we maybe defer our next battle until I have this IV out of my hand?" I asked, not even looking at him.

Instead, I leaned up and kissed his sister.

He muttered a curse beneath his breath, and I smiled against V's lips.

Fletcher disappeared from the bed, and the sound of the curtain ripping back made all of us look around. He stomped over to where Daeshim was lying on his back, propped up on several pillows, eyes closed.

"Excuse me," Fletcher announced, standing beside him.

I saw my brother's lips twitch before he opened his eyes to look at Fletch.

"What?"

"Are any more antis going to come for my brother?"

"Antis?" he echoed.

"Yeah, you know, people he's probably gonna have to kill."

Daeshim chuckled.

"What's so funny?" Fletch scowled.

The smile on my brother's face grew. Ethan appeared, pulling Fletch into his side, giving a stony, uppity look to Daeshim. "Mine."

Fletcher patted Ethan on his chest but looked down expectantly. "Well?"

His smile faded. "No. I don't think anyone else will be coming around."

Fletcher nodded, satisfied. "Good. So we can put all this behind us and move on," he said, taking in the entire room.

I didn't think it would be quite that easy, but I didn't bother telling him that. Feeling safe was something important to Fletch, and I wouldn't disrupt that.

Judging from the look Ethan gave me, I could tell he was thinking along the same lines and was grateful I didn't disagree.

After they left, Beau said his byes and followed behind. Neo went for Virginia again, and she sighed. "I don't want to go."

Leaning up, I brushed my nose against hers. "It's only one night. If you stay here, I'll just worry about you."

"I do need to get Zilla under a heat lamp," she said, eyes going to the gecko sitting in a small plastic carrier on the bedside table.

The thing had been lucky the lid to her habitat didn't fly off in all the commotion back at the Tower.

"You sure you'll be okay?" she asked.

I nodded, kissing her quickly. "Call me when you get there."

She nodded.

When she was in her chair, Neo and I shared a look, but I shook my head. "Later."

He nodded and headed to the door with V and Ivory.

"Neo?" I called out to him.

He looked back.

"Take care of her."

"As if I wouldn't." He scoffed.

We both smiled.

When they were gone, the silence in the room seemed loud as I adjusted against the pillows and contemplated pulling the IV out of my hand.

"I'm glad you haven't been alone." Daeshim's quiet voice brought my head around.

He was still lying in the bed, bandages covering one half of him and bruises the other. Feeling my stare, he rolled his head on the pillow to look at me.

"What about you, Hyung? Have you been alone?"

"You know the Black Rose is a big organization."

Something squeezed my chest. I might have been cast out, but I was the lucky one.

"You wanted me to let you die," I said, still hearing his breathless whisper echo in the recesses of my mind.

"Would be better than going back."

"You don't have to go back now. She's dead."

"Yeah."

There were a lot of things I wanted to ask. But instinctively, I knew the answers, and not a single one would be good.

I wondered if Daeshim Hyung was broken or if he'd managed to somehow keep a piece of himself unscathed.

Thick emotion welled up in me, pressing against my chest and then nearly squeezing my throat. The lump it formed was uncomfortable, and it seemed I might choke. I hadn't seen my brother in over ten years. The last time I did, he'd put a bullet in me.

And tonight, he'd jumped in front of one to keep it out.

"Thank you," I said, voice kind of hoarse.

I felt his eyes sharpen. The air hung thick between us.

Clearing my throat, I went on. "For getting me out all those years ago and for helping me tonight."

"I didn't come here to help you." He reminded me.

"But you did anyway." I reminded him too.

The silence was heavy but not uncomfortable.

"You really trust those people?"

Those people were my family, and I did. I trusted them with my life. "Yes," I said, hoping all those feelings resonated in that simple reply. "And you will too once you get to know them better."

I heard his intake of breath. "I didn't come here to stay."

"But you will," I told him, and we fell back into companionable silence.

Much later, after I'd spoken to Virginia and wished her good night, I was partially drifting off when I whispered, "Welcome home, Hyung."

Forty-Five

Virginia

"Did you sleep well?"

His gruff voice tickled my ear even through the phone. Chills raced over my body, prickling my skin, making it hum with awareness.

It wasn't even eight in the morning, yet he woke my body in a way no one had before—not even me.

"My room at Ivory's is very comfortable," I told him. In truth, I lay awake half the night, longing for his touch and replaying everything that happened. "What about you? How's your shoulder?"

He made a dismissive sound, and the chills tingled my scalp. "I'm fine."

"I'll have Neo bring me over soon," I said, knowing he wouldn't tell me even if he were in pain.

"No."

My stomach bottomed out. *He doesn't want to see me?* "No?"

"Fig and his merry band of morons are coming by to ask me a thousand questions. I don't want you involved."

"Oh." Did that mean he was just trying to protect me? "Well, what about after?"

"After, I'll come to you."

"You will?"

He sighed, his voice gentling. "Did you think I didn't want to see you?"

"You sounded grumpy."

"I always sound grumpy."

"Well, usually, I can see your face, and I know you don't mean it." I defended, feeling kind of silly.

"My face is always grumpy too."

"Not to me." If my voice was smaller than before, I pretended not to notice.

Of course, he wasn't that polite.

He sighed again. I could almost see him scrubbing a hand over his face. I wondered how much stubble had grown on his jaw overnight and if it was rough against his palm.

"There will never be a time when I don't want to see you, sweetheart."

My heart fluttered. Lips curling in on themselves, I smiled secretly.

"Okay?" he pressed, though his voice was soft.

"Okay."

"I'm sorry I wasn't there to adjust you in your sleep last night. Is your body feeling okay after everything?"

"I miss you," I blurted out, feeling my face heat even though no one was looking at me. Physically, I was fine, but mentally… I longed for him.

I wanted his arms. His voice. The scent of his skin. Despite how close we'd grown, we were still too far apart. I wanted more. Needed it.

A low growl vibrated my ear, and then the rest of me vibrated too. The hand clutching the phone tightened, and my other pressed against my middle.

"I'll be there as soon as I can." His voice was husky. All I could think about was kissing him.

"Call me if you need anything," I said, completely breathless.

"That's my line."

"Hurry," I whispered, then ended the call before I could sound any more desperate.

The phone went off again before I even put it down.

"H-hello?" I answered, heart beating wildly.

"You'd better be ready for me when I get there, sprite, because I'm coming for you, and nothing—and I mean *nothing*—will keep me away."

This time, he hung up first.

The phone dropped into my lap, and I released a shuddering breath. The want he pulled out of me was shocking. For so long, I wasn't sure I could feel… desire.

Obviously, I'd thought longingly of kisses, physical closeness, and of love. But I worried having no feeling below my waist would inhibit my sex drive, would inhibit even the natural *want* of someone else's body. And that, in turn, would mean I might never find true love.

The kind of love where the bonds of physical and mental connection fused, where two bodies melded into one for extended amounts of time. I worried so much there might be a disconnect for me.

But the way I felt now—*so needy*—I thought maybe there was a chance. A chance to connect with him completely. On every level. In every way.

And with those powerful feelings came fear. What if we tried and it didn't work? What then? Would he walk away from me, and if he didn't, would I be strong enough to shove him away? The last thing I wanted was for Earth to be bound to someone who couldn't satisfy him because he was too loyal to leave.

I might have been young, inexperienced, and sheltered, but I wasn't stupid. Sexual compatibility, sexual satisfaction was a big part of a relationship.

What if I couldn't deliver?

I already knew he could. He proved it the first time he even tried.

Nerves knotted inside me, warring with the excitement his dark promise elicited. There was a swift but gentle knock on my bedroom door, and despite its friendliness, I jolted.

"Come in!" I called, heart all the way in my throat.

Ivory let herself in, looking fresher than anyone had a right to this early in the morning.

"Good morning," she said.

"Morning," I chirped back, hoping I looked and sounded half as enthusiastic as she.

Her bright-blue eyes narrowed a bit, hands coming up to rest on her slim hips. Ivory was tiny, so I don't know how she pulled off the wide-legged jeans or how the high-waisted style didn't swallow her narrow midsection whole, but she managed to look perfect in them and the cream lace tank top tucked into the waistband.

Her small bare feet were practically invisible beneath the wide hem, but a couple red-painted toes peeked out when she shifted.

"What's the matter?"

"What?" I squeaked. "Why would anything be the matter?"

A look of horror flashed in her eyes. "Is Earth okay? Did something happen at the hospital?"

"No!" I quickly assured her. "I just talked to him." I gestured to my phone. "He's okay. He said his shoulder is fine."

She tilted her head, pursing her lips. "Then?"

"He said he would be here later." I was pretty sure the blush blazing across every inch of skin on my face said a lot more than my words ever could.

"Ahh," Ivory replied.

I really wasn't up for some awkward conversation. I mean, really, there was nothing she could say to alleviate all my worries and unique doubts.

I should have known, though, that my sister likely knew that, so she didn't press.

"Well, it's a good thing I called Marco. He's on his way. He'll have that hatchet job Earth did on your hair fixed in no time."

I gasped, reaching up to finger my uneven strands. I hadn't even thought about my hair. "Oh, thank you!"

Ivory smiled. "We have some time before he arrives, so let's go look in my closet. You can borrow a few things until we're able to move your stuff over."

The Tower was pretty damaged by the fire on the lower floors, and it had been closed off for investigation and repair. I wasn't sure how long it would be until everyone could go back, but as of right now, they weren't even allowing patients back in to get their belongings.

I couldn't even imagine what I would have done if I didn't have this place at Ivory's. All the equipment I needed to make my life easier would have been locked away, possibly even damaged from smoke.

What about the people who didn't have a family to help them? Or money to get what they needed?

It made me feel guilty for the things I had.

"Virginia?" Sensing my inner turmoil, Ivory turned in the hall to look at me.

"I was just worrying about the other residents of the Tower. I'm lucky because I have family to help me."

Ivory nodded. "I'll make a few calls and see what I can find out. Maybe I can help."

I gasped. "Oh! I didn't mean it that way. I would never ask you to do that."

She made a face, waving away my words. "Of course not, but I want to. What's the point of having all this money if I can't use it to help people?"

My heart swelled. She was so kind. So unlike the high-society prima donna the social pages made her out to be. "My brother is very lucky to have you," I whispered. "We all are."

Her eyes shimmered a little with tears, but she sniffled and blinked them away. "Ugh, enough! These past few days have been a rollercoaster. Let's have some fun with some clothes and hair for a while."

The morning and early afternoon whirled by much quicker than I expected, thanks to Ivory and her team. By the time Marco—who self-proclaimed himself my fairy godmother—was finished gasping over and fixing my hair and I'd gotten a manicure and chosen some clothes out of Ivory's closet, it was well past lunch.

I thought I'd be much more upset over the loss of half my hair, being that it represented so much to me. But surprisingly, I just felt lighter. It was still long enough to braid, the strands falling over my shoulders. Marco added a few layers beneath my chin so it curled in a little, framing my face.

It was the first time I'd had a haircut in almost seven years, and I had to admit it felt nice. He'd even blown it out into long, smooth strands that felt like silk when they slipped over my shoulders and caressed my throat.

My nails were a neutral shade, but the manicurist hand-painted flowers on some of the nails, and that small detail made tears rush to my eyes.

So much had changed recently that at times I was a little overwhelmed. Looking down at the newly painted flowers, I was comforted. It was a small thing, but they rang with familiarity.

"So," Ivory said after everyone had gone. "I told Neo I had to go to some dinner tonight and I couldn't get out of it. So naturally, he will be escorting me."

"You couldn't get out of it?"

"Well, I could have called and given an excuse, but I figured you might like some time alone with Earth."

Nerves exploded inside me, making my stomach churn and my chest feel tight. "You didn't have to do that," I said, trying not to show my anxiety.

"If Neo is here, he will never leave you two alone." Ivory sighed. When I said nothing, a wary look came over her. "Unless you would rather not be alone with him. We can stay—"

"No!" I cut her off swiftly. "I... I want to be alone with him for a while. We never get that."

Ivory relaxed and nodded. "Well, I need to go and get ready. We probably won't be back until late, so don't wait up," she called, letting herself out of the bedroom.

My stomach flipped over and over again as I stared at the empty room.

The nerves didn't go away. Not the entire time I was in the bathroom emptying my bladder, bathing (for a second time that day), and making sure my hair still looked as good as it did when Marco left.

There was still a tremble in my fingers when I slid on a casual sage silk dress and then added a white cashmere cardigan over the spaghetti straps.

I didn't bother with shoes or socks, opting to leave my feet bare, nor did I bother with jewelry or makeup.

My face was so blushed from nerves—*or was it desire*—that there really was no point.

When I'd attempted and failed to distract myself, I wheeled out into the large living area, parking in front of the huge floor-to-ceiling windows to hopefully lose myself in the incredible view.

It partly worked. But the other part of me listened for the door, hyperaware of every sound.

And then the door was opening. The guard stationed outside said something, and the low murmur of Earth's voice carried through the penthouse, making my pulse race.

Unable to breathe, lost in a sea of butterflies, all I could do was turn and wait for him to appear.

Forty-Six

SHE WAS SITTING IN HER CHAIR, THE PICTURE WINDOW AT her back framing a breathtaking view of the beautiful parts of the city. The sun was sinking in the sky, its rays a burnished gold that shone around her as if revealing the halo I always knew she hid.

The room was silent but charged with so many emotions it made my footsteps falter. The air was thick but not uncomfortable. Somehow her small body managed to overflow and fill the room. She was nervous, scared… eager.

I practically tasted desire in the air, and it created a low chant inside me, which pounded louder than the sound of my rapidly beating heart.

Claim. Claim. Claim.

I took a breath, feeling the way the oxygen shuddered in my lungs as I told myself to chill the fuck out because I didn't want to make the cacophony of everything she felt worse.

Somehow throughout this endless, increasingly annoying day, I'd managed to convince myself that Virginia probably didn't know what I meant when I said I was coming for her. She was too innocent and sweet.

But oh, feeling the undercurrents in the room, just looking at her across the space, watching me with awareness, I wondered how the fuck I even believed that lie.

She knew.

She knew, and she was waiting.

The sound of my swallow echoed in my ears as I started across the room, eyes never once leaving her.

My God, she was absolutely beautiful. Far more beautiful than anything I'd ever seen, and I myself was an expert on beauty because ugly was so prevalent in my life. I knew all the faces of ugly, even the pretty ones good at pretending.

But this girl, *my* girl, was real. There was not one ounce of ugly in her. Her beauty reached far beneath her exterior and into her gorgeous heart.

How the hell had someone like this chosen me? How had she kept her eyes open and looked into the ugly of my world and still held out her hand?

Most people probably looked at Virginia and saw fragility.

But not me.

I saw strength beyond measure. Strength to live with the fragility everyone else saw and to find beauty in my ugly.

I didn't deserve her, but I didn't care. She was offering herself, and I would take. I would take and take until I owned her, but I would never make her regret.

My knees hit the floor in front of her, reaching for her hands. "You're waiting for me."

"You're late."

"Are you afraid?"

"Yes. But not of you."

I stood, picking her up out of the chair, holding her

up so it was like she stood in front of me. Her hands curled into my jacket, chin tipping back. I was a whole head taller, and I reveled in the fact that my body overwhelmed her.

Her eyes were already slightly dazed, but preventing them from glazing completely was the wariness in their depths.

I liked when people were afraid of me. I enjoyed making them nervous, and intimidation was something I didn't necessarily practice but was good at nonetheless. It was likely because I didn't bluff. I followed through with action, and people knew I played no games.

I didn't want her to be afraid of me. I wanted that wariness gone. I wanted to wipe out every doubt she might ever have and be the anchor of her world.

Instead of crushing her to me, instead of reaching up the mouthwatering silky dress she wore, I ignored the instincts I usually followed and listened to the ones that loved her.

Carrying her to the window, I shifted her, pressing her back against my chest and locking my arms around her waist. Her delicate hand reached out, flattening on the glass, and we stood there in silence, watching the evening sun play a game of hide-and-seek with the tall buildings below.

She smelled of fancy shampoo and something softer, something unique to her. Leaning down, I nuzzled into the side of her neck, inhaling sharply. Her head tipped to the side, offering more access, so I nipped and kissed, dragging my tongue across her skin.

She made a small whimper, her body sagging even more against mine.

"Where's your brother?" I whispered, voice already half gone.

"Not here."

"Tell me yes, Virginia."

"Yes."

Swinging her up, I carried her bridal style down the hall going into the bedroom she indicated and, using my boot, kicked the door closed.

When she was sitting on the bed, I backtracked to throw the lock and prowled back toward her, peeling my leather jacket off as I went.

It hit the floor with a low smack, and her hungry eyes ran over my chest. I pulled my shirt off too, not even bothering to wince when I felt the tug in my shoulder from the movement. Every single stitch could rip out and blood could drip down my back, but I wouldn't stop.

I gritted my teeth at the sight she made sitting on the side of the bed, her face level with my torso, closer to my rapidly hardening cock than anything else.

She lifted her fingers, reaching out, but then glanced up. I angled closer, silently giving permission, and then her cool, delicate fingers were slipping over me like silk. They trailed over my torso, across my stomach, and curled around my back.

My eyes closed at the way she traced my spine before dragging her nails lightly across my skin.

A low groan filled the room when her lips pressed against my ribs, and she trailed moist, tentative kisses down my stomach and over my navel. I felt her hesitate, and I made a sound of impatience, then peeked down to make sure I didn't upset her.

My breath caught.

Her wide, luminous eyes stared up my body, pupils already blown and staring directly at me. Her wheat-colored hair framed her flushed cheeks, and the soft strands tickled my middle.

"I'm so afraid," she confessed, not even glancing away.

Making a sound, I buried my hands in her hair, fingers sinking into her scalp. "Don't be afraid of me, sweetheart. Please."

"Not you," she confessed, wrapping her arms around my waist and pillowing her cheek on my stomach. Her heated cheek felt delicious against my skin, and her breath made goose bumps race over my body. "I'm afraid of me. That I won't be able to please you."

I laughed. It was low and throaty, all I could manage. "Oh, I'm already pleased."

She pulled back, a hint of the bravery she carried inside her sparking in her eyes. "Let me try."

Deft fingers went to the button on my jeans. I sucked in a breath, all humor draining out in one second flat.

"Sweetheart…" I was going to tell her it wasn't necessary, but then she looked up my torso with those damn brunet eyes, and I was gone.

All I could do was nod, and the next thing I knew, she was stroking my stiff cock with her gentle hands. "It's big," she marveled as if she didn't realize she was speaking out loud.

Pride as well as amusement shot through me, and a little piece of my heart crumbled away. "Your hands are small," I allowed.

"Humbleness doesn't really suit you," she said, still stroking.

Reaching down, I grasped her chin, allowing my eyes to meet hers. "I want to please you too."

She smiled and wrapped her thumb and pointer finger just around the head. A choked sound ripped out of me, and my stomach muscles jolted. She made a soft sound and did it again.

My fingers found themselves back in her hair, and

then her tongue was licking over the tip like I was some kind of dessert.

I whispered a curse up to the ceiling, eyes sliding closed.

Oh, that tongue of hers. Licking, gliding, tasting. I was shaking before her lips even closed around me, and when the wet heat of her mouth enveloped me completely, I nearly lost it right there.

I jolted, intending to push her off, instead, I pushed deeper.

She made a surprised sound, and I felt her gag slightly. Cursing, I pulled back, but her hands gripped my hips, and she sank over me again.

She took the entire thing. She took me until I felt the sensitive head nudge against the back of her throat.

I whispered her name and rocked a little, feeling her nails drag over my stomach.

When she pulled back, I used the modicum of sanity I clung to and slipped from between her lips. She made a sound, reaching for the slick, hard-as-granite member like she was going to swallow it again.

"No," I rasped, rotating away.

"Did I do bad?" Her lips were swollen and red, hair mussed from my fingers.

I couldn't even laugh because I was too busy fighting the urge to push back into her mouth. "No." I panted. "So good, but I want to touch you too."

Carefully, I slid the cardigan down her arms, tossing it away. Next, I slipped the thin straps on her shoulders away, allowing all access to her creamy shoulders.

I kissed across them first before using my teeth and then sucking her collarbone between my lips.

Her body melted into the palm I pressed against her lower back. When her chin fell back, all her hair fell behind her shoulders, and the long column of her neck was finally exposed. I loved her neck, and I knew there was an area there that aroused her.

I dove in, making my way to that spot at the back. The second I found it, her body arched up.

Satisfied, I eased back, making sure she could support her weight before withdrawing my hand and then removing her dress. She wore nothing at all underneath it, and my still-hard cock jerked at the sight.

"If anyone else ever touches you, I will kill them," I growled, possession nearly boiling in my veins. She was so incredibly beautiful that my thoughts instantly turned to murder, to the most extreme thing I would absolutely do to keep her.

"I don't want anyone else. I only want you."

Oh, she was good. Instead of calming the beast inside me, she was encouraging him.

Slipping my hands beneath her arms, I dragged her up the bed, laying her out against the blankets and pillows and arranging her like my own personal doll.

"Okay?" I asked when I was finished, needing to know she was comfortable.

"When are you going to kiss me, Earth?"

I pounced, our lips and bare chests meeting at the same time. Both of us groaned into the kiss, but we kept kissing, lips moving together in a dance only they knew.

I don't know how long we kissed, how long I explored her mouth and feasted on her neck, but when I finally pulled back, her eyes were pleasantly glassy, her lips were wrecked, and her face was flushed.

Her gaze strayed down to my cock, which was leaking like a faucet and flushed an angry red. My jeans were still around my hips because I'd been too distracted to take them off.

Some of the pure passion in her eyes dimmed, her teeth sinking into her already puffy lip. "I wish I was able to feel you in me."

"Shh." I soothed her, bringing our bodies back together. "I'll make you feel everything I can."

I kissed her once. Twice. Three times. And then I left her body to strip away the rest of my clothes. Her eyes were hungry, roaming over me, and I climbed onto her body, straddling her waist.

Her eyes widened at the position, but then her attention was stolen by the cock pointing right at her.

Leaning down, I took her lips, plunging my tongue deep. Using one hand, I held her open and made love to her mouth while the rest of me started to move.

Panting, I lifted my head to slide up, bracing myself over her to skim my rock-hard dick over her stomach and chest, rocking it between her boobs. I'd only meant to let her feel me, to know what it was like to have me thrusting against her. I didn't expect it to be a test of my control at the feel of her hot little mouth running over my stomach, lips reaching up to close around a nipple. A hoarse moan floated up to the ceiling while my weeping tip basically smeared her skin with lubrication as I rocked against her again and again. It was torture at its best. The weeping tip smeared her skin with lubrication, and I rocked my hips into her again and again.

I let my forehead fall just above her shoulder as I fought for control. I wasn't even inside her... but I wanted to release. Just rutting against her silky skin, hearing her gasp and coo at the contact, made me want to blow.

"Can you feel that?" I whispered in her ear.

"Oh, yes."

"Can you feel me all over you, pushing you into the

mattress and dragging my leaking dick all over your pure skin?"

She moaned, arching up.

It created new pressure against my shaft, and I groaned, sliding a hand beneath her to hold her body against mine.

In my haste, I slid down a little, my hips rocking into her stomach.

"Can you feel that?" I whispered. "Too low?"

"I feel it." Her voice was husky and thick.

It turned me on.

Leaning close, I latched on to her neck, on that erogenous zone, and sucked deep. She made a keening sound and arched up again. She squirmed as I pinched and tugged at her nipple while I worked her neck.

I couldn't rut against her and do everything else, so I finally crawled down her body, latching on to her nipples to suck and play. She whispered my name, tugging my hair, trying to get me closer.

When her nipples were swollen, I moved down her torso, swirling my tongue around her belly button before licking in deep.

"Please, Earth. *Please.*" She was pretty far gone, didn't notice that she was asking for more, and I wanted to point it out, but I also didn't want to pull her from the headspace.

Sex with Virginia wasn't just physical. It was mental. The mind was so powerful. This I knew. Because of her injuries, she needed more mental stimulation. She needed me to map her body and find her most erogenous zones and love them.

Everything didn't center between her legs like every other sexual experience I'd had. This was more... intimate. I had to be more patient.

Moving down her body, I pushed her legs wide, peeking up to make sure she wasn't upset.

"Wider." She beckoned, and I did as she asked, pushing them as wide as I was willing. Just because she couldn't feel pain didn't mean I would take advantage of that.

Hurting someone because they couldn't feel it was a dick move, and I might be a villain, but I was not a dick.

Her trust meant more to me than anything ever had because she *did* trust me. Even though she had every reason not to.

Kneeling between her legs, I gazed down at her center, which was surprisingly bare. "Can I touch you?"

She nodded, and I instantly dragged my finger over her smooth, hairless skin.

"It makes it easier," was all she said as I continued touching.

"Can you feel this?"

There was a pregnant silence. "I'm sorry, but I can't."

"Hey, it's okay," I murmured. "It's gonna take a while to figure this all out, but I'm looking forward to it."

Climbing back up her body, I kissed her, then trailed my lips down to nuzzle her center. She was slick. Dripping actually.

Reaching for her hand, I pulled it down her body, into her middle. "What are you doing?" she asked nervously, hand tensing.

"Feel, sweetheart. I want you to feel how ready you are." Dragging her fingers up her slit, I watched her eyes widen.

"Oh..."

"Your body likes me."

She giggled. "There's the arrogance I'm used to."

Her laughter fell away and her brown eyes turned

deep when I lifted her fingers and sucked them between my lips. Lapping at all her silky desire, I moaned around them, sucking her digits a little deeper.

Her eyes glazed over.

"You taste so good," I whispered, reaching for the condom I'd tossed at the end of the bed.

She watched quietly as I rolled it on, and when I was done, I caged her in with my arms. "If you want me to stop, I will."

"I don't want you to stop."

"If something hurts or feels weird, anything… just tell me."

I saw a flicker of something in her face, kind of like sadness, but then it was gone.

Leaning in, I kissed her, tangling our tongues and pushing into her body in one long stroke. I groaned the second her tight heat clamped around me, my forehead falling onto her shoulder.

"Jesus, V. *Jesus.*"

"Is it bad?" She worried.

"Christ, no." I panted, then pushed up onto my elbows to stare down into her eyes. I started moving in her, pulling out and plunging back in.

She made a soft sound, gripping my shoulders and watching the emotions flicker over my face.

Leaning down, I took her breast in my mouth, and she arched up into it as I snapped my hips forward.

"Oh," she crooned.

I snapped in deeper.

"*Oh.*"

Pushing up onto my palms, I glanced down, pulled out, and pushed deep. Her eyes rolled slightly back.

"I-I think I feel that."

Elation made my heart pound, and I did it again. "So

you like me deep," I murmured, grabbing her hips and pushing.

She cried out, one of her hands grappling for the blankets.

Thinking fast, I grabbed the hand, pressing it against her stomach. "Feel me inside you, sweetheart. Feel."

Pinning her hand there, I moved, snapping my hips over and over.

She gasped, eyes filling with tears. "That's you."

"That's me."

"I c-can feel you moving."

I pushed her hand down harder, swiveling my hips while bending to take a nip at her breast.

She gasped and squirmed. I kept up the steady pace. Tension built in my stomach, quivering my muscles. The need to let go was indescribable, almost too much to bear.

Not yet. Give her something else.

Slapping my hand onto the headboard, I used it as an anchor and went *deep.*

Her mouth fell open.

Holding on to the headboard, I went rough, her body rocking with every thrust, my balls slapping against her.

Her muscles started to tighten. I glanced down, wondering if she could feel it, but her face was already blissed out.

Her walls clenched against me, and I moaned, body coming undone. Before every thought fled my brain, I slipped a hand between us and pushed down on her belly, rocking my hips.

I heard her cry out, but then my body took over. White light exploded behind my eyes, my cock nearly bursting inside her, the orgasm going on and on.

I was shaking when I finally came down from the

high. My hand ached from the grip I'd had on the headboard.

With a groan, I rolled, pulling her with me, allowing our legs to tangle as I hugged her into my chest.

My softening dick slipped out and I knew I needed to take care of the condom, but goddamn, I couldn't move. That was... *amazing.*

After a few more moments of my mind being blown, I realized that she was awfully silent. All my bliss turned to panic as I looked down.

"Sweetheart?"

She sniffled.

"Oh, baby, did I hurt you?" *I was too rough. Too rough!*

Despite the weakness in my limbs, I lifted her, her entire body like a rag doll draping against mine. "Virginia," I said, concern making my voice firm. "Look at me."

She looked up. Her eyes were wide, pupils blown. Her lips were well and truly fucked, and sweat glistened on her forehead.

"Did I hurt you? Scare you?"

Her lower lip wobbled, and I contemplated murdering myself. I meant it when I said I'd kill anyone who hurt her. I was no fucking exception.

"I felt it," she whimpered, hand grabbing at my chest. "I felt it a little."

"And it hurt?"

"No!" she wailed. "I came!"

And then she started to cry, curling into my chest, streaking it with tears.

I blinked up at the ceiling, not sure if that was good or bad. I mean, she had an O... That was good, right? That was the goal. But why was she crying?

"I'm confused," I admitted. My hands hovered over

her back as she drenched me with salty tears. "Tell me what you need."

She looked up, eyelashes wet, nose pink. "I hadn't hoped. I'd been so worried that I would just be this… lifeless body and you would be turned off. But it wasn't like that at all. It was… It was *everything*. It was more than I could ever have hoped for."

"And it felt good?" I wanted to be sure.

"Oh my God, yes."

I blew out a breath. "Thank God."

"B-but…" Her voice was wobbly, and another tear tracked over her damp cheek. "Was it okay for you?"

I laughed and rolled, caging her against the mattress with my body, letting our chests rub together.

"That was literally the best sex I've ever had."

"Don't lie to me."

Pursing my lips, I pushed up, reached down, and pulled off the condom, tying the top. Then, without a second thought, I held it up. "See how full that is?" I said proudly. "I fucking loved it."

Her eyes went between the condom I held up like an award and my face. A giggle slipped out, but she swallowed it down. "This is unnecessary."

Tossing the condom aside, I gathered her up, shoving my arms under her body to hold her against me. "I'll do whatever it takes to make you believe."

Her eyes roamed my face, and the way she stared made me want to preen. There was awe in her eyes, happiness… love.

I kissed her nose. "No more doubts about bedroom stuff. I think we just proved we are definitely compatible."

She smiled shyly, burying her face into my neck. "You talk kinda dirty."

"You like it." *Mental stimulation.*

"Yeah," she confessed.

I pulled back so I could look into her gaze. "Was I too rough? It seems the more... aggressive and deeper I am, the more you can feel."

"It was perfect."

I pulled back and looked between her legs. She screeched, trying to cover herself with her hands. I grasped them and continued looking. It was a little late to be embarrassed. She appeared unharmed, so I decided it was okay.

The grabby hand motion she made turned my insides to mush, and I wrapped her up in my arms, settling us both into the bed. "We'll clean up in a bit. Let me hold you."

"What about your shoulder?" She worried.

"It's fine." I assured her. "You can change the bandage for me later."

"Will you stay?" Her voice was soft, breath fanning out over my chest.

"I'm never sleeping without you again."

"I love you."

My heart tumbled. I wondered if I'd ever get used to hearing her say it. Knowing she meant it.

I hoped I didn't.

Forty-Seven

A SLIM CRACK OF LIGHT SHONE THROUGH THE HEAVY curtains, stretching across the floor and snaking across the bed. The rest of the room was dim, but that thin line was persistently bright and only stopped when it touched Earth.

I lay on my side, Earth spooned against my back. I'd fallen asleep on his chest, so at some point, he'd shifted us like this. I smiled into the pillow at the way he'd kept his promise to adjust me in the night.

I'm never sleeping without you again.

Memories of last night washed over me, making me tingle and my chest expand with awe. I'd been half a girl for a long time, told I might never be whole again.

But I wasn't half a girl. I never was. I'd always been whole, capable of feeling *everything* that mattered. I'd just been afraid. Trapped in a tower but not the one I lived in, the one where I'd placed my heart.

Afraid of love. Afraid of losing. Afraid of trying and proving all my fears wrong.

It took a villain to give me courage. A villain to reach into my darkness and only see the light. If Earth hadn't shown up to drive me to an appointment, none of this would have happened.

Maybe I wouldn't have found the courage to tell Neo my dreams.

Yeah, Earth took lives. But he saved some too.

Mine being one of them. Perhaps every villain has a little hero in them. Maybe that's what makes them so good at being bad.

Hero. Villain. It didn't matter. Earth was Earth. The man I loved.

As if on cue, he made a deep sound, and his hand dragged across my waist, settling in the dip in my side. "I like waking up to you." His voice was sleepy in my ear.

"Me too."

He kissed my cheek and then my ear before slipping out of bed.

"Hey! Where are you going?" I scowled.

He padded around the bed to pull open the curtains. "Opening these so you can look out."

"You're naked!" I gasped as he stood in front of the glass.

He grinned lazily. "You don't even need a window to have a view."

I giggled. "Come back to bed."

He stepped forward, and I noted the tattoo on his hip.

"Come here," I murmured, holding out a hand.

He did, and I dragged my fingers down the black rose inked into his skin. "I didn't even notice this last night."

"I'll take that as a compliment."

I smiled. "You should." Focusing back on the art, I said, "So this is your family's symbol?"

"It's more like a gang symbol." His voice was tight.

Letting my fingers fall away from the rose, I glanced up, catching his black eyes. "You did well, sweetheart," I told him, using the endearment I loved him to use. "You endured them well, surviving until you could get away."

Emotion filled his expression, and he looked away. He started to retreat, but I caught his hand, tucking mine inside, warmth blooming in my chest when his fingers curled around mine, clutching tight.

"I know you think you're like them, but you aren't. You're so much better. And yes, you've done bad things I don't like, but I love *you*. All of you. Always. Unconditionally. We all do."

He made a sound and crawled back onto the mattress and over my body to curl his around mine. I could feel the heavy pounding of his heart against my back and how he buried his face in my hair.

Maybe he hadn't needed to hear that, but when I finally felt like I was enough for him—just as I was— something inside me settled. I wanted him to have that too. Or, at the very least, to know that I wasn't secretly judging him for the path he took that led him here.

He clung to me, saying nothing, but we didn't have to speak for him to know I was here.

"Thank you," he whispered after a long while, breath ruffling my hair.

I smiled.

Forty-Eight

Bang! Bang! Bang!

"Get your ass out here, Earth!" Neo demanded while steadily pounding on the bedroom door.

"We're getting our own place," I declared.

Virginia twisted at the waist to stare at me, surprise lighting up her face. "What?"

"There's two units available on lower floors in this building and one available in Ethan and Fletch's building. Pick one."

Gaping, she scrambled to sit up, and I slid my arm around her to lift. She looked fucking gorgeous sitting there in the middle of the rumpled sheets we'd had sex in last night. Her hair was a wreck, her chest was bare, and her lips were still swollen.

Satisfaction hummed bone deep inside me this morning, which was why I was probably ignoring the still-hammering hothead at the door.

Bang! Bang! Bang!

"You can't be serious!" Her eyes were owlishly wide.

Tucking a strand of soft hair behind her ear, I said, "You don't expect me to live with *that*, do you?" I hitched a thumb over my shoulder.

"Earth! I'll bust down this door!"

"I'm naked!" I yelled.

Neo roared.

"Well, I guess I could get used to it." I amended. Riling him up on the daily sure sounded fun.

V crossed her arms over her bare chest and scowled.

"You're blocking my view, sweetheart," I drawled.

Her cheeks pinkened, and her eyes dropped. Chuckling, I pushed up her chin to kiss her softly.

Bang! Bang! Bang!

"Don't you realize how much these buildings cost?" she asked when I pulled away.

"Killing paid very well, sweetheart."

Her mouth fell open.

"We'll go look at them later. Then you can pick one," I said, getting off the bed to find my jeans.

The door was shuddering under Neo's assault.

"Hold on. Let me get some pants," I called.

"You son of a bitch!"

I winked at V and handed her my T-shirt. She pulled it on, and then I scooped her up, placing her in her chair. "Go do whatever girly stuff you gotta do, and I'll go see what he wants."

"If he punches you, don't come crying to me."

"You won't kiss it and make it better?"

She blushed. I was gonna have to flirt with her more. She was cute when she was shy.

"Come out when you're done," I said, giving her a noisy kiss and letting the sound of her laugh seep into my skin.

I unlocked the door and slipped through a slim opening.

"What the hell is going on in there?" Neo demanded.

I smiled slow. "You really want to know?"

He swung.

I ducked.

"You got any coffee in this fancy place?" I asked.

"You're getting decaf," Neo declared, stalking toward the kitchen.

"That's the meanest thing you've ever said to me."

He made it as far as the kitchen island before swinging around, a hard set to his mouth. "You spent the night with my sister."

All the teasing I'd been thoroughly enjoying evaporated.

"Yes," I said honestly.

"Did you touch her?"

"I think you know the answer to that."

His hands balled into fists at his sides. Despite the anger radiating from his body, his voice was concerned. "Is she okay?"

"I promise you she's okay."

Some of his anger ebbed, but there was still worry in the lines of his face.

"I love her," I told him honestly. Teasing him was fun, but I also wanted him to know I was serious here. V wasn't a game to me.

His hands relaxed. "You aren't good enough for her."

"No." I agreed.

"But if anyone could come close… it would be you."

It took a moment for the words to register. Surprise rendered me quiet. Of all the things he could have said, I never would have imagined that.

"Someone so *good* needs someone a little wicked. I know you will do anything to keep her safe."

"And happy," I added. "I'll do anything to make sure she's happy."

"Even go against me."

"Even go against you," I echoed.

"No one else was willing to do that." He smirked, proud of himself.

"Jake was a wanker," I cracked. "Thanks for getting rid of him."

Snorting, Neo went to the coffeepot, which was already full, and poured two mugs full. When he was done, he picked up one and leaned against the counter to sip.

"Being with her isn't going to be easy," he observed. Or maybe it was a warning.

I went over, picked up the other coffee, and leaned against the counter beside him. "I'm not too good at easy anyway."

Neo nodded.

"She—" He stopped as if the words were stuck. He drank coffee. Blanched. Drank more. Staring down into the black brew, he finally whispered, "She probably won't walk again."

My mug made a low thud on the counter when I set it aside and turned to him. I knew it was the first time he'd likely ever admitted that to himself. After seven long years of pushing, fighting, and denying, he was finally coming around to accepting.

I hoped that meant he was finally also starting to forgive himself.

"She doesn't have to walk to have a good life. We'll make sure she has a great one no matter what."

"We?"

"I'm not taking her away from you, Neo. She needs you, and she always will. I'm just hoping you'll share her with me."

"You did take a bullet for her," Neo said coolly,

glancing at my shirtless shoulder, seeing the edge of the bandage taped there.

"I would die for her."

"I actually believe you."

"Because it's true."

"I've been a jealous, unreasonable asshole," he finally admitted.

I smiled. "I was wondering when you'd get to that."

"Fuck you."

I slapped him on the shoulder and picked up my coffee again. "I deserved it. I wouldn't have respected you if you acted any other way."

We swallowed down some coffee, and I waited for whatever else Neo wanted to say.

"Look," he said at last, voice low. "I'm… sorry about the shit you went through. You, ah, had a rough time as a kid."

"And?"

"And I want you to know that I don't blame you for it, but I have to think of V." His dark eyes settled heavily on mine. "I need to know if there is anyone else that might come after you. Did the vendetta against you die with that woman? Is my sister in danger?"

That woman. Not your mother. But he was right. She had never been a mother to me.

"The Black Rose won't be a problem anymore. My family is gone except for Daeshim, and the organization will be chaos while they have a power struggle to figure out who's the new boss."

"And we can trust him? Daeshim?"

"Yes."

Neo gave me a sidelong glance. "Because you honestly believe that or because you want to believe it?"

"Both."

"And what about… your other business."

My business of killing. "I'm done."

Neo nodded. "I know. But are there loose ends? Anyone or anything that could come back to bite us?"

"Us?"

His eyes turned fierce; loyalty shone in their depths. "Yes, *us.* We have a family to protect. I certainly wouldn't ask you to handle it all on your own."

"But it's my mess."

"You aren't alone," he insisted.

I've missed him. All these months that we've been at each other's throats. I missed my brother.

I cleared my throat, trying to dissolve the emotion stuffed there. "There are no loose ends."

Neo scrutinized my face. "Are you sure?"

"I would never put your sister in danger like that— any of you. If there was a loose end, I would tie it."

Neo nodded. "Okay. Good."

Silence fell between us.

"So, ah, we good?" I asked.

He blew out a breath as though some giant weight were finally being lifted from his shoulders. "Yeah. We're good."

Straightening from the counter, I pushed my hand between us.

He glanced at it, then shoved it away.

Before I could react, he leaned in and hugged me. I froze, shocked.

"I missed you," he whispered.

And then I was hugging him back, more of that emotion shit clogging my throat. "Me too," I rasped.

We broke apart, both looking away to chug the horrible black coffee.

"You and your sister are turning me soft," I muttered at last.

Neo made a rude sound. "Yeah right. We all know it was Fletch."

"Fuck you."

Neo laughed.

Movement across the room brought my head up.

Virginia looked sheepish. "Is it safe to come in now?"

Neo and I glanced at each other.

I smiled. "Yeah, sweetheart. It's safe."

She was still wearing my T-shirt. The sight of it draping her small frame made possession and want war within me.

Poisoning Guaranteed. The shirt proudly proclaimed the logo for my brew. But really, it had been an honest logo for *me*.

It should have bothered me to see those words written across the woman I loved. It should have been proof I was anything but good for her.

It wasn't.

Yes, I was filled with venom. I might always be.

It didn't matter.

She was my antidote.

"His shirt?" Neo muttered, gazing at his sister. "Really?"

I grinned at him before scooping her up to deposit her on the island. "At least she has on pants," I ribbed, glancing down at the loose shorts she'd pulled on.

Once she was settled on the island, legs dangling toward the floor, I pecked a kiss to the tip of her nose and pulled back. "Coffee?"

She nodded.

Since I put her on the island, she was more eye level with us, something I liked. I never wanted to somehow make her feel small or like I was lording any kind of power over her.

I mean, she was small. Tiny in fact. My little sprite. But in truth, she was the one with the power.

I poured her some coffee and then fished some fancy creamer out of the fridge. "What the hell is this?" I muttered, looking at the ornate glass bottle.

"It's organic," Neo muttered, a small smile playing on his lips.

"Money has changed you, bro."

He snorted.

I held the mug while V added what she wanted and then watched her take a sip.

"Mmm," she hummed. "This is way better than what we have at the Tower."

"I'll get you a coffeemaker just like it," I said.

"She already has one. Here," Neo retorted.

"We're getting our own place."

Neo stiffened. "Excuse me?"

"Did you really think I would live apart from her?"

He frowned. "Your apartment isn't good enough."

I wasn't offended because it was true. "I'm not talking about my apartment. Besides, Daeshim is crashing in my room now."

"Just stay here, then." Neo concluded.

"I can take care of my girl," I spat, upper lip curling.

"Is anyone going to ask me what I want?" Virginia cut in, voice mild and slightly amused.

The neckline of the shirt was a bit big on her, so it exposed a creamy collarbone, her hair pushed behind her shoulders. Some of the newly cut layers fell forward to frame her chin. Both her little hands were wrapped around the mug, and she regarded us over the rim as she sipped.

I wanted to kiss her.

"Of course, sweetheart," I murmured, shifting away from Neo to swivel entirely toward her. Both my hands settled on the counter on either side of her hips. I was close enough that her knees brushed against my waist, but because she couldn't feel it, I fit one palm against her waist.

"Brother in the room," Neo muttered.

"Exactly why we're moving out," I tossed over my shoulder, then pushed her cup down to kiss her softly.

Her lips were warm and tasted of coffee. The way they turned pliant under mine was fucking heady.

She pulled back first, face flushed pink, and ducked her chin shyly.

Stomach doing a weird fumble, I glanced over my shoulder at Neo to draw his attention and give her a moment. "There's two apartments, if you could even call them that, in this building. And there's one in Ethan's. I told her to pick one."

Neo's eyes bulged. "Bro, the prices in the Upper East Side are not like the Grimms."

"I can afford it."

Glancing back at V, I rubbed her side. "You'll never want for anything."

Her eyes were soft. "All I really want is you."

Neo made a gagging sound. "You mean you're going to take care of my sister using blood money."

My eyes narrowed. Who the fuck cared what color my money was as long as it provided for her? The fact was he should be glad I had a fat bank account from all my misdeeds because that meant I could afford everything she would ever need and then some.

Virginia rubbed a palm against my jaw, her eyes silently telling me it was okay. Leaning around me, she glanced at her brother. "You've been taking care of me for years with money you stole. Don't you think that's a bit hypocritical?"

That shut him up.

Pulling away, she swept us both up into a rigid look. "It isn't easy accepting financial care, you know. It makes me feel like a burden, like I can't depend on myself."

"You aren't a burden," I said, voice hard.

"I don't want a fancy house."

"Well, none of the available units are penthouses, so they aren't—"

"I want to live in the Grimms."

"No!" Neo and I both declared.

Setting aside her coffee, she pinned me with a stubborn look. "You said to pick a place to live. I just did."

I glowered. "I gave you three choices."

"Well, I added one!"

"The Grimms is no place for you, Virginia. I won't have my sister living in the ghetto," Neo argued.

Her arms crossed over her chest. "But you lived there for years. Earth and Beau still live there. It was good enough for you."

"That's different," I said.

"Why?"

"Because you're better than that."

Her arms fell to her sides. "No," she whispered. "I'm not. I'm a girl who, up until the fire, was trapped in a tower. A tower that sat on the edge of the Grimms... It might not be fancy and elite like all the places you're offering, but it has something the Upper East Side never will."

"What's that, sprite?" I asked, voice soft.

"It's a place that shielded me and kept me when I had nowhere else to go. I met Emogen there. I learned to live in my body there. Some might consider the Grimms the ghetto, and yeah, maybe it was… but it's home."

With a gruff sound, I pulled her into my chest, palming the side of her head and holding her tight. Her cheek rubbed against me, and her fingers splayed against my side.

"You told me to choose, and I have," she whispered.

Her lips grazed my pec when she spoke, and I had to resist the shudder that moved through my body.

Pulling back, I cupped Virginia's face between my palms. "If that's what you want."

"You can't just give in to her!" Neo spat.

"Why not?" I asked, looking over my shoulder with a raised brow.

"If you didn't have a bullet hole in you, I'd deck you," he grumbled.

I grinned.

"Actually," I said, moving back to lean against the counter near my brother. "Living in the Grimms might actually work out better for some of my other plans."

"I expect you to live clean now that you're with my sister."

I didn't bother to remind him that he didn't own me, and he sure as hell wasn't my boss. "You know that building I own, the one up the block from the bar?"

"The one where you keep your car?" Neo asked.

I nodded. "It's empty. I'd been thinking about renovating it into some affordable housing, nothing fancy but something better than what the people there are used to."

"Oh, that's a wonderful idea!" Virginia exclaimed.

The pride in her eyes when she looked at me elicited a feeling I could get used to. No. It was a feeling I could become addicted to.

"Instead, I'll just renovate the entire building for us.

Make it handicap accessible. Add an elevator, a room for physical therapy." Glancing at Neo, I added, "I'll have Beau install the best security system."

Neo frowned, but I noticed he didn't argue.

"We don't need an entire building," Virginia put in.

"How about we make the ground floor into a flower shop."

Her head came up.

"*Your* flower shop."

Tears flooded her eyes, making the brown turn more translucent. "Y-you would do that?"

I'll do everything for you. "You can work as much or as little as you want. You can put flowers on the sidewalk and in the windows. Home will be right above you, and the bar will be just a short walk away."

She burst into tears.

Pushing off the counter, I went to her, pulling her hands down from covering her face, allowing her to bury it in my chest instead. Tears smeared my skin, and I swear I felt them seep in. I felt their warmth all the way to my core.

Definitely my antidote.

"We could bring some beauty into the Grimms." She sniffled.

"Well, with you there, it will already be the most beautiful place."

Neo made a sound, but we ignored him.

Her face was wet, eyes shimmering when she looked up. "You'd really do that?"

I nodded.

"Can we get a cat?" She was hopeful.

"No. Snort will eat it."

Her lower lip stuck out. "But you were gonna let Fletcher bring Gwen."

I made a sound. "Fine. Pick a cat."

Her eyes lit up. "I'll have Fletcher go to the shelter with me!"

"I'll warn Ethan," I muttered. No way in hell that kid wouldn't drag home another animal. Ethan was worse than me. He'd never say no.

"Pushover," Neo quipped.

I gave him the finger.

"I really like this idea," she said, but a frown drew her eyebrows together.

"But?"

Sheepish, she looked up. "But what about all the people who would have had a nice place to live if we didn't use the building for us?"

I made a sound and turned to Neo. "About that... I was thinking of buying a couple more of the rundown buildings to fix up. Nothing fancy because then no one would be able to afford it. Just basic small apartments. But safe." I paused. "If Fletcher had somewhere like that, then maybe you wouldn't have found him in that alley."

"And maybe you wouldn't have had to bring me home," Neo added.

"I don't regret that," I told him honestly. Dragging home some guy I didn't know with holes in his clothes and a bad habit of stealing was the worst idea I'd ever had. But then it became the best.

Look at everything it brought me.

"I could maybe go in with you on the buildings. I earned a bit from my gallery showing. I've been wanting to get a respectable job... something to maybe be proud of." *Something for Ivory to be proud of.* He didn't have to say that for me to hear it. I understood.

"Making the Grimms a little better is definitely something to be proud of," Virginia said.

"I was hoping you'd say that. I could definitely use a business partner."

Neo eyed me a minute longer. "You'll make sure your building is secure?"

I nodded. "We'll need somewhere to stay until all the renovations are done."

"You'll always have a place with us," Ivory chimed in, making us all look up as she walked into the room, wearing a deep-blue silk robe that was belted at her waist.

"Were you eavesdropping?" I scowled.

"It's not eavesdropping if the conversation is taking place in your own home," she told us as she got herself some coffee.

I rolled my eyes. *Such a princess.*

Neo looked down when she settled against him, dark eyes softening as something passed quietly between them.

"Let's do it." He nodded, looking up to meet my stare.

"Yeah?"

"Yeah."

Virginia squealed happily, holding her arms out for me. I moved into them of course.

Her nose nuzzled the underside of my jaw, followed by the softness of her lips. I glanced down, the venom in my veins still there but definitely subdued.

She kissed me softly. "I love you, Earth."

Everyone always said villains don't get happy endings.

They were wrong.

Forty-Nine

You know, I always thought I'd end up in a place just like this. A place with watchtowers, armed guards, and high walls topped in barbed wire.

Since I was conceived, crime and violence were a given. Venom surely flooded my veins. Even still, I was careful. Meticulous even in protecting myself and eventually those around me.

Regardless, I knew the odds of me ending up locked away were in my favor.

Grumpy. Crass. Cold. Just a few words that described me. All of them were true. In fact, those might even be too kind.

Despite it all, I wasn't the one in the hideous orange jumpsuit. I wasn't the one being led by armed guards and escorted into a chair behind a large glass shield. The old-school phone on the wall had one of those spiral cords.

They shouldn't allow those here. They make perfect weapons.

She was the last one to enter the visitation room. Even though she'd been locked away for many charges, including murder, she walked with an air of superiority and arrogance. I mean, really, I'd be impressed if I didn't loathe her.

Her hair was styled. Nails painted. And I was pretty sure, as she perched on the chair on the other side of the glass before me, her lips were stained with lipstick.

Clearly, Audra White's money had influence even behind bars. And it wasn't her appearance that proved it. These details just hammered in the truth I'd already known.

Her eyes flicked to mine as though I were a peasant she deigned to share her time with. In truth, I knew this little impromptu visit likely caught her off guard. For all her riches, popularity, and once-high rank over New York City elite, she was now nothing but a shunned jailbird.

And *oh*, how angry that made her.

We regarded each other for long, quiet moments.

I know you called the Black Rose. I spoke through my eyes.

So what if I did? She was haughty even in silence.

You don't have the power to take me down, so you called someone who did.

I'm not so powerless. After all, I figured out your true identity. Huntsman. Her eyes boasted that she did indeed find out what no one else had ever been able to.

She was so arrogant it never once occurred to her that prying into my secrets would only put a target on her back.

I spread my hands, palms up, gesturing to the room in which we sat. *But here you are.*

Her stare narrowed into thin slits, and her nostrils flared. Oh, the amount of control she must have been exerting to sit there and not explode. The woman was a live wire, a firework just waiting for a match.

She'd made it abundantly clear that, even from her jail cell, she would try and take me down. Take us all down.

And that I would never allow.

My family closed ranks around me. They buried secrets, lied, and accepted me even though I didn't deserve it.

Virginia loved me. With her eyes open.

They protected me, and now it was my turn to do the same. A villain's protection was absolute. There was no limit to what I would do to ensure the safety of those I loved.

And the people who threatened them? Poisoning guaranteed.

Leaning forward, I plucked the phone off the wall, holding it up to my ear.

She held out for a moment, maybe trying to exert some power she didn't have. I sat there bored, waiting for her to finish her game.

Eventually, she picked up her line, holding it gingerly against her ear. "Why have you come?" So haughty.

"I brought you a gift," I told her, motioning at the guard behind her.

Her mask of indifference slipped, surprise flickering in her stare. "What?"

Her thin frame flinched when the guard brushed her shoulder as he placed the large wicker basket on the counter in front of her.

"How lucky for you the warden here allows gifts." I spoke into her ear.

The guard melted back against the wall, and Audra's wide stare wavered between me and the basket, which was piled high with shining red apples.

"I know how much you love a good apple."

Panic flared in her expression. The hand holding the receiver against her ear tightened. "What have you done?"

I kept my face innocent. Polite. "I've brought a thank-you for everything you've done."

My eyes turned flat, and I allowed the true depth of my anger to show. The phone in her grasp shook. Genuine fear slurped all the color from her cheeks.

I spoke quietly into the line, keeping my voice even and flat. "You never should have touched her."

Confusion flickered in her eyes. "Ivory?"

"Sending scum after a girl in a wheelchair is low. Even for you."

Realization dawned. She sat forward in the chair. I saw her lips move, but I didn't hear her voice because I returned the receiver to the wall.

I stood from the chair and turned my back. Her conceited self-importance was suddenly gone. The glass rattled from the way she pounded on it, begging for my attention, pleading for me to come back.

I left her like that and walked away.

Not once did I turn back.

I promised Neo there were no loose ends.

And now there weren't.

Two weeks later...

Ivory lowered the cell from her ear, her milky white skin taking on a translucent tone. "Oh my."

Neo's fork clattered against his plate. One arm went across the back of her chair, and the other wrapped around her middle, curling around her hip. "Princess? What's wrong?"

She placed the phone on the table, swallowing thickly before her ultra-blue eyes lifted to Neo.

"Th-that was the warden at the state penitentiary."

"That's where your stepmother is, right?" Fletcher asked.

"She—she's dead."

Virginia gasped.

Reaching over, I cupped the back of her neck lightly with my palm. She sank into the touch, clearly comforted by it even though her eyes remained on Ivory.

"How awful! I'm so sorry, Ivory."

Ivory was quiet a moment, her body leaning into Neo. Her red lips parted. Then she glanced at the family sitting around the table. "It's all right. I mean, it's not like she and I were close."

Not close = the woman tried to kill her. More than once.

And yeah, maybe I tried to help.

"It's okay to be upset," Ethan said, concern darkening his features. "All of us would understand."

Everyone nodded. Except for me.

"Ethan says it's okay to be upset when someone evil gets hurt because it just makes us human," Fletcher told her.

Ethan rubbed his hand over Fletcher's hair, smiling slightly. Thoughts of Fletch's mother darkened my thoughts, but I shoved them away. Killing that woman would only hurt him more.

"I'm not upset. I'm just surprised is all." Her eyes turned a little guilty. "And maybe just a little relieved."

"What happened?" Beau asked.

"He didn't say. Just that she was found dead."

"Will there be an investigation?" Ethan inquired.

She shook her head, shiny black locks swinging. "I

don't think so. She's just… gone."

Silence blanketed the family breakfast. Everyone sat unsure of what Ivory might need.

Virginia's hand went to my thighs, her delicate fingers tucking between them. I gave the nape of her neck a light squeeze, brushing the pad of my thumb along her pulse point.

Suddenly, Ivory's chair scraped back, and she padded around the table, stopping beside me. I glanced up, noting the tears shimmering in her stare.

Thin arms wrapped around my shoulders, and her hair brushed my cheek. I froze, completely taken aback.

"Now would be a really good time to finally hug your sister back," she whispered against my ear.

I swallowed an odd feeling in my chest.

Virginia tugged her hand from between my legs and patted my thigh. I glanced at her, unsure what to do, and she lifted her eyebrows.

Ivory was still locked around my shoulders, and I tore my gaze from V to look at Neo. He smiled lightly and nodded.

My arms slid around her as I angled to pull her into a hug. She was soft and small like Virginia, but she didn't set my pulse racing. She didn't make me want to bury my face in the side of her neck and inhale.

But there was warmth. Comfort. Connection.

Ivory and I started out as a princess and a huntsman, and along a long and winding path, we found ourselves here as brother and sister.

As family.

"Thank you, Earth," she whispered.

"I didn't do anything," I told her.

"I know."

I hugged her a little tighter.

Epilogue

VIRGINIA

VIBRANTLY COLORED FLOWERS SPILLED FROM THE windows and out of the flower shop door, trickling onto the sidewalk.

Autumn had a complete grip on the city, and it was positively magical. The air was crisp and sweet, the sun shone golden rays over the buildings, and there was an underlying excitement of renewal swirling in the wind.

The city sounds were secondary because, inside, K-pop played through the small speakers on the counter. I listened to it more and more these days because Earth liked it.

He'd never admit it, though. Don't tell him I told you.

My chair was tucked under a low marble counter. A freshly prepared vase of long-stemmed yellow roses sat off to the side as I worked on a sample arrangement of the seasonally classic chrysanthemums, which would be presented in hollowed-out pumpkins. Ivory was hosting a dinner for her fashion line and had hired Tangled Stems, my little shop, to do the centerpieces.

A gust of chilly air rushed in through the open double doors, ruffling the strands of rapidly growing hair falling around my shoulders. Goose bumps rose along my arms beneath my sweater, but I didn't mind. It was so nice to be able to feel the outside air.

"What the hell is this door doing open?" a loud voice bellowed.

I glanced up, forgetting the bunch of golden blooms clutched in my hand, to smile at Earth's scowling, grumpy face. "You know I like to let in the fresh air."

He frowned, already pulling off his leather jacket. "It's too cold for that. You're gonna freeze."

His boots were heavy over the smooth tile, but his movements were gentle when he draped the jacket around my shoulders, the weight of the leather settling against me with familiarity. He still smelled faintly of bread and stale cigarette smoke, but now there was also a hint of flowers.

"I won't freeze. You'll keep me warm," I replied, absolutely certain.

Grasping my face between his palms, he pulled me around, penetrating my eyes with his enigmatic stare. "Always," he murmured, pressing our foreheads together before caressing my nose with his.

A little shiver prickled my scalp, and I tilted up my chin. The brief kiss wasn't enough, though. It never was. I always wanted *more, more, more* of Earth. I always would.

With a gruff sound, he lifted me out of the wheelchair and sat down on the counter with me in his lap.

Squealing, I smacked his shoulder. "Earth! My flowers! You'll crush them!"

"I'll buy you more," he murmured, dipping his head once more.

I melted into his chest, his mouth, parting my lips wider to invite him in. Our tongues tangled together, brushing softly before his pulled back to swipe over my lower lip. I whimpered a bit as he nipped the sensitive flesh while the pads of his fingers massaged my scalp.

As I arched into him, my arms wound tighter around his neck so he would go deeper. Before I knew it, my lungs were on fire, and the world around us was blurry with only the feel of him around me and the scent of flowers mingling in the air.

"Are you done here?" His voice was husky, and the promise of it made butterflies take flight beneath my ribs.

"Almost."

He groaned. "Give me another, then, to hold me over."

I giggled but lifted my face.

We kissed again, this time his tongue delving deeper, more aggressively, as if he really was trying to take his fill until we got home. I never thought anyone would crave me the way he did. I never thought someone would ever be powerful enough to make me burn.

I was breathless when he pulled back, his eyes glittering with promise and his lips slick from mine. "What do you need me to do?"

I told him, and he reluctantly put me back in my chair, then helped put the flowers and arrangements into the cooler at the back of the shop.

"The baker came in today and got a small arrangement for the bakery down the block," I told him.

He grunted.

"And a nice lady who lives one block over stopped in to get a bouquet for her kitchen."

"Your flowers are making the Grimms look pretty, sweetheart."

"I made an arrangement for the bar!" I said excitedly.

Turning from the cooler, he crossed his arms and glared. "I told you flowers don't belong in a bar."

"But I made it for you." I stuck out my lip in a pout.

He sighed. "Fine. Where is it?"

Beaming, I rolled to the other side of the cooler to reach into the lower shelf and pull out the arrangement. "Ta-da!" I exclaimed, holding it out.

Earth's lips twitched. "What the hell is that?"

I grinned mischievously, holding out the empty (and washed) beer bottle with a single daisy sticking out the top. "Do you like it?"

Giving up, Earth chuckled. The warm sound made my insides feel like jelly. "Thank you, sweetheart."

"You'll put it on the bar?"

"No." He was back to being grumpy.

"Why not?"

"Because every drunk idiot who comes in will try and drink it, and then I'll have to smash their heads."

I made a face.

"I'll put it in my office instead, where it'll be safe."

Squealing, I made a grabby motion at him with my hands, and he came over, slipping between them easily. His lips brushed in my hair, then kissed across my temple.

"Come on. I'll take you back to Ivory and Neo's, then come back to the bar."

I sighed. "I wish our apartment was done."

"Soon." He promised, glancing at the elevator shaft at the back of the shop.

The three floors above this shop were almost finished but weren't quite ready. Earth basically gutted the entire building and started from scratch. The only thing that looked the same was the outside and the small garage in the back off the alley.

Everything was updated and brand new. Everything was state-of-the-art and handicap-friendly. All the finishes were white and bright. Big windows overlooked the street.

It was honestly more than I ever hoped for, more than I needed, but everything Earth said I deserved.

"Earth?"

He turned.

"Can't I just come to the bar with you tonight?"

"You know I don't like you being there around all those drunk assholes."

"But I want to stay with you."

His eyes glinted stubbornly.

I added, "I missed you today."

"Fuck," he muttered under his breath, and I suppressed a grin.

Stalking forward, he reached into the chair to haul me up. Over the past few months, Earth had become an expert at maneuvering my body, knowing where to hold and how to pick me up. After a moment, he was between my thighs, his arms under my butt, and it was like I'd wrapped my legs around his waist. I wished I could lock my ankles at his back and squeeze his body with my thighs, but I couldn't and that was okay.

Instead, I looped my arms around his neck and leaned in, pressing our chests together.

"I don't want to go home without you," I whispered.

He made a rude sound, then hitched me up a little. "Fine. But if anyone looks at you cross-eyed, I'll punch them."

I considered it progress that he didn't say he'd kill them.

When we entered the bar, music was already playing (not K-pop; I told you he doesn't tell people it's his favorite), and there was already a crowd. The neon lights on the wall were glowing, colorful Christmas lights draped around, and my brother's graffiti covered the brick.

"Hey, Virginia!" a bunch of men called out the second I rolled over the threshold.

I felt Earth grumble and glare, but I ignored him.

"Hi, everyone!" I called out. "Thank you so much for the welcome. And thank you for supporting my flower shop!"

When Tangled Stems first opened, I wasn't sure if people would like having a cheerful little flower bar in the middle of the Grimms. I didn't really expect many visitors, but people came. At first, I thought maybe Earth intimidated them all to show up. But then I realized it was out of curiosity. The woman who "tamed" Earth (as if there were such a thing) was quite a draw.

I gave out free flowers to everyone who even stepped in the door. Some people tried to refuse; some people looked at the beautiful buds as though they were foreign. It made me a little sad but even more determined to bring some pretty here. Everyone deserved beauty and kind words. It didn't matter where you lived, how much money you had, or even if you could walk.

And some people had already come back. A few simple bouquets here and there gave me hope. Some came in and didn't buy anything at all, but that was okay too. Everyone was welcome in my flower shop. Smiles and kindness were free.

I would admit, though, having Ivory and Ethan using my shop for their business needs definitely would help me on the financial side. It also made me extremely proud that my beautiful creations were being fashioned in the Grimms and sent into the Upper East Side.

Perhaps that would also help bridge the massive gap between the two worlds.

It was a long shot… but hey, it was my dream.

"Come over here, little one, and play poker with us!" One of the men waved me over. He was sitting at a table off to the side that was filled with other men.

"Okay, but don't be upset when I beat you all."

They all laughed and hooted.

Earth grabbed the back of my chair, stopping it from rolling. "Her name is Virginia," he announced. "And she's not playing."

The men at the table all muttered and glanced away.

I smacked Earth's hand. "I am too!"

He growled.

I growled back.

His lips twitched, and I gave him a sweet smile.

"You're lucky you're so cute," he muttered.

I tugged the hem of his shirt, and he leaned down to kiss me.

Catcalls filled the bar.

He stiffened, and I kissed him again.

"Go work," I said, heading toward the poker table.

All the men shuffled their chairs around to make room and deal me in.

Snort barked, bounding into the room, my chair jolting under his front paws when he leaped up. "Hey, boy!" I said, scratching behind his ear.

He licked my arm, and I patted my lap. He jumped up, settling on top of me like he belonged.

I showed him my cards, and we got to playing.

A while later, I had a massive pile of money in front of me, and all the men at the table were groaning.

"You little hustler!" one of the men yelled.

"You should have told us you were an expert," another said.

I giggled. "Now, gentlemen, I did warn you."

"Earth, your woman is robbing us blind!"

"I can assure you I play fair."

"Double or nothing," the man beside me slurred. He really shouldn't play drunk.

"You'll just lose again," I told him.

He leaned over the table, laying a hand on my arm. "Teach me your secrets." His breath was hot and smelled like beer.

Did I mention I never developed a taste for it? I still thought it was gross.

"I play sober," I told him, glancing at the bottle of Perrier at my elbow.

"You're pretty." The man giggled.

I'd never seen a grown man giggle before.

A hand slapped onto his shoulder, and he was wrenched back. "Hey!" he bellowed, dropping his handful of cards. "What the—"

Earth stood over him, eyes black, face like stone.

Drunk poker guy gulped. "Earth."

"You touching my girl?" His dark eyes slipped to my arm where the man was still clutching.

"Oh, Earth, it didn't mean nothing. I was trying to learn how to win."

Clutching the back of his neck, Earth ripped him up by his hair and dragged him to the door. The bell overhead rang when someone scrambled ahead to hold it open for him.

The man was tossed out onto the sidewalk.

The door shut behind him.

Everyone in the place stood quietly, staring at Earth, who literally commanded the room.

"Do not touch," he barked.

I giggled.

A few people sucked in a breath, looking at me like they were scared of what Earth might do.

Stomping across the room, he leaned over me, his glittering eyes intent on my face.

I pecked a kiss on his cheek. "That was unnecessary."

He grunted. "No one touches you."

"Whatever you say, my villain."

His eyes darkened, and hunger washed over his face. My tongue darted out to wet my lips, and beneath his breath, he groaned.

Leaning so close his lips brushed my ear, he murmured. "I'm gonna be in you so deep tonight you won't be able to *not* feel me."

Tingles raced over my scalp, and I shivered lightly. "Can't wait," I whispered.

He straightened. "We're closing early! Last call!"

There were a bunch of groans and protests from the crowd. Earth ignored them all to move behind the bar.

I smiled. It didn't matter how many times I told him he wasn't a villain; he believed he was. I stopped arguing long ago. It didn't matter to me anyway. I loved him regardless.

But it seemed to mean something to him when I would acknowledge the antihero inside him, claim even that piece of him too.

I'd come to realize that was all he really wanted. Acceptance for he who he was. What he'd done. He wanted to be loved in spite of it all.

Isn't that what we all wanted?

Everyone deserves a fairy tale, no matter who you are. They can be found in the most unexpected places.

When I looked up, he was already staring. Love made me feel light.

A girl doesn't need legs to fly.

I blew him a kiss, and he rolled his eyes, but his lips curved into a smile.

Don't be afraid to reach for your dream. You might find it just like I did. And just like me, you too can live…

Happily Ever After

AUTHORS NOTE

Once upon a time, there was a writer...

Who refused to give up on her dream.

And though her dream shifted and changed, became work instead of something magical, she wanted it still.

I just typed the end of this book... and I felt some tears well up in my eyes. This book took *months* to write. I wanted to release it much sooner, but the process was a bit daunting. I think I always say it, and it's true: Writing does not get easier for me. In some ways, it gets harder. This series in particular has been a bit of a challenge for me. I feel like it's been a lot of world-building, which is a little odd because it's a contemporary book/series. Perhaps it's the fairy-tale tie-ins I try so hard to weave through. And honestly, I don't even know if I'm completely successful, but I try anyway.

Huntsman originally set out to be a book about the huntsman, you know, the man who was supposed to kill Snow White but didn't. Whatever happened to that guy anyway? When Earth surprised me in *Ivory White* with his true identity, I knew I wanted to write his book. He was loud and demanding in my head. For a while, he definitely flirted with the idea of making a play for Ivory. But he didn't. He knew she wasn't the one for him.

I wanted to write someone who was "bad" but also likable. I wanted to write a flawed man that, honestly, we probably shouldn't like but did anyway. I mean, sure, I wanted to make him human… but I also wanted to make people root for him even if he was bad. I hoped to inspire loyalty toward him regardless of his killer ways. When I set out to write this book, I thought, "I won't have him kill people on the page," because that would make him "unlikable." And then I was like… "That's lame." And it was also counterproductive. I mean, we kept hearing him say he's killed people, and we already saw him try to kill Ivory. I didn't want to gloss over who he was for the sake of him being more "human." He IS human. Even as a killer. Lol. So he killed some people. I think it made him more authentic to his true character. What do you think?

Also, when I started this book, Virginia was not his original love interest. Interesting, right? I had originally planned to have his family send an assassin after him (a woman) and have them fall in love. I pondered that plot for a long time. Even as I was writing *Prince*, I plotted, made notes, etc. But there was something off about it. Earth was always so loud, but about this, he was kind of quiet. It was odd.

Then a friend messaged me. She said, "I guess Earth and Virginia are getting together."

I was shook.

Like shookened!

I had never once thought of that. LOL. I know. Some writer I am. But really, I hadn't thought that. I had always just thought I would write Virginia a story of her own (even had the photo cover picked out).

The second that idea was in my brain, Earth was kinda… wild. That quiet, off feeling disappeared. Earth was like, "YES!" He was like, "She's mine, and I'll fight Neo for her." I was like, "Oh dear."

But I was also very intrigued. I mean, the dynamic between Neo and Earth was already hella strained. This was just icing on the cake. It was like asking for a battle.

And then I realized how alike he was to Flynn Ryder (who is like my favorite "prince"). He's a criminal. In with a bad crowd. Moody.

Virginia was my Rapunzel—a girl trapped in a tower. And Earth was really the only one courageous enough to get her out. The only one willing to battle Neo.

She's light where he's dark. But she's also very accepting.

They make a great match—in my opinion.

Originally, with Virginia, I was going to have her walk again. I had plotted I would have her do that surgery Neo went on about forever and that she grew close to Earth in recovery.

It felt wrong.

It felt like I would be sending a message that to get a happily-ever-after you had to walk. That you couldn't be in a wheelchair.

I want this entire series to have the theme that fairy tales are for everyone. No matter your race, sexual preference, social status… It doesn't matter if you are disabled, disfigured… or a villain. You can be happy. Everyone deserves that.

For some research, I watched some YouTube videos made by people who are paralyzed and in wheelchairs. I read some articles, etc. as well. One thing someone said that truly, truly stuck out to me was, "People always assume the thing we want most is to walk again. That's not true."

I realized, while I hadn't really contemplated what someone who was wheelchair-bound might feel, I would probably think that. Not because I'm ignorant or ill-meaning but because I didn't know better. Because I never thought about it.

So I thought about it. A lot.

And Virginia revealed that she didn't think she'd ever walk again—something we all thought because that's what Neo told us. We had HIS side of the story. Not hers. Here she was, frustrated and exhausted, tired of making walking again her only goal. She just wanted a life and to be happy.

I really felt that.

This story became about a lot more than a feud between brothers or the huntsman. It's about acceptance, forgiveness, family. It's about how others see you but also how you see yourself and the balance between those two things.

I don't know if Earth "deserved" a happy ending, but I really wanted him to have it. I wanted Virginia to have it too.

It was such a challenge to write a paraplegic. I would like to say if I portrayed any of this incorrectly, I sincerely apologize. I did do research, but I can't possibly know everything. I've never been in Virginia's position. It was a gamble writing her because it is something I'm unfamiliar with, but at the same time, I wanted to be a voice. I wanted to bring some awareness and some romance to those in a wheelchair. Maybe you've never thought about it just as I hadn't before. Maybe now you have.

On top of Virginia, I was writing an assassin. An Asian man who came from a bad past and turned into a killer. That wasn't easy either. I'm not an assassin (though I've offed some people in books... lol). Alternating between a killer and a wheelchair-bound woman was difficult, to say the least. I'd also like to note that, for the little bit of Korean language I added into the book, if there are any errors, I apologize. I did my best to look up the translations, and I read a few articles and watched a few language videos. I do watch a lot of K-drama, so a lot of the phrases are familiar to me, but I am not fluent. So any errors are mine and mine alone. I would also like to note I used informal tone for Earth when he was speaking (a more casual way of speaking) because it was his brother and Virginia he was speaking to.

It took me almost four months to write this book, which is pretty long for me. It's just a little shorter in words than *Prince* (my longest book to date), and at times, I considering quitting. I considered stopping this series after this book was over—even though I wanted to write books for Beau and Emogen. Oh yeah, what did you think of the beast? 😉 I still consider dropping it because it's overwhelming. It's a lot. And I worry no one will read them. It's hard to put hours upon hours, months upon months, into something people may or may not like.

But really, how can I not write the rest of the series? I want this series too much. I believe in the message, the themes... the characters. I love this family.

I hope you do too.

I hope you think I did justice to Earth and Virginia. I hope he was villainous enough but also human enough.

I want to thank YOU for reading. For coming on this journey with me and for your support. It really keeps me going. Also, please consider leaving a review online for *Huntsman*. Reviews help. Even just short two-sentence ones. I'm grateful for them.

Now, if you will excuse me, I have to go clean because I neglected my house while finishing this, and I have to start brainstorming the next book!

See you then!
XOXO~
Cambria

ABOUT CAMBRIA HEBERT

Cambria Hebert is a bestselling novelist of more than fifty titles. She went to college for a bachelor's degree, couldn't pick a major, and ended up with a degree in cosmetology. So rest assured her characters will always have good hair.

Besides writing, Cambria loves a pumpkin spice latte, staying up late, sleeping in, and watching K drama until her eyes won't stay open. She considers math human torture and has an irrational fear of chickens (yes, chickens). You can often find her running on the treadmill (she'd rather be eating a donut), painting her toenails (because she bites her fingernails), or walking her chihuahuas (the real bosses of the house).

Cambria has written in many genres, including new adult, sports romance, male/male romance, sci-fi, thriller, suspense, contemporary romance, and young adult. Many of her titles have been translated into foreign languages and have been the recipients of multiple awards.

Awards Cambria has received include:

Author of the Year 2016 (UtopiaCon2016)
The Hashtag Series: Best Contemporary Series of 2015
(UtopiaCon 2015)
#Nerd: Best Contemporary Book Cover of 2015
(UtopiaCon 2015)
Romeo from the Hashtag Series: Best Contemporary
Lead (UtopiaCon 2015)
#Nerd: Top 50 Summer Reads (Buzzfeed.com 2015)
The Hashtag Series: Best Contemporary Series of 2016
(UtopiaCon 2016)
#Nerd Book Trailer: Best Book Trailer of 2016
(UtopiaCon 2016)
#Nerd Book Trailer: Top 50 Most Cinematic Book
Trailers of All Time (film-14.com)
#Nerd: Book Most Wanted to be Adapted to Screen:
(2018)
Amnesia: Mystery Book of the Year (2018)

Cambria Hebert owns and operates Cambria Hebert
Books, LLC.
You can find out more about Cambria and her titles by
visiting her website:
http://www.cambriahebert.com

BOOKS BY CAMBRIA HEBERT

The Heven & Hell series

The Death Escorts series

The Take It Off Series

The Hashtag Series

The GearShark Series

The Amnesia Duet

The Public Enemy Series

The BearPaw Resort Series

The House of Misfits Series

Standalone Titles:

Moth To A Flame

Mr. Fantasy

Distant Desires

Maneater

Blank

Whiteout

Check out all these and more here:

https://books2read.com/ap/RQDG6x/Cambria-Hebert